HIGH RAGE

James K. Burk

Wolfsinger Publications Security, Colorado

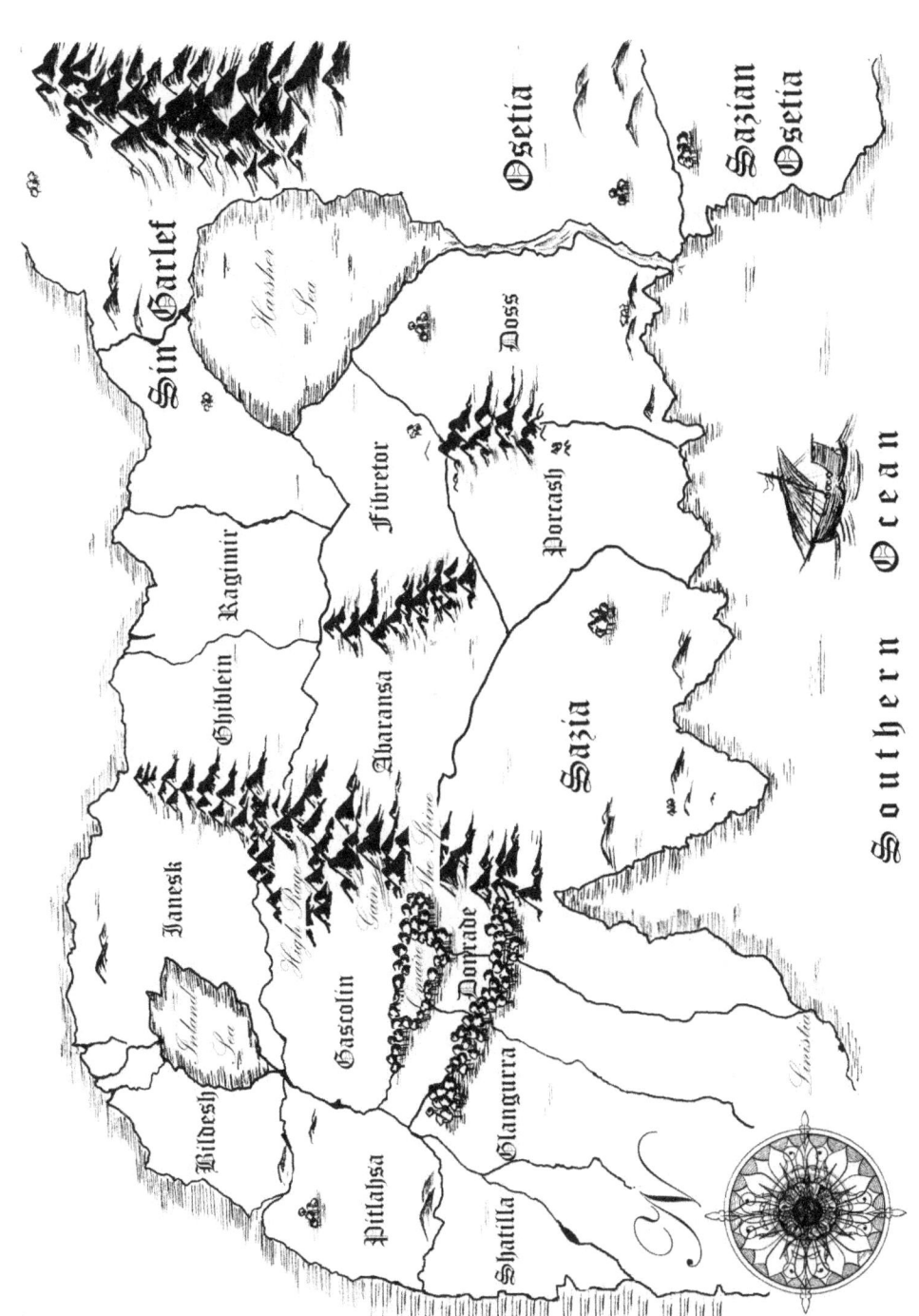

Dedication

To all my roses, each of them unique in all the world, especially Tara Elaine-Renee (Olive Tara), Whitney Dawn, Erika Alana-Morgana, Orion Salvador, Olivia Isabelle, and Scarlet Francesca.

Chapter 1

Staying in the deepest shadows, Scarface crept to the wall and along its outer base until he stood midway between two of the guard towers he'd observed earlier. The stone wall, with its ill-fitting blocks, gave purchase to gloved hands and booted feet. He considered using a spell of concealment but not being able to see his own hands and feet would make the climb more difficult. And if he fell from that imposing wall, being seen would be the least of his difficulties. Pausing, he made sure the scabbard across his back was well secured so the sword wouldn't snarl his legs or clatter against the rock.

He gripped the stone wall nearly as high as he could reach, and his toes found crevices. The wall was more treacherous than he'd expected. The stone was soft, its edges rounded by weathering. Alert to any sounds, he began to climb.

Looking neither up nor down, he could only guess at how high he'd climbed by the ache in his shoulders, arms, and calves. Time became measured by breaths. The sound of his climbing seemed loud in his ears but he heard nothing to warn him he'd been detected. As he reached for the next handhold, rock crumbled under his foot. An icy hand clutched at his heart and guts and he clung to the wall in a panic.

Trembling with exertion and fear, he forced himself to breathe slowly.

When he could trust his body, he reached upward and resumed his climb. To Scarface, the sound of his clothing rubbing against the stone was as loud as a crowded tavern and he stopped once more to listen. He could, at the edge of hearing, distinguish a guard muttering but the voice came no nearer or louder.

He reached the top, his right hand finding a solid grip, then drew up his right leg. Staying low on the top of the wall to avoid being silhouetted against the night sky, he slithered across it like a lizard and lowered himself to the wooden walkway between the guards' posts.

Once on the walkway, he crawled across it to keep the wood from creaking, found a support, and lowered himself down the sloping timber.

The worst moment came when he hung over the edge of the walkway, his feet dangling at least ten long strides above the courtyard. Finally he managed to wrap his legs around a support and let himself down until he reached the stone wall.

The inner wall was even more difficult than the outer because his feet had to grope for footholds and his arms and legs again trembled with fatigue, and because there was always the risk that a servant might look outside the residence and see him on the wall.

At last he sank gratefully into the grass and scanned the courtyard. With all the blazing torches, there were still pools of shadow. When he was ready to move he slunk between the deeper patches of darkness till he was only a few paces from the gravel trail that described a circle in front of the large doors of the residence.

He moved into position and daubed more clay onto his cheeks and forehead to hide his scars then unslung the scabbard from across his back and thrust it into his belt, where it was readier to hand but would still be clear of his legs when he had to run.

Carefully, he examined the courtyard and the walls, trying to anticipate sources of danger. His only escape route was also the greatest trap, the open gate beyond which a single halberdier paced, his weapon over his shoulder.

After removing his gloves and making sure they were tightly secured in his belt he wiped his hands on his sleeves and glanced up at the moon, trying to guess the hour from its position. Every delay now was an added danger. The Ghiblin princeling he'd left in the alley might waken or be found. Even worse, the Abransans might let their dogs into the courtyard, forcing him to flee, his task unfinished, his carefully laid plan a disaster. Again he wiped the sweat from his palms and licked his lips with a tongue as dry as a stick.

He thought he heard the clatter of hooves and the rattle of wheels on paving stones and he waited, almost holding his breath, until he was certain of the sound. It came nearer and he coiled into a crouch, drew his knife, and gathered his muscles for the rush. The carriage slowed as it entered the gate and turned onto the circular track of gravel. Ignoring the guard on the rear platform, Scarface sprang at the door, tore it open, and lunged inside, then cursed in Sinn.

He'd expected only the Abransan noble but another man sat beside him. The man shouted in Abarsa and his right hand reached for his dagger while he flung up his left hand to block Scarface's thrust.

As the man raised his hand into the light Scarface caught a glimpse of a heavy green ring on his hand but didn't hesitate to strike the hand aside and plunge his poniard into the man's chest, feeling resistance as the narrow blade spread the links of a mail shirt. He twisted the blade and wrenched it free then drove deeper into the coach toward the Abaransan noble, who cowered in the dark corner, almost paralyzed with fear.

"Die, you damned Abransan land-bandit!" Scarface roared in Ghiblin, and drove the point of the poniard under the man's chin and back into the base of the brain.

The brake shoe squealed against the wheel and Scarface seized the doorframe to keep from falling. Hearing the guard drop to the gravel, Scarface sprang outside, tossed the dagger to his left hand, whipped out his sword, and parried a slash at his head. Steel rang then rasped as Scarface slid his blade up to slash the guard over the eyes.

The man screamed and fell back and Scarface leapt at him like a tiger, his sword tearing through the man's collet and sinking deeply into his neck.

A crossbow quarrel slammed into the side of the carriage and Scarface raced for the gate, hearing another bolt hiss past. His dark blue cloak made him all but invisible in the shadows. Just inside the gate he confronted the halberdier, who thrust at him. Scarface dodged and was almost pulled off his feet as the halberd snagged his cloak, stumbled, then lashed out desperately. His blade caught the guard across the forearm, biting through the light mail and driving the shorn links into the wound.

The guard howled and dropped his weapon.

Scarface recovered his balance, snarled a curse in Ghiblin, and slashed at the man's knee. He felt the steel bite, heard the man howl again.

Another bolt whined past Scarface, who whipped his cloak free and dashed through the gate into the street. While the crossbowmen reloaded their weapons he darted into an alley. The guards raised the hue and cry and, within moments, Scarface heard shutters flung open above him and the alarm taken up all around him. He raced down the alley, shot across another street, and followed another alley to the place he'd left the Ghiblin prince.

As he neared the place he fumbled into the pouch at his belt and scattered a handful of herbs which, when crushed by footsteps, released a sharp, pungent odor that deadened the ability of hounds to follow a trail.

The man he'd left hidden in rubbish and shadows still lay unconscious. Scarface tossed the sword he carried beside the man's outflung left hand, reclaimed the plain sword he'd left in the prince's scabbard and the dagger in its sheath, then wrapped the Ghiblin's right hand around the grip of the poniard and drove the point into the man's throat. Then, before slipping back into deeper shadows, Scarface used his sword to tear the man's cloak; if the halberdier lived he might remember his weapon had caught the assassin's cloak. It was better to leave no annoying loose ends on which to hang a supposition.

The spell of concealment required moisture applied to the forehead and Scarface felt a stab of panic when he found his mouth dry from fear and the run. He picked up a pebble from the dirt, slipped it into his mouth and sucked at it until he could wet his fingertip enough to trace the sigil on his forehead, and muttered the incantation.

He lurched as power drained from him, running from his scars. Then he pressed his back against the wall.

Running men approached the alley, the sound of their footsteps growing louder, and he pressed still further back, as though trying to force himself through the wall. Carrying torches, three men in Abransan livery pounded into the end of the alley, swords in their hands. They saw the body and warily advanced on it.

Scarface sidestepped slowly toward them, carefully putting his feet down only where he was sure of his footing. A Ghiblin, wearing only his nightshirt and grasping a club, appeared at the other end of the alley and shouted a challenge in his guttural language.

One of the Abransans shouted back in his own rolling tongue and gestured with his sword. More Ghiblins, some armed with knives or short swords, joined the crowd, which grew rapidly, and curses were shouted in two languages.

Scarface permitted himself a grim smile. If no one stumbled over him in the press of the crowd, the confusion would ensure the success of his mission.

The Ghiblins and Abransans were at the point of trading blows when a Ghiblin night patrol arrived and, laying about them with clubs and staves, forced their way into the alley.

The crush of the crowd grew dangerous as Scarface crept past the mob. He heard one of the Ghiblins shout, "This smells of the power. We need a magus for this."

Feeling new urgency, Scarface made his way carefully past the throng. He'd planned his route with care and, within an hour, reached the old tree behind the inn. Springing, he caught a lower limb and drew himself up then crawled along the branch that ran over the kitchen at the back of the building to the slanting roof. He cautiously lowered himself from the branch, crouched on hands and feet, and climbed the steep pitch of the roof to where his open window gaped.

In the relative safety of his room he stripped, then wiped the disguise from his face and the blood from his hands with a dampened cloth. The clothing he bundled into the torn cloak and stuffed into a saddle pouch. He snapped the blade of the knife he'd worn then dropped the pieces and the sheath into the bag. He'd wait until morning with its usual street noises to break up the plain sword and add its pieces to the contents of the pouch. He'd again be wearing his own, more distinctive weapons, and he preferred not to be asked why he carried another sword.

There were still a few risks to be run and the return to High Rage to survive but his mission had been all but accomplished. The Abransan envoy was dead and a Ghiblin lord would be blamed for the killing. He wondered about the man with the green ring, a double to the one in his pouch. How deeply was the Union involved in the fragile peace between Ghiblein and Abaransa? And why hadn't the clan been notified of that involvement? The questions might bear deeper thought but that was something to be dealt with later.

He sank to the pallet with a grateful sigh and in little more time than it had taken him to kill the two men in the carriage, he was asleep.

~ * ~

He brushed the dust of many leagues off his clothing and adjusted the set of his sword and knife before he stepped inside the door of the inn. His eyes adjusted quickly to the dimness—lighter than the darkness outside. A small fire blazed in the central fireplace and over it turned a lamb or kid, glistening with butter like sweat in the glow. The surge of saliva and the rumble in his stomach reminded him his last few meals had been cold, meager rations.

Hunger never overruled his caution. His eyes had, by habit, continued their study of the room. Kegs and casks and shelves lined the far wall and dried roots and vegetables hung from the rafters. Between the door and the fireplace stood two large tables with a double handful of travelers sprinkled along them. A middle-aged woman and a man, slightly older, carried cups, flagons, and platters to the tables from the back. To both sides of him sets of stairs led up to the lofts. He guessed no one was in the lofts.

The man serving the travelers left his tray at the table and approached Scarface. "Greetings, traveler," His pale blue eyes flicked as his assessment took in Scarface's clothing, weapons, and jewelry, then paused at the black ritual scars on his forehead, temples, and cheekbones. "How may I serve you?"

"Wine, meals, and a pallet in the loft. What's the price?"

Again the evaluation of the worth of what he wore. "A mark of silver."

"Fifteen copper."

"But, sir—" The gaze was fixed again on the scars and on the cold, pale green eyes they bracketed. "Fifteen marks of copper."

Scarface hid his satisfaction at the double usefulness of his scars as he fished in the front pocket of the pouch at his belt and handed three large copper coins to the innkeeper.

The man looked at the coins then glanced up at his face, "These are Gascalan *sanciams*. Did you come from there? Through the mountains?"

"I'm returning."

"Most of the travelers at that table," he gestured with his thumb, "are going that way. It might be to everyone's benefit to have more protection."

Scarface nodded. He strode to the foot of the indicated table, drew up a stool, and sat down. Most of the travelers were a nondescript lot but two stood out. His attention was immediately drawn to the woman, tall and attractive.

Her dark brown, almost black, hair was long but drawn back rather severely from her pale, oval face. Her high forehead curved at the top, her nose looked as though it'd once been broken, her wide lips seemed both determined and sensual, and she had a strong chin. He noticed her fingers, long and tapering, with closely trimmed nails. She carried on an animated conversation with the man at her right and Scarface observed that she spoke and laughed freely, as though the conversation was the border of her world.

The man to whom she spoke was more than half a head shorter than she, with a thin face and a full black beard. He had the olive complexion of a westerner and the frequent grin of a man who sold carriages he didn't own.

As the innkeeper moved past, Scarface glanced up and said, "Red wine."

The man brought a flagon and cup then rounded the table, leaned over the woman, and whispered to her. She seemed annoyed the interruption but looked down the table toward Scarface as though he were a long-lost friend.

Her voice was deep, for a woman. "I'm Mendarian, and these are Stego," she indicated the short man,"Timos, and Arv lat Paldisan." The last two names apparently belonged to the men sitting across the table from her. Timos had the look of a veteran, a thug, or, probably, both. Lat Paldisan was short, with a paunch and a drooping moustache and seemed to have a perpetually hangdog air in spite of the nobility implied by his name. Two or three others at the table also gave their names.

"Honored. I'm called Scarface." He accepted the food placed before him as a welcome distraction. The wine had made an almost complete transformation to vinegar, the meat was unseasoned, the green and orange bits had been dried so long boiling had only made them mushy rather than aiding the favor, and the bread was coarse. His hunger made it all taste like delicacies.

Stego leaned forward and turned his head to look past the people between Scarface and himself. White teeth flashed in his black beard as he produced another grin. "I can see how you gained the appellation. Those are really fascinating disfigurements. I'm sure the story of how you acquired them would be equally interesting."

"I doubt it." Scarface forced himself to eat slowly, savoring the meal. He had to keep his back straight to hide the scepter thrust into his belt at the small of his back.

Mendarian sipped at her wine and looked at him. "The innkeeper says you're also going to Gascolin. Would you like to ride with us? Since the latest declaration of war between Ghiblein and Abaransa, the bandits around here have become bolder and more numerous."

A half-smile flickered under Scarface's moustache. "I'll be pleased to offer you my protection."

Mendarian's smile seemed genuine. "And I'll be pleased to accept."

Scarface poured himself another cup of the sour wine and finished his meal.

"If you'll excuse me," he said, and walked outside. The bright stars and the full moon shed enough light to let him survey the rugged countryside, and he heard enough animal noises to feel secure. Apparently the brigands weren't yet bold enough to attack the inn itself. He strode along the front of the building to the door of the stable and entered. The stableman looked up from his bread, cheese, and beer.

"I just wanted to see to my horse." Scarface moved to the third stall and ran his hand down the animal's nose. It'd been rubbed down and given a blanket and a meal and was already dozing. Scarface patted its neck then returned to the inn. Mendarian and Stego passed him on their way out, as he reached the door. He nodded to them and paced into the inn, feeling a twinge of envy.

Most of the travelers, muttering in flat, tired voices, still sat at the tables. Scarface had, on hearing of the declaration of war, learned all he needed to know and had nothing he wished to share with trail companions. He nodded absently at them and climbed the stairs to the loft.

In the loft, he sat down on the pallet that looked cleanest and pulled off his thigh-length boots. He slipped the scepter into the right boot and pushed it all the way to the toe. After he unbuckled his belt and removed the pouch he shoved the purse into the top of the boot. He laid his sword beside the mattress, placed his other belt with its knife by his head, then lay back on the pallet. He added his cloak to the thin blanket provided by the inn and drifted into slumber.

~ * ~

He slept undisturbed and rose early the next morning, dressed, and made his way down the stairs. The innkeeper, still sleepy, tended a steaming stewpot, and Mendarian sat at the same table she'd dominated the night before. She'd heard the creaking of the stairs and looked up from her stew. "Good morning."

He nodded at her greeting and sat down across the table from. Strangely uncomfortable with the leaden silence, he finally said, "I hope you slept well."

"Very well, thank you." She stared frankly at him for a few seconds. "You seem high-born. Why are you traveling through dangerous country alone?"

He threatened to smile. "Because I can. But you're far too attractive to be traveling with such a small escort."

Mendarian grinned. "Then adding you will double my protection."

The innkeeper set a bowl of stew before Scarface, who stirred it to cool it. "Where are you going? Shatilla?" Stego's accent had marked him a Shatillan.

"No, I'm bound for Forgren's holding to discuss a treaty between he and Cerco. I understand he has considerable power."

"That's what I've heard." Scarface sampled some of the stew, tore a piece of bread from the loaf on the table. "You might also want to visit High Rage."

Mendarian looked up from her stew. "Oh? And who's lord there?"

"Hadrian Darkmoor rules there in the name of the Winged Dagger Clan."

"You don't like him." It was almost a question.

"I didn't say that."

"You don't need to. Your eyes and the tone of your voice said it for you."

"We've disagreed in the past." Scarface leaned back in his chair and considered the question for a moment. "I respect him. I respect anyone who could kill me with very little effort."

"You're afraid of him but you want me to see him?" Her voice rose.

"I didn't say I was afraid of him, only that he could kill me, something very different. He's only dangerous to those who threaten, and you don't seem the sort to threaten others. His word is good, but only so far as he gives it. I don't believe anyone knows what he thinks."

Mendarian finished her stew and sopped up the last traces with a piece of bread. "Hadrian Darkmoor, I seem to remember that name."

Stego chose that moment to come down the stairs. "Who are we discussing?"

Mendarian turned to him. "Good morning. I was just wondering where I'd heard the name Hadrian Darkmoor."

Stego dropped into the chair beside Mendarian's. "There was a Hadrian Darkmoor who was a count of Doss. He fell out of favor with the new godhead and was exiled. Correct?" His stare at Scarface was almost a challenge.

"Near enough." Scarface turned to Mendarian. "Which horse is yours? If we want to leave soon, it'd be better to have the mounts ready."

"Thank you. The roan in the stall nearest the door."

Scarface strode to the stable and saddled his black and Mendarian's roan then bought two large bags of oats. He paid the stableman for the grain and the services and led the horses into the wan sunlight.

Mendarian emerged from the inn with the rest of the party. Stego, Timos, and lat Paldisan walked to the stable to ready their own animals while Mendarian swung into her saddle. She wore all black, including soft leather boots.

The rest of the travelers in the group were apparently afoot. One of them had drawn on the gray cloak with the white handprint of a pilgrim. Scarface led his horse toward the man. "Palmer, are you sure you want to travel with us? Alone, your cloak may afford you better protection than a handful of swords and, if there's trouble, the brigands might not take the time to notice you've been touched."

"Thank you for your concern," the elderly man said, "but I prefer the company to whatever special protection I might have alone."

Scarface mounted his stallion. "The choice is yours." He urged the horse into a trot until he was ahead of the rest of the party, scouting the broken country ahead.

These mountains were part of the rocky backbone of the continent, dividing Gascolin from Ghiblein and Abaransa and sheltering the tribes of Cerco. Here, they were a barrier twenty leagues wide, although the trail winding through the passes was almost twice as long and boasted some of the country best suited for ambush.

By midmorning Timos had joined Scarface as vanguard. As he rode forward he held out his left fist, displaying a green ring that matched the one Scarface now wore. Scarface vividly remembered the last time he'd seen another such ring.

"Greetings, Scarface," Timos said. "What are you doing out in these wastes?"

Scarface gestured at the trail ahead. "Trying to make sure we don't step into something we can't step back out of. And you?"

"I was wondering how you'd happened to arrive here. The woman I'm escorting is a guest of Forgren."

"Forgren's a fortunate man."

"Was it clan business that took you to Ghiblein?"

"Curiosity. I hadn't seen a real court since the old days in Doss. The Ghiblins do it in purple. Their High Warlord has done a fine job of castrating the princes and making them his housedogs. As long as they vie with each other for the privilege of handing him his napkin as he eats away their power, they stay out of the power engine. And the endless small offices accomplish just enough to run the country while providing an impenetrable defense against common sense."

Timos laughed obligingly. He was silent for a time and Scarface could almost observe the engines of his mind winding. "One of the problems we have is similar to those of the Ghiblin court. Either the leaders of the clan and the Union aren't speaking to each other or they're not telling us at the bottom about their decisions." He lapsed into another brief silence. "While you were at court, did you have a chance to talk to minister lat Dromyn?"

Scarface's lips twitched with a momentary flicker of amusement then he asked, "Would you stick out your tongue?"

"Why?"

"I just wanted to see if you'd stained it brown licking Forgren's boots."

Timos drew rein sharply and his hand dropped to the hilt of his sword. "I don't consider that remark amusing, even coming from a fellow Unionist."

Scarface also drew up his horse. "Well and fine; I wasn't trying to entertain you. For the moment, we have a common cause—trying to get this group over these mountains alive. Do you want to die on this side of the mountains ahead or would you rather wait until we'd crossed them?"

Timos scowled. "You're pressing the fact you're a Unionist and a member of the clan too far. One of these days that loose mouth of yours will get you pitched out of High Rage, and I'll be standing outside, waiting."

"Why not? It's what you—and vultures—do best."

Timos glared at him for a long moment then rode as far away from Scarface as the trail would permit.

Late in the afternoon Scarface rode back to the party with word they were approaching a place where they could pitch camp. Mendarian gestured to him then offered him a drink from the wineskin tied to her saddle. He rode beside her and reached for the wineskin. As he leaned toward her, Mendarian murmured, "I saw words cross between you and Timos and he's avoided you since. What happened?"

Scarface sipped at the wine, swished it around in his mouth, spat it out, and then drank deeply. "We both thought we smelled something rotten. At least one of us was right." He handed back the wineskin. "Thank you, lady."

"Are you a gambler or a fool?" she inquired. "I can appreciate gamblers—when they win, but fools don't live long."

"An excellent question, well worth deep consideration when I'm too old for anything more strenuous than reflection."

The place he'd chosen was near the top of a mountain called Keep. The trail widened until it became a plateau a good stone's throw across and almost twice as long. A rivulet, from a spring nearer the peak, threaded its way down to the place. The mountain's slope was gentle here, so rockslides would pose little danger.

Scarface carefully trod across the area, frequently stopping to look around, then pointed to a depression holding ashes of old fires. While the rest of the travelers sat or lay down on the rocks he prowled among the stones around them, occasionally stopping to murmur and scratch patterns on the rock with the point of his knife. Finally he returned to the group.

After he'd hobbled his mount he pulled off the saddle, rubbed the animal down, and resaddled it before he blanketed it. He fed it and Mendarian's roan the oats he'd bought at the stable.

At last he ate his own meal, a couple of biscuits and some strips of dried meat, and washed it down with water from the stream.

Stego, stretched out on a boulder, was basking in the last, wan light of the day. He rested until the roseate light had almost drained from the sky, then he yawned and grinned. "I think I'd like a nice fire."

Two or three of the party chuckled and Scarface said, "Then you'd better wish for the wood to build it with. If there are bandits about they already know we're here, but I don't see anyone who had the foresight to bring kindling."

"Just wishing," Stego said.

"Never wish small," Scarface replied. "It's as easy to wish for a palace as for a stick of wood." He drew his cloak tighter around himself as twilight's chill seeped into him. "I'll stay awake until the moon is overhead. Who wants me to wake him?"

"I'll watch after that," Timos said.

"And I'll help you keep watch," Mendarian said to Scarface. "Stego, why don't you watch with Timos?"

In the dimness, Scarface could barely see Timos shrug.

One of the other men had a bow. Scarface told him to string it and to sleep with it to keep it warm. With a last glance at the horizon, he clambered up a sloped boulder at the edge of the camp and perched himself with his back to the camp. Mendarian joined him and moved to sit back-to-back with him, then flinched. "What did I bump against?"

He pulled the scepter out of his belt and shoved it into the top of his boot. "Just a bauble I picked up in my travels."

"From where?"

"The eastern continent. I doubt you'd even recognize the name of the place."

"Try me."

"Near a place called The Shield of the Saint, in the Empire of the Book."

"That's farther east than I've ever gone. Isn't it near Myslan?"

Scarface settled himself more comfortably. "It's on the border."

"What were you doing there?"

"Satisfying my curiosity."

Mendarian leaned back until her head touched his. "Curiosity, they say, killed the cat."

"Cats have only nine lives." He stared at the moonshadow of a boulder until he was reassured that he hadn't seen movement in the darkness. Gradually the shadows all but disappeared as the moon rose higher until it seemed directly over them. He drew up his cloak. "It's time to wake the other two."

"Would you like to sleep with me tonight? *For warmth*." The last two words were spoken with authority.

"I'm agreeable." He climbed down from the rock and walked, scuffing his boots against the stone, to where Timos lay. Five paces away from the man he halted and said softly, "Your time to watch."

Timos lurched to his feet, strapped on his sword, and walked to the boulder Scarface had chosen. Mendarian wakened Stego, who joined Timos.

Scarface let Mendarian lie down where Timos's body had warmed the rock then laid down beside her. He found the nearness of her body and the heat of her breath very tempting, then realized the weight of her left hand had left his right side moving down toward his waist. He covered her hand with his. "Hold my hand," he whispered.

"This is just for warmth," she reminded him.

"I feel warmer in knowing my weapons and articles are safe."

"Are you accusing—" she hissed.

"Not at all. I'd never suggest such a thing. But to remind me where *my* hand is supposed to stay, I'd appreciate your protecting me from myself."

She chuckled then snuggled closer and seemed to doze off. He waited a short while then let himself slip into the warm pool of sleep.

~ * ~

The howl brought him instantly awake. He looked past Mendarian, who'd also been wakened, to see a man writhing in a red-orange glare. As they watched, the man's skin blackened and shriveled, then he collapsed. A bandit had found one of the traps Scarface had left. Stego and Timos shouted an alarm.

Scarface murmured the incantation and, with a saliva-wetted finger traced a design on Mendarian's forehead. She tried to sit up and he gently pushed her back down. "Stay here and you won't be seen." He unclasped his cloak and rolled to his feet, drawing the scepter from his boot. With the scepter in his left hand, he whipped out his sword.

One of the bandits was atop Stego, trying to nail him to the ground with a short, leaf-shaped Sazian stabbing sword. Stego had caught the brigand's wrist but was too close to use his own longer blade.

Scarface struck with the scepter and the robber instantly aged and withered. Stego was so surprised by the reaction he almost released the bandit's wrist. He rolled out from under the man and struck down at what was already a lifeless husk.

Scarface hadn't stayed to observe the end of the struggle. A large man, mailed and armed with a sword and shield attacked him. He parried the cut aimed at his head and swept his sword around to come in over the shield, cutting with the upper edge of his blade. He felt his sword bite and heard a grunt, and he side-stepped past the man to face another robber, this one armed with a two-handed sword. Scarface sprang forward, closing so that the longer blade was almost worthless and slashed at the man's left forearm. He parried the awkward return cut. As he deflected the heavier blade he touched the bandit's wounded arm with the scepter. Again he felt the vibration of the rod as he willed it to drain its victim, and the man before him withered.

Then there were no more bandits around him so he wheeled to attack the man he'd wounded. The brigand was unsteady, stumbling and leaning on his sword and he'd dropped his shield. Scarface lunged, the point of his sword taking the man in the belly. The bandit screamed and fell. Scarface bent over him and wiped his blade clean on the man's cloak.

He remembered to cancel the spell he'd cast and looked up to see Mendarian staring at the bodies.

If he hadn't exhausted his welcome he'd at least exposed something he'd prefer to keep hidden, and the scepter's power was now obvious to the whole group. He stepped over a corpse with an arrow in its chest, picked up his cloak from the rocks, and caught up the reins of his horse. As he stepped behind the stallion he slashed the hobble.

Mendarian faced him, smiling. "That's a very impressive 'bauble.'"

Scarface backed away from her, the scepter still in his hand. She moved toward him. "Are you afraid of me?"

He returned part of her smile. "I've seen that predatory look before." Then the smile, which had never reached his eyes, went away from his lips. "You're entirely too charming for me to want to see you grow old before your time—so keep your distance." Timos, Stego, and lat Paldisan had heard the exchange and drew nearer.

Scarface continued to back away. He turned his head to see the way behind him, expecting one or more of them to follow him, but Mendarian shouted for the men around her to halt. Scarface turned his face toward them again and kept backing away, leading his horse wide around him. He reached a certain stone and stopped, said a word they couldn't hear, and retreated another dozen paces.

"Stego," he said, "you're very quick, and you others may have abilities not apparent, but I don't need to defeat you, I only need to touch you with this. As good as you all are; can you keep me from just touching you?"

He sheathed his sword and, one-handed, drew on his cloak and clasped it. "You may remember the brigand who lit up in the night. You may also recall I scratched that sign more than once. There isn't enough light for you to go looking for scratches on rocks, especially when your life might depend upon finding them."

After tracing a circle around himself and his mount with his knife he muttered and added more patterns to the circle then turned his back on the others, took off the horse's blanket, and folded it,

Muttering and gesturing, Timos slowly advanced on Scarface. A bright bluish glow sprang up around the edge of the circle and Scarface, just tying the blanket behind the saddle, turned and smiled at him in the faint light.

Timos murmured again and advanced. Framed by a glare, he screamed as his skin turned red and blistered. For a moment he seemed suspended in the fire, then it vanished and he fell to his knees.

Scarface sprang into the saddle with a laugh. "Your spell of protection damned near worked." He glared at Timos writhing on the stones. "I should kill you where you are, you bastard. You owe every breath you take to your green ring and the woman. If ever you press me again, you won't be on your knees; you'll be flat on your back."

"Scarface," Mendarian called, "we'll meet each other again."

"I hope so," he replied. "You do make life interesting." He urged his stallion through a maze-like pattern around the signs he'd drawn. When he reached the place where the trail narrowed he turned and shouted, "You'll be able to read the signs and obliterate them after the dew's risen."

He followed the trail out of sight around the mountain then dismounted and led the stallion until sunrise brought enough light to let the horse see the way. By late morning he'd reached the base of the mountains and, an hour later, had crossed the River Etaine at the town of Varish. There he visited a stable in the foreign quarter and changed mounts.

The liver-colored bay he'd chosen had both speed and heart and by midafternoon he'd reached the outpost outside the pass to Vale Shanna. There he changed mounts again and started the final dash to High Rage, making good time on the wide road to the town and the citadel.

He slowed at the outskirts of town. Hadrian might have his city yet. Seven years ago the place had been a farming village in the shadow of a decrepit hulk, then King Laranin had awarded the valley to the clan as a fiefdom. The castle looked almost new again and the town had grown as Hadrian had brought in artisans and craftsmen. Traders had begun to visit, some to settle, and the town had flourished. The quarries in the mountains had been reopened, a distillery had been built, and tribute to Gascoyne had been paid in Shannan marble and brandy.

His horse's steel shoes rang on cobblestones as he followed the wide, straight street that led up the hill atop which stood High Rage. He halted an arrow's flight from the wall, and stared up at the parapet above the gate. The flag of the clan scarcely billowed in the still air, its winged dagger of gold and silver and black stood out clearly from the red field.

Below the great flag hung six pennons. Scarface noticed Hadrian's banner was not among them, and cursed. He'd wanted to see him immediately, if not sooner. As he watched, a seventh pennon, his own red sunburst eagle on black, was hoisted by two of the guards.

He shook the reins and his horse's hooves sounded like a drumbeat on the wooden drawbridge. Liveried guards saluted as he passed and in the courtyard another man waited to take his mount to the stable.

After dismounting stiffly, he handed the man the reins then hobbled through the great bronze doors. Martina, in the hall, ran toward him, threw herself at him, and hugged him fiercely. "My favorite sadist! Are you well?"

He returned the hug. "Tired is all, my favorite wanton witch, and dry. When will Hadrian be back?"

She put an arm around him and walked with him to the great hall. "He should be back later this evening. Is your news for his ears only?

They entered the hall where servants were setting a place at the table for Scarface. Travesty, Hawk, Wolf, Lantee, and Raven were waiting for him. He nodded to each of them then dropped into the chair before the platter and cup.

"No need to raise an army," he said, and drained the cup. "Ghiblein and Abaransa have decided they'd rather continue to nibble at each other's borders than try to gobble up Gascolin." He found the carafe and refilled the cup then began to eat.

Travesty leaned on the back of the chair across the table from Scarface. "How much persuasion did that take?"

"None. I'd hardly begun to thread my way through the maze of petty officials when some Ghiblin prince killed the head of the Abransan legation. Stabbed him to death right outside the Abransan embassy. When the guards chased him into an alley he committed suicide. The Abransans were probably suspicious he'd killed himself to protect someone higher in the Ghiblin court. The Ghiblins, perhaps driven by guilty consciences, seem to have declared a new war immediately.'

Travesty's fingers toyed with the gold ring in his right ear. "Those seem rather suspicious circumstances."

"All the more appropriate, in view of the suspicious people involved." Scarface took another sip of wine. "Oh, did I mention the Ghiblin prince was from a border province where there hadn't been enough time for all the bodies to cool since their last border skirmish?"

As Scarface dined, his cousins, one by one, wandered out of the room until only Martina remained and she'd sat down in the chair beside his. "That was a long chance you took."

He chuckled. "The hard part was getting the Ghiblin prince drunk enough to get him to follow me into the alley. You know what guzzlers the Ghiblins are. The rest was simple. I'd seen him earlier in the day, so it was an easy matter to dress like him. After I got him into the alley I knocked him unconscious before laying a spell of slumber on him. Then I waited for the duke to return from his party. When he arrived I killed him, along with one of Forgren's guard dogs, dashed back to the alley, killed the Ghiblin with his own knife, and used a spell of concealment." He finished the venison and bread and chose two plums from the bowl of fruit on the table. "Anything interesting happen here in my absence?"

"Not much. Hadrian's son Damon and his new wife, a girl named Jeshka, have gone to the outpost in the Empire of the Book. Poker's coming back from there. That's why Hadrian isn't here. He went to meet Poker's boat in Varish."

"Damn! I just missed seeing him, then."

"You seem even more excitable than usual. What else happened to you?"

"I had a disagreement with one of Forgren's crowd—"

Martina sighed. "When are you going to stop antagonizing them?"

"Whenever they learn manners or you grow a beard, whichever comes first." He overcame an odd reluctance. "And I met a woman."

Martina leaned back in her chair, smiling. "So, that's your problem." She leaned forward, reached out, and stroked his cheek. "If you weren't my cousin, I'd take you myself."

He took her hand and kissed it. "And I'd accept, if you weren't my cousin—and weren't so damned fond of that little palm dagger." He stood. "I'm going to take a hot bath and fall into a soft bed. Tell Hadrian to wake me if he has to."

Without waiting for her answer he trod to his rooms. His needs had been anticipated and steam was rising from the water in the wooden tub. He placed the scepter on the bed, along with his weapons, so they were within easy reach of the tub, then undressed and lowered himself into the hot water.

Once he'd adjusted to the scalding heat he relaxed, almost falling asleep. It'd take the rest of the party he'd left in the mountains until at least tomorrow to reach Forgren's court at Gain. He could imagine Forgren and his lackeys falling over themselves and each other, trying to impress Mendarian. Imagining her in bed with Forgren smacked of bestiality, and the sycophants around him were as morally, if not physically, repugnant.

Mendarian had tried to steal the scepter, and if he'd allowed her to get close enough to him to reach it he couldn't have guessed what she might have attempted. He also remembered her chuckle and her manner after he'd thwarted the attempt. Apparently, there'd been no rancor and, certainly, no cowardice. He doubted he would've tried such a theft under the same circumstances in the first place but, if he had, he'd also have known when to give up and cut his losses. And he recalled that she'd tried to call off her two-legged dogs after he'd avoided her.

He felt more resentment toward the men. They'd been so eager to please her they'd have tried to kill or humiliate him for a smile from her. He had to admit her smile was a worthier prize than a king's favor—though not, he suspected, any more durable. He respected her. He could also trust her—to do what she thought was in her own best interests.

It seemed to take all the energy he could gather to bend tired joints and climb out of the tub. He rubbed himself dry with an old blanket then crawled onto the bed. He'd said nothing but the truth when he'd told her she made life more interesting.

~ * ~

The first tap on the door brought him awake. He had the scepter in his hand before the second rap. "A moment." He put down the scepter and, forcing his body to move despite its stiffness, pulled on a robe then picked up the scepter again.

Hadrian pushed open the door. He still wore his black leather armor and his weapons—two swords and at least three daggers. He signed a greeting then asked, "Did you want to go back to the hall to tell me of your trip?"

"How about the library? There's wine there and greater privacy."

Hadrian walked to the door and waited there while Scarface put on slippers and thrust the scepter into the belt of his robe. He led the way down the corridor and past the great hall, where Poker looked up from his dinner and waved to Scarface, then strode to the corner room with its dark wood shelves for books and bins for scrolls. Raven reclined on one of the couches, reading a scroll. She glanced up when they entered then stood and took the scroll with her out of the room.

Hadrian paced to the low table by the couch, held up a bottle of wine, red as blood in the firelight, and Scarface nodded. Hadrian filled two cups, handed one to Scarface, and sat on the couch Raven had just quitted. "I understand your 'diplomacy' was successful."

Scarface sat one the other couch, across the table from Hadrian. "Yes, Ghiblein and Abaransa have given up their plans to combine for an attack on Gascolin. Any clues they dig up will point to each other or the Sazians. I also had to kill a man with the Abransan legate, a man who wore a green ring." He paused but Hadrian said nothing. "And I ran into a little trouble on the way back; a group of travelers. One of them wore a green ring and called himself 'Timos.' From his build and his manner, it was probably Murtry. He never gave me his real name, and he persisted in asking prying questions."

"And you replied characteristically." Neither Hadrian's soft voice nor his expression revealed whether he was pleased or annoyed. "You'll have to learn to be more diplomatic."

"Horseshit." Scarface sipped his wine. "We both know I'm more valuable to the clan as unpleasant as I am than I'd ever be as just another ass-kisser. It's common knowledge you have trouble keeping me on a short rein, so you and the others can look pious, keep your hands clean, and tsk with the opposition while I get things done that couldn't be accomplished by any number of 'pleases' or 'by your leaves.'"

"How serious was the breach between you and Murtry?"

"He sizzled a little. I trapped the campsite with wards. I warned him and he still set one off." Scarface finished his wine, groaned as he extended his arm and placed the goblet on the table. "He'll be using a lot of aloe but, unfortunately, he'll survive." He sighed and leaned back on the couch. What do you know, or can find out, about a woman named Mendarian?"

Hadrian finished his own cup of wine, leaned forward, and refilled it. "You've been missing the gossip, haven't you? She's the new ruler of the Dieri, the largest single tribe in Cerco. She's been a roamer and in her travels found the lost crown and wolf's-head staff. From the stories, the staff and crown have some powers of their own, as well as being symbols to the Dieri and some of the other tribes. She's a good one to watch, if my information's correct. She's supposed to have played the same games our little cousin talks about. If you embrace her, be sure you know where all the knives are."

"Two more names. Arv lat Paldisan and Stego."

"Stego? Little man with a beard? Grins a lot? He's a Shatillan. He's gained some renown as a scholar of thaumaturgy, among other things, and it's been said he's been seen around objects that later disappeared. The other name is less known. If you met him on the road and not on your mission to court, I'd guess he's a younger son or from one of the families that's spent everything but the name." Hadrian stroked his thin moustache. "It sounds as though your trip was more interesting than your 'diplomacy.'"

"Very much so. Mendarian mentioned a treaty between Cerco and the Union, and I gather Forgren would like to seal that with a state wedding. It might be worthwhile to invite Mendarian here in two or three days."

"You, of course, have no interest in the matter beyond the tactical and the political."

"Hadrian, have I told you lately you can be a real prick? No fencing. Yes, I'm interested in the woman but I also think it'd be a good idea for you to meet her. You can claim that, as part of the Union, the clan should be involved in any treaty signed by Forgren as head of the Union.

"It might even be advisable for the clan to have a separate treaty with Cerco. Trusting Forgren and his lackeys as I do, I think it's possible Cerco may need more protection from the Union than it may ever get from them." He refilled his cup and drank half of it. "I'll also admit I don't fully trust the woman. Your warning about her mixing romance and cutlery rings true. I just wonder whether her hand was reaching for the scepter or my dagger."

Hadrian said nothing, only raised an eyebrow.

Scarface stared into the fire. "If she represents a threat to the clan, how much greater the danger if she gains the favor of the Union and joins it against us in open conflict? We should at least identify her as an enemy if she is one. If you can't be certain, a private interview with her might yield more information. It's well known you and I have had our differences in the past, and if I were to try to make common cause with her against the clan, and if she agrees and doesn't warn you, then we'd have knowledge we need and couldn't get any other way."

"The idea has merit." Hadrian stood and stretched, cat-like. "I'll let you get back to sleep, if you'd like. I should get back to Poker."

Scarface forced himself to his feet. "He might be the best man to deliver the invitation. Give him my regards."

"I'll do that," Hadrian said, and walked from the room.

Scarface scowled. It'd been like talking to a damned statue. Hadrian hadn't made a single commitment, he hadn't offered a trace of either support or opposition, and he hadn't even raised his soft voice. It was infuriating to compete with a man who wouldn't play. There was, at least, the chance Hadrian would favor the course he'd suggested. He wished there was a way to apply pressure, to force his plan into inevitability, but at this stage the likely result would be the opposite of what he wanted.

Again the dilemma. The clan did need him. Hadrian had simply told him Ghiblein and Abaransa were preparing to forge a treaty and combine to attack Gascolin, and had "asked" him to see to the matter. Hadrian had certainly been able to guess at the methods that would be employed when he chose Scarface for the mission.

It rankled Scarface to admit he also needed the clan. It afforded him a measure of protection and assured him of vengeance, when and if he fell. No one man could have enough agents in enough places to accomplish what the clan could achieve effortlessly. Were the clan merely a ruling family, leaders of a single nation, no matter how great, their power would be only a fraction of what it was now. The diaspora had actually made the clan more formidable than it'd been before. Its secretive ways were a source of strength. Clan members needn't wear crowns or ermine trim when they could force the alternatives between which crowned heads had to choose.

The Union operated in much the same fashion, although they lacked subtlety. Scarface had been able to observe the heavy hand of the Union at the Ghiblin court. They supported the High Warlord, and why not? If the Ghiblins attacked Gascolin they'd strike where the clan was responsible for defense. Clan members might be lost in the fighting. Certainly, the clan would lose prestige and power in Gascoyne, and Scarface was willing to bet High Rage itself that Forgren and his lackeys would've been called out of town just before they were called upon to honor their pact with the clan. It was long past time for some of the Union to do some of the worrying.

The Union was only one horn of his dilemma. Without clan protection, the Union would see Scarface as vulnerable, and he'd annoyed Forgren and his underlings often enough to be considered dangerous as well as personally detested. At the same time, the clan would execute him if he struck openly at the Union or its members unless he could prove he'd only killed in self-defense.

The clan existed to provide for all its members. Well and good, when all they wanted was their crumb of refuge. Hadrian had no ambitions beyond High Rage and the other outposts. He wanted nothing more, as chief of the clan as well as its executioner. His word was binding on all its members, but Hadrian's vision of power was too limited and limiting. Precarious safety wasn't power. In a world of ravening beasts, one couldn't afford to dine politely. He who eats least is eaten. There were kingdoms sprinkled across the map ripe for the picking, and sweeter than Shannan plums. Scarface knew that with a throne and ten years' grace he could build a force that'd stand firm, as firm as a rock in a spring's breeze.

The other nail in the boot was Hadrian's diplomacy. The rest of the Union outnumbered the clan by a wide margin and some of them had made their bargains with Powers or delved deeper into the Art than most of his kin. Scarface knew that, in any war, the clan would take losses, but the low cunning that had kept them all alive when the clan should've died favored its members in any battle. Still Hadrian insisted upon maintaining a posture of generosity and apparent weakness, of an almost dog-like eagerness to please.

Forgren owed even Gain, his holding, to Hadrian who'd stalked and destroyed the presence that had threatened Forgren's life and those of his household. And what was his reward? Forgren still treated the clan as underlings, pawns to be judged and used, trusting them no more than he had before.

That, at least, was something. Scarface didn't want the Union's trust; he wanted its fear. His contempt for most of its members could eat holes in iron. To have to pretend respect for them, to be silent in the face of their absurd pretentions, was gall in his mouth.

Returning to his room, he regretted that he was too tired to visit with Poker. Placing the scepter on the table beside his bed, he lay down. He'd have to find a silversmith to copy the scepter. Already a nagging worry and a plan became clearer. He blew out the candle and, still plotting, went to sleep.

~ * ~

Mendarian silently cursed Timos for a fool, even as she comforted him and applied a salve offered by the palmer. When Scarface had stopped smiling and told her to stand back, she knew she stared at death. If she'd stepped toward him, not all her charms or her power would keep that death away, and in that moment she knew she wanted Scarface more than any other man she'd ever met. Here was an equal, who treated her as an equal.

Arv pulled Timos' charred clothing off him and Mendarian used it as an excuse to go back to her cloak. The spell Scarface had used apparently caused the body to burn itself. Neither Timos' heavy robes nor the mailed shirt beneath them had protected him.

Mendarian recalled hearing of such a spell. It was a relatively simple one, she guessed, though not much known or used. It certainly wasn't the thing she'd expect of just a warrior, even one as well-traveled as Scarface seemed to be. That meant he was death spelled at least two different ways.

He'd caught her interest from the start. When he'd entered the inn he'd been cautious but his carriage had been confident, as though he considered himself the equal of any—or all—who were there. And the black scars on his upper face looked like the fingerprints of a demon. If Stego hadn't opened his sarcastic mouth at the wrong time she could probably have gotten the tale of how they came to be.

Timos was still moaning and she took some secret satisfaction in that. The scepter had been Scarface's—or hers if she could've gotten it. She'd told Timos to halt and he'd ignored her, so his pain was well-deserved. Now Scarface would be doubly on his guard around her.

That also pleased her. It made the challenge more interesting.

~ * ~

Arv woke her at dawn. She sat up and saw the other travelers eating whatever cold, dry food they carried—all but Timos who sat huddled in a blanket. His skin was peeling and he looked different, as though more than a layer or two of skin had been burned away. His features were more refined than she remembered, with thinner nose and lips, and his eyes were less deep-set, his cheekbones less pronounced.

She took a piece of cheese and an apple from her saddle pouch and sat beside the palmer. "Can you make him ready to travel?" She jerked her thumb at Timos.

"Perhaps I can relieve his pain but his burns need time to heal."

"Then relieve the pain. I need to be on my way again."

He stared at her as though she'd slapped his face. "I can do it but his burns need time in which to heal. Besides, we can't leave the camp with those signs out there."

"You tend to Timos. I'll take care of the other matter." She finished breakfast and strode to where Arv and Stego were sitting. She nodded at their greetings and pointed to the half-dozen dead bandits. "It's too stony to bury them here. I suggest we make pyres."

"But there's no wood here, either," Arv observed.

"But there are signs scratched on rocks. Take spears and push the bodies over the rocks until we've cleared a way out of here."

Stego grinned. "Ingenious! I should've thought of that."

Mendarian left them and went to Timos, whose moaning had stopped with the ministrations of the palmer.

"Can you ride?"

"Yes, my lady."

"Good we should be ready to leave here within the hour." She turned and watched as Arv and Stego pushed a corpse toward the trail.

They'd almost reached where the plateau narrowed when the body was obscured by a sheet of flame and reduced to little more than a smoking skeleton. They shoved another body along the path cleared by the first and it burned within four paces after the first remains. Four corpses were used to clear a path wide enough for three men walking abreast to march from the campsite to where the trail wound around the mountain.

The palmer approached Mendarian as she swung into her roan's saddle. "We can't leave yet. There may be more such signs left, and they might endanger other travelers."

"That's *their* problem," Mendarian snapped. "I've already been delayed longer than I want to be. If you want to play with the other bodies, or wait for the dew to rise from the rocks, that's your choice to make."

"You're a beautiful lady," the old man said. "Such a shame that when L'Istrim made you he forgot to give you a heart."

Mendarian glared at him then wheeled her horse and urged it along the cleared path.

Arv and Stego led the way, Timos rode beside Mendarian, and three other travelers followed on foot. The palmer and two others, one of them wounded in the night's attack, remained to clear the rocks of wards.

By noon Mendarian wished she'd brought the palmer, as his spell and medications to ease Timos' pain had worn off. Timos moaned and cursed, and each step of his horse seemed to add fresh anguish. She comforted him as best she could but was relieved, that evening, when she saw the rooftops of a large town.

Timos identified the place as Varish, and led them to an inn. The innkeeper sent for a healer and Mendarian sat down to a late dinner. She almost forgot her meal when a healer in his yellow robes and two other men entered the common room. One of them was a head taller than Timos, who was only slightly taller than Mendarian. The tall man wore doublet and hose of dark green and a sword and dagger at his belt. The other man was shorter, half a head shorter than Stego, dwarfish in the shape of his head and the disproportionate shortness of his limbs. He wore brown leather armor and carried an ornate battle-ax in his belt. She noticed all three of the men wore green rings.

They greeted Timos in Gasgoran, then changed to Porcashian. Mendarian smiled to herself. She spoke the language badly but understood it well.

Timos responded in Porcashian. "This is the woman I was to take to Forgren. Aren't you, my dear?"

Mendarian glanced at him. "I'm sorry; I don't understand what you said. Did you ask me a question?"

Timos reverted to Gasgoran. "Sorry, just asked if the food here was any good. Please excuse my friends and I. Their Gasgoran is limited, and I haven't seen them for some time."

"No offence taken. And the food here is at least better than trail rations."

"What happened to you?" the tall man asked Timos, in Porcashian.

"We met Scarface crossing the mountains—"

"Scarface? That whoreson!" The little man slammed his hand down on the table. "He was through here today, riding like there were a dozen creditors at his heels. Did you do something to him?"

"No such good luck. I found out he'd been in Ghiblein, though he wouldn't tell me what he'd been doing there. I'd guess he had a hand in reigniting the war between Ghiblein and Abaransa."

"I'll tell Forgren, although he's going to be more than a little annoyed," the tall man said. "But what happened to you?"

"We made camp together and he left some traps around it. I tried a spell of protection that kept the trap from killing me, but only barely. If you run into him, be careful. He has a scepter that causes whoever he touches with it to age. If you can get it away from him, Forgren would probably give almost anything for it."

The little man turned his eyes toward Mendarian and grinned.

Timos noticed the leer. "I said almost anything. He gets first claim on that. Maybe he won't like her."

"Not much chance of that," the tall one said.

Timos sipped from his cup, which held only water. "Anything interesting happen while I was gone?"

The short man caught the innkeeper's attention and called for mead, then leaned across the table and lowered his voice. "My old teacher was in town today."

"What was Hadrian doing here?"

"He met a barge from downriver. There was a man on it who, from a distance, looked like Poker."

Timos sighed as the healer's pain-easing spell took effect. "Poker? He's been gone for quite a while. Wasn't he at their outpost in the Empire of the Book? Do you think something's afoot there?"

The innkeeper delivered four mugs of mead to the table, caught the coin the tall man tossed him, and trudged back to the kitchen.

"Not likely," the tall one said. "I've heard Damon, Hadrian's boy, had gotten married. I haven't seen him lately, so I'd guess he's gone to the empire and Poker's returned."

"Shit," the little man snapped. "Before long we'll have another damned generation of them to worry about."

"Maybe not," Timos replied. "I hear Runa's being sent to the empire to make some contacts for us."

Mendarian recognized only a couple of the names but she could understand the sense of their conversation and guess at the rest. Scarface had mentioned Hadrian ruled in the name of the clan and it was obvious the Union, at least these members, but probably the whole Union didn't trust the clan. This was worth knowing. The best weapon was knowledge of the weaknesses of possible enemies.

"Excuse us," Timos said to Mendarian in Gasgoran. "I'm going upstairs. The healer will be treating my burns. Ivo, the tall fellow, and Valdemar will escort you to Gain tomorrow."

"I'll miss you. We'll have to try to see each other again, soon."

Timos stood and bowed then plodded up the stairs, the healer following him.

Mendarian made small talk with her new escorts, whose Gasgoran was much better than Timos had claimed. The little man should have been clad in motley. She was tempted to toss a stick for him to fetch. Ivo was more reserved but obviously eager to impress her.

Finally she pleaded weariness and climbed the stairs to a small room. She undressed and, using the pitcher and the basin, washed herself as best she could and lay on the pallet. Sleep came softly, like a thief.

~ * ~

She came awake to the sound of tapping on her door. "Who is it?" She'd already slipped her dagger under the blankets.

"Ivo. We'll be leaving in half an hour."

"I'll be ready." She sprang from the bed and pulled fresh clothing from her pack. Like the clothes she'd worn the day before, they were black, differing only in cut and material. She dressed quickly; made sure the dagger, now strapped to the inside of her left forearm, could be quickly drawn but was well-concealed, then went downstairs.

Stego glanced up from the stew he'd almost finished. "Join me, my dear. It's my last chance to converse with you before we part company."

Mendarian sat beside him, Arv on her other side. Stego was, as always, witty and exceedingly sharp. Mendarian was amused and enjoyed the attention but caught herself wondering what he was trying to prove by displaying his learning. He wiped his bowl clean with a piece of bread then stood. Mendarian gave him a hug and considered a kiss, but was very conscious of the presence of Ivo and Valdemar.

They walked to the stable as a group, claimed their horses and gear, and parted, Stego continuing to the west, Mendarian and her group riding south.

It'd seemed like early fall in the mountains and Mendarian was almost shocked to realize that here, in the rolling, grassy hills, it was still midsummer. The warm wind stroked the once-green crops, turned to gold and brown. She looked to her left to see the blue mountains and tried to guess what was happening beyond them, in Cerco. She'd left the story that she was in a cave, meditating, drawing nearer the old gods of the place.

The hills through which they rode became flatter and the crops gave way to grassland dotted, here and there, with small herds of half-wild cattle. Twice she saw deer and when they stopped at noon by a tree-shaded spring she recognized the paw prints of a bear.

In the early afternoon she saw the spires of turrets and an hour later they rode through the main gate of Gain.

Chapter 2

Scarface rose early and reviewed his thoughts of the night before. While he still had no clear plan, he had ideas enough that should be acted upon as soon as possible. He wanted a copy made of his scepter. He'd need to study Cerco. He had the feeling he might be seeing the place soon, and he wanted to know the history he might want to change. And he might need some help that could best be given by Martina.

A silversmith was easy enough to find in the town Hadrian was trying to coax into becoming a city. Without complaint, Scarface paid three prices for the work, even though the replica couldn't be a perfect copy. One price was for the work, the second was for promptness—he wanted the copy in his hands within three days, and the third price was for discretion,

Scarface refused to allow the silversmith to even touch the scepter. Instead, he held it up and turned it so the craftsman could make sketches, and he took the dimension himself by stick and drew them on a sheet of parchment.

His study of Cerco was, of necessity, confined to the library of High Rage, which contained only two books and a scroll on the place, although there was also a very good map.

He read the scroll first, as it was the oldest, and immediately found mention of the crown and the staff Mendarian had found. Beyond conferring leadership of the Dieri, the articles also gave some powers to their possessor. Both crown and staff were relics of the Age of Building. The crown was an oracle of sorts, in that its wearer could receive the answers to some questions. The staff was supposedly more powerful. If the wielder of the staff also wore the crown, he or she could control the weather in Cerco. These relics had been given to Wolf, the father of the tribes, to make the people of Cerco great.

Scarface returned the scroll to its bin, nodded to Raven who'd just entered the room, then returned to the couch and the books. What the scroll hadn't said had been, perhaps, more valuable than the information it imparted. It would've been helpful to know what questions Mendarian could ask of her crown and the sorts of answers she might receive, although oracles were notoriously enigmatic. If the crown's last wearer had been well served, why had the staff and crown been lost for so long?

The scroll had also given no clues as to the limits of the staff's power, although it must have some. Scarface had long since learned that, no matter the greatness of the maker of an artifact, each item's power was limited in some ways, just as was his scepter. A mystical balance was always maintained. Man alone had only the limits he set upon himself.

The first book was in Oldtongue and dealt with the magic, religion, and customs of Cerco, especially of the Dieri, the largest single tribe. The magicks apparently practiced by the Dieri were only shamanism and charlatanism. He doubted he could learn much from their magi.

Their religion was more interesting. Father Wolf was worshipped, although the Cercans believed in the existence of a higher power or, perhaps, more than one greater deity. The greater power, or powers, was reckoned to be so far above man that it or they had no interest in man or his struggles. That was the reason for creating Father Wolf—to intercede for man. The howling of a wolf was taken as a prayer for the tribe.

Among the tribes, wolves were honored. A share of each game animal was left to the wolves and, during winter, when food was scarce, as many as half the sheep and goats of each shepherd's flock might be given as an offering to the wolves. If a Cercan had to kill a wolf he always asked pardon first and kept the pelt as an object of veneration. A man was only permitted to wear a wolf skin if he'd killed the animal with his bare hands.

Scarface smiled and stroked the black scars around his eyes and forehead. It seemed each society had its own little tests for the devout and the ambitious.

The values of the tribes were apparently the usual code of hunters and reluctant warriors, or even willing warriors among some tribes. Boasting, for instance, was perfectly acceptable if a man was prepared to make good his brag. All this could be very useful.

He rose to return the book to its shelf and barely noticed that Raven had left and Travesty sat on another couch, reading a scroll.

Scarface walked back to the couch and the third book. This was a history and written only a decade or so ago. According to the history, Cerco could hardly be considered a nation; it was more a collection of tribes, with frequent wars between them. What little commerce existed between the tribes was chiefly confined to barter.

A little over eight hundred years ago the Dieri had either conquered or allied themselves with the other tribes and had even begun to expand into neighboring countries, then, after four hundred years of conquest, had slid into consolidation, then into decadence. The beginning of their decline had coincided with the loss of the staff and the crown. The eastern tribes had broken away from the crumbling empire and the western tribes, after a single generation, had declared their independence from the Dieri.

This could be dangerous. Or an opportunity. If the recovery of the staff and crown heralded the recovery of an empire, then Cerco would be a force that must be dealt with.

The Nevenii, the northernmost eastern tribe or tribes, spoke Ghiblin and sometimes allied themselves with Ghiblein. They'd begun to carve out a minor kingdom for themselves, conquering and taking slaves from some of the smaller tribes around them. Something would have to be done about these matters, Scarface decided.

The Tuati, to the southeast, seemed to be a confederation of tribes. They spoke Abarsa and raided and traded in Abaransa, while to the west the Senshenni spoke Gasgoran and carried on some trade, although they hadn't raided into Gascolin since at least a decade before the clan had been awarded High Rage.

A thought struck him. Most such peoples entertained the notion that women existed only to bear sons or to cook and mend. If so, the Dieri and other Cercans were likely to learn more from their new ruler that they could guess. Mendarian was no man's slave or toy. Her nerve and determination would be a surprise for her subjects.

He took the third book back in its place and felt the distorted sense of not-time. He couldn't guess whether it was late morning, early afternoon, or midnight. The candles must've been changed while he'd been reading for they were longer than he remembered them.

From the library he strode to the hall. Dinner was being served and his stomach twisted with hunger. An empty chair stood between Poker and Martina and, when they saw him, both motioned for him to occupy the place so he sat down with them. A servant brought him a platter of food and a cup of wine.

"We've missed you," Martina said with a grin. "All the flies I've seen still have their wings and all the spiders have all their legs. Are you feeling well? Where've you been hiding?"

"I had some reading to do. One or two of the things involve your specialty. May I talk with you about it later?"

"Of course. My rooms? That way, if you annoy me I can kick you out instead of having to walk out on you. I hate long, angry walks when I'd rather just pout."

"I'll be the perfect gentleman."

"You always are. In some ways, you're a real disappointment to me."

Scarface had to grin. "You don't mean there might be some chance for me to become more intimately acquainted, do you?"

"No, but you might try. It's good for my self-esteem to have to slap a face now and then."

Poker's grin revealed his very long canine teeth. Scarface caught Poker's forearm, felt the other man's strong grip wrapped around his own arm. "You've been gone a long time, brother. Is your god being kind to you?"

"Ianno is kind to everyone," Poker replied, "but I'm especially blessed. I've become a priest and now I teach in a small seminary in The Shield of the Saint." He sipped his wine. "And you? Have you found something to give you contentment?"

"Not yet, but you give me hope."

"True, we were very much alike before my conversion."

Scarface chewed and swallowed a bit of lamb before he spoke again. "If it doesn't bother you to talk about the old days—how do you reconcile your present love of man with your former skill as an interrogator? Early in the Doss wars you had the reputation of being able to make a stone talk, and you were never lied to, as far as I know."

Poker washed down bread and meat with more wine. "It's my honor and duty to love all people. How can I withhold that love from myself?"

Scarface's smile was sardonic. "So, your deity relieves you of the unnecessary burdens of remorse and recrimination?"

Poker laughed. "Not at all. I wouldn't be human if I had no remorse or regrets, knowing what I do now. I don't justify the things I did. I use the memories as a spur to avoid that kind of thing in the future. What I did then I did out of misguided religious convictions."

Scarface stopped, his cup halfway to his mouth. "None of us, or the Union either, believed in Das. We fought for the clan or the Union." He sipped his wine.

Poker carefully carved his meat into smaller pieces. "I wasn't referring to the false god of the sword, I was talking about another false god, whose name is 'expediency,' and I think we all worshipped him with the fervor of fanaticism."

"I notice you seem to regard all gods but Ianno as false."

"Not quite, but a god should give as well as take. If he accepts our offerings and gives us only bloodshed and strife, then he's a false god. A true god gives his followers peace and joy. What joy have your dark death-gods given you? Gods are like the wind; they're invisible but their effects are observable to all. The proof Ianno exists is the love and gentleness he's inspired in his worshippers. I'm not saying you're evil or a fool, only that you've been defrauded."

Scarface felt uncomfortable with the conversation and tried to conceal his discomfort by concentrating on his meal. When he finished he leaned back, then remembered the errand. "Cousin, you may be escorting a certain person back to High Rage—"

"Yes, Hadrian mentioned that. A woman named Mendarian? I'll leave the day after tomorrow, and I should be back with her by evening of the following day, if she chooses to come with me."

"Very good. In the odd event she asks any questions about the clan or any of us individually, I give you leave to answer fully and honestly as much as you know."

Poker again showed his fangs in a smile. "I'd have answered honestly anyway. As for fully—I'll answer any questions about you if, indeed, she does ask. As for the others, their privacy is their own."

"Fair enough." Scarface rose. "I hope to see you again tomorrow. It's been too long. Do you think you can still beat me at Gods and Kings?"

"Perhaps we can play a game tomorrow and see. If memory serves, your weakness was rashness but your strength was improvisation."

Scarface nodded and turned to Martina. "Would it be convenient for you to discuss the Art with me now?" He drew out her chair as she rose.

"Oh, all right. You know, when you have an idea or a problem you're impossible until you've acted. If you've really taken an interest in this Mendarian, I don't know whether to pity you or her."

He held out his arm and she linked hers through it. "I can understand why you might feel sorry for her, but why waste sympathy on me?"

"Because your shadow's grown darker since you returned."

Scarface almost missed a step and had to make a conscious effort to avoid looking down at his shadow on the floor.

Without speaking again they followed the corridor to Martina's room, which was bright with hangings and rugs and pillows, all jewel-bright. Instead of a bed she had a large, soft couch, and her armor and weapons, clean and well-oiled occupied one corner of the room.

She kicked her soft ankle-boots into a corner and sank onto a mound of cushions. "What, in particular, did you want to know?"

"Two spells." Scarface sat on the floor, facing her. "I may want to assume a different appearance, perhaps for several days. It can be illusory but it needs to be good enough to fool people who aren't easily gulled. I may also want to assume a different form. A hawk, maybe."

Martina laughed. "You don't want much, do you? Just most of what I know. This is much more involved than your battle-magic. I'll have to do the ceremonies myself, but I'll need to draw on you for power. Do you just want to change your appearance or do you want to mimic someone in particular?"

"Mimic."

"Do you have something that belongs to the one you want to impersonate?"

"No, dammit."

"That makes it more difficult. Do you know him well?"

"Too well."

Martina grinned. "Oh, one of the Union. You can use your green ring for that, since it can be used to reach anyone who wears a similar ring. That's probably why Forgren hands them out." She paused for a moment. "How soon do you need the spells cast?"

"I'm not sure. I'm not even certain I'll need them, but it's always best to know the way to the back door."

"I'll get some things ready tomorrow and we can build the first spell the day after. We'll do the spell of transmigration first, since it's the more difficult. You know the risks, don't you?"

"I think so. If, when I try to change form, the body I wish to change into is dead, then I die. And if something happens to my body while I'm in the other form, I may be trapped in that form until it dies, then I'll die, too. Anything else?"

"You have the major points. There's also the chance of madness or, in your case, possible sanity." Martina leaned back into the cushions and stared at Scarface until he became uneasy. "Perhaps I shouldn't ask, but since I'm casting the spells, and since I'm taking a chance on losing a cousin of whom I've grown fond—for no good reason, mind you—I'd like to know what you want to do, and why."

"I'm not sure myself. If I need to use the magic I'll tell you what and why. That much, at least, I owe you."

Martina laughed again. "I think I can tell you why. I think you may be in love and, if so, I'm sorry for both of you. From what I've heard of her, she's a very self-willed woman. You'd do better to take a wife like Hadrian's; one who'll care deeply for you and make you the center of her world. This Mendarian sounds as though she'd fight you for the tiniest scrap of power, or lash out at any perceived threat."

"Then I'll have to make sure I never give her cause, or take anything from her."

"That's not enough protection. I'm afraid of what she'll take from you. And if she hurts you enough, I'll be afraid for her. We know each other too well, cousin. You're the kind that doesn't like to have enemies, at least not living ones, and those never really touch you. I hope I never find out what you'd be like if you were cut to the bone."

Scarface smiled. "As to dealing with enemies, we're just discussing shades of annoyance. How many imps can dance on a nailhead? How many ways are there to die painfully?"

"That's what bothers me; you're inventive. It's for your sake I hope I never have reason to regret helping you."

"What time do you want to start, the day after tomorrow?"

"Half an hour before dawn, so be sure to get to sleep early tomorrow night. These rituals take time and a good deal of power, so be sure you're ready to give me both."

He drew his legs under himself, then rose to his feet. "I'm very fond of you, too. It's a pity we're blood kin because you do have a wonderful body, which should be properly appreciated. Is that sufficient to get my face slapped?"

Martina's smile was weak. "Somehow I've lost the desire. Good night."

Scarface trod back to his room, cloaked and cowled in deep thought.

~ * ~

Mendarian undressed for bed and tried to sort out her perceptions and opinions along with her clothes. Forgren was attractive, in the sense any man who held and wielded power was attractive. Physically, he was less desirable. He was taller than Scarface, and heavier. He'd obviously once been a formidable fighting man and still retained some vestige of that power, but the massive muscles had grown slack. For some reason, Mendarian had been repulsed by his walk and his boots, both of which showed the strain of supporting so much weight.

Still, he was charming because he was so obviously charmed. They hadn't yet discussed matters of substance but Mendarian suspected he wouldn't be a hard bargainer.

She'd only seen one woman in Gain who hadn't seemed to be a servant. She was large, blonde, and aggressive, and seemed to be a warrior from Bildesh. The other members of the Union she'd met had been a disparate lot, from as short as Valdemar to as tall as Ivo; from as blonde as Lidhyar, the woman, to as dark as Valdemar with his swarthy face and black eyes and hair; and speaking with many foreign accents, most of them Porcashian but a few were accents she couldn't recognize.

As obvious as the members' differences were their similarities. With the exception of Lidhyar, they'd all gone out of their way to be charming and they'd each observed their own position in a definite hierarchy. This was a thing she sensed rather than reasoned.

The prospect of a state wedding was made less appealing by Forgren's bulk. She might be able to accomplish the same ends by marrying some other member of the Union but she found herself mistrusting Forgren's generosity. Besides, marrying an underling was not a promising beginning for an empress.

She wondered what Scarface was doing. It was a pity his power and his resources were so limited. It was also unfortunate she couldn't trust him. No one could be trusted completely, not even Arv, but most could at least be expected to follow certain patterns. Scarface was someone who relied upon surprise, which could also be a fatal weakness.

She finished stacking her clothes in the chest, her gowns and robes on top, her traveling clothes, clean again, at the bottom. Finally she blew out the candle and climbed into bed.

One could adjust to luxury so quickly. A year ago she'd never been nearer a bed than a straw pallet at an inn, and now she slept in real beds between sheets of silk.

~ * ~

Her education in the ways of the Union began the next day when she learned how the Union influenced nations as far away as Doss and even had contacts in the Sazian court. Most of the members were mere lackeys and messengers doing Forgren's bidding. The other power in Gain was Harma, the old, bald magus. As much as Mendarian enjoyed power and the company of men who wielded it, Harma made her skin crawl.

His bulging eyes dominated a face in which the nose was little more than a tip and the mouth a gash. His attempts to charm her seemed more oily than suave, and his ego was at least a match for his considerable abilities.

When Forgren took her riding in the afternoon she observed the town near the castle was obviously under the tight control of the Union and large squads of soldiers, usually under the command of men wearing green rings, patrolled the roads. When she saw one of the squads stop a tinker and search his wagon she raised an eyebrow at Forgren. "Does some danger threaten?"

"Not now," he said with a laugh. "And not likely to as long as we keep our precautions."

She suggested the race back to the castle and enjoyed her victory almost as much as Fogren's ill-concealed displeasure at being beaten. She guessed there weren't many in the Union who'd dare best Forgren at anything.

That evening, after dinner, several of them gathered in Forgren's suite of rooms. Valdemar teased Mendarian until Forgren picked him up and set him on the mantel. Mendarian felt very relaxed with the men, none of whom could threaten her, and all of them trying to entertain her. She was even becoming used to Harma, who created fabulous birds and dragons and even a unicorn out of flames from the fireplace.

Finally she left them and walked to her room. Nothing had been mentioned about a treaty but she guessed she could get almost any terms she might want. While the center of Union power was tightly controlled, that control was Forgren's, and he could be dealt with. As she undressed she tried to decide what terms she might choose and wondered what she might have to trade for them.

She woke up once during the night with the bitter taste of a dream still on her mind—a fire-demon like one of Harma's conjurations, reaching out with clawed fingers and touching a face, then withdrawing. The face, whose eyes were now framed with black and smoking scars, was her own.

~ * ~

The memory had faded in the morning, leaving only a vague sense of foreboding. Late in the morning she found herself alone with Forgren in the great hall, at the head of a long table. Forgren's immense chair was almost a throne.

"Yesterday," Forgren reminded her, "you were speaking of the security of Cerco. Would being accepted as a member of the Union set your mind at ease about the safety of your rule?"

Mendarian suddenly felt cold. She heard herself, in a calm voice, ask, "And what's the price of admission to membership in the Union?"

"No price. It's in the interest of the Union to have some of our members on thrones."

"But I thought the Union was an exclusive organization."

"It is, to the extent you must be invited to join and your membership must be ratified by a number of members and several leaders, but I doubt they'll raise any objections."

"Who are the leaders?"

"Myself, of course, Harma, Hadrian Darkmoor—"

"I've heard of him, that he can be deadly."

Forgren smiled. "Of course. As can we all, but I know how to handle him. And neither Misetel nor Wilkan pay much attention to the internal affairs of the Union. You'll be readily accepted as a member if you decide to join."

"As a member of the Union, what do I give and what will I receive?"

"You'll be asked to give assistance to the Union, which will, in its turn, guarantee the safety of your throne and your person."

"Very generous." Mendarian left her reservations unspoken. It'd occurred to her this agreement might leave her a figurehead, carrying out the Union's orders, and her payment would simply be the right to continue being a live slave. She would actually be giving up the power she already had. She'd underestimated Forgren as a haggler.

He noticed her preoccupation. "Does something bother you?"

"No, just tired. I didn't sleep well last night. By the way, how's Timos?"

"For a moment Forgren's eyes reflected confusion, then he squeezed out a smile. "His real name is Murtry. I regret having to deceive you but, since he was traveling in unknown country it was decided he go in disguise. He's doing well and will probably return to Gain within the next week or two."

"I'm glad he's well." She paused. It might be interesting to see Forgren's reaction to being reminded of his fallibility, and it would put her back on the offensive. "It's interesting that he was apparently recognized by a man called Scarface."

Forgren pressed his lips together so tightly they turned white. "Scarface is also a member of the Union. He may have recognized Murtry. More likely, he only knew he was facing another member of the Union." He steepled his fingers and stroked his second chin with the tips of his index fingers. "Scarface is a disappointment to me. I had greater hopes of him."

"What do you mean? That he's a member of the Union, too? How did that happen?"

"All the members of the Winged Dagger Clan are also members of the Union. That's one reason Hadrian has so much power in the Union."

"I talked to this Scarface. He never mentioned he was a member of any group but he suggested there was bad blood between himself and Hadrian."

Forgren eked out another tight smile. "There seems to be bad blood between Scarface and almost everyone. I've heard he and Hadrian had some sort of disagreement and Scarface had to back down. When Scarface first came to our attention he was quiet and courteous. Each success has made him bolder, until he accepts no power higher than himself. It may be necessary to re-educate him."

Mendarian stood. "If you don't mind, I'd like some time to think about your offer. I'd also like to have a drink."

Fogren heaved himself to his feet. "Very well. I can provide the drink." He led the way to the back door of the hall, into the kitchen, and to a great keg of wine. "Shannan wine. Hadrian has many uses."

Mendarian had noticed the quality of the vintages she'd drunk at Gain and at the inn in Varish. She'd heard of Shannan wine and now knew how it'd acquired its reputation. "What's the connection between Hadrian and Shannan wine?"

"The same as the connection as Shannan marble. Hadrian's trying to build a city in Valé Shanna. His first step was to have the farmers establish vineyards and orchards in addition to their grain crops, and to hire vintners. Then he reopened the quarries in the mountains. He used the marble and the wines and brandies as trade items to draw merchants to his town, and where buyers and sellers gather, the artisans soon go to ply their trades. He may have that city on his hands one of these days."

"Why haven't you done the same thing here?"

"Cities tend to be noisy, crowded, smelly things. I'd rather have a simple hamlet near me."

Mendarian finished her wine and excused herself, then went looking for Arv. She found him playing Gods and Kings with Valdemar. She entered the room and gestured for Arv to ignore her but hadn't crept more than four paces when Valdemar, without turning around, greeted her.

"That's a neat trick. How did you know I was here?"

"I heard the door open and the light footsteps. And Arv, here, can't keep his face expressionless." Valdemar moved a piece on the board. "Your last god has no worshippers. You owe me a keg of beer."

Arv stared at the board. "I'm still not sure about that last move, but here." He dug into his pouch and drew out three large silver coins. "This should pay for the keg. I'll try to win it back later."

Valdemar grinned. "Why wait? Have you a coronation to attend?"

Mendarian put a hand on Arv's shoulder. "He's coming with me. I don't think Arv's been out of the castle since we arrived. I'm going to see he gets some sunlight and fresh air. Come on, Arv, the woods are waiting."

Valdemar looked up at her and grinned. "I've been sitting a lot, too. Maybe I should go out and stretch my legs."

Mendarian replied without thinking. "Fine idea, but I don't think it'll work." Then she noticed a faint narrowing of the little man's eyes and an ugliness flicker in their depths and knew she'd just discovered a chink in his armor. "Just joking. I hope I haven't given offense."

"I can't be offended by the truly beautiful."

"Why, Valdemar, you have the soul of a poet. But I really need to talk to Arv. I hope you don't mind."

"Not at all."

Arv had stood and together they strolled out of the castle and to the fringe of trees, well out of bow-shot of the buildings. As soon as they reached the shade of the trees, Mendarian turned and caught Arv by the shoulder, making no attempt to hide her excitement. "Arv, I've been invited to join the Union!"

Instead of the answering excitement Mendarian had expected, Arv's usual expression of gloom seemed more deeply etched into his face. "I'm glad to hear that."

"You don't look it. What's the matter?"

Arv stared at the toes of his boots. "How long have we known each other?"

Mendarian's face went rigid. "Over five years, since you plucked me out of that alley in Havamn. You don't need to remind me how far I'd fallen nor how I lasted until you found me and took me with you. Yes, I'm grateful for all you've been to me and all you've given me."

Arv still didn't look up. "We've taken care of each other a lot in those five years. I just don't feel comfortable getting involved with people we don't know. Is this Union going to take care of you, or are they just going to use you?"

Mendarian stood, legs apart, fists on hips. "They'll use me no more than I'm going to use them. Of course they're going to try to control me, but I think I can handle that. I'll give what I must and slide as much by them as I can. And, in the meantime, my throne will be secure."

Arv finally looked up, his expression unchanged. "I just think that with me taking care of you, you don't need all of these others."

"You've done a great job, too," Mendarian said sarcastically. "*I* was the one who found the crown and the staff, and once you knew what they were, you wanted to turn your back on them. If you had your way, I'd still be following you around, patching you up after every petty border dispute or whatever war you could sell yourself for. Maybe you want to be a whore to war all your life, or wait for your older brothers to die off without acknowledging any of their bastards, but I know opportunity when I see it, and I'm not letting it slip by me. Now, you can follow me for a change or you can go your own way. It's your choice to make."

"I'll stay with you, but I don't think these people are going to be much help to you."

"They'll be more help than you can be at this point. We aren't playing soldier anymore. For the first time, we have real power. Whether they mean to or not, they're going to teach me the use of power."

She watched him staring at his boots, then she turned on her heel and strode back to the castle. Her long legs rapidly carried her over the ground and she took satisfaction in knowing Arv had to run to keep up with her. When she reached the list, the sandy strip between the outer wall and the main building, she met Ivo, who congratulated her on becoming a member of the Union.

"But I haven't decided to accept, yet," she protested,

"In that case, I'll congratulate you when you do decide. In the meantime, would you like to go riding or hawking?"

"I've spent most of the last week in the saddle, but I haven't had a bow in my hands lately. Would you like to help me get used to shooting arrows again?"

Ivo flashed a smile and nodded toward a squat stone shed. "Over there's the armory."

For over an hour Mendarian practiced with the bow. When archery bored her she borrowed Ivo's sword and attacked one of the pells, and when that lost her interest she returned Ivo's sword and found Harma to teach her about the workings of magic.

Although Harma was very friendly and amusing, she learned next to nothing from him but a spell of warding. Every peasant had some magical protection, usually crude and ineffective, varying from carved wooden amulets to crossed fingers.

Harma's spell was more elaborate and seemed to resemble the circle of protection Scarface had used when Timos—or rather, Murtry—had attempted to use a spell against him. The spell seemed simple enough, with little to memorize and only the design scratched on the floor or ground and only a few motions but she found, after practicing the spell, that she was exhausted.

Harma was just beginning to explain why she was so drained from executing the spell when a servant announced the dinner hour. Mendarian accompanied Harma to the great hall and had just sat down when one of the guards trod into the hall and whispered to Forgren.

Forgren took the interruption with ill grace and she caught his reply, "What does he want here?"

The soldier whispered again and Forgren frowned, then said, "Well, show him in then."

As the guard left, Forgren turned to Mendarian. "You'd expressed some curiosity about the Winged Dagger Clan. One of their members—a man called Poker—is here to join us for dinner. He's just returned from the Empire of the Book, where he's been for some time, and I've heard he's become a priest."

Within moments a man wearing blue-gray and black walked under the arched entrance to the great hall. He was of medium height, almost as tall as Mendarian, and slender. His hair and beard were blue-black and tightly curled but his most arresting features were his slanting eyebrows.

He approached the head of the table and gave Forgren a nod that was almost a bow, then he smiled and Mendarian noticed his long canine teeth, half again as long as the rest of his front teeth.

"Greetings, Forgren," he said. "It's been a long time. You look well."

"Thank you. You seem to wear the time well, too. I believe you know most of us, all but our guests, Mendarian of Cerco and her man down there," he gestured at Arv, "Arv lat Paldisan."

Poker turned to Mendarian and she was surprised to see his eyes, as black as his hair, were remarkably gentle and pacific. "It's she I came here to meet." His voice, though rich, was as mild as his eyes. "I'm here to offer her an invitation in the name of the clan. Hadrian wanted me to tell her he'd be honored if she'd accept the hospitality of High Rage."

Mendarian glanced at Forgren and observed his smile was a thin lie, then she looked again at Poker. He was an attractive man and, if the eyes could be believed, his other features only added a dash of the exotic to a face that was almost handsome.

"I'd be honored to visit Valé Shanna and High Rage. I've heard so much about them."

Forgren ordered the servants to set another place at the table and asked the members of the Union already present to move down a space. Mendarian noted that Poker's place at the table was on the other side of Forgren from her and the men asked to move down the table did so with ill grace. She shouldn't find it difficult to drive a wedge between the two groups, she decided.

Poker ate and drank well, and abstained from neither the meat nor the wine. Mendarian finished her own meal and drained the last of the wine in her cup, then held it out for more, a motion Poker copied.

"I've noticed," she said, "that you're hardly ascetic. I thought it was the lot of priests to live lives of abstinence."

Poker smiled. "For some priests it seems proper. For others, abstention is a source of pride, which is an affront to Ianno. Indulgence is only wrong when it distracts us from worship or good works." He held up his cup. "If I were to permit wine to become my master I couldn't serve Ianno as He should be served, but so long as it's only a pleasant thing I may do without, there's no reason to avoid it."

Mendarian answered with a smile of her own. "Are you also married?"

Poker laughed. "No, I fear a woman would be my soul's fatal weakness. I'd become too devoted to her to be a good priest."

"That's interesting. Some men would consider it a form of cowardice to avoid a weakness. They'd try to conquer it and make themselves stronger."

"That would be arrogance, and the price of my victory would be paid by someone else, in unhappiness. Even if I won the battle, I'd lose the war for my soul. I can't gain salvation by condemning someone else to unhappiness or worse."

"But a woman of the night—"

"Is still a woman. If I didn't care for her I'd only be using her and if I really cared for her, I'd want her to love me. If I saw her only as a creature for my pleasures I would, I suppose, be able to convince myself I'd overcome some weakness, but I'd have lost much more, for I'd have thought of her only as a body, an object and that, for me, would be a greater loss than loving her."

"You're a very strange priest."

"There are some very strange gods."

For a moment she toyed with the handles of her dinner knife and spoon. "Speaking of the strange, you have a very strange name."

He nodded. It's only strange because it's foreign. In Sinn, 'Poker' means 'proud.'"

"Then the name was well-chosen."

She found the rest of the evening most pleasant. She discovered that, by paying attention to Poker, she could cause Forgren and his men to redouble their efforts to charm her, and she enjoyed the game for a time. Finally, just before she retired for the night, she agreed to leave early the next morning with Poker.

As she lay on her bed she let her mind drift. It was disconcerting to like a man, particularly one she'd just met, and especially one whose beliefs were so counter to her own. Poker was pleasant and affable without apparently trying to charm her. She also found interesting the fact that, in some ways, Forgren seemed to fear him.

~ * ~

She rose early the next morning, dressed in her traveling clothes, and packed two changes of clothing in her saddlebags. She stopped at the kitchen to nibble on a piece of bread and an apple, then strode to the stable where she fed what was left of the apple to her roan then saddled and bridled him. As she finished buckling the cinch, Poker and

Arv entered the stable together. Poker greeted her then walked to a stall holding a blue roan, led him out, and began to saddle him. With a glance at Poker, Mendarian beckoned for Arv to follow her outside.

"I want you to stay here," she said softly. Even in the wan light of early morning she could see the perpetual expression of gloom on his face deepen. "I need you here to be my eyes and ears. I want you to find out what you can about the Union, especially whether they can be trusted. You might also try to find out everything you can about the Winged Dagger Clan."

"Mendarian, I think you're on a trip from adder to viper."

"Maybe, but I don't think I have anything to fear from Poker and I think I can count on him to protect me. Besides, no one in the Union has suggested that what I'm doing is dangerous."

Arv's reluctance showed in the sag of his shoulders. "All right, I'll stay here, but you be careful. Remember, you're walking into Scarface's place of power."

Mendarian mounted then watched Poker lead out his blue and swing into the saddle. "I'll remember."

Poker set an easy pace for the ride and commented on the beauty of the rolling, grassy hills.

"Why," Mendarian wondered aloud, "would Hadrian want a city just outside his walls?"

"For civilization. It takes cities to foster art and commerce to improve goods. Hadrian believes everyone benefits from both art and commerce."

"And, of course, the lord collects more taxes," Mendarian added.

Poker frowned as though Mendarian had disappointed him. "That's a common mistake. More people are taxed, but the tax on each is less. The peasants gain in that the merchants bear some of the load the peasants would otherwise have to carry alone. At High Rage we keep the taxes to a minimum, since high taxes are no inducement to anyone. Instead, we supplement the taxes by buying the fruit, berry, and grape crops at market value, then ferment and sometimes distill them, then sell them at a profit. Shannan wines and brandies support most of the upkeep of the fief, and most of the rest of the income is from Shannan marble. The low taxes are one reason High Rage has grown so quickly."

"You seem to have a high opinion of this Hadrian Darkmoor."

"He's my cousin, and I have a high regard for his understanding of some matters. As for Hadrian the man, I respect him."

It'd be interesting to bait Poker, Mendarian decided, and any information she might gain would be a gift. "I've heard stories about him, that he was run out of Doss."

Poker chuckled. "'Run out' is an inappropriate description. Hadrian and the clan had a disagreement with the new 'godhead' of Doss and declined to accept the castle we'd been awarded for our service in the war. We gave some consideration to open rebellion but decided the people had suffered enough in the last war, and starting another one wasn't in the best interests of the people or the clan."

"I've heard Hadrian can be very dangerous."

"Anyone or anything with great power has the capacity for great good or evil. Power itself is dangerous. Every river is equally a source of life or death but, like a river, Hadrian isn't vicious."

He studied the terrain ahead of his mount before urging it carefully over a patch of rough ground to a clearer area. "Also, you should remember Hadrian's reputation is both necessary and a logical consequence of his being the clan's executioner. It's his responsibility to avenge any member of the clan cut down, as well as to punish clan members who attack those outside of the clan."

"Has he, as executioner, killed anyone inside or outside of the clan?"

"Not that I know of. The threat seems sufficient."

"What about Scarface? From what I've heard of him, he seems an excellent candidate for the headsman's block."

"I feel rather sorry for Scarface—"

"Sorry for him! Why not be sorry for a snake?"

"I am, rather. Serpents seldom attack. Their bad reputation is caused by the fear of others, and so it is with Scarface. He uses the fear he inspires to keep others at a distance. He trusts no one and wants no one to trust him."

"That's strange. It's easier to destroy someone who trusts you."

"Misplaced trust might provide the opportunity, but having the will to betray that trust is another matter. I suspect that Scarface, however much he might deny it, tends to try to live up to the expectations of others. By lowering their expectations, he increases his options. He's not given to trust, but if he were to give his trust and it were betrayed, he'd probably be implacable. For that reason, I think, he seldom gives his own word and, when he gives it, he's prepared to make it good to death."

"Apparently his lack of trust extends to giving his own name. What is it?"

Poker shrugged. "I don't know."

"Would anyone know?"

"Hadrian, maybe. Or one or all of the elders."

"It's hard to believe you're related to him and don't know his real name. Why does he hide it?"

"I've never asked him his name. As for why he doesn't use it—in the place he grew up, giving someone your name gave him or her power over you. There's some truth to the superstition, in that some spells require the true name of their object."

The answers reminded her of another question. "Do you know how he got those scars? They look like the finger-marks of a devil."

"Do you know of a country called Sin Garlef?"

Mendarian searched her memory, then shook her head. "No, the name isn't familiar."

"I'm not surprised. It's east of Porchash and Doss, beyond the Talgan mountains, on the Harsherf Sea. It's where Scarface, Hadrian, and I all grew up. The country's under the heavy thumb of a theocrat who had an elite guard and elite troops in the army, all distinguished by scars like that. The scars were caused by branding, one burn at a time, with two weeks' time between brandings.

"Each fresh burn was treated with an astringent salve mixed with ashes, so the scars would come in black. The wait between brandings were to give the man who'd chosen to be scarred the opportunity to remember and think on the pain, to let anticipation burn him a dozen times before the iron ever touched him. Many did choose to die on the headsman's block rather than finish what they'd started."

"Why didn't they just run away?"

"It would've done no good. No one ever had less than five fully-healed scars. Anyone with less than five scars, all healed, would've been treated like a mad dog—he'd be killed on sight. I've never heard of anyone with similar scars who didn't have all five."

Mendarian thought of the pain of being branded on the face and the other pain of a salve that would burn like the iron itself. "Those with the scars must either have been paid very well or they enjoyed rare privileges."

"No, they were paid the same as the rest of the army, and their discipline was much more severe. The 'Marked Ones,' as they were called, had the 'honor' of being in the forefront of every battle. No, their only reward was prestige. Most of them, apart from their glory-hunger, were unimaginative brutes. Scarface was an obvious exception. With his imagination, it must've taken vastly more nerve to submit to the brandings. Sometimes I think about the force of will it took to submit, and I think of what a great priest of Ianno he could be." He drew on the reins as his horse topped a rise and they stared down at Varish. "Still, he got a reward, but not before he began to dabble in the Art."

"Magic?"

"Yes. Pick an inn. I'll buy us lunch"

"You probably know the place better than I. Why don't you choose?"

"Just a few days ago was the first time I'd set foot in Varish in over three years, but I'll try to find a place where the food and drinks are good."

They urged their horses down a trail that wove across the face of the ridge and joined a traders' road that followed the river. In a little more than half an hour they were wending their way through narrow, winding streets. The way Poker had chosen was unfamiliar to Mendarian, and she didn't see the inn to which Murtry had led her earlier. The dirt tracks gave way, in places, to cobblestoned streets, then to a wooden bridge across which they clattered.

Poker led the way to a small inn, which had apparently been set in a tangle of goat pens and chicken coops and surrounded by the arcane designs, scratched in the dirt, of children's games.

The urchins playing in front of the doorstep scurried around the building at the sight of strangers, all but one tall, sullen-faced boy who'd come, still carrying a hammer, from some job behind the building. When he saw Poker he dropped the hammer. With a shout, he raced toward Poker with his arms spread and caught him in a hug.

Both the boy and Poker talked rapidly in a language Mendarian didn't recognize, then Poker untangled himself from the embrace of the boy who was, awkwardly, almost a man, and turned to Mendarian.

"Mendarian of Cerco, this is Yosh. His family is one of those who followed us out of Doss." He faced the boy again and gobbled some more in Dasht. Mendarian could gather that Poker was asking something or suggesting something and the boy, while he was well-inclined, was unable to comply. Finally Poker fished in his pouch and handed the boy a silver coin, then gestured at the horses. He spoke a short phrase in Dasht, then indicated Mendarian should dismount.

The boy shouted at the children who came out of hiding, and some of the older ones seemed to recognize Poker and approached him. He greeted each of them, probably with names, although Mendarian couldn't tell for certain, then, at the edge of a curving line scratched into the dirt, he halted.

He stared at the pattern a moment, then walked around to an opening in the design and hopped and skipped through the maze, sometimes coming down with both feet, sometimes with only one, until he looked as though he were having a seizure. Just before he reached the other opening he stumbled and his foot smudged one of the lines. He stopped and, with a huge grin, made an elaborate show of embarrassment, which caused peals of laughter from the children. Game ended, he pushed open the door of the inn and motioned for Mendarian to precede him.

The place had the strong smell of foreign cooking but was much neater than suggested by outside. A scrawny woman with stringy hair approached Mendarian, then saw Poker. Again he was hugged and exchanged greetings in Dasht.

While Poker and the woman talked, Mendarian glanced around the room. Three men in rough clothing sat at one of the tables, two of them playing a game involved moving colored pebbles around a design chalked on the table. One of the men leaned across the table, indicating the newcomers with his thumb, and said something to the other two. All of them rose and strode toward Mendarian and Poker.

Before Mendarian could warn Poker of the possible threat the men had surrounded him, then all of them were trying to clasp his arm or clap him on the back. When Poker had finally finished all his introductions he led Mendarian to a table. He held out the chair for her to sit in before dropping into the chair facing hers. "Do you want me to order?"

"Yes, please. I wouldn't know what to ask for."

"All right, but do you want wine or *akvad*? *Akvad* is a plum brandy that'll make you consider having your throat re-lined."

"If you can drink it, I can drink it."

Poker grinned. "On your own head be it." When the woman came to the table with a basin he washed his hands and dried them on the cloth she offered. While Mendarian followed his example he said something she guessed to be the name of the food he wanted and the brandy. The woman nodded and carried away the basin and cloth.

"You brought me here just to impress me with your popularity, right?"

He grinned again. "Absolutely. And also because I haven't had good *sukaris* in three long years."

"What were you saying to the boy outside?"

"I was trying to get him to convince his mother to move to High Rage. He wants to go, but his mother is staying here. Maybe he'll be able to go when one of his brothers is old enough to take care of the family. I wish I could get Arshara to move to High Rage, but she wants to stay here to wait for her husband."

"So?"

"He'll never come. He's dead in Doss. Everyone's told her that but she's still going to wait for him. I don't know whether to give her my sympathy or my admiration."

"You said you were brought up with Scarface and Hadrian. What were they like as children? Or were they ever children?"

"I really don't know." He looked up and smiled and thanked the woman as she brought a bottle and two cups to the table, then poured some of the golden liquid into the cups. "I grew up in the north of Sin Garlef and they were brought up in the south, by the sea. I never met them until the clan gathered for the war in Doss, when we all fought together in the Das war. Some of us were late to the gathering, even then.

"I still remember the first time Scarface and I worked together." He sipped the liquor in his cup, treating it with obvious respect.

Mendarian sniffed the mouth of her own cup, then wet her lips with the brandy and licked them. It had the burn of liquid fire but an oddly pleasant taste. She sipped cautiously and was grateful for Poker's warning. "Go on, you were telling me about the first time you and Scarface fought together."

Poker's laugh was self-deprecating. "Nothing is more boring than someone else's old war stories."

Mendarian took another sip of the sweet fire. "I'll chance it."

"Well, it was early in the war. In those days I had many of the same attitudes Scarface still has. About a dozen of us, new to the game, decided a little brigandage was in order. Most of the merchants were in the purse of the priest-king we were fighting anyway, so we could always claim it was a military action. We ambushed a caravan and they nearly wiped us out." He chuckled. "We'd underestimated the quality of their guards, just as we'd overestimated our own abilities. They were cutting us to rags when Scarface, single-handed, started a crossfire. Ivo and another member of the Union, a man called Runa, were along. That was the beginning of a grudge between Scarface and the Union."

"How so?"

"Because Runa was basically a bully. Scarface and I were both very aware of our vulnerability at the time, and we didn't argue with him or Ivo when they took first choice of the spoils. I believe we both thought goodwill was worth more than booty. Eventually I was able to see the emptiness of it all. I was more fortunate than Scarface who, I'm sure, still burns at the humiliation.

"I'd learned better. And when the clan set up an outpost in the Empire of the Book, I asked to go. I'd already converted and was fascinated by the church. Scarface continued to struggle, learned some of the Art—ah, the food is here."

Mendarian watched as Poker tore off a piece of bread from the loaf and ate from the platter with his fingers. The meal consisted of the bread and a platter of thin-sliced kid mixed with bits of raw fruit, vegetables and melon. Some of the items were unfamiliar to Mendarian. Half of the mixture was covered with a cheese sauce and the rest with a strong sour cream. After her first bite reminded her it had been several hours since a light breakfast, Mendarian ate with a good appetite. She discovered one of the strange red vegetables was tart and juicy and the small green vegetables with the yellow pulp were even hotter than the *akvad*.

Finally she dipped a last piece of bread in the sour cream, washed it down with some of the brandy, and leaned back, picking at the meat between her teeth with a thumbnail. "That was delicious."

"I'm glad you enjoyed it." Poker finished his meal and tipped back his cup. When the woman approached the table with another basin and cloth he washed his hands again, said something in Dasht, then changed to Gasgoran. "It was excellent, Arshara. I think it was the best meal you've ever made."

The woman carried the basin to Mendarian and watched as she also washed her hands again. She seemed to be trying to avoid looking at Poker but finally said, in heavily accented Gasgoran, "It was for you."

Poker bowed. "Then I'll be pleased and honored to accept it, and I'll ask you to accept this to remember me by." From his pouch he took a small, silvery icon and handed it to her. "Thank you again," he said, then went to the men at the gaming table and spoke a few words to each of them and clapped them on the back or the shoulder. He finally returned to where Mendarian sat. "Shall we go? It's still a half-day's ride to High Rage."

Mendarian stood and followed him out, squinting at the brilliant sunlight. The boy/man tightened the cinches of their horses' saddles, then led the animals to them. "Have a good ride," he said, in Gasgoran less accented than his mother's.

Poker hugged him again, assisted Mendarian in mounting her roan, then climbed into his blue's saddle. Side-by-side, they rode down a maze of crowded streets until they'd left Varish behind them and faced what appeared to be a wall of mountains. "Those," Poker announced, "are the Shannan Mountains."

As they rode, Mendarian tried to pick up the thread of conversation that had been cut by the arrival of food. "You were saying something about Scarface learning the Art, and earlier you said something about his having some advantage or reward."

"Oh, yes." He studied the mountains ahead through narrowed eyes. "You know the basic kinds of magic and their laws, don't you?"

Mendarian felt uncomfortable with the idea of admitting ignorance. She'd observed that magic was a chancy thing upon which to depend, and that most magic was too limited to be of any real value. Also, magi tended to be lonely or aloof people who had the resources to spend their time studying. Several of the courts kept magi—just as most of them also kept jesters. She'd never had the resources or the excessive interest in dabbling in magic, and she was uncertain how much of what she thought she knew was merest superstition. "It may be a matter of... interpretation. Why don't you tell me how you see it?"

"Well, like anything else, magic has a cost." Poker, without being aware of it, had slipped into a tutorial manner. "A large stone can be lifted but it requires very great effort by a very strong man, less effort from a group of men, and even less by a man with a lever. Still, the man with the lever can lift the stone only so far, and the lever and the fulcrum are under great stress.

"So it is with magic. All spells must be learned. Some minor effects aren't too difficult to learn and can be performed very simply. Usually, the greater effect of a single spell, the greater its cost in will or concentration or energy.

"Some spells can be accomplished by magi working together, but it's very sensitive work. The timing must be precise and a strong will is required of each magi. Such spells are like chains in some ways, like ropes in others. The weakness is that of a chain. You know the strength of the weakest link is the strength of the chain. On the other hand, the strengths of the magi are, like the strands of a rope, braided together. Such spells can produce enormous effects but they're rare, because magi working together must trust each other completely, while the practice of magic tends to appeal to the solitary individual.

"The cost of a spell is sometimes in energy, sometimes in time of preparation, and sometimes even in pain. Eventually Scarface learned he had the power to work some spells without apparently having to pay for them, other than learning them. This is because of the pain he bore when he was scarred. The will-force was spent and the pain accepted without any thought, at that time, of gain. What he'd paid for and what he received were disproportionate, so now he can draw on that reservoir of determination and anguish and weave a spell that would drain the energy of most other magi, or would, at least, require more time and preparation."

"I see," Mendarian said. So that was how Scarface had conjured his traps and his circle of protection so quickly and easily. She thought about comments and stories she'd heard. "Does that mean all magic is the same? Just learning a spell and applying it with enough force?"

"Oh, no," Poker replied. "No, there are at least three kinds of spells. Some spells require only a limited knowledge but great force. I'd call those brute spells. Most battle-magic is made up of brute spells.

"Then there are lever spells. They require varying amounts of force but a great and deep knowledge of the spells themselves and by the principles by which they circumvent the usual natural order.

"Finally, there are…let's not call them spells but summonings. There are certain forces at large which will, for their purposes, deal with magi and others, trading certain powers for things they want."

"Like trading power for souls?"

"That's an oversimplification, like most of what I've been saying. It's more subtle than that. Each of us has the power to call up forces, benevolent or malevolent, not so much by summoning them but actually being a part of them. These forces reflect some part of us and by our own actions, by following our own desires, we give them their gifts of love or discord , and the gifts are mirrored back, so the mind that drew the presence becomes even more like the presence.

"As I serve Ianno I become more and more, if I do well, a reflection of Ianno and his love. Scarface, whether he knows it or not, whether he even believes in them or not, serves deathgods and gods of battle by creating strife and so he comes to resemble them in his ruthlessness."

Mendarian rode in silence for a while, wondering what gods she served and what they might offer her for her services. Between her preoccupation with gods and powers and her fatigue, she didn't immediately notice Poker had raised his arm as a signal to halt, then she realized he was standing in his stirrups and pointing. "That fortification is the entrance to Valé Shanna. We'll dine in High Rage tonight."

Chapter 3

The pattern around Martina blurred and Scarface's eyes burned as sweat ran into them. His legs had long since gone to sleep, his knees felt as though he had been kneeling on knives, and his back was stiff and knotted. Still he remained motionless. He was tempted to draw relief from his scars but put that thought back into the dark corner from which it'd crept. The mystic pool wasn't infinite, and someday the well would be dry.

Finally Martina stood, her body glistening with sweat. For a moment, Scarface was reminded of a kid or lamb turning on its spit. She bent and picked up the knives before her and used the black-handled dagger to scratch a line through the pattern painted around her on the floor, then walked to the smaller pattern around Scarface and opened it with the white-handled knife.

He commanded his legs to straighten, to hold him up. Martina walked away from him to a much smaller circle and again used the black-handled dagger to release the spell around a glass rod a hand's length long and as big around as his little finger. She picked up the rod and carried it to him. After handing it to him, she glanced back at the remaining pattern, still closed, around a caged falcon.

"He'll be at least as safe with his pattern intact. I'll be sure to take care of him. When you leave, let me know so I can move him to a cage large enough to hold your body." She gestured at the piece of glass. "When you want to change into the falcon, break the rod to release the spell stored there."

Scarface accepted the rod, wiped his face with his forearm, and nodded. He was becoming aware Martina was not only naked but also very appealing, with large but firm breasts and a slender waist and hips. He picked up his robe and wrapped it around himself, then caught up Martina's robe and held it up between them. She slipped into the red silk and drew it around herself.

"I owe you for this," he said, his voice almost a croak.

"Not really. You're the one who'll be taking the risks, and most of the power I used came from you."

"Still, you've worked very hard on this spell. I wish there were some way to repay you."

She stared at him and her lips flashed into a dangerous smile. "I know how you hate to owe anything to anyone. The fact you feel obligated to me is payment enough. If you really want to repay the favor, you might find some way to annoy that snow-hearted bitch, Lidhyar."

The sound Scarface made was almost a laugh. "I'll do what I can. Anything that annoys a member of the Union must be worth doing." He stepped closer to Martina and embraced her, then strode to the door, the glass rod in his hand.

That hug had been dangerous, reminding him of how desirable he found her. He went to the bath, left the glass rod cushioned on his robe, emptied a bucket of icy water over himself, and felt his desire momentarily extinguished. After scrubbing at himself with a cake of coarse soap, he dumped another bucket of water over himself, dried and put on a fresh robe.

After taking the rod to his room he groped for and found the key he'd wedged into a knife-cut in his bed frame. It was useless to try to keep things like this from Hadrian or Martina, either of whom could pick a lock as quickly as he could open one with a key, but neither of them wanted anything he had and Martina, at least, was welcome to anything he owned.

He turned the key in the lock, pressed a part of the chest's inlay, and raised the lid. Beneath some clothing was a smaller chest wrapped in an old robe. He unrolled the robe and opened the box. His scepter was still there, in a scrap of wool. After tearing another scrap from the old robe he wrapped it around the glass rod, then put it into the box with the scepter. Replacing the box in the chest, he concealed it again under old clothing. He closed the lid and slid the key into his belt where the stitching had loosened between two thicknesses of leather.

His body still complained of fatigue but he needed to feed it before letting it rest. He was glad Martina had been slow to go to the bathhouse. Too much closeness could cause him to either make an unpleasant acquaintanceship with a palm dagger or—better not to think about it. Among the few mores of Sin Garlef he'd never quite been able to shrug off was a stern prohibition against incest.

As he trudged to the kitchen he considered the relationship between Martina and himself. She had always been a tease but she'd also let the men around her know the teasing was a game, and games stopped short of consummation. She'd probably had a few affairs with men outside the clan, but her first loyalties seemed always to be to the other members of the clan.

Poker had been a battle-comrade and a fellow conspirator, and Hadrian had been a rival with power. What was Martina? Perhaps it was her easy laughter, her teasing, her charm that made her company a refuge from the somberness of the rest of the clan. Travesty, with his paternal attitude and his caution; Raven with her arcane studies; and all the rest had seemed distant.

Poker, even after his conversion, had still been a comrade, though his deepest drives were utterly foreign to Scarface. If Martina's pursuits weren't the same as his own, he could at least understand them. Perhaps she represented another side of him, with many of the same drives but without his hunger for power, his reservations, or his superficial control. Of all of them, only she, Poker, and, ironically, Hadrian could claim any measure of his trust.

He pushed open the door of the kitchen. The cooks had long since gone to their pallets. He took a deep breath, savoring the scent of the stew simmering over the coals, found a clean bowl and spoon, tore off a large piece of bread, and ladled stew into his bowl. He set the bowl on the table in the corner of the room then selected a dry red wine from the racks of bottles. He'd just sat down to eat when Martina entered and also helped herself to bread and stew.

He held up the bottle. "If you've no objections, we can drink out of this."

Martina sat across the table from him. "No objections."

They shared a companionable silence along with the wine until he stood to refill his bowl. "May I get you some more, too?"

"No, thank you."

He tore off more bread, ladled more stew, and brought back a bottle of pomegranate wine. Martina watched him eat, then, abruptly, asked, "Why are you so interested in this woman Mendarian?"

"I'm not sure. Some of it may be the fact that she's dangerous. As dangerous, in her own way, as anyone I've ever met."

"That doesn't surprise me. You have a taste for danger. But it's something more than that."

Scarface ate and considered the question. Finally he washed down his last mouthful of bread with a pull from the wine bottle. "Physical attraction, of course. Perhaps it's because we're kindred spirits. She's willful, determined, and very much alone. I'll be interested in your reaction to her."

"From your description, I don't think I'll like her. And you're more than just those qualities."

He lapsed into a brief self-conscious silence, then, "Why do you care about me?"

Martina tipped back the bottle, taking a long drink, then grinned at Scarface. "Any other time I wouldn't answer that question, but right now I'm just a little tipsy, so neither of us will remember what I say. I'm going to tell you a secret." Her tone became conspiratorial. "I love you. If you and Hadrian weren't my cousins, I'd want one or the other of you for lovers. You're both beautiful men. Not pretty, but beautiful. Yes, even with the scars. And you're both powerful men. Power is an aphrodisiac. And both of you can be very, very gentle."

She leaned toward him and lowered her voice to a whisper. "And one more secret—you really aren't the devil you think you are."

Scarface's self-consciousness returned in a rush and he tried to hide it behind a grin. "You want to be careful. I've been drinking, too." He leaned forward and stroked her cheek. "At this moment, you're the most beautiful woman in the world to me, especially with those soft, brown eyes. I don't want to take advantage of you."

"Like I said, not the devil you think you are, or you wouldn't give a damn."

"Let's just say I like to give my respected opponents a fighting chance. Not fair to take advantage of someone in her cups."

Martina's eyes welled with tears. "I'm afraid that may be what kills you."

He laughed. "No, I don't think so. It's what you can't laugh at that kills you." He stood. "Let me take you to your room."

"All right." Martina got unsteadily to her feet. Scarface put his arm around her waist and walked with her, half-supporting her, until they reached the door to her room. Scarface shoved the door open, then looked down at her.

Impulsively, he covered her mouth with his own and his tongue stabbed at her lips. She flinched, then relaxed and returned his kiss with equal passion.

He could feel himself becoming aroused, and he knew her palm dagger had been forgotten.

With an effort that was like tearing the flesh from his own chest, he brought his hands up to Martina's upper arms, then slowly backed away from her until he held her at arm's length.

"Good night," he said, and paused. Something more seemed needed. "It's a bad joke of fate that we're kin, but we are." He looked into her eyes. "I do love you, very much." He dropped his hands, turned, and hurried away, afraid to look back.

Some noes are forever. This would not come his way again. He wanted, desperately, to go back; to gently touch and make love to her, but that "no" was permanent, though he might regret the decision a thousand times.

The corridor was dim as a cavern, lit only by candles a dozen paces apart, and he had the sense of stalking through a tunnel. A moment after he'd strode past the open door of the library he heard his name called by a voice he thought was Travesty's, but he continued to his room, closed the door, and locked life outside.

He strode to his sword where it hung by its belt from the peg, drew the blade from its scabbard, and stared at it, running his fingers across the convolutions of the bat-winged guard. The sword felt almost alive in his hands, gave him a sense of barely-controlled power, reminding him of the fragility of the other things in the room. He fought back an urge to attack everything within reach. Instead, he performed a few simple practice slashes and thrusts, ended the exercise with a moulinet, then returned the brand to its sheath.

He snorted at a sudden perception. Inner desolation seemed to invite external destruction. The nagging emptiness he felt as only the sharper pang of a dull ache loneliness with which he was unpleasantly familiar.

He undressed, crawled into bed, and stared at the ceiling. What was Mendarian doing now? Poker should've reached Gain earlier this evening. Would she come to High Rage with Poker or had she been gulled by the Union? Even if she did come to High Rage, what could he say to her? She…he tried to pick at a thought, to tease loose a strand from the tangled web of ideas…might be dangerous to the clan. There was a relatively simple way to probe that, depending only on the degree to which she believed him. It should be interesting…

~ * ~

Scarface came awake as suddenly as if he'd been plunged into icy water. Today was the day Mendarian would come to High Rage—if she were coming at all. After springing out of bed he dressed in soft clothing and armed himself. The silversmith should've finished the copy of his scepter by now.

He paced quickly through the corridors, slowed only as he passed old Imshar, probing the hallway before him with his stick.

In a few moments he was striding the cobblestoned streets of the town. Vendors were already pushing their carts and tradesmen arranging their wares for display. He stopped at a cart and bought a loaf of fresh bread, tore off the end, gave the rest to the hawker from whom he purchased a cup of cider.

The silversmith met him at the door of his shop, a grin of satisfaction alternating with the forced nonchalance of nervous self-effacement. He led Scarface through the blanket-covered door to the workshop in the back of the building, then gestured at a piece of black felt, upon which lay the silver scepter.

Scarface picked up the copy and examined it critically. The size and weight were close enough to the original and, at any distance, the engraving and piecework would pass. He shoved the copy into his belt and dropped another gold piece on the felt. "For prompt delivery," he said.

Without pausing to watch the smith's reaction, he strode out of the shop and out of the town, back to the castle. As he crossed the list he heard his name shouted and turned to see a man in practice armor, a bucket helm on his head hiding his face. From the red and light blue quartering on the battered face of the man's round shield, he knew it was Travesty.

Travesty approached him, pulling off the helm. "Wasn't that you in the corridor outside the library last night?"

Scarface nodded.

"I went to Varish yesterday. There's a story going around that you provoked a fight with Murtry, then tried to kill him."

"You shouldn't listen to stories."

Travesty brushed back some of his shoulder-length hair from his cheek, where it had been plastered by sweat. "What's your side of the story?"

"I don't have one. Murtry is still alive, isn't he?"

"Yes, but recovering from some nasty burns."

"Then I couldn't have tried to kill him. If I had, he'd be dead."

Travesty frowned. "I'm not over-fond of the Union either, but—"

"Especially since they once 'disciplined' you when your nerve broke. They're very free with their threats and their displays of power when someone else lets them down, but are very forgiving of their own shortcomings."

Travesty's face flushed and became set when Scarface reminded him he'd once been afraid and had submitted to being threatened. "That's beside the fact the clan and the Union are allies."

Scarface spat. "I'd rather be allied with the lowest gutter sweepings in Sazia. At least they wouldn't act pious. When an 'ally' can't be trusted or respected, they're no longer an ally."

"The Union is stronger than we are..."

"They might be, if you convince yourself of it." He glanced back to where one of the castle's garrison stood waiting for Travesty. "I haven't had my exercise yet today. I need to take something to my room right now. Why don't you get some rest while I'm gone? I'll give you a chance to work off some of your worry."

Travesty stared at him a moment then signaled for the other man to practice at the pells. "I'll be waiting for you."

Scarface grinned at the memory of Murtry's similar promise a few days earlier. "Don't let it become a habit." He turned and hurried to his room where he tossed the scepter onto the bed then strode to the armory, a cave-like room in the base of the keep with the thickest walls in the castle. There he pulled on a heavy, padded gambeson which reached past his knees and covered that with a chain mail hauberk and a heavily-padded bucket helm.

The wide variety of practice swords reflected the clan's catholicity of tastes. He chose one with a straight, double-edged blade and ran his thumb along the carefully-dulled edges and around the thick, rounded point. Finally he took down his practice shield and picked up a heavy leather gauntlet.

As he strode back into the list, Travesty rose from a bench, put on his helm, and walked toward him, swinging his curved sword from side to side.

Scarface crouched, his sword drawn back over his shoulder. For the first few exchanges he and Travesty both swung easily, going through the simpler drills of attack and defense, then Travesty changed the pattern of attack. Travesty was a better than adequate fighter but Scarface noticed his cousin caught each blow on the edge of his shield, then twisted the shield. Were they using weapons with a real edge, this maneuver would give him a chance to snap an opponent's blade or wrench it out of his hand, but each time he twisted the shield he immediately brought it back up, its upper edge at the level of the bottom of his helm.

Without conscious thought, Scarface threw a cut at the bottom edge of the shield. Travesty swung his shield down, twisted it, and snapped it back up. Scarface slammed the face of his own shield against the bottom edge of Travesty's, driving the upper rim under his chin.

Before his cousin could recover, Scarface struck, hard, against the side of Travesty's helm. The blow hurled Travesty to the ground and Scarface sprang forward. His left foot stamped down on Travesty's right wrist and he drew his sword back for the kill-stroke, then realized he'd actually hurt Travesty, perhaps badly. Instantly he stepped back and lowered his blade.

Travesty rocked back and forth on the ground then rolled over and lurched to his feet. His hands fumbled at the bottom of his helm before his fingers could loosen the straps and tug the helmet free. His eyes were still unfocussed and he swayed on his feet but when Scarface took a tentative step toward him he stumbled backward. "Stay away from me!"

Scarface took another step back. He knew he should apologize but the words froze in his throat.

Travesty's glare finally settled on Scarface's eyes. His face had lost its pallor and now was flushed. "This was supposed to be practice, not mortal combat. You damned nearly broke my neck."

Scarface was grateful for the blank steel face of his helm. Again he struggled with an apology but the words still wouldn't come to his lips.

Suddenly he was aware Hadrian stood before him.

"I haven't practiced yet today, brother," Hadrian said, in his soft, precise voice. "Will you provide me with some exercise?"

Travesty stepped closer, almost between Hadrian and Scarface. "No, Hadrian, it was my fault." He forced his lips into a semblance of a grin. "Scarface just took the training more seriously than I did. It's better for me to learn my mistakes in practice with dulled blades than in the field, where a real enemy might've taken my head off." He glanced at Scarface. "I'm grateful for the lesson." His voice sounded as though he were trying to mean what he said.

Hadrian ignored him. "Now, brother?"

Scarface studied Hadrian a moment and knew his chances of beating the little man stood somewhere between nonexistent and impossible. Not trusting his voice, he nodded.

Hadrian bent and swept up Travesty's sword from where it had fallen, then signaled the soldier, now ignoring the splintered pell before him, to throw his sword. The man tossed the sword underhanded so it flew in a steep arc, tumbling end over end. Hadrian caught it by the grip and let the momentum of the throw swing the blade through a series of circles, then confronted Scarface, a sword in either hand. "Do you mind if I don't bother with the armor?"

Scarface swung his shield into a defensive position and raised his sword. Both of Hadrian's blades flashed into movement, constantly striking from unexpected angles, impossible to defend against. Scarface's helm rang with a blow and twice his sword arm was struck with bruising force.

There was no way, with normal tactics, Scarface could both defend himself and still attack the other man, so he waited for an opportunity. For a moment he saw a slender chance. He deflected a blow with his shield and immediately tried to lock blades with Hadrian's left-hand sword then shoved forward with the shield, trying to push Hadrian off-balance, only to find the smaller man had already moved to the side and was attacking again.

Frustration at not being able to reach his opponent quickly turned to rage, which Scarface snuffed before it could defeat him. Hadrian was obviously toying with him, most of the light taps falling on his shield or the blade of his sword.

Abruptly, Hadrian stepped back, swords crossed. "Thank you for the exercise. Do you mind if I call for a halt? I seem to have tired more quickly than I thought I would."

Scarface's helm concealed his bitter smile. He'd been given the choice of continuing a hopeless battle or accepting a face-saving gesture that, to him, represented a debt. He transferred the practice sword to his left hand and lifted off his helm. "Thank you for the lesson. I'm sure I'll remember everything you taught."

Hadrian tossed the swords he'd used to Travesty. "Very good," he said in his quiet voice, devoid of inflection.

As Hadrian walked away, Scarface nodded to Travesty. "Thanks for the words." He still couldn't dredge up an apology but he did manage to say, "I'm on edge today."

Travesty grinned. "Your apology is accepted. But why didn't you tell us about the trouble with Murtry when you returned. If you'd had a complaint to make, the proper steps might've been taken to have the Union discipline him."

Scarface laughed. "Your honesty is only exceeded by your naivete. Personally, I'd sooner believe King Ogaard and all his court had been resurrected. Besides, I've given Murtry a lesson in manners and the limit to 'friendly' inquisition. If I have to repeat the lesson, I'll make sure it leaves a permanent impression."

"And," Travesty said, "just incidentally embroil the clan in a struggle with the Union or chance having yourself outlawed by the clan. If you'd told us about your trouble with Murtry and he'd attacked you again, we'd be more liable to believe he'd provoked the trouble."

"And do what? Thank you, but no thank you. Your problem, cousin, is that you're too reasonable. You'd still be listening to everyone's arguments until all the bodies were safely out of sight."

"Just don't overreach yourself."

Scarface returned to the armory and left the weapons and armor he'd used in their proper racks, then went back to the library where he read again those passages about Cerco he considered most important. If Mendarian meant to rule in Cerco, these were things she—or an advisor—would need to know. He drummed his fingertips against the cover of one of the books, then left, with the scroll and the books, to find a scribe in town.

He was literate but his handwriting was distinctive and he'd not want Mendarian to know the source of the information. It was too much like trying to buy her affection.

He found a scribe who'd write all afternoon for a *dusiam*. By an hour before sunset he had five parchment pages of notes. He paid the scribe and returned to the castle, where he learned from a guard Hadrian was in his rooms with his family.

Scarface was always reluctant to enter Hadrian's suite, perhaps because he always felt like an intruder. Hadrian's wife, Vornarei, was of the race of the lords of the Harsherf seaports and, like many of them, was pale, fine-boned, white-haired, and very reserved. Her little warmth seemed spent only on her immediate family and Scarface couldn't escape the feeling her reserve was a form of disapproval. He'd have preferred some indication of warmth, or even open hostility, either of which would pluck less at his nerves.

He knocked at Hadrian's door, which was opened almost immediately by one of the twins. Scarface stared down at her and was forced to smile at the solemnity of her expression. "Are you Corina or Coriss?"

"I'm Coriss. Please come in. I'll get my father for you."

Scarface stepped into the room but remained by the door. The furnishings, though simple, were colorful and comfortable, leaving Scarface to wonder at the source of personal warmth in the room. Neither Hadrian nor Vornarei had ever impressed him as other than colorless, almost insubstantial.

Hadrian entered the room and, for a moment, Scarface thought he detected something in the other man's manner unlike his usual impersonal courtesy but the impression faded almost as soon as it was recognized. Scarface inclined his head in the direction of the doorway. "Your five-year-olds should learn to smile more. They're as polite as castellans."

"I'm glad she showed good manners."

Scarface tried to hide his discomfort by glancing down at the sheets of parchment he held. "I took the liberty of gleaning some basic information about Cerco from what we had in the library. I thought perhaps the clan might make a gift of this to Mendarian when she arrives."

Hadrian smiled. "Very well, thank you. I'll add it to some notes on the present state of arms and power we've prepared for her."

Scarface returned the rare smile. "Apparently we think alike on this matter. Do you think an alliance with Cerco is likely?"

"At present, nothing stands in the way. As a matter of fact, the elders will meet with her after dinner this evening. Presuming, of course, she dines with us."

Scarface permitted an eyebrow to arch but resisted an impulse to whistle. The elders showed themselves to clan members only infrequently; and to outsiders almost never. "They must, then, consider it of some importance."

"They wished to meet Mendarian and determine for themselves how she should be dealt with." Hadrian paced to a cabinet, picked up a decanter, and looked over his shoulder at Scarface, who nodded.

Hadrian poured two glasses of deep purple brandy, handed one to

Scarface, sipped at the other. "What was your impression of her? Can she be trusted?"

Scarface tasted the pomegranate brandy before he answered. "I wish I could answer 'yes,' but I'm not certain. As you said, she's been an adventurer and she has a high degree of cunning but I don't know whether she's learned statecraft or, if she has, it's been affected by suspicion and opportunism."

"In other words, you don't know whether she'll see the value of an alliance with the clan on its merits or whether she'd try to play the clan against the Union."

Scarface took another sip and finally nodded.

"I see." Hadrian finished his brandy and placed the glass on a shelf. "I'm having dinner delayed until Poker arrives, with or without Mendarian. I presume you'd like to be a member of the welcoming party." He didn't wait for Scarface's response. "I gave the guards orders to sound their horns when they see riders."

~ * ~

As Mendarian and Poker cleared the shadowed pass to Valé Shanna she halted to gaze at the valley, still basking in the red-gold light of early evening and heard the faint echo of a horn. She ignored the sound and studied the rolling terrain. The fields looked like a golden-green carpet for the valley, at its center the town and its castle, surrounded by its shining ribbon of moat. The town's buildings, most of them constructed of the same tan stone as the castle itself, clustered around the wall and turrets like sheep around their shepherd.

Poker also drew rein and waited for her to finish her survey, then offered her his wineskin. She drank deeply then pointed at the sun, just beginning to sink behind the teeth of the western mountains. "It'll be full dark by the time we reach the castle."

"Yes, evening comes early around here. All the more reason to hurry." He urged his mount to a canter and Mendarian did the same. Before they'd reached the outskirts of the town the dusk had risen and shadows crept up the eastern mountains. The horses slowed to a walk. Squares of light appeared in the dark blocks of buildings as lamps and candles were lit.

Mendarian saw no patrols and the few merchants still closing their shops seemed tired but content. Once, someone shouted Poker's name and he had to twist in the saddle and wave, but most of the town had closed for the night. Soon they were on their way up the hill to the castle.

The crenellated walls stood out in stark relief, lit by torches, and through the open drawbridge and gates she could see a knot of people waiting for them in the list. The sharp clatter of her horse's hooves on cobblestone changed to a hollow booming as they rode across the wooden drawbridge, then fell to a soft padding as they reached the sand of the list.

She and Poker approached the crowd and she recognized Scarface in the front rank. She started to draw rein but Poker leaned toward her and whispered for her to ride directly toward the men. Mendarian did so and halted when she reached the place where they stood.

Scarface held up his hand to her. "May I take the reins to your horse?"

She handed him the reins, then a smaller man stepped forward and held her stirrup. She glanced at Poker, who whispered, "This is a customary honor extended to royal visitors."

She hid a grin that struggled to appear, dismounted, and faced the short man, who was no taller than Arv and slenderer, although if the leather breastplate he wore were actually formed to his chest, he was wiry and strong. He wore his black, wavy hair cut short and his beard carefully shaped and trimmed to two points. Unreadable black eyes dominated his thin, refined features. On his breast rested a small metal plate bearing a stylized black eagle clutching a white skull on a field of red. She also noticed he wore two swords, one on either hip, and he moved in his black leather armor as though he'd never worn anything lighter.

The man bowed. "In the name of the Winged Dagger Clan, I welcome you to High Rage. I'm Hadrian Darkmoor. We're honored that you chose to visit. I invite you to share dinner with us."

"I'd be delighted." Mendarian held out her arm to him and allowed him to lead her to the great hall. As they entered the high-ceilinged room she was surprised to see the floor covered with carpets instead of rushes and the stone walls were largely hidden by tapestries and hangings. A linen cloth covered the table, and on it sat platters and cups of chased silver.

Hadrian nodded toward the table. "Where would you prefer to sit?"

She was surprised by the question and tried to decide if it was some sort of test.

Hadrian apparently perceived her confusion. "If you sit near the center of the table, more of us will be able to see and hear you. If you're uncomfortable with such informality, I'll lead you to the head of the table."

Mendarian glanced at him and still found him inscrutable. "I'll be happy to sit at the center."

He led her to an elaborately carved chair, drew it out for her, then turned and held out another chair for a small, white-haired woman. He sat between them and leaned toward Mendarian. "I should like to present my wife, Vornarei."

"Honored," Mendarian said, and looked around the table at the people taking chairs. Poker sat down at her left and Scarface sat across the table from her. Beside him, to his right, sat a woman who spoke only once to introduce herself as Martina, and Mendarian felt she was being examined like a piece of dubious merchandise at a fair.

The clan was unlike the Union in that almost all its members seemed to bear a family resemblance. Aside from the man called Wolf, with his prematurely gray hair and green eyes, and Scarface's pale green eyes, all were dark of eye and hair, and all were lean. Most were also short of stature, Scarface being the tallest. The man called Travesty, who tended, when thinking, to turn the golden ring in his right ear and to brush his hair back with his fingers, was about as tall as Mendarian. The quiet woman named Raven was as tall as Poker, the rest being shorter than he.

Despite the physical similarities, the traces of accents and tastes in dress suggested the membership of the clan came from as many different nations and cultures as the people of the Union, but they all seemed at ease with one another, and the conversation was light and pleasant. After the platters had been cleared from the table, servants carried in glasses of a deep purple drink, which Mendarian found to be a rich brandy, and drank slowly, savoring it.

Hadrian again leaned toward her. "After we finish here, if it wouldn't be inconvenient, I'll take you to meet the clan elders."

"Shouldn't I bathe and change clothing first?"

"Only if you're uncomfortable in what you're wearing."

She swallowed the last mouthful of brandy. "I'm ready now."

Hadrian rose and drew out her chair, then guided her through the dim corridors to another room, perhaps half as large as the great hall, and lit only by candles on a table. As her eyes adjusted, Mendarian realized three old men sat behind the table. One of them wore a strip of cloth over his eyes and Mendarian saw, from the folds in the robe of the man in the middle, that he had no legs.

Hadrian led her to the center of the table opposite the men, drew out a chair for her, moved down the table, and sat at the end, away from the light of the candles.

The men nodded to her, almost bowing, then the man in the middle spoke. "I'm Taranto, this is Nembli Crow," indicating the man to his right, who stared intently at her, "and this is Imshar." Imshar was the man with the cloth across his eyes. Taranto's voice was soft but surprisingly steady for one so old. "We're honored by your presence."

"It's I who am honored," she replied.

"One of our members has suggested an alliance be formed between Cerco and the clan. For that reason, you were asked to visit us. What, if we may ask, are your intentions in ruling Cerco?"

"To try to unify the country and stop the squabbling among the tribes, to make the country secure and its people happy." The answer seemed appropriate.

"Very admirable," Taranto said, "although I fear you'll discover happiness is a most elusive state."

"It thrives best in a climate of peace and prosperity," she replied.

All three men smiled. Mendarian let a breath slowly leak out. She'd apparently said the right words. She grinned back at them, then took the initiative. "You'll forgive me if I ask what each of us would gain by an alliance."

Taranto picked up a quill pen and stroked its plume. "We'll respect your rule in Cerco, defend it with arms if need be, and try to provide some of the things you might need to achieve your goals. On your part, you would respect our rule in High Rage."

"That seems very little to ask."

"Not really. You'd be able to sign treaties with Ghiblein and Abaransa, but not to ally with them against Gascolin. You may deal with the king at Gascoyne, but not to try to influence him against the clan."

"It's hardly necessary to state such prohibitions to an ally, but you've made me curious. How would you find out about such dealings, and what could you do about it if I broke my word?"

"In a more settled world," Imshar said, "such secret agreements wouldn't be possible or desirable but could be kept secret. In the here and now, such a treaty could be signed but you could never keep it secret.

As for how we'd protect ourselves—I regret to say that we'd consider a false ally the most dangerous possible enemy."

Mendarian turned slightly and let her gaze travel down the table to the shadows in which Hadrian sat.

Nembli Crow's lips twitched and he turned his head and gesticulated rapidly at Taranto, who said, "My brother wants me to tell you that, yes, you have the nub of it."

When Nebli had turned his head Mendarian had seen a flash of scar at his throat and ear, and she guessed he stared at her so intently to read her lips.

"I'm also curious about some other things." She stared frankly at Taranto. "Perhaps you can answer some questions about yourselves."

"It's necessary for allies to know and understand each other. That's how trust is built. We wouldn't expect you to sign a blank document with strangers. Please ask."

"I've noticed everyone in the clan seems to share a family resemblance, and I can't help but see the three of you are maimed. There are other strange things about the clan that seem to be part of the same puzzle."

Taranto laid down the pen, leaned back in his chair, propping his elbows tightly against the chair's arms, and folded his hands in his lap. "All this is true. Nembli Crow, Imshar, and I once ruled a nation. Does it matter to you which one it was?"

"Not really, as long as it wasn't Cerco."

"It wasn't. Imshar was the war leader, Nembli was the Voice, the one who spoke for the three, and I was the mover, the Lawmaker. Some of the ambitious nobles of the country gained allies among some of the neighboring rulers. There was a war, then revolt. We were defeated." He seemed to be staring into infinity, just above Mendarian's head and years in the past. "We were all maimed, just as you see, and banished. They mutilated us but left us alive to show how little power we had. That, for our conquerors, was the cream of the jest.

"With what we had left of our families, we were forced to flee. We sent our children out to foreign places, to survive if they could, and to bring up their children. At the end of twenty-five years, the children's children were to gather.

"All this was done for a variety of reasons. Our grandchildren would've learned to survive and even to prosper in places where they might've been expected to die, so they'd been taught self-reliance and cunning. Also, scattering the clan would prevent their all being wiped out by petty rulers jealous of their stolen thrones. High Rage you know of and, probably, The Shield of the Saint in the Empire of The Book. There are other places where the clan has holdings so it can't be destroyed by a single stroke.

"There are differences among us. Poker's mother was of the old race of Niphtenic, and he shares some of their traits. Some of our grandchildren have their secrets and they're entitled to keep them, just as we have some secrets of our own. No one is forced to the gathering of the clan. We offer freedom and some power. In return, we see the blossoming of our families. None of us will ever again sit on a throne. We've learned. But we'll never again be shattered or harried. The clan, some part of it, will always survive and the dead will be avenged.

"Are there any other questions you'd like to ask of us?"

Mendarian stared at each of the old men in turn, then shook her head. "No, no questions. Do you want to sign the treaty now?"

"Not yet," Taranto said. "You've just met us. It'd be an agreement to which too little thought had been given. At least sleep on it before you decide to sign."

"Until tomorrow, then," Mendarian said, and stood.

"If you choose to sign, Hadrian will sign for us. He speaks for the clan. Good night, Mendarian, it was a pleasure to meet you."

Hadrian stood by her again. She followed him out of the hall and down the corridor to a room, the door of which held a key in its lock. Hadrian opened the door and handed Mendarian the key. A tub of water set steaming in one corner and Mendarian's saddle pouches lay on the room's one chair.

"Is there anything else you need?"

Mendarian glanced around the room, then walked over and tested the bed with her hands. "No, nothing else. Except company."

"I'm sorry, I thought you'd be tired and wanting a bath. Also," he gestured at a small writing table by the bed, "there are one or two items you might want to read yet tonight. If you'd rather wait before retiring I can show you to the library."

Mendarian glanced at the table and saw, along with a candle in a silver holder, an inkwell, a quill pen, and a roll of parchment bound with a black ribbon. "Then I'll see you in the morning?"

He bowed slightly. "At your convenience." After he'd closed the door,

Mendarian locked it, then undressed and stepped into the tub. The warm water relaxed her and opened the door she'd closed on weariness. After she'd relieved her sore muscles she stepped out of the tub, dried, and drew on a robe. Within a short time servants knocked at her door and took out the water and the tub.

After closing and locking the door she sprawled across the bed, the parchment sheets spread before her. Her learning was limited and so some of the words escaped her, but the notes seemed to be filled with information about Cerco, the relations between the tribes and the nations around them. This alone would've been worth the trip.

She rolled the parchments up again and slipped the ribbon down the roll, placed it back on the desk, the wriggled out of her robe and under the sheets.

It'd been an informative day, as well as a puzzling one. Hadrian had been a surprise. She'd expected a much larger man, one who walked with a swagger, one who was accustomed to giving orders and having them obeyed, one who might try to bully her into accepting terms less to her advantage than to the clan's. She was almost shocked by the difference between her expectations and the reality of the soft-voiced little man with faultless courtesy. On the other hand, she wasn't sure how much of his fearsome reputation was simple fabrication.

From Forgren's attitude, she could guess he considered Hadrian easy to manipulate or intimidate. If Forgren actually believed that, she wondered who was being fooled. She thought she could charm Hadrian and, with a good sword in her hand, she thought she could face him and give at least as well as she got, but those eyes of his showed nothing of what went on behind them.

The story the elders had told her might be true, and that would explain something she'd sensed but hadn't quite understood. Because they were all related, all family, there was no maneuvering for prestige and no one treated Hadrian as anything but the titular head of the clan.

Hadrian's wife had been another surprise. Mendarian had known he had a son but, somehow, his reputation suggested he was more wolf than house-dog. She'd been tempted to start undressing while he was still in the room. Married or not, he could probably still be manipulated that way. If not, he'd be the first man she'd met who was immune, at least of those who didn't prefer boys to women.

Perhaps that was why she and Arv had stayed together so long. She'd been the daughter he'd wanted, and her contempt for him as a man had been mitigated.

If she assumed the unlikely, that Hadrian couldn't be manipulated, what other way was there to reach into the clan? The elders had been easy; almost too easy. She had, in other days, given better performances for a bowl of thin soup and a bug-infested pallet. Who else had power within the clan? Travesty was a slow, patient man, the sort of man everyone listened to, but not very much or for very long. Poker had obviously taken himself out of the power game. Hawk and Wolf, from what she'd seen, were simply good fighting men, and content with that.

What about the women? There'd been something almost protective— or defensive—in the way Hadrian's wife sat beside him and talked with him through the dinner, and Martina was obviously hostile. She'd been so watchful. The other two, Raven and Lantee, had been quiet but had lacked Martina's intense cat-waiting-outside-the-mousehole air. She'd have to deal with Martina soon, either to disarm her or neutralize her.

That still left Scarface, who was more like the man she'd expected Hadrian to be. She guessed that, even with his knack for annoying those in power, he still had more real power than almost anyone else in the clan. And he was attractive as well as dangerous. Or was he attractive *because* he was dangerous?

She wondered why a mouse like Hadrian ruled here instead of a wolf like Scarface. Still, there was something about Hadrian, something that tugged at the hem of her memory. As she tried to follow the thought she became lost in sleep.

She remembered waking long enough to snuff out what was left of the candle, then slipped back into oblivion.

~ * ~

Sleep went away from her like a tide ebbing and she yawned and stretched and lay wondering, for a moment, where she was. Her gaze roamed over the hangings and the ornate woodwork of the bed and table, stopped at the silver inkwell and quill on the table. Then she remembered. This was High Rage.

She slid from the bed, enjoying the cool morning breeze on her body. She rummaged in her saddle pouch until she found a soft green gown that hadn't wrinkled, put it on, then tied on a belt of silk and thrust her feet into pliable slippers. She balanced on her fingers the dagger she always carried then slid it into its sheath and strapped it to the inside of her left arm where it hid beneath the robe's full sleeve.

She found the key where she'd tossed it on the table and opened the door. Hadrian stood waiting and she couldn't guess whether he'd been waiting for hours or had just arrived.

"Good morning," she said.

"Good morning. Would you care for breakfast?"

"No, thank you. I seldom eat breakfast."

"What would you like to do?"

"If you don't mind, I'd rather just stroll around High Rage. After a long day in the saddle, it's a real pleasure to walk. You might show me the library you mentioned, and I'd like to meet some of your family." She started to close the door, then remembered the information on the parchment sheets. Slipping into the room, she snatched up the pages and rejoined Hadrian.

As they walked down the corridor he said, "The library is one of the three best places to find the brothers and sisters of the clan. The other two places are the practice yard in the list, and the town. Do you want me to stay with you or would you prefer to be left alone?"

"If you show me the library, I think I can find my way around."

A dozen paces later, Hadrian stopped and gestured at a doorway. "This is the library. I'll probably see you again at lunch, if not sooner."

"I'll look forward to it."

Hadrian bowed, a precise declination of the head, and walked away. Mendarian stared after him for a moment, something still nibbling at the edges of her perceptions, then she entered the library.

The place was twice the size of her sleeping room, occupied by two couches and a low table and dominated by a massive fireplace. The woman called Raven sat at one of the couches while Martina lay lounging across the other. The table between them held a couple of bottles and several cups, along with candles, blank parchment, inkwells, and quill pens.

The walls were rack after rack of books and bins of scrolls. Mendarian had never seen so many volumes in one place. She approached one of the shelves and stared at the titles. All the books on that shelf seemed to be geographies, many of them representing places with which Mendarian was only vaguely familiar. She took out a book about Bildesh and covertly watched Martina.

After a short time Raven stood, returned the scroll she'd been reading to a bin on the far wall, and left.

If Mendarian were going to deal with Martina, it'd best be soon. She returned the book to its shelf, walked to where Martina lay, and bent over her. "I'd be grateful if you'd look at something for me." She handed Martina the parchment sheets that had been left in her room.

Martina looked up from under arched brows, then wordlessly sat up to make room for Mendarian on the couch. She accepted the pages and read them aloud, explaining one or two passages Mendarian found confusing, then handed back the sheets.

"Thank you," Mendarian said, as she tucked the notes into her belt. "I don't read Gasgoran very well yet. I'm rather better at reading people. I haven't reasoned out, though, why you seem to dislike me."

Martina showed no surprise, only smiled. "Because you have no shadow."

Mendarian recoiled. "That's absurd!"

"Not as absurd as not having a shadow," Martina replied. She paused a moment. "You're hollow. The only things within you are hunger and fear."

Mendarian glared at her then made her eyes as cold as chips of ice and lowered her voice. "Those who make themselves my enemies most often find life unpleasant and short."

Martina had been clenching her hand into a fist. She reached across to the table with her other hand and picked up one of the candles. Something in her fist made a snapping sound and a short blade shot out. She slowly cut through the candle in a single motion. "I suppose you know the clan law—that we always have a weapon in hand's reach."

Mendarian laughed, then stood. "A wise rule to follow." She strode to the door of the library and turned. "Good day," and she left the room.

Martina had nerve, at least. There might be polite verbal fencing around the others but Martina was a deadly enemy, one who'd never turn her back on Mendarian, one who might strike at the first misstep.

Mendarian took the notes back to her room, left them on the table, and followed the corridor back to the great hall, then outside.

The day was still cool—the sun barely above the mountains, and the shadows of the walls left most of the building in shade. The rich, heady scent of growing crops mixed with the equally rich odor from the stables and she could hear, from around the corner of the building, the clangor of metal striking wood.

She decided to follow the sounds, still savoring the taste of the game with Martina. Martina's enmity and wariness added spice to what might've otherwise been a dull contest. In her present combative mood, the sounds of arms practice drew her like music. She crossed the list and climbed a set of steps beside the gate, reached the walkway around the wall, and passed a guard in gleaming mail wearing a red surcoat with the winged dagger on the breast. He saluted her and she nodded in reply, then she trod along the boards around the corner, enjoying the feel of the breeze in her hair.

Again she heard the din of weapons' drill and looked down into the yard to see Travesty drilling with a glaive, a weapon like a heavy curved sword set at the end of a shaft. He seemed to have mastered the use of the rather difficult weapon. Eventually he stopped, leaned on the haft, wiped the sweat from his face and pushed back his damp hair, then strolled through a doorway.

He'd hardly disappeared through the arch before Hadrian came out the same door. He wore the leather armor that seemed almost a part of him, both swords, and a pair of daggers strapped to his forearms.

Mendarian, watching him closely, suddenly realized what had been nagging at her. When she'd seen him before, he'd been too near for her to really observe his movements. She'd noticed he didn't swagger but now she could see that he moved with the fluid, boneless grace of a cat.

He stopped beside the pell nearest the door and faced the post thirty paces away. For a long moment he stood relaxed with his arms crossed, then his hands whipped out. Mendarian saw two blurs of motion speed away from him, then he spun and faced the nearest pell. Both his swords rang against the wood before Mendarian heard the knives strike the far post.

The swords had become almost living entities, weaving bright patterns about their master so that one or the other seemed always to be lashing out, while both made an almost impenetrable defense. Mendarian could detect no rhythm to the strikes; making any defense nearly impossible then she realized he was cutting through the pell at neck level and at waist level. The blades continued their attacks, biting deeply at the wood and spewing chips.

Finally the left-hand sword chopped through the bottom cut and, as the upper part of the post toppled, the right-hand blade hacked it into two pieces.

No, Mendarian decided, she wouldn't really want to have to face him, sword in hand. She could now understand the source of his reputation.

Still, there were weapons other than swords or knives, more deadly than blades and more basic than magic, and she was confident she knew their use. She watched as Hadrian returned the swords to their scabbards then paced to the other pell and pumped the knives free.

As he turned around, Mendarian clapped her hands. He glanced up and—was that a smile—bowed.

Another set of stairs stood to her left and Mendarian ran down them to the list. He waited for her, again exhibiting that air of infinite patience. As she approached he bowed again and said, "I'm delighted I was able to entertain you."

Mendarian grinned. "It was most instructive. Since you're obviously capable, would you escort me into the town. I've heard you're trying to make it into a city."

"Honored." He walked with her to the gate, across the drawbridge, and down the road that crossed the cleared area separating the castle from the town around it.

Halfway down the hill, Mendarian turned to look back at the castle. "High Rage is very impressive. Like its rulers."

"The Shield of the Saint in the Empire of The Book isn't as high but is more defensible, but then it's a border warden. Here, defense is secondary. The castle was built before the clan came here."

The streets in the town were broader and straighter than in most of the cities she'd visited. She'd noticed the fact last night, riding through the town, and now she remarked on it.

"Most cities are built that way for defense," Hadrian answered. "If a city's built here, I want it defended at the outer walls, the mountains themselves. And if an army breaches the mountains, then nothing is gained by making our city a battleground. If the natural fortress is stormed, then the people can still retreat to the castle."

"And when they come out, their city will be gone," Mendarian said, "carried away."

"Most of the buildings will remain. Will an invader carry away paving stones? And what will have been stolen or destroyed can be rebuilt. Lives aren't nearly as replaceable. It's people who make a city, not goods."

Mendarian saw some shops whose wares would be far too expensive for the locals to buy, and few merchants would dare pack such valuable goods out of the valley. She mentioned that as they passed a shop in which a silversmith was engraving a goblet.

"Caravans come to High Rage three times a year. I want their reasons to be more than wine, brandy, and marble. Within a few years I expect Valé Shanna to be at least as well-known for its artisans."

The town was cleaner than Mendarian had expected it to be. All the merchants seemed to know Hadrian by sight and, while all were polite, none were obsequious. As they returned to the castle, she said, "I must admit I'm surprised. Few towns enjoy such tranquility."

"Today was a good day. High Rage has its problems, too. The town already has its own constables and I'll be relieved when it has its own court. For the present, Travesty sits as judge."

"It must be easy for you, having so many of your own people here, each able to deal with some part of your responsibilities."

He nodded. When they reached the great bronze door of the castle proper he opened it and they followed the corridor back to the great hall, where several of the clan had already sat down for lunch.

More trenchers and cups were brought in and Mendarian saw Poker sitting where he had the night before. The place beside him was still empty and she sat in that chair. "I haven't seen you since dinner last night. Are you avoiding me?"

He grinned. "Hardly. One of my vices is that I'm a late riser. I hope you're enjoying your visit."

"Very much." She glanced beside her to be sure Hadrian had taken the chair on her right side and noticed neither Scarface nor Martina were at the table. She faced Poker again. "I'm ashamed to admit I'm a little surprised that everything you've told me about High Rage is true. I'm very impressed, and eager to have any assistance you can give me to make Cerco so peaceful and prosperous."

Poker drank then set down his cup. "I'm pleased you're so favorably disposed toward us. I hope you don't mind that I'll be escorting you back to Gain tomorrow."

"I suppose I do have to return then, but I'm sorry my visit to High Rage has to be so brief." She turned to Hadrian and placed a hand on his arm. "Could you accompany us?"

"While I'd be honored, matters here demand my attention."

Hadrian still spoke in that quiet, even voice. She couldn't be sure her flattery was reaching its mark. She ate and drank sparingly, using most of her time at table to social advantage. She complimented Travesty on his skill with the glaive and made pleasant conversation with Lantee who was, like Raven, a magus. A few words here and there seemed to be all that was needed to gain acceptance from the clan, and words were a commodity she could well afford to spend.

In the afternoon she rode out with Hadrian to see the vineyards, orchards, and quarries, disappointed Vornarei had decided to ride with them. She made appropriate responses and asked the polite questions of one who pretends interest. Evening was deepening as they returned to the castle, just in time for dinner.

Scarface and Martina were both at dinner, and both of them looked as though they'd worked a long day. Scarface tried, twice, to start a conversation with Mendarian, while Martina only watched her like a fencer studying an opponent searching for weaknesses.

During the meal, Mendarian asked Hadrian if he could meet with her in her room after she'd had a chance to bathe and had treated his answer almost as a favor. She also noticed he made a series of hand signals to one of the serving girls.

With a final cup of brandy, Mendarian returned to her room and found servants waiting for her with the tub and buckets of water, and she understood then the signals Hadrian had made. After the servants had gone she bathed, dressed in another soft gown, and hid her dagger under the pillow on her bed. She called the servants to remove the tub and water, then brushed her hair. She'd just finished brushing it to a fine sheen when she heard a knock at her door.

"Come in." She sat on the edge of the bed and, when Hadrian entered, gestured toward the chair. "Please, sit down."

He stopped at the door. He'd apparently left his swords behind and seemed to be wearing only one dagger, which he drew from his boot and placed on the floor before he entered.

"I thought it was clan law never to be more than a hand's reach from a weapon."

"It's also bad form to be armed in the presence of one with whom one is signing a treaty—if you still wish to sign."

"I do, and I'm not armed." Her lips twitched. "You can search me if you'd like."

His dark eyes stared at her for a moment from under black brows and she couldn't guess whether he was amused, annoyed, or considering the offer. "That will be unnecessary," he said, then reached inside his sleeve and withdrew two pieces of parchment. "Would you like to have me repeat the terms of the treaty to you? I suggest you read these to be sure they're the same, and they're the terms that were stated before."

"No need. I remember the terms quite well, and trust must begin someplace. Where do I sign?"

He moved to the desk, opened the inkwell, dipped the quill into the ink, and signed both copies of the treaty. "You need only write your name above mine."

Mendarian rose, reached the desk in two steps, and signed both documents. Hadrian sprinkled fine sand over the signatures, then shook it off into a groove in the desk. He kept one of the pages. "The other is yours. Is there anything else you require?"

She faced him, smiling. "How long can you stay?"

"Unfortunately, my time isn't my own. And I believe you have another visitor waiting to see you."

"Who?"

"Scarface. Did you want me to stay while he's here, would you prefer to see him alone, or do you wish to see him at all?"

"I'll force myself. You may leave, but I hope to see you tomorrow morning before I set out for Gain."

He nodded, caught up his dagger from the floor, slipped it back into his boot, and opened the door. Scarface stood just outside. For a moment, she seemed to sense a tension, as though two tigers passed each other in a narrow corridor, then Hadrian stepped out of the room and Scarface entered.

He closed the door behind himself. "Well, we've met again."

She stared at him for a moment, then glanced at his sword and knife. "Hadrian put his knife down while he was in here."

Scarface shrugged, unbuckled his sword belt and the other belt with the knife on it, and placed them by the door. "The gesture is meaningless for Hadrian. He *is* a weapon."

"And you?"

He shrugged again. "Perhaps."

He locked stares with her and slowly advanced. "And you?"

She smiled. "Perhaps,"

A hand's length from her he halted. "You're a weapon in the truest sense of the word. You're an elemental woman."

"Do you want to see if I'm carrying any other weapons?"

His fingers closed around her wrists, then slid up her arms and across her shoulders then down to the small of her back. She was surprised his hands were so gentle. Slowly, almost timidly, he leaned forward and kissed her. The tentative kiss became more passionate. Another surprise was her own response, as her own passions struggled with her control.

Finally he released her and stepped back. Without ever removing his intense attention from her, he sat in the chair, legs crossed, fingers laced together around his right knee. "If a state marriage is what you really want, I can arrange a better match than Forgren."

"To you?" Her voice dripped sarcasm.

"To me. What flag would you like to see flying beside Cerco's?"

"If I were interested in such a preposterous thing, what about the banner of the Winged Dagger?"

"That'll come in time, when I take back what should always have been mine." He laughed at the astonishment reflected on her face. "Haven't you guessed yet? Yes, Hadrian really is a little bastard, a bastard child, a street urchin adopted by the clan. He's no more a member of the clan by blood or birth than any other mongrel in High Rage. And someday I'll take back what is mine. There will be a battle, and at the end of it a two-pronged beard will be pointing to the sky."

"What would you gain by marrying me?"

There was a long pause. "Besides the opportunity to enjoy your undeniable charms, I'd ensure our child would be a ruler, a legitimate ruler, in his—or her—own name."

"I'm not interested in being your baby-maker, or any man's, for that matter. *I* will rule. If you want to pay court, holding a kingdom like a handful of flowers, you may do so but, so far, your hands are empty. And if you try to cross me or my friends, you'll find that I have a very long arm. Do you have anything else to say? If not, I want to go to bed."

He grinned. "As a matter of fact, so, at the moment, do I."

"Then I suggest you leave and find your room. Good night."

He stood and she sensed again his ruthlessness and she was exhilarated, then he stalked to the door, picked up his weapons, and buckled them on. "It's my turn to say it this time. We'll meet again."

As he strode out the door, Mendarian caught herself thinking his answer to her when she'd said the same thing to him. *I hope so. You do make life interesting.*

~ * ~

Hadrian stared out the arrow-slit at the clouds scudding across the face of the moon. That cloud looked like a horse's head, with storm-tossed mane, and the one behind it resembled a hand, its ring finger gone. The chill night air raised gooseflesh on his bare skin.

Scarface was a brother. Not by blood but in some deeper sense. There was, however, one great difference between them. Hadrian now had someone, several someones, he could really trust. He wondered if Scarface actually thought that he, Hadrian, really trusted the Union, or the king in Gascoyne, or even the elders. Did Scarface comprehend the difference between trust and predictability? Even if Hadrian couldn't see farther into the future than anyone else he could, at least, sense the current of events, predict the most likely consequences, influence some of the reactions of those around him, and still stay ready for the inevitable dagger-thrust in the dark. But he was no longer alone, not in these rooms.

Suddenly he sensed Vornarei standing behind him in the darkness.

Her hand brushed his cheek. "What troubles you, my love?"

"That woman, Mendarian. She's going to be the death of most of the clan."

"Then kill her. Or have her killed. She's not worth your regret."

"I don't know if she means to destroy the clan or if she's only a pawn of chance. And killing her would only precipitate friction with the Union. I really don't know if she's as selfish and unprincipled and as cunning as I fear, or whether she's only a victim of something else. No, this is a storm the clan must weather."

"She's full of resentment. She radiates it as you radiate warmth."

Hadrian put an arm around Vornarei's thin shoulder, noticing, in the pale reflected moonlight, her pallor contrasted with his own darker skin. "It doesn't matter. A storm will break, sooner or later. And the one who'll be the most wracked is Scarface."

Chapter 4

Mendarian had finished her preparations for the ride to Gain before the belated sunrise of Valé Shanna. The mountains around High Rage made the days shorter and the climate cooler than in most of Gascolin. When she at last opened the door of her room she again found Hadrian waiting in the hall with that stone-like air of patience, and their exchange of courtesies met all the requirements of hospitality. Again she was impressed by how unreadable he was, yet how apparently bound by convention.

At the stable she found her roan saddled and waiting, and Poker already mounted on his blue. The rest of the clan had gathered in the list by the main gate.

She led her horse from the dark shed into the dim morning, then faced Hadrian. "I want to thank you again. The treaty we've signed has been the greatest triumph and the finest gift of my journey from Cerco. I hope to see you again."

He bowed. "The clan is pleased to have found such an earnest ally. And we may all see each other before you return to Cerco. If you choose to join the Union, there will probably be a meeting." He moved to the side of the horse and held her stirrup. "I wish you a pleasant ride."

Mendarian slipped her foot into the stirrup and swung up into the saddle. From her higher vantage, she could see Scarface standing in front of the crowd. As soon as their gazes met he performed a slight bow, little more than a nod, and with an indefinable air of insolence.

"I want to thank you all for your courtesy and hospitality," she said, staring at Scarface. "The entertainment was all that could be asked." She shook the reins and rode under the portcullis and across the drawbridge, Poker at her elbow.

In the town the merchants were opening their shops or bringing out their wares for display. She halted her horse and stared at the place one last time, then she set out on the road to Gain.

Mendarian waited until midmorning to break her silence.

"You were right about Hadrian. He was most courteous, but I could see he's earned his reputation. I'm not so sure of your opinion of Scarface. He came to my room last night and, well...I felt he was threatening me."

"Are you sure he was threatening? That wouldn't be at all like him. He has a deep contempt for bullies, and he'd perceive threatening someone in his own place of power as cowardice. He might threaten on neutral ground, or in an enemy's stronghold, but not where he has the upper hand."

"You sound as though you admire him!"

"I can and do admire some aspects of him. Ironically, I probably most admire those qualities about him that he sees as weaknesses." Poker drew rein and drank from a wineskin then offered it to Mendarian.

As they urged the horses back to a fast walk, he continued. "And I see his hunger for power as his greatest weakness. I'm hoping he'll someday learn that power is ashes and strive instead for strength."

Mendarian raised an eyebrow. "But they're the same thing."

"No, not at all. Power is our command over others. Strength is the steel within us that lets us exercise control over ourselves."

"So, you'd control yourself and, all in the name of courtesy and self-discipline, let any petty tyrant take what he wants from you, like handing your gold to a thief holding you at knife-point."

Poker threw back his head and laughed. "You seem to have confused sanctity with stoicism—or worse. Everyone must answer to the voice within himself—or herself, but we must also cultivate the wisdom to know whether or not the voice speaks true. We often lie to ourselves and convince ourselves we're opposing greed out of principle, when the truth is we're opposing greed with avarice and fighting treachery with treason. One must be certain the conflict is genuinely for a principle, then fight the battle while keeping the principle."

Mendarian was almost surprised by the sight of Poker's fangs when he laughed. She'd become so accustomed to his gentleness she'd almost forgotten his appearance. Immediately she distanced herself from him. It was foolish to forget, even for an instant, that he was one of the enemy. All his talk was a subtle trap, a mask to convince her he was different from the other men around her, that he didn't have the same drives, the same appetites. He was more dangerous than most men she'd met because he was more subtle. She began to understand why Forgren had been uneasy around him.

Her time with the clan had been educational as well as interesting. She'd learned the Union wasn't as powerful as she'd thought at first, almost certainly not as powerful as the Union thought itself. Despite the Union's drive for power, the clan might well be the more dangerous group.

A thought occurred to her, one which, if voiced, would probably gain her some information and might cast a pebble into someone else's pond. "Poker, I've noticed the Union seems to crave power, rather like one of your cousins. Do you think they might represent a threat to the clan?"

"All things are possible. I'd hope that possibility would never be tested."

"But, if it were, what would you do?"

"Ask me what I'd do if goats grew wings or the moon turned purple."

"But you could do something about the Union."

"What could I do? Live in constant fear of treachery? Would my suspicion make someone else more honest? It'd likely have the opposite effect. And the price I'd pay would be dear: I'd have violated my own ethics. There's nothing to be gained that even approaches the cost."

Mendarian drew rein and stared down at the town of Varish. "Hadrian doesn't think like you. Does the Union have anything to fear from the clan?"

Poker halted his blue beside her roan. "No. I didn't see the treaty you signed with the clan, but I can guess at its terms. The same terms govern our relations with the Union."

"Do you know the inn favored by the Union here in Varish?"

He nodded.

"Will you take me there to eat?"

"Very well." He drew a green ring from his pouch and slipped it onto the middle finger of his right hand, then urged his mount along the track toward the maze of buildings clustered along the river.

Mendarian noticed a subtle difference in her perception of Varish after having seen High Rage. High Rage was a town with a purpose, while Varish had simply grown up around a place where farmland, commerce, and the water that fed both all joined. The hawkers chanted the same litanies and the merchants displayed many of the same wares, but without some undertone of pride that marked the people of High Rage. Somehow, Varish seemed drabber and more dispirited that it had on her previous visits.

After following Poker through a rabbit's-warren of streets, Mendarian recognized the inn she'd visited before. The sign had been taken down and was leaning against a wall, fresh paint gleaming on its face. As they approached the building she saw a chimney-sweep climb out of the chimney.

She halted. "I'm not sure we should stop here. They seem to be standing the place on its ear,"

"Just cleaning. I expect to carry back to High Rage an invitation to attend a meeting of the Union here."

In spite of an attempt to conceal it, Mendarian smiled. "Can you also read the purpose of the meeting in wine spills?"

He chuckled. "It has to be just the right vintage. I can guess, though, that it's to announce that you've either joined the Union or signed a treaty with them. They'll want the clan to ratify the treaty and your membership."

"And?"

"And of course the clan will ratify it."

Her smile became impish. "Even if I choose not to sign their treaty or join the Union?"

He chuckled again. "Then, my guess is, we'd be standing around commenting on how clean the inn is and discussing the quality of the wine." He clicked his tongue and urged his horse to the stable behind the inn, dismounted, and showed off his green ring as he handed the reins to the attendant. Mendarian also swung down out of her saddle, not waiting for Poker to hold her stirrup.

"Rubdowns and a little water and fodder for our animals," Poker said. "We have many more leagues yet to travel."

As they walked into the inn they had to thread their way through a constantly shifting maze of servants and hirelings who were frantically cleaning everything that could be cleaned and polishing everything that could be made to gleam. The dogs had been ejected from the building and the rushes on the floor had been changed.

The innkeeper bustled toward them, his face set in an expression of professional regret, but that changed to an obsequious manner as soon as he saw the green ring on Poker's finger. "Milord, milady." He bowed toward Mendarian. "How may I serve you?"

Poker nodded to Mendarian, who gestured at a table. "Wine and a meal. And is 'Timos' still here?"

"Yes, milady." He led them to the table Mendarian had indicated and called for the servants to bring them wine, meat, and bread. "The man called Timos is still here, but he's not to be dist—"

"Tell him Mendarian of Cerco is here. I suspect he'll deign to join us."

"Very well, milady."

Mendarian sat in the chair Poker held for her and, when the servant brought food and wine, attacked the meal with enthusiasm. She'd just finished eating when Murtry descended the stairs, moving with obvious difficulty.

"I was hoping to see you again," Mendarian said, and nodded at a third chair at the table. She raised her cup and stared over it as she drank, a coy mannerism that let her study Murtry without putting him on his guard. He'd obviously been wearing a disguise before, for his features were much changed from their previous meeting. His nose was thinner and straighter, his cheeks had lost their puffiness, and his lips were less full. He smiled with his whole face at Mendarian and with his mouth at Poker.

"I was hoping to see you at Gain," Mendarian said. "While I've grown fond of most of the Union, I've missed you."

"Your concern makes the pain worthwhile," he replied.

"I'm flattered that you place such a high value on my feelings." She glanced at Poker then returned her attention to Murtry. "I suppose you two know each other."

Poker grinned. "Yes, we've met…." He left a diplomatic pause.

"Murtry," The other man condescended to smile. "The lady knows my true name by now." He glanced sharply at Mendarian. "I hope you were made comfortable at Gain."

"Very," Mendarian replied. "And also at High Rage."

"Oh?" His manner became forced casualness. "Did you encounter Scarface again?"

Mendarian recognized again the signs of tension members of the Union seemed to display toward the clan. She drank deeply from her cup to buy a few more seconds in which to phrase a perfect response, considering the men at the table. "Oh, yes. Poker, here, assures me he becomes less abrasive with longer acquaintanceship."

"He seems prepared to shorten some acquaintanceships," Murtry observed.

Mendarian leaned back so she could see Poker's reaction. He leaned forward, thumbs under his chin, his lips resting on his hands, one hand clasped over the other. Mendarian wondered if he weren't hiding a smile but he said nothing, neither with words nor with his eyes.

She turned toward him. "I hate to impose upon you like this, but would you please see to the horses? I'll be out shortly. I haven't seen Murtry for some time, and I'd like to have a moment to speak with him."

She was disappointed by Poker's reaction. Without the slightest apparent reluctance he rose, nodded to them both, and, after paying the innkeeper for the meal, stepped out the door.

Murtry watched him leave the room. "What do you think of that one?"

"He's very charming," she said, and sipped the wine in her cup, "and so, very dangerous. I'd trust him almost as much as I would Scarface." She looked keenly at Murtry. "I hope I haven't said anything wrong."

"Not wrong at all. Those are my own feelings. And Hadrian?"

Mendarian smiled and traced the mouth of her goblet with a fingertip. "Very courteous, like a viper who begs pardon before striking, but not the man I'd expected. He seems not to understand the uses of power, and negotiates from weakness. And he seems a small man for such a large reputation."

"Oh, he's dangerous enough, with all his little tricks, but he lacks vision. He's easily led."

That statement caused Mendarian's finger to stop in its circuit around the rim of the cup. Perhaps Murtry was right. It might be that those eyes revealed nothing because they belonged to just another face and mouth through which the clan elders issued their edicts. It was a possibility, though somehow she doubted it.

Her finger resumed its course around the cup. "To keep them happy I signed a treaty with the clan. I doubt it's worth the parchment or the ink, but there were no demands of territory or sovereignty, and my signature on it seemed to please them."

She stood. It was time to leave and let his imagination play with what she'd given it. "I must be going if I'm to reach Gain before nightfall. I do hope to see you again very soon."

Murtry slowly got to his feet. "I'll look forward to it."

The brilliant sunlight dazzled her eyes as she stepped out of the inn, and she was forced to squint. Poker, holding the horses, stood only a few paces from the door. Mendarian caught up her mount's reins, stepped into the stirrup Poker held for her, and swung into the saddle. "Let's get out of here," she muttered.

Poker mounted and led the way through the tangle of streets. Varish was a town that ended abruptly. One moment they were on a crowded street, looking at fields framed by walls of mud and wattle and, a moment later, they were following a road that ran like a scar through those fields.

Mendarian frowned and urged her horse to greater speed until Poker shouted for her to slow. She tugged at the reins and drew her mount to a halt, then clicked her tongue to order it back into a walk. She kept the frown.

"Is there a problem?"

"No," she snapped. "I don't want to talk about it."

She waited in vain for other questions or apologies but there were none, so she waited for what she considered the proper length of time before she grumbled, "I think you're likely right about Scarface. At least he'd probably threaten openly." She allowed herself to seethe, let that slip into her voice. "Those satin-covered vultures of the Union prefer to hint and sneak."

She glanced at Poker, whose face was a mask, then sighed. "I suppose I may as well join the Union. Tell me, Poker, will the clan take advantage of the terms of the pact the Union wants me to sign, or will you honor the compact I signed in High Rage?"

"The treaty you signed with the clan contains all the provisions you'd be asked to honor. And, on its part, the clan will accept the terms of either accord, should the Union be more generous than we've been."

She barked a short, bitter laugh. "You can rest easy on that account." She waited another few moments to suggest reluctance. "And would the clan honor its obligations to defend my rule in Cerco, even against the Union?"

"I'd hope that provision would never be tested, but, yes, we'd defend your throne, even against the Union."

"How could you do that? Don't you have a treaty with them, too?"

"True, but the important word is 'defend.' One cannot defend an aggressor."

She rested a hand on his arm. "I want you to know that I'll depend upon the treaty with the clan, and nothing else."

To her surprise, Poker laughed aloud. "When I put my faith in something, it's less visible but more faithful than man—or even men."

"Anything or everything is more faithful than man or men," she muttered behind her teeth.

"I beg your pardon?"

"Nothing. Just trying to add up the leagues back to Gain."

Not all the fatigue Mendarian permitted to show, to escape further conversation, was feigned. Elaborating too much on what she'd hinted at would be too obvious. Besides, Poker would undoubtedly stay overnight at Gain, and she wanted some plan of action to keep him and the Union at a cool distance from each other. Playing a game against two sides at once was risky, when the best manipulation could be destroyed by the briefest of conversations.

She was also disturbed that Poker couldn't be made to react as she might wish. Her dismissal of him to talk to Murtry alone should've made him suspicious, just as her presumed annoyance should've redirected the suspicions, but his opacity made her wonder if he hadn't already seen through her maneuvers. It didn't matter how gentle he might be; if he could see through her, he was too dangerous. How to answer that question for herself without having it occur to him? Perhaps the best defense was a good attack.

She drew rein and untied the wineskin from her saddlebow, drank, then offered it to Poker, who'd drawn his horse up beside hers. He drank, then returned the skin. As she tied the thong to a ring on her saddle, she said, "I'm sorry. I hadn't meant to be such poor company."

"You haven't been."

"Thanks, but I know I've been in a sour mood." They nudged their horses back into movement. "And I've taken it out on you and my poor animal. It's really my own fault, for trying to take on more responsibility than I may be able to handle.

"Before a mere accident I was just a simple roamer, one who survived from one day to the next. Then I found the staff and that crown and, to be honest, my first feelings were of pride and a sudden hunger for power. If one's starved too long and then sits at a banquet table, one tends to be a glutton and eat so much you make yourself sick. Then I looked around at the people who're my subjects and, to tell you truly, that terrified me. Suddenly it was on my shoulders to try to provide peace and prosperity for them.

"As I said, I was only a simple roamer, and that's what I remain, for the most part. So all these courts and intrigues and alliances leave me feeling like a rabbit who's wandered into a pack of hounds. Even the clan, as friendly as its members are, frightens me a little. And if I make a mistake, it's my people who'll have to pay the price."

"I think you'll do well at this business," Poker said. "You seem to learn quickly and, as long as you place the needs of your subjects foremost, you should do well."

She tried to examine his face and voice for any hint of irony, and could detect none. After another, shorter silence, she returned to the other question. "If the members of the clan are also members of the Union, how do you keep your independence?"

Poker smiled. "Partly, it seems, by not being royalty. And partly because Forgren trusts no one outside his own household. So he makes few requests of the clan. We cannot be responsible for duties we aren't asked to perform, nor are we bound to support plans or policies of which we haven't been told. Forgren keeps his own counsel, to which he's welcome, and silence often gives consent."

Mendarian chuckled at Poker's overplayed naiveté. "And so, if Union policy were to differ from, say, the needs of the clan or the will of your god—"

"Then Fogren would be too considerate a man to mention those to us, and we can hardly be expected to defer to a proposal that was never made."

"You, on the other hand, harbor no secrets from the Union."

"None. They may ask anything—almost anything—of the clan and will receive an honest answer. We do, of course, have clan policies which have nothing to do with the Union, and so do not consult with them on every matter, but these things aren't kept secret, only discreet."

Mendarian observed that Poker was, with difficulty, hiding a smile. She grinned openly, making it a shared joke. "And I assume Forgren asks questions as often as he explains Union policies."

"With almost the exact frequency."

Mendarian laughed outright, then wiped her brow with the sleeve of her blouse. The summer heat in this lowland region, unmoderated by mountains, was draining her. She looked again at the grasslands around her; the green tinged with brown, a deeper patch of green and a stand of trees showing where a small creek snaked its way across the steppe. Her horse had apparently caught the scent of water and she had to keep a firm hand on the reins to control him.

At the rivulet they let the horses drink lightly, then set out again. Once, they saw vultures ahead and to their left and rode a little out of their way to see what had died. It was a dead calf. Poker murmured, perhaps a prayer, and they continued.

"As you've observed," Mendarian said, "you have the advantage of not being royalty or, at least, not crowned. But Forgren and the Union might ask rather more of a member who sat on a throne."

"Ah," Poker replied, "but as a member of the Union, you may always call for a broader debate on issues affecting your people. There's also the difficulty of translating from one language to another. And the natural imprecision of messages and messengers. The possibilities for not quite understanding are almost limitless."

"I'll remember that."

Mendarian considered Poker's remarks in light of what she'd already decided about the clan. She'd been treated with faultless courtesy and had been offered an agreement that bound her to very little while granting her some measure of security, but she still had the nagging question of what the clan wanted from her.

She suddenly understood the difference between her visit to High Rage and the way negotiations were normally conducted. Men in power usually flexed their muscles, ranted and stormed, presented impossible demands, and tried to get at least half of what they'd been demanding. The clan had flexed its muscles—Hadrian's display of swordsmanship at arms practice had either been planned or was remarkably coincidental—but the show hadn't been accompanied by threats or demands.

That made no sense at all. A show of force was the preliminary to taking something from someone else. The clan had power enough that she'd have gone to High Rage at a peremptory summons and the courtesy, her treatment as an honored guest, had been unnecessary, since the treaty itself had been inducement enough to sign. The clan was obviously up to some unseen game. Perhaps they were trying to alienate her from the Union.

These ruminations faded into a sort of traveler's stupor, in which leagues vanished while the rider was only aware of dim discomforts. By late afternoon they'd encountered one of the patrols and Poker had needed to exhibit his green ring. He had to show it twice more before they reached the guards at the castle gate, and Mendarian's patience was whittled shorter with each delay. By the time they drew rein in the courtyard she had to remind herself that it was necessary to keep a clear head when dealing with dupes with power.

Arv met them in the list with Ivo, Valdemar, and two other men Mendarian had seen but didn't know. She ignored Ivo's attempt to assist her and dismounted, then hugged Arv.

Valdemar grinned. "Is this some special ceremony, or may I entertain hope?"

"Certainly," Mendarian retorted. "All you need do is be my best friend for five years." She hugged Arv again, then slipped one arm under his arm, the other under Poker's, and strode into the castle.

Forgren and Harma were descending the stairs as Mendarian and her escort entered the main building. Both men bowed and Forgren, with a glance at Poker, said, "I hope you enjoyed your visit to High Rage."

"Very much so," Mendarian answered, "But you'll forgive me if I prefer to talk at dinner. I could eat an ox—hide, horns, hooves, and all. And I'd like to do it on a cushioned chair. All this riding has taken its toll of some of the softer parts of my anatomy."

Forgren grinned and rubbed his hands together. "I could, if you really want revenge, order horse for dinner."

"Don't you dare." Mendarian said. "A sore backside is a small enough price to pay for not having to walk all the way to High Rage and back."

Forgren led them to the dining hall and held out a chair to the right of his throne but Mendarian took a step back. "I was introduced to a different custom at High Rage. Let Poker sit there and I'll sit between him and Arv. Besides, I have some amends to make. I've been gone three days from my faithful Arv, and I'm afraid I may have hurt Poker's feelings on the ride back." That should give everyone something to think about. "And, tomorrow, Poker will be gone again." She was amused to observe that Forgren's tight smile seemed to make his face hurt.

"It's always good to remain open to new customs," he said, and lowered himself into his throne.

The meal was brought in and Mendarian ate ravenously, listening to the conversations around her. Poker generally confined himself to giving polite answers and even more polite evasions to questions from Forgren or Harma. She noticed the absence of the sort of badinage and shared reminisces one might expect at a reunion of old friends. She also noticed interesting gaps in the Union's information. Poker admitted an ignorance she couldn't quite believe about the location of two clan brothers, men named Eagle and Gisli, about whom Forgren had indicated curiosity.

Arv spoke little and, with an odd significant glance, let her know he wanted to speak with her privately. She directed his attention to her hand and as she reached for her cup she made the sign for "tomorrow," then scanned the faces at the table to be sure no one else had seen the silent communication. No one else had observed the exchange, everyone else being involved with trying to entertain her or listening to the talk between Poker and Forgren.

Harma finished a last mouthful and leaned back in his chair, staring at Poker. "Do you still play Gods and Kings?"

Poker smiled. "I still play at it, and I appreciate the invitation, but the ride and the heat have exhausted me, and I have another long ride to take tomorrow. I'd be even more grateful for the offer of a bath and a bed."

Before Harma could reply, Mendarian said, "That sounds most agreeable to me, too. I'm not used to this lowlands heat." She politely covered a broad yawn.

"We'll have tubs taken to your rooms," Forgren said, as he crumpled his napkin and tossed it onto his platter. He drained his cup then stared at Mendarian. "We still have matters of importance to discuss."

"Not tonight, please," she said, and covered another yawn with the back of her hand then massaged her temples. "I'm afraid the weariness and the headache from the heat would leave me a very poor negotiator. You're much too considerate a man to take advantage of me while I'm unable to think clearly."

Forgren stood. "In the morning, then?" At her nod he shouted to a servant. "Halkett, tubs for our guests, in their rooms." He watched while the man hurried out the door, then stepped around behind Mendarian's chair and drew it out for her. "May I show you to your room?"

"That would be very nice."

As Forgren led her to her room, she gestured toward the doors they passed. "Which room will be Poker's?"

"Why?"

"Because something just occurred to me about something he said on the ride here, and I wanted to ask him about it."

"Oh, what was it about?"

Mendarian sensed an opportunity to end the questions and to tweak Forgren's guilty knowledge. And it would help set another barrier between

Poker and the Union. "He claimed he and Scarface had known Murtry and a man called Runa from long ago. Something about having been robbed of spoils."

Forgren rubbed his hands on the sides of his robe. "I wouldn't know about that. You'll have to ask Murtry." He stopped at a door. "This'll be Poker's room." He resumed his walk down the corridor and led Mendarian to her room, thrust open the door, and gestured at the bed and the dress draped across it. The gown was gorgeous; blue silk and satin with intricate patterns picked out in gold and silver threads, and sparkling with gems set in the fabric.

"Oh, Forgren," Mendarian breathed, "it's beautiful."

He beamed. "For you." He took Mendarian's hand in his. "A throne is a lonely place. I'd like to share mine with you."

"Forgren, I really don't know what to say. This is something I hadn't expected at all. Please, at least give me until tomorrow to think about it."

"Of course." He wheeled at the sound of footsteps at the door and watched two servants carry in a tub. "They'll bring the water next. "I'll leave you now." His tone made it plain he'd like to be invited to stay longer, but his words had made it possible to misunderstand.

Mendarian chose to misunderstand. "I'll see you in the morning, then."

She watched him retreat, then strode to the bed and gazed down at the dress. It was an impressive piece of work, and it looked as though it had been made to her measure. That worried her. She went to the chest at the foot of the bed, opened it, and took out the clothing she'd brought with her. Everything that was supposed to be in the chest appeared to be there, although one of the blouses was missing a button. Had she lost it or...?

It was probably nothing but it made her uneasy. She picked up the gown and carefully laid it across the back of the room's solitary chair. A dull noise at the door startled her, and she saw the servants had returned and one of them had bumped a bucket of water against the door frame.

They poured water into the tub, then backed out, bowing. As the second one retreated, she closed the door behind them and slid the bolt shut, then undressed and slipped into the tub.

The water could've been warmer, but it and the coarse, scented soap removed the odors of horse and sweat.

She had, until now, played a difficult game and it was going to become even more intricate and lively. She needed a plausible excuse for not accepting Forgren's proposal that wouldn't give offense. If he'd indeed been the most powerful man in the region, she could've accepted marriage with him, but now her freedom seemed better traded on an open market. Once it'd been given for an alliance, it'd be a very hard thing to take back.

She climbed out of the tub, dried herself, and put on another robe, anticipating her visit to Poker. The visit could serve several purposes, not the least of which was to inspire a bit more jealousy in Forgren and some of his underlings.

She left her room and crept down the corridor, the stone floor cool against her bare feet. She counted the doors and approached the one Forgren had indicated, then pressed her ear against the wood. She heard nothing through the door and she wondered, momentarily, if Forgren had lied about which room was Poker's, then she tapped with a fingernail.

"Enter." It was Poker's voice.

She pushed open the door and found him sitting cross-legged, like a tailor, on his bed, and he held a fine chain of jewels or jewel-bright beads. As she stepped into the room he stood and slipped the chain up his sleeve.

"Good evening," he said. "To what do I owe the honor?"

"I was just feeling lonely. Besides, since you'll be leaving tomorrow, it'll be my last chance to see you for a time. I'll miss you. I've enjoyed your company and now I'll have to do without it." She gestured toward his sleeve. "Was that a chain of beads you were holding just now?"

He smiled and lowered his arm to let the beads slide down his sleeve and into his hand, then held them out for her inspection. "These are prayer-beads. Each bead is a different color, each signifying a different attribute of Ianno. One touches the bead, offers a prayer then meditates on that attribute and how one may strive to cultivate it. And, of course, thinks upon the greatness of Ianno."

"Interesting," she said, and sat on the other side of the bed. For a moment she arranged her thoughts. It was essential to remember Poker's might not be the only ears to hear what she said in this place. She grinned at Poker. "There are times when I regret you're a priest who doesn't permit himself to enjoy closeness with women."

He laughed. "There are times when I regret it, too, but it's a thing I chose and daily choose again. And there are many kinds of closeness."

"True." She paused. "May your choice bring you happiness and pray that mine does as much for me. I'll see the clan in Varish. I've decided to join the Union."

"I'll pray for that," he replied, "that you find happiness."

She stood. Her performance was at an end and it'd be foolish to stay for either applause or criticism, since remaining would only increase the risks. "I'll see you in the morning, then."

"Until then."

She returned to her room. The tub was gone. She closed the door and slid the bolt, undressed again, then lay on the bed and tried to frame her response to Forgren.

~ * ~

She and Arv met Poker at the stables as he saddled his mount. She embraced him just before he climbed into the saddle, and then he was gone. By glances and gestures she led Arv into the woods by the town, finding a secluded clearing. When she was certain they were alone she turned on him, eyes afire. "Why did you let them handle my clothing?"

"I didn't know anything about it until Forgren told me they were making you a dress for the ceremony."

She let him realize she was still angry but she might ignore the mistake this time. "Did you discover anything worthwhile?"

"Only that most members of the Union here seem to actively dislike the clan. They make all the polite disclaimers, but almost all the remarks about them are derogatory." He chuckled. "Rolling dice badly is called, 'doing a Scarface. Apparently, he's had bad luck with the bones."

"Were any remarks useful? Anything that gives away weaknesses or habits?"

"Mmmmmm, there's a man called Travesty, who tends to be over-cautious, and one of the men Forgren asked about last night—Gisli—he was apparently badly wounded in the fighting in Doss. No one's seen him for quite a long time and some of the people here think he may be dead."

Mendarian knelt on one knee, plucked a stalk of sweetgrass, and sucked at the stem, watching Arv with calculating eyes. "Have you found out anything about the people of Gain that might be useful? How many of them have given away something about the Union itself?"

He shook his head. "Nothing. They consider me an outsider, and are careful around me."

"Very well." She spat out the stem. "We'd better go back now. Forgren expects to have a talk with me this morning. I do wish you'd been able to give me something to either hold over his head or dangle in front of his nose."

She stood and led the way back but dismissed Arv before they reached the great hall. She found Forgren sitting on his throne at the head of the table but he came to his feet when she entered the room. He drew a chair out for her, lowered himself into the chair beside it, cleared his throat, and then stared down at the spot of the table he was rubbing with his thumb. "Have you thought of what I asked you last night?"

"I've thought of nothing else." She covered his hand with hers. "I think it would be unwise for me to marry at this time. Part of my power in Cerco comes from the fact I'm not a wife. You know how barbarians are. I must be an empress, not a woman, if I hope to command them. Besides, I have to prove myself worthy of the honor you've given me. You'll be able to see from my administration of Cerco whether I'd aid you or be a liability." She gazed down at her hands. "I guess I'm really just not ready. This was all such a surprise to me."

Forgren's eyes narrowed and his voice deepened almost to a growl. "Then your answer is 'no.'"

"No," she said softly, "the answer is 'not yet.' I've things to prove to myself before I could accept such an honor, but I'd be pleased to become a member of the Union—on one condition. I know it's outrageous to ask, but Arv's been my advisor and, more importantly, my best friend for many years. Could he also be invited to join the Union?"

Forgren leaned back in his chair. "That's little enough to ask. And you say, then, that there's hope?"

She smiled. "There's always hope, and I hope to prove myself worthy of your respect and affection."

He patted her hand. "I'm already sure of it, but I'll respect your decision." He stood. "Will you be our guest in Varish tomorrow night? And would you wear the dress I gave you?"

"I thought it was a wedding-dress. I'd rather save it for that occasion. As for a celebration, I accept the invitation with pleasure."

He drew closer to her. "Is there anything else I could do for you?"

"Yes," She grinned. "Teach me to play Gods and Kings."

He put his arm around her. "Harma probably has a game going on in his room now."

Together they strolled to Harma's room and Forgren explained the rules of the game. Gods never contested directly with each other but attacked their rivals through the kings under them. Gods and kings alike depended upon armies; the kings for soldiers, the gods for worshippers. The object was to separate a god from all his worshippers.

Mendarian watched Harma beat Valdemar and be beaten by Forgren, then Forgren challenged her. He beat her, but made it seem more difficult than it had been.

As her last god was finally surrounded she stood, pleaded weariness, and trod to her room. As she paced the corridor she had the sense of being watched but saw no one. With a last glance down the hallway, she entered her room. She'd barely knelt before the chest at the foot of her bed before she heard a light tapping at her door. She leaned on the chest and levered herself to her feet. "Who's there?"

"An old friend." It sounded like Murtry's voice.

"A moment." She lifted her sleeve and removed the scabbard from her arm, slipped it under the pillow, then sat on the bed. "Come in."

The door opened and Murtry stepped into the room. "I've missed you," he said, his voice changing with his features, which wavered as though she were seeing them reflected in choppy water, then the face relaxed but it was a different face.

"I just wanted to let you know you aren't the only one with a long arm," Scarface said.

~ * ~

Scarface had stood at the ramparts watching Poker and Mendarian until their horses were mere dots raising dust on the road to the pass. Mendarian could be almost as hard to read as Hadrian. He wasn't sure he hadn't overplayed his rivalry with Hadrian—that he hadn't made himself too transparent. Even though Mendarian hadn't responded to his approach, Hadrian hadn't told him of being warned by her, either. She might assume Hadrian already knew of his feelings, and not many people wanted to step into a family quarrel, but he was still troubled by feeling his loyalties being drawn in two different directions.

With a last glance at the fading dust cloud, he strode to Martina's room. She stood waiting for him, wearing bright robes.

She glanced up from the mortar in which she was grinding an herb. "It should be easy enough to finish the spell we began yesterday. How soon do you want to change?"

"Sundown tonight would probably be best."

"You know the consequences?"

He let a trace of humor past his guard. "Yes, I will be much uglier for a while. And the other consequence is that you want me to explain all to you, correct?"

"You always were very quick and observant."

He sat on the edge of her couch. "I intend to masquerade as Murtry to get into Gain and pay a visit to our recent guest. Once there, I intend to let her know who I am—"

"Going into the stronghold of the Union strikes me as a little over-dramatic, as well as a very complicated way to commit something as simple as suicide. Do you mind telling me why you're playing this game at all?"

"Several reasons. She's told me she can reach into any place. I think the remark was intended as a threat. I want to establish that many of us have that knack, and some of us don't need agents to do our dirty work for us. I'm still not sure about her motives as regards the clan. And I find I enjoy her company. If nothing else, she offers challenge." He stood and stretched. "Between the disguise, perhaps a spell of concealment properly used, and the spell of transmigration in case I need to leave in a hurry, I should be safe. You do have that falcon in a safe place, and in a cage large enough to comfortably hold my body, don't you?"

"Yes, but I wish I could convince you of how foolish all this is."

"You might, but it's my chosen folly, and I have a weakness for self-indulgence."

She held up a small, dark, wooden figurine, carefully carved to resemble Scarface, placed it on the low table before which she knelt, then lit a gray candle and let the hot wax drip over the face of the carving.

Scarface gritted his teeth as he felt as though something hot and heavy settled over his features and dripped down to cover the rest of his body. From far away, it seemed, he heard Martina's voice. "I'm sorry about the discomfort, but it should go away quickly."

His face seemed set in stone as Martina sculpted his appearance into the wax, then the sensation of heat ebbed, leaving only the feeling that he was covered by some invisible but hardly yielding substance. At first, it was difficult to move even his limbs and his face was a rigid mask. All the better, he decided. He approached Martina and folded his arms around her. "No matter what happens, little cousin, always remember that I love you very much and always will."

He released her, stalked to his room, and opened the chest. He would have need of both the scepter and the copy, the glass rod, a bit of money—he tossed a pleasantly heavy purse into the air and caught it again—and his weapons. He'd also need to get some other weapons from the armory.

His preparations for the trip, not knowing when or if he'd return to High Rage, took most of the morning, so it was only a little before noon when he set out on the road to Varish, wearing green and gray. A few daubs of the proper clay hid his scars, at least at a distance, and so he wasn't hailed as he passed the outposts of the pass guards, riding out of Valé Shanna almost unnoticed.

As he rode to Varish he kept one part of his attention directed at the sun. Sunset came earlier in the valley and he needed to find a secure place for the time when Martina would finish her spell. The foothills held their stands of trees, but woodcutters had been known to come this far from Varish for fuel. When he judged the time to be near he found a clump of trees and investigated it quickly, then tied his mount's reins to a low limb and laid down on the ground to wait for the change.

His wait was brief, then he paid the real price for the spell.

This spell had been simpler and far less draining than the spell of transmigration, but the cost for this spell was to be paid in a more bitter coin. He felt warm and opened the collar of his shirt but found no relief. The heat became oppressive, as though he were being held over a fire. Sweat ran down his face and body then the wrenching began. He felt as though the bones of his skull were being bent and twisted, and he could almost hear a grating sound through the bone. His muscles were also being kneaded and re-formed, cramping and stretching into new positions. Within moments his entire body convulsed with the agony of being pressed and pulled by an unseen giant. All the soft parts of his body screamed in protest, and the skeleton groaned with the pressure as parts were bloated or pinched into different shapes. He fought to stifle a moan, then realized he was alone; no one could hear him. He screamed, then, and it seemed to lessen the pain.

Time lost all meaning as the agony that gripped him crumpled him like a piece of discarded parchment. He felt as though he'd always endured the pain, that it would never end, then the worst of it was gone.

He stretched out as best he could on the ground, finding this wouldn't relieve some of his cramped muscles. This discomfort, he knew, was a necessary part of the spell, to make him believe, as he wished others to believe, he wore some other man's face and body; one that looked different from his own, one that moved differently.

After using the truck of the nearest tree to haul himself erect, he caught at the reins of his horse, dragged himself into the saddle, and rode to Varish.

The sun had been down almost an hour before his horse's hooves clattered across the main bridge linking the two parts of Varish divided by the river. His passage would be noted, he knew; few traveled after sundown, but he wasn't sure his disguise could survive fording a river, and the other bridges and ferries that crossed the River Etaine were far out of his way. At least the darkness would provide a welcome anonymity.

Once, as he rode through the town, he saw two or three men gathered in the street ahead and several other shadows skulking in nearby doorways, but the moon shed enough light to let the length of his sword gleam, and the men hurried into alleys. Rats. If the woods produced both wolves and weasels, cities produced only rats, less predators than scavengers. It might've been better to have cleaned out this nest but the less attention he attracted, the better.

He found himself breathing easier when he saw the moonlight limning only grasslands again, and the ruts and depressions in the road could be seen well enough to avoid. Out of sight of the town, he turned off the road, followed a track used by farmers to cultivate their strips of crops, and took a winding trail up to a hill topped by a rock formation that looked like a resting bull.

Halting at the foot of the hill, he draped the reins over the limb of a stunted, twisted tree, gathered the items he needed to bury, and clambered awkwardly up the slope.

He chose the steeper slope and, well down from the best vantage point to observe either the rock formation or the surrounding countryside, he sought and found an erosion runnel that ran straight for almost the length of his own body. After running the point of his sword down the runnel to make sure it wasn't inhabited, he thrust his hand into the crevice and scraped away some of the gravel. He'd made a bundle of his own clothing and boots, one that was almost too bulky to be concealed, but he widened the lower part of the niche. Into the straight section of crevice he placed his sword and knife, the stiletto he'd taken from the armory, and the scepter, all of which he'd wrapped in a drab woolen blanket.

After he'd covered his cache over with dirt and gravel so the fissure looked undisturbed, he returned to his horse, obscuring the marks of his passage as well as he could. At the bottom of the slope he looked back up. In the moonlight he could see nothing to excite curiosity. Satisfied, he led his horse back down to the road, which he followed to a copse.

Finding a place reasonably secure and discreet, he hobbled his horse and let it graze while he gnawed dried meat and sipped sour wine, and finally tried to find a comfortable position in which to rest. Wearing Murtry's body was like wearing an ill-fitting suit of armor. There seemed to be no position in which he didn't feel bound and cramped. At last he struggled to a half-sitting position, his upper back and head resting against the rough bark of a tree trunk.

Why, he wondered, was he hurrying so cheerfully into a snakepit? The gamble appealed to him, of course, but he tended to game carefully. And for what stakes was he playing? If he guessed wrong or hesitated the Union would send his head back to the clan. Even if he won, Mendarian wasn't going to ride out the gates of Gain with him. He took another sip of wine and snorted at a fresh perception.

He was behaving like a love-struck boy, showing off for some adolescent goddess. Was that why he enjoyed being around Mendarian? Because she made him feel like a boy again? Again? He'd never really been a boy. He winced at memories that still stung through the years—a belt and a rough voice, rasping and hissing, vehemence only controlled by the fear of being heard through thin walls. His father had been obsessed with hiding among the peasants of Sin Garlef, and each time Scarface excelled or took some chance there'd been another appointment with the strap. The memory was as sharp and metallic as the blade of a knife. He burned again with resentment at each tear shed, a humiliation that hurt worse than the blows.

Why all the memories? It reminded him of stories he'd heard, of dying men reliving their pasts. Despite his carefully controlled self-assurance, a trace of doubt crept in.

No, he wasn't going to die in Gain. He'd made his preparations well, and he had the advantage aggressiveness gives the hunter.

And what was the goal of his game? Why was he so mad to see Mendarian again? He'd seen prettier women and been less attracted, although he'd never met one with such electric intensity in the eyes. And there was something else there, too. Challenge? He knew if what he felt was love, Mendarian would be the last one he should tell of it. That's why he'd lied to her about wanting an heir, when what he'd really wanted was Mendarian. She was too used to ruling and manipulating men, and to admit he loved her would make him, in her eyes, a subject, far less than her equal. Obviously, she was devious. She used her charm to bind men to her, men she'd sell for the price of a bottle of watered wine. She had the advantage. He cared for her while she would cheerfully rob his dead body. He respected her independence, as he'd respect any wild thing, while she'd fit him with a slave collar if she could, and discard him when she'd found some new toy or challenge.

Some of the charms of the situation, he decided, were the deplorable odds.

~ * ~

Breakfast, eaten and drank quickly in pre-dawn darkness, was more dried meat and sour wine. By the time the sun had risen he was already riding the vague trail to Gain.

He waited until midmorning before he veered away from the track to Gain and became alert for signs of a rider approaching. Poker would take this way back to High Rage, and Scarface preferred not to test either his disguise or Poker's conscience.

At last he saw the rider he'd expected, in his blue-gray and black, off on the far left. Scarface had, as much as possible, kept to the hollows and wooded areas. When he saw Poker he was near enough a copse to move, unseen, into deeper cover. He dismounted and waited, his hand over his horse's nose, until his cousin had disappeared over the crest of a hill, then he resumed his ride to Gain.

The first patrol stopped him less than an hour later. His green ring and a haughty manner took him past them. Successive groups were treated with indifference or, if they were too inquisitive, convinced of the urgency of his mission, but they delayed his arrival until after noon.

Nonchalantly, he rode through the gates of Gain and handed the reins of his horse to the first man he saw who wore livery. His sole visit to the place had been years ago, but he remembered where the rooms of Forgren and Harma were located, and he had a vague idea where guests might be roomed. Eager to conceal himself, knowing every moment he spent in the open was another unnecessary risk, he stepped into the cool dimness of the main building and was relieved to see no one in the corridor. He licked his finger and traced a pattern on his forehead, repeating the words of the simple spell, concentrating on pronouncing the words precisely. His hidden scars throbbed for a moment, then he relaxed. He wasn't truly invisible but he blended with the walls now, and anyone who looked in his direction would be misdirected to look past him.

The corridor he followed led to the great hall, then another corridor to the room he remembered as Forgren's. Pressing his ear to the door, he listened but heard nothing.

Farther down the corridor he found the door of Harma's room standing open and, through the doorway, he could see Mendarian and Forgren playing Gods and Kings, surrounded by Arv lat Paldisan and members of the Union. Scarface watched the game for a few moves. Mendarian was a talented novice, and Forgren was showing generosity in his moves. The game would probably go on for quite some time.

With a last glance at Mendarian that was almost a caress, he moved silently away from the door. He could guess which direction she'd take on the way back to her room, and so he slipped down the hallway, his back to the wall, easily avoiding the few servants he encountered.

He was still trying to find a comfortable stance against the wall when Mendarian stepped into the hallway. She approached, then passed him, and he tried to become a stone in the wall as she appeared to sense his presence. He stood motionless, holding his breath, afraid to reveal himself yet.

With a last, sharp look down the corridor, she entered a room.

He let his breath out slowly. His heart pounded and his palms were moist. He'd gone into pitched battles more calmly. Slowly, he approached the door and lightly rapped on the panel.

"Who's there?"

He couldn't bring himself to lie so baldly as to use Murtry's name. "An old friend."

"A moment." The pause was just long enough to tighten his nerves by one more turn. "Come in."

He pushed open the door and strode into the room. "I've missed you," he said.

Those were the words chosen for the release of the spells and he almost stumbled as a wave of relief swept over him, washing away the illusion that had wracked his body like a confining costume.

"I just wanted you to know you aren't the only one with a long arm." He smiled at the small flicker of surprise she couldn't quite hide.

He moved slowly toward her. "You have only to call the guards. In this place, they'd kill me, throw my body on their dung-heap, and count it the best thing they'd done all year."

She stood. "I'd hate to have them disgrace their dung-heap."

The words were a razor drawn across his face, but he tried to hide the blood they'd drawn. "You won't find anyone here who can feel disgrace or dishonor."

He took off the sword belt he wore, placed it on the table beside Mendarian, laid the dagger at his belt and the copy of the scepter beside the sword then continued his patient advance on Mendarian until he stood before her. With deliberate motion, he took her wrists, slid his hands up her arms, across her shoulders, and down her back. At least she wasn't wearing a knife in any of those places. He drew her closer, waiting for and dreading the least resistance. There was none.

He leaned forward and pressed his lips against hers and, when she opened her mouth, he kissed her deeply and passionately. For a time he was lost in that kiss, experiencing nothing else. Her arms were around him, holding him as tightly as he held her.

Finally they drew a little apart. He slid his hands around her waist and his fingers teased at the knot of her belt until it slid down the robe to the floor. Still waiting to be stopped, he opened the front of her robe and touched the silken skin at her waist.

He grinned. "Would you care to share a religious experience?"

"What sort of religion?" Her voice had never sounded so soft.

He kissed her again then moved his mouth down her chin, down her smooth neck, to her chest. He bent and gently kissed her nipples, noticing her breasts were large and well-shaped. He bent deeper and his mouth moved from between her breasts down her belly. She smelled fresh and sweet, and her skin was a pleasure to touch.

He knelt and probed into her navel with his tongue, his hands resting lightly on her hips. He looked up at her and smiled. "My religion. This is divine."

He'd touched her abdomen with his lips and she stepped away and closed the robe. "That's enough." She snatched up her belt from where it'd fallen and secured her gown. "Why are you here? I'm sure you didn't come all this way for just a social call." She sat on the edge of the bed.

He stood up and smiled again. "As I told you, I wanted to let you know you aren't the only one who can reach into strange places, and some of us don't need catspaws to take our risks for us. And," he took the glass rod out of his purse, unwrapped it, and tossed the scrap of blanket on the table with the weapons, "aside from that, it was indeed a purely social visit. I wanted to look again into those lovely gray eyes and see if your lips were really as delicious as I remembered them."

"Then you're a fool," she snapped, her tone hard, almost brutal.

He was caught off-guard by her attack. His defenses crumbled with his smile but he forced the remains of his bravado to keep his lips curled. "You value your company too cheaply."

"And you place too high a value on yours. Now get out of here."

He struggled to hold his rictus steady. "Another time, then," he said, and strode to the window, the glass rod in his hand. "I've lost track. Whose turn is it to say 'we'll meet again'?" Without waiting for her answer, he jump-stepped to the frame of the window and flung himself out as he snapped the rod in his hand.

Instantly, he was in a different world. Colors vanished. The jumbled shapes of gray seemed distorted, most of them becoming flat, with no more depth than the figures in a painting, but very clearly perceived. He spread his wings, caught the wind in them, and beat strongly upward.

The walls of Gain loomed above him, and if he touched stone he'd again be in his own wingless body. With reflexes that weren't quite his own, he gained the needed height and cleared the wall. He heard a shout and, as he sped away from the castle, a quarrel whined past him. He dipped and turned frantically, then climbed. Even Harma would need so long to work a similar spell that pursuit would be impossible. His only worry was the guards, and he should be above bow-shot in moments. Once he'd gone too high for arrows to follow, he fled northeast, in the direction of Gascoyne, until he was certain he was out of sight of Gain, then he turned north by northwest.

Away from his enemies, he could appreciate the body he wore. He hadn't needed to learn to fly or dodge in the air. Some part of the habits, if not the mind of the hawk, must remain in this body, and both that part that was falcon and the part of him that occupied this body exulted in the sensations of flight and freedom. He'd become a part of all that lay beneath him, but free. He was more a predator than ever before, and so he experienced the wild, keen sense of kinship with all that lived and, simultaneously, breathed in, deeply, the ultimate freedom and self-reliance of the true hunter.

Some sense he didn't recognize and couldn't understand screamed in warning and his wings snatched at the air and threw him into a diving turn. Sudden movement, like a lightning bolt with feathers, shot past him with a harsh cry.

Surging upward in the crisp air, he saw the other hawk below him spread its wings and flash across the treetops then struggle to gain height again. Circling, he watched his opponent as its speed fell while it labored upward. Catching a column of air rising from the ground, he rode it higher, still circling, still watching the other bird. He could clearly see each feather and the wild rage in its eyes.

He allowed it to approach, some part, not himself, knowing when to strike. Now!

He became a thunderbolt, dropping like death from a war-god. At the last moment the other hawk, larger than he, faced him and raised its legs, the thumb talons pointing at him. His own lower talons were already like spears thrust at his enemy's breast. The world shuddered with the impact of their combat then they were tumbling and flapping in the air, attacking, locked in a duel in which neither knew defense, only attack. He felt and smelled his own blood and that of his enemy, and the battle-lust of the hawk whose body he wore somehow merged with his own ferocity in the struggle with the bird defending its territory. He struck, again and again, felt the claws of his enemy tear at him then the other bird was gone, diving away, fleeing.

He gave a harsh scream of triumph then wondered whether it was him or the falcon who'd done this thing.

Rising again, he searched the terrain below for some familiar landmark. The battle had drained him, made him hungry, and he became conscious of the slippage of the hawk's mind into the madness of yark. He'd seen falcons, mad with hunger, attack horses with armed riders.

In the distance he saw the flash of sunlight on water and a jumble of walls and roofs. It must be Varish, but the land around it looked different. Stone formations, seen from the sky, took on shapes he didn't recognize.

He dropped lower, desperate, fighting the mindless hunger that increased his aggressiveness until he was afraid he'd attack the first moving thing he saw. Level with the tops of hills, he sped like a crossbow bolt, his hawk's brain sorting the images he saw on both sides. He fled his fear over a copse and along a trail like a bare wound in the grain fields then he spied a hilltop that looked like a resting bull.

Banking, he swept toward the hill, shutting out everything else until he reached it, spread his wings to halt his flight, and alighted beside a large stone. He reached out with a taloned leg and touched the rock.

He sprawled on the ground, unable to stand. Wings he no longer wore clutched at the air he could no longer ride. Pain was something sharp and red on his left wing. Left arm. Colors flooded back into the world, coming like a shock. More pain, dull and black, along his left shoulder. He thrashed about on the ground, scrambling madly for an outcropping of reality. His mind caught at the ground itself, the hands that clutched at it, took those bits of the real and clung to them as a drowning man clings to flotsam.

With the shards he found, he began to rebuild his world.

A fine sheen of sweat covered his body, chilling him. He drew the cloak he wore tighter about himself and waited for the last of the confusion of transference to pass. He became aware of his own heartbeat, weak and thready, and he forced himself to relax. Within a few moments his pulse became stronger, a steady pounding, and the chill retreated. Some dislocation remained but he looked down at his left arm, the source of pain. The hawk must've panicked at being thrown into a strange body so different from its own, and thrashed about the cage, numbing and bruising the left upper arm and shoulder.

The chill finally passed and he took off the dull cloak and let it drop to the ground. He paced along the slope above him until he saw where he'd left his clothing and weapons. Still clumsy from the shocks his body had survived, and with his left arm still numb—useless for climbing— he used his right hand to shove his left hand into his belt then selected the safest route of ascent. He scrambled up the dirt and gravel until he reached his cache.

First, he fumbled out the bundle of weapons. The scepter he thrust into his boot, the knife and stiletto into his belt, and the sword belt he threw over his shoulder so the sword could be easily drawn but kept away from his legs for the descent.

The clothing and supplies, all but the wineskin, he tossed to the ground. The strap of the wineskin went over his right shoulder, beside his sword then started back down.

At the base of the hill he tore open the bundle, found the dried meat and bread. He gnawed at them ravenously and washed them down with wine. Even after reclaiming his own body he still felt traces of the hawk's maddening hunger.

He quickly finished what little food he had hidden then considered his clothing. No reason to change now. His body reeked of fear-sweat and, despite his desire to resume his own colors, he decided to wait.

The fingers of his left hand began to tingle then he felt the pins and needles sensation that meant the numbness was receding. Awkwardly, he buckled his sword belt around his waist and picked up the gray cloak from where he'd thrown it, put it on, and began the long walk to the River Etaine. He wanted to reach a place downriver of Varish, one easily forded.

An hour before midnight he finally reached a bottleneck in the river, threw his boots, clothing, and weapons across, then walked upriver to a wide shallows where he splashed across, stripping as he waded and swam. Once across, he recovered his equipment and set out for the foreign quarter of Varish.

~ * ~

He slipped out of the night shadows and rapped at the door of the most imposing house in the quarter. He waited then rapped louder. The third time, he pounded at the door. He was considering trying to break into the building when the door was snatched open and a bearded man, club in hand, glared at him.

"Rastig," Scarface said, "I need your services again."

The bearded face glared at him a moment longer then was split by a wide grin. The man laughed, a deep, rich rumble of pleasure, clapped Scarface on the shoulder with the hand not holding the club, and drew him into the house.

They shared a bottle of *akvad* and stories of the Das war. Rastig had plainly done well since coming to Varish as a refugee. He'd risen from thief to fence to usurer, and now he owned a share of half the businesses in town.

"It sounds as though you've prospered mightily," Scarface observed. "Do you, then, own everything on this side of the river?"

Rastig roared with laughter again. "No, by Ragma's girdle, my friends are here. I only rob those crooked Gascolans. They fancy themselves merchants, traders, and thieves. It's a pleasure to teach them how a Doss horse-trader can eat their dinner and make them pay me for the privilege of watching me do it."

Scarface laughed with the former bandit.

Rastig refilled their cups. "And what sort of horses are you interested in trading for?"

"No horses. I suspect there'll be a large number of people coming to town tonight, all wearing green rings. I'd like to be sure this is the case, and I'd enjoy visiting with you until after they've all arrived."

"Will Forgren be there?"

"Almost certainly."

Rastig's curse was half disgust and half admiration. "If you buy a horse from that bastard, be sure to count the legs first."

Scarface chuckled. "It's not a horse, it's not his—at least, not yet—and I've counted the legs. She has two, and nice ones they are, too."

Rastig fell victim to another bout of hilarity and produced another bottle. Scarface saw a blurry dawn before finally taking to a pallet.

~ * ~

The heat of early afternoon eventually drove him from the pallet. Another cup of *akvad* helped steady his hands and stop the pounding behind his eyes. Two buckets of cold water dumped over his soaped body completed his resurrection. As he dressed he received confirmation of his guesses. The Inn of the Three Crowns would be the site for the meeting of the Union.

There was a final gamble to be taken, the biggest of all. The Union would, at the very least, demand Scarface's outlawry. Forgren still found the clan too useful to outlaw the entire family, and Scarface had acted in such a way the clan could easily disavow his actions.

He'd cut himself loose from everyone. Now he must either form an alliance the Union would be forced to respect or prepare for a brief but unpleasant and eventful life. Mendarian was the key and he must stake everything on her. He felt a bond between them, one not reducible to logic but stronger than logic.

After borrowing a horse from Rastig he rode out of town and returned later without sword, knife, or scepter.

He wrote a note to Mendarian, telling her the location of the hidden scepter. If the gamble failed and he died by her hand, it was only fair she should win as prize the bauble that had drawn them together and made them opponents. And, with some of her allies, she'd need all the protection anyone could give her.

The afternoon dragged interminably, it seemed, until the time came to ride to the inn. Rastig refused to sell him a horse but offered to lend him one and ride with him to the meeting. Scarface was grateful for the company and rode slowly, savoring the companionship, taking pleasure in each sight, sound, and smell, immersing himself in life. If one is gambling life itself, one should appreciate it the more.

When they reached the inn Scarface dismounted and handed the reins of the borrowed horse to Rastig. "I'm sorry you'll have to miss the excitement." He displayed the green ring on the middle finger of his right hand. "You need one of these to enter here."

He watched his comrade ride away then faced the guards standing in front of the door, waved his ring at them, and stepped forward. They advanced and crossed their spears in front of him.

Scarface stood, legs apart, hands on his hips. "I'm surprised that even Forgren and his lackeys need four armed men to protect them from one man who isn't even wearing a sword. This trinket entitles me to enter here, and it's mine until he or you can take it from me."

One of the men stepped closer, his spear pointed at Scarface's belly, then Travesty stepped out the door of the inn. "Hadrian said I should wait for you here. Are you coming in?"

Scarface smiled at the guard. "Would you like to discuss this with Hadrian?"

The guard scowled then gestured and the other men took a step back, no longer barring his way. Scarface strode past them, nodded to Travesty and, in a low voice, said, "Step inside then pretend you don't know me."

Travesty's eyes widened then he entered the inn and trod to an empty chair along the right wall.

Scarface studied the seating of the membership. The tables formed a hollow square, open at the bottom. All the clan who'd been at High Rage except Hadrian sat at the table Travesty'd gone to, to Scarface's right. Hadrian sat at the head table, along with Forgren, Harma, Wilkan, and Mendarian. Behind the head table was a door leading to the stairs to the upper floor.

The clamor and movement in the room stilled as Scarface watched. Even the servants stopped and stared, their trays and flagons almost forgotten. Conversations at the tables died or faded into silence, and all the faces in the room were turned toward him.

"I seem to be the subject of conversation here," he said, and began to stride to the head table.

Chapter 5

Forgren nibbled a piece of meat covered with melted cheese, washed it down with a deep draught of wine then leaned forward to talk past Mendarian to Hadrian. "Did you know that Scarface entered Gain in disguise and threatened our guest?"

"No." Hadrian's eyebrows rose and he turned to Mendarian. "What did he say or do?"

She sipped her wine. "Nothing, really. It was more of a social visit. I'm just very particular who I talk to in my bedroom."

"He refused to leave when you told him to?"

Mendarian grinned. "No, although his departure was as unorthodox as his arrival."

"Still," Forgren rapped at the table with his knuckles, "he abused the hospitality of Gain. If the clan has some excuse or explanation for this, I'm willing to listen to it."

Hadrian ran the tip of his finger around the rim of his wine glass. "The clan was unaware of his visit."

"I've heard his banner was still flying at High Rage until sunset of the day before he came to Gain, and the horse he rode was almost dry."

Mendarian leaned back so she wouldn't be caught between the two men and tried to conceal her surprise that Forgren would make such an obvious admission that he had spies in Vale Shanna. She cast a quick glance at Hadrian to observe his reaction. He seemed not to have understood the implications of the question. Was he really that dense or....

"We only discovered his absence at sunset. He'd left without farewells and the guards also apparently failed to recognize him and note his leaving."

Forgren's voice deepened and he spoke through clenched teeth. "If the clan has no knowledge of his actions—which turned out to be sneaking into Gain and threatening our guest—and the clan doesn't approve of his actions, does the clan then withdraw its protection from Scarface?"

"Not until he refuses to explain—" Hadrian paused then gestured at the door. "And now would seem to be an opportune time in which to ask."

Mendarian stared with the rest. There, framed in the doorway, stood Scarface, gazing into the room. When all the faces were turned toward him, he approached the head table. His walk was inexorable, as though had mountains or deserts or a thousand armed men stood in his way he would've trod across them, too.

Valdemar rose from his seat and stalked toward Scarface. Both men stopped, an arm's length apart, and Valdemar snarled, "You've finally signed your death warrant. Your walk stops here."

Valdemar's hand moved toward the dagger at his belt while Scarface held out his right hand and intoned a phrase. The spell seemed to weaken him a moment but Mendarian sensed a blackness flowing around and through his fingers, and she knew that death now rode in that hand.

Hadrian leaned toward Mendarian and Forgren and whispered, "Forgren, I suggest to find a way to let Valdemar save both his face and his ass, because if he doesn't move, he's dead meat."

"That goes for Scarface, too." Forgren was obviously struggling with his own rage.

"Is it easier to clean up after two or more corpses than just one? If I know my cousin, he'll want more company than just Valdemar on his hellride."

Mendarian felt as though she were watching a rope holding some great weight beginning to unravel. Neither of the men in the center of the room seemed prepared to take a step back.

In the electric silence, Hadrian's mild voice was clear and knife-sharp. "Valdemar, we've asked him here to explain his actions. Allow him to approach."

For half a dozen heartbeats the two men stood, then Valdemar turned and stamped back to his place at the table, as though he had a personal grudge against each reed on which he trod.

Scarface muttered again and Mendarian sensed the death retreating from his hand and could almost see it flowing back into his scars. He resumed his advance on the head table. He halted across the table from Forgren and herself, turned slowly making a complete circle, and faced them again.

He pulled the green ring off his finger. "I renounce my membership in the Union." He flung the ring onto the floor, where it rang like a dropped coin. "I renounce my kinship with the Winged Dagger Clan." He paused a moment, then said, "I renounce all gifts and holdings, all attachments and obligations." He stared directly at Forgren. "I declare myself outlawed."

Mendarian was stunned by the words. Scarface was throwing everything away, discarding whatever protection had brought him this far.

She was hardly aware of the others in the room. She'd never seen anyone build his own gallows with such deliberation, then realized he was staring now into her eyes.

"If I'm to be executed," he said, "I demand it be done by the only one of you I respect." His voice stopped but his lips finished with the words, "and love." With a sudden snap of his wrist he whipped out a small dagger and extended it, hilt-first, to Mendarian.

Staring back into his eyes, almost without being aware she'd moved, she reached out and took the knife. She had to tug, as Scarface apparently had to open his fingers by force of will, but open them he did.

She stood, the stiletto pointed at him and side-stepped around the table, always facing him, always with the blade of the dagger pointed at his chest. She was vaguely aware of Forgren sputtering, then rumbling that Scarface had no right to make demands.

As she rounded the end of the table she seemed to see Scarface more clearly. He knew she could kill. He'd even provided her with the opportunity to do it openly and by her own hand, and even to be congratulated for the killing. She'd fed him scant hope, had faced and fought him at every meeting, and now he was placing—almost negligently tossing—his life into her hands.

As she paced toward him she became aware of the vein pulsing in the side of his throat. He was afraid: He was hiding it, standing like a rock with his arms at his sides, his only movement to turn to face her squarely, as she came nearer with the dagger, but that throbbing blood vessel in his neck gave him away. He feared!

He was gambling! Without knowing how she knew, she was certain he was gambling. If she chose, she could kill him where he stood. Again her feelings came in a rush, as when she'd seen he could've once killed her.

The enormity of his risk appealed to her. If she left him alive she'd always, in a way, be responsible for him. He'd have lost the clan's protection but gained hers. She knew if she let him live, neither the clan nor the Union could strike at him without breaking their agreements with her. She hid a grin as she observed all the calculations that had gone into the construction of this one scene.

The throbbing pulse in his throat was proof he was gambling—that he didn't know whether or not she'd strike him dead.

An advisor who could scheme so successfully and be willing to back up his hunch with his own life was perhaps the best thing she could take back from this trip.

She halted, so close to him she had to hold the dagger vertically under his chin, then she spun and whipped her arm out, sending the dagger into the door behind the table.

As she turned back toward him she saw him exhale a long-held breath. He did it slowly, silently, but it'd been a held breath, and she knew a bonding had occurred. By sparing his life she'd become responsible for him to all those present, but now he was also tied to her by an obligation he'd find stronger than any chains.

She stared at the members of the Union. "This man is under my protection. We leave immediately for Cerco. It's for you to decide what treaties you choose to make and honor. Arv will follow me in a day's time with your decisions." To Scarface she quietly said, "Follow me." She seized his arm and strode from the hall, leading him past the stunned faces of the astonished guards. If nothing else, Scarface had bought his life with the entertainment he'd provided.

She led the way to the stable. While she saddled her roan she saw Scarface drawing tight the cinch of a black saddle he'd thrown onto a clean-limbed black stallion. In a few moments they were riding out of Varish. Scarface took the lead across the river and along a road running northwest, then veered off into heavy forest. He dismounted by a dead tree, paced away from it, counting his steps, and began to dig.

From the trench he extracted a long bundle which he unwrapped. He unwound his sword belt from around the scabbard and clasped it around his body, mounted the knife on his belt, then strode back to Mendarian, carrying the scepter.

"You seemed interested in this. It's yours. I left a note for you so, if I'd died, you'd still know where to find it."

"Keep it." She grinned. "With your scepter and your staff, you'll comfort me." She swung her leg over the pommel of her saddle. "Are you going to help me down, or was courtesy one of the things you forgot to pack?"

Again she saw a lightning-flash of amusement then he caught her under the arms and lifted her off the saddle. As he lowered her to the ground he drew her to him and, after a momentary hesitation, pressed his mouth against hers.

She felt the thrill of the closeness of danger but this danger was of a different sort. His hand crept upward from her waist, and she permitted it.

There was no need for hurry. She doubted the Union would choose to follow and she suspected Hadrian would discourage the idea if it were proposed. And, for the moment, the grass, shaded during the last part of the day, was cool and soft, the exploring hand was gentle, and the evening sound of birds and insects soothed her.

Perhaps it was the sound of the cicadas that took her back to the day she carried a bucket of milk on the path from the barn to her house. That day had been warm and well-used, like a comfortable pallet. Each of her chores had been carried out with a curious sense of rightness, and it was the end of a perfect day. She was tired but there was nothing of exhaustion in that pleasant weariness partly built of contentment.

For that moment, everything—the great tree's shade through which she walked; the last sunlight turning the fields of grain to cloth-of-gold; the heft of the bucket; the warm, heady scent of fresh milk and it shifting weight swinging the bucket with each step; the battered but beloved house before her; her mother in her coarse smock, waiting—it all seemed perfect. She felt the resonance of a perfect note being struck, the perfect chord being played, of belonging. And that resonance of inner peace had returned like a gift from her childhood. The memory faded but the feeling continued to reverberate within her.

And here she stared up from a bed of soft, fragrant grasses at a man who was stroking the bottoms of her breasts. She found his features pleasing. Even the black scars seemed attractive, proper to his face, a face she wanted to see often, and she felt again that resonance of the perfect note being perfectly struck; that same sense of belonging.

His hand crept down her belly and tugged the bottom of her blouse free of the waist of her riding trousers, then slid upward, under the cloth.

"Scarface—"

"Morgan." For a moment she failed to understand and he read her confusion. "My true name is Morgan."

She realized then the importance of the gift he was giving. Rolling the taste of his name around her mind, she decided it was also right. "Morgan, when you visited me at Gain, you knelt before me. Never do that again. Not for any reason. And never expect me to kneel before you. Not for any reason."

The tips of his fingers and been teasing one of her nipples. Now the hand moved down her belly to the hollow formed by her hipbone. "We're both lying down right now." He fumbled with her belt. "So, if you have no religious objections, I'll finish my devotions."

She laughed and meant it, a pure release of contentment. "I may even become a convert."

~ * ~

Mendarian woke first and, for a time, just lay on her side gazing at Morgan. Asleep, his face lost its harshness. She could remember no harshness from the night before, so perhaps his sleeping face was his true, unguarded self.

What sort of gamble had she taken? What kind of bargain had she made? She'd offended the Union and, probably, the clan, all for an advisor who was also a bed partner. Or was he a bed partner who could advise? Did she enjoy having him around her because he could be ruthless and calculating, or—

She looked at him again then recoiled from him as though he were a pit that had just sprung open beside her. In a sense she indeed stood at the lip of a pit or the edge of a cliff. A single step forward could take her into the void, and what would become of her then? She realized she was afraid of losing herself in Scarface, afraid that nothing would be left of her but an echo of his voice.

She had to protect herself, had to keep a distance between herself and Scarface, to take what he offered and give only what she chose to trade away. She couldn't permit herself to believe he was other than an enemy like any other man, putting his own wants and interests foremost. He would use her if he could and, when his interests were taken by something, or someone else, he'd abandon her.

He stirred and rolled over, wrapped an arm around her, and tried to draw her toward him. She resisted and he lay back, grinning with sweet insolence. "How lightly some take their religion."

"It's politics before religion in this case. We must return to Cerco."

He rolled free of the blanket and dressed. For a moment she lay watching him. His body appealed to her—large-framed and strong but slender, hard enough to look good, soft enough to want to lie with.

The sense of belonging returned and she fought it back, then she also rose and dressed. They returned to Varish where they purchased a meal and supplies, and Scarface stopped at a large, impressive house where he left the black stallion and obtained a rangy gray gelding.

He chuckled as he set a new saddle on the gray and remarked, "It seemed only proper, yesterday, to take Hadrian's horse and saddle."

She rolled her eyes. "Do you think you left any possible source of annoyance untouched for future use?"

"Opportunities always arise," he said, and mounted the gray.

The ride back to Cerco was a fast one. By nightfall they were well into the foothills and, three nights later, they were in Cerco, in the country of the Dieri. Mendarian was able to lead them around or past patrols of Dieri soldiers to a mountain she identified as "Crown."

At the base of the mountain they had to dismount and the two of then scaled the slope to a place where a ledge and an overhang concealed a fissure in the rock, one barely large enough to admit Mendarian crawling on hands and knees. They crouched on the ledge, gathering back the breath they'd lost on the climb.

"Take the horses around to one of the main caves. The guards will stop you, but show them this." She handed him a carved baton she'd taken from her saddle pouch. "This, and the names Arv lat Paldisan and Orhan Ustruatha should be enough to get you into the throne room today and, with luck, we'll have you moved into the imperial apartments by tonight."

She kissed him and watched him make his way back down, then ducked into the crevice and crawled into the mountain. Three spear-lengths into the tunnel, it widened and deepened enough to let her move quicker, even in the utter darkness. She ran her left hand against the stone wall and passed the first three gaps in the stone, false exits, turned at the fourth passage, used her other hand to guide her through two more turns, then climbed a ramp of loose stone. The air had a musty odor, but that was being carried away by moving air. She was nearing the niche where she'd supposedly been meditating the last fortnight.

It shouldn't be difficult to get Morgan—Scarface...she must remember to call him by his use-name in public—to get Scarface a room in the imperial chambers. Knowing his true name was not an advantage to be taken lightly. It was a thing best hoarded for a time when the scales neared balance and the need was greatest.

Ahead, a dim light flickered. Another turn and she could see the source, a candle, as well as a bundle of cloth that would be the old woman who'd told her of this meditation cave and its hidden exits.

Nearer, and she observed the candle had burned until it was little more than a puddle of wax on its stone shelf. In the candlelight the old woman's white hair was almost yellow. She knelt beside the dais on which the pallet lay and shook the woman's bony shoulder. "Sabriye."

The old woman moaned and rolled over, her face a knotted mask of deep wrinkles which slowly relaxed into a sleepy smile.

"Sabriye, my 'meditation' is ended. Go back now and return for me two hours after dawn."

As Sabriye rolled to her hands and knees and lurched off the pallet, Mendarian laid down in the same place and let the tension and excitement seep out of her. Today should prove most interesting.

~ * ~

Scarface left Mendarian beside the tunnel, made a precarious way down the mountain, then mounted and rode until he was challenged by a sentry. After he'd displayed the baton he was led to a cave that seemed natural, although the floor had been worn smooth by the passage of countless leather-shod feet.

Scarface and the men who guarded him followed the tunnel for the length of a bow shot, then reached another opening, trimmed and shaped into an arched portal. Through this doorway he could see the squared and smoothed walls of the next cavern, and pillars of what had once might've been stalagmites and stalactites.

The room to which he was led appeared to be a guardroom or barracks, with racked weapons and pallets on stacked wicker frames.

A man from the barracks had taken the reins of the horses and led them away, and the sentry who'd first stopped him indicated a stone bench. Scarface sat down and used the time to study the soldiers. In the march to the barracks his escort had increased to four men, all of them stocky and of medium height with broad features, fair-haired and pale-eyed. Racially, they looked to be more closely related to the people of Porcash than to their nearer neighbors.

They all carried spears, bows, and knives. Two of them wore short swords, while the other two had light hatchets thrust into their belts. Their armor was varied. His first guard wore a helmet of boars' tusks topped with a horsehair crest, a rattling bone breastplate, and breeches of leather. Two of the other men also wore leather, although the one with the Ghiblin pot helm had his leather studded with metal. The fourth man was clad in a coif and tunic of chain mail.

All of them looked as though they knew the use of their weapons. If these men were garrison troops, their army was better than most he'd seen. He'd have matched his guards against any but the Marked Ones of Sin Garlef, the Sazian Elites, or the reavers of Bildesh when the bloodlust was on them. Other men had entered and left the barracks singly and in pairs, and all of them seemed to have an air of grim competence that spoke well of their leadership.

Twice the guards had tentatively tried to speak with him. From their tones, they were asking him questions but, apparently they spoke only Dieri, and his Dieri was limited to no more than a dozen words, and none of them responded to his own questions in Sinn, Ghiblin, or Gasgoran. After the brief attempts at communication they all simply waited.

Half an hour after Scarface had been brought into the barracks, another man, wearing no armor but with a sword at his side, strode into the room. From the way the guards shifted, trying to stand more erect, the new arrival was their commander. Scarface rose from the bench and faced the man.

"Greetings, outlander. I am Orhan Warleader." The man's Ghiblin was heavily accented, much less guttural than the language usually sounded, but at least they could talk to each other. "I've been told you carry the sign of the favor of the empress."

Scarface drew the baton from his belt and handed it to Orhan. "Since it's served its purpose, it'd probably be best to return it."

They studied each other. Scarface was impressed by the man's confidence and air of command. He was taller than any of his men and looked as though he'd be the last to fall in any contest of endurance or determination. Scarface hoped he was being as favorably assessed.

Abruptly, Orhan turned and motioned for Scarface to follow him and led through more caverns that had obviously been enhanced by decades of labor and were dimly lit by the walls themselves, which glowed faintly. Scarface followed Orhan through another barracks and a kitchen, then into an area where the rooms were smaller but more ornate, with carved

and fluted pillars and bas-reliefs on the walls. Orhan finally stopped
before a heavy, richly decorated door curtain. He drew the curtain aside
and waved Scarface past him into the room beyond.

The commander lit a lamp on a low stone table. On the wall opposite
Scarface hung a wicker rack of weapons, all of them looking well-used
and well cared for, flanked by a mannequin, also of wicker, in full armor
and with what appeared to be wings on its shoulders. Another doorway
stood to Scarface's left, covered by another heavy door curtain, this
one decorated in simpler designs executed in muted reds and tans and
browns. A pair of stools flanked the table and Orhan motioned toward
one of them, then, catching his scabbard and swinging it forward to lie
across his thighs, sat on the other stool.

Almost before Scarface had seated himself, Orhan leaned forward
and asked, "What service do you offer the empress?"

Scarface steepled his fingers. "It's for you to tell Mendarian how
battles should be fought. I'll advise her on what's to be gained by battle
or suggest ways to win wars before battles or instead of them. I'm
intimately aware of the leaders of the nations around you, their fears
and weaknesses, and I'll see you Dieri and your Cercan enemies through
different eyes. And, I can fight."

"All to what end?"

Scarface was tempted to lie but rejected the thought before it was fully
formed. "To please Mendarian."

Orhan's face grew a lopsided grin. "An honest answer." He rose,
ducked through the doorway into the darker room, and returned with
two goblets and a flagon. He handed a goblet to Scarface and filled it,
then filled his own. "To honesty," he said, raising his cup.

"To honesty," Scarface responded. He sipped the liquid in the cup.
It was mead, too sweet for his taste, but he drained the cup. Orhan's
behavior smacked of ritual, and sometimes a drink shared is the best
mortar for building an understanding.

Orhan refilled the goblets. "And how do we pay you?"

Scarface's grin was as crooked as Orhan's had been. "I was given to
understand that your ruler would think of something appropriate. And
you might like to invest some information. I know the countries around
you and I'm familiar with the ancient history of Cerco, but I haven't
heard much lately about the Dieri. How, exactly, did Mendarian come to
rule?"

Orhan moved about on the stool, apparently settling himself for a long talk, more difficult because it had to be delivered in a foreign language. "It all goes back to when the staff and the crown were lost. It is believed the last emperor who held them had hidden them because he knew they would not serve his son. He felt it more important his son rule after him than the empire remain strong.

"With the loss of the gifts of Father Wolf," he bowed at the name, "the empire fell and the weak rulers who followed could select their own successors, so bad became worse. The last emperor without the crown was the maddest and most corrupt of a long line. Then, almost a year ago, Mendarian came to Crown Mountain with the staff and the crown, and she still had to fight for what was hers by the will of Father Wolf." He bowed again. "The last ruler had an army of slaves of the Nevenii, with a picked guard of Nevenii soldiers."

"What happened to them?"

"The Nevenii we killed or ransomed. The slaves are still here, some of them tending gardens, others finishing tunnels."

"Where did they come from, before they were slaves?"

"They are men of conquered tribes or outland captives. The Nevenii are not a single tribe but a..." he had to reach for the word, "a confederation of six of the largest tribes in the northeast. They have conquered the smaller tribes around them, using the men as slaves, sometimes as soldiers, though never in or near the slaves' own former territories."

Scarface made circles with the goblet, watching the golden liquid swirl in the bowl, then, suddenly, he stared into Orhan's eyes. "You'll excuse my blunt nature, but I prefer to know well the men to whom I entrust my life. What do you want from Cerco?"

For a moment Orhan stiffened and his lips became a narrow, pale line, then he shrugged and relaxed. "I was the captain of guards at the Snake Mountain garrison, facing the Senshenni. It was through my border post that Mendarian entered Cerco and my troops and I were the first to swear our lives to the staff and the crown. It was we who led the army that toppled the old ruler." He took another deep drink of mead. "As for my reasons and ambitions—" He barked a laugh. "If I guess yours rightly, there will be no conflict between us. I do not want the throne, nor to stand beside it. If I were to come too close to Mendarian, my lady Marikaa would have my hide made into gloves.

"I do not care who sits on the throne, so long as the crown and the staff will answer to them. It does not matter whose voice Father Wolf," again the bow, "chooses to speak through. And as long as you advise her well, we will serve together."

Scarface had swallowed his first yawn and hid the second but Orhan saw the third.

"You look as though you need rest." Orhan stood. "I can provide a pallet in the barracks until we find some more suitable place for you."

Scarface hauled himself to his feet. It cost more effort than he'd thought it would, with weariness riding his shoulders. He followed Orhan through the warren of tunnels to another large room with pallet platforms and a few resting men. He was only dimly aware of what Orhan said and even less sure of his own responses. When Orhan had gone he stipped off his weapons and put them on the mattress, peeled off all but his shirt and hose, and lay down beside his sword.

~ * ~

He felt he'd only closed his eyes when he felt a hand on his shoulder. It was one of the Dieri soldiers, clad in full armor. The man motioned for him to dress and put on his weapons and, when that was done, led him through the caves. Scarface was beginning to learn his way through Crown Mountain but he noticed something that had puzzled him before. In most corridors the light was provided, not by torches or candles, but by the walls themselves, which glowed with ghostly phosphorescence.

When Scarface was convinced he was simply being led on a tour to learn the tunnels, they reached a room a spear's cast long and wide, and almost as high. Bars of sunlight fell from openings in the ceiling, to be directed around the room by mirrors of polished metal. Everywhere in the room the light danced and shimmered off jewels and ornaments of intricately crafted metals.

Dieri of all ages crowded around the edges of the room so he couldn't see the center until the soldier had escorted him past a knot of men and women, who stepped aside for him.

At the center of the room, illuminated only by the indirect sunlight, stood a dais of deep green and purple stone on which rested a throne that might be made of jade. On the throne, wearing a golden sunburst crown and robes of deep red, holding a plain wooden staff with a carved wolf's head at the top, sat Mendarian.

She spoke in the staccato language of the Dieri, then, in Gasgoran, she told him to approach the throne and turn to face the people, then to step onto the dais and stand beside her throne. He noticed this would put him closer to her than either Orhan or lat Paldisan, both of whom stood at the edge of the dais. He did as he was told and stared out at the people, not quite listening while Mendarian spoke again to the Dieri.

By slightly turning his head and looking sidelong, Scarface studied Arv. The Ghiblin must've arrived a little before him and Mendarian, since he'd been able to ride into Crown openly, but he looked as though he hadn't yet had much rest. Not all the sagging lines on his face could be attributed to weariness, however, and Scarface suspected the drooping ends of his moustache hid grim lines bracketing the mouth.

At the end of Mendarian's speech the crowd filed out of the hall, the soldiers of the imperial guard the last to leave, so he was alone in the hall with Mendarian, Orhan, and lat Paldisan.

In very good Ghiblin, Mendarian said, "Now we go to the council chamber and talk." She led the way to a huge, ornate hanging at the back of the hall and pushed through it. Scarface, following her closely, found the chamber beyond the curtain was small, only half a dozen strides long and not quite that wide, with a stone table surrounded by heavy wooden chairs at its center.

Everything in the room was intricately carved and again the light came from the walls themselves. Scarface stepped to the wall and touched the glow, and found that his fingertips, which now glowed, had left dark smudges on the wall.

"It is something that grows on the stone," Orhan said. "We discovered it centuries ago. Most of the smaller rooms are lit that way."

"Interesting." Scarface stared at his glowing fingertips.

Mendarian had sat in the massive chair at the head of the table. Scarface dropped into the seat to her right, and Arv took the chair opposite his, with Orhan beside him.

Arv rubbed his hands together as though he were washing them. He glanced up into Scarface's eyes then stared down at the table. "I'm not sure it's wise to have this man as an advisor." He cast a side glance at Mendarian then returned his attention to the design cut into the stone before him. "I had a chance to talk to several people about him, and he has a very unpleasant reputation." He hazarded another look at Scarface. "What do you say to that?"

Scarface laughed then stared directly at Arv. "The fact that I have a reputation instead of a funeral eulogy is some recommendation by itself. Another is that reputations are earned; no one gives them to harmless nonentities. Yet another point in my favor is that the reputation is perhaps understated. I rather doubt Forgren and his bootlickers know every way in which I've thwarted them. Any cunning I have, any power I might wield, is now in Mendarian's service."

She stared at Scarface. "I know Scarface and I vouch for him. That should be enough. I'll brook no jealousies among my advisors. We're all friends here."

The humor of the scene caused Scarface's lips to twitch. "My name is Morgan."

For a moment neither Arv nor Orhan seemed to comprehend what he'd told them.

"Then it's settled," Mendarian said. "I appreciate your concern, Arv, but from what you told me earlier, taking Scarface as my advisor hasn't greatly damaged our relations with either the clan or the Union."

Arv prodded at part of the table's raised design with a fingertip. "That's true, although I'd have given much to have overheard the meeting upstairs in the inn between just the leaders of the Union. Both the clan and the Union will honor all the commitments they made to us, and," his feeble grin at Scarface was a weak concession, "your outlawry was set aside. A warning, though. Forgren read the announcements, but as grimly as a man reading his own sentence of execution."

Scarface hoped his hid his annoyance well. It rankled that the pronouncements had probably been forced on Forgren by Hadrian, to whom he wanted to owe nothing. Rivals should have the grace to always oppose.

"The warning is taken," Mendarian said, "but the commitments remain, so we've won for now. Do any of you have any other business to discuss?"

"Yes," Scarface said. "I advise you to release the prisoners you're holding, the former slaves of the Nevenii."

Orhan raised his eyebrows but said nothing. Mendarian was more vocal in her surprise. "There must be some devious reason for this novel idea. It'd be simpler to kill them."

"Not at all. In the first place, is the labor they do worth the time of the men guarding them? I'd doubt it. If we kill them, we offer their tribes only another enemy, just like our enemy, the Nevenii.

"On the other hand, if we give them back their weapons and, perhaps some small gifts and send them back to their peoples, we've gained allies. Do you really think they'd return to being slaves of the Nevenii? They know the Nevenii would kill them on sight. But if we send them back with the message Father Wolf has seen their trials and he's coming to help them, they'll be ready to be half our army against the Nevenii."

"And we warn the Nevenii we're coming," Arv objected.

"If you were in their place, would you believe it? I suspect they'll think we're making an empty gesture. And I doubt they'll be ready for an attack in late fall."

Orhan laughed. "I doubt I'm ready for that, myself. Do you know how difficult it is to move an army through the mountains when the snows begin?"

"Yes, and so do the Nevenii. That's one reason it'll work. With luck, by spring we'll have reunited the tribes of Cerco under the Dieri."

Mendarian raised an eyebrow. "And without luck?"

Scarface shrugged. "With or without luck, we're all dead in the long run."

Her eyes burned into his. "It's not just your life you're gambling now, it's all the Dieri."

Suddenly he had the sense she was lying, if not to him, then to herself. It wasn't the Dieri she was afraid of losing, it was her crown. He pushed the thought away and grinned to hide where he'd buried it. "I'll gamble on your people no less carefully than at a certain dinner in Varish, and I'm still alive."

She smiled back at him with her whole face. "I've made arrangements for you to stay in the room next to mine. Shall we go look at them?"

Arv and Orhan both understood they'd been dismissed. They stood and left by the curtained doorway through which they'd entered.

Mendarian led Scarface out a massive door of stone that pivoted at a touch. Despite the fact Crown Mountain was only a collection of caves and tunnels, it was still a palace that could rival any in any nation he knew.

His rooms were large and luxuriously furnished—and connected to Mendarian's apartments by two doors. After he'd seen his rooms she showed him hers. The last room she led him into was her sleeping quarters. He strode to the bed, tested it with his hands, and turned in time to see her remove her crown.

It took longer for him to undress and they sampled the bed and each other. He gave himself completely to her and the excitement they shared, several times. After a time they lay holding each other, enjoying the lingering sensations and the velvet lassitude.

Finally she rolled over and stared into his face. "Do you really believe you can have all Cerco re-conquered by spring?"

His amusement bubbled out as a laugh. "I didn't say 'reconquer,' I said 'reunite.' We'll beat the Nevenii and, if necessary, the Tuati in the field. The rest you can probably control through diplomacy and a strong dose of charlatanism. It also costs less."

She considered that for a long moment, then grinned. "That should be enough." Then the grin went away. "I think Orhan will have to meet his doom before the victory celebration."

Scarface could feel the hair at the nape of his neck stir. "Why?"

"He could be dangerous to me. His troops are personally loyal to him—"

"Which means he's a fine commander, one well worth keeping. And to kill him would be to throw away his troops, who are your finest soldiers."

"And he's had a taste of power. I named him regent when I left, or rather, when I 'went into seclusion.'"

"And he's loyal to you as long as you have the staff and crown."

"Are you afraid? Would you kill him for me if I asked you to?" Her eyes chilled him. He saw a coldness and a distance in them that made him feel as though a monster made of ice were hiding in her body, that at core she was an almost elemental force of ambition and greed for power. He prided himself on his own ruthlessness, but now he felt overpowered by her frigid detachment.

"No, I'm not afraid and, yes, I'd probably kill him for you if you really wanted it, but you don't want it or need it." He tried to make her believe that.

She brought the grin back from where it'd been hidden. "Especially if you really can give me all of Cerco."

"I've said it and, for good or ill, I take my words very seriously."

"I hope so. Much depends on it."

That evening, alone in his rooms, he thought long and deeply upon what he loved. He'd heard the unspoken threat. He'd already known that Mendarian would keep him—and let him live—only so long as he could support and enhance her rule. If he failed her, it'd be just as easy for her to ask someone for his death as it'd been for her to ask him to kill Orhan. He'd been reminded he was living on the knife's edge.

~ * ~

The next day he began his preparations for the war against the Nevenii. He observed the captives being given back their weapons, gifts of food and clothing, and being sent back to their peoples with a message of hope and revolt. The first and strongest wing of the Dieri army should be in enemy territory within the next day or so.

Not all the Nevenii slaves had been Cercans. They'd also used captured mercenaries taken in some of their battles with Ghiblein. Most of the foreigners chose to be repatriated and were sent on their ways, but a handful were willing, for a price, to serve the Dieri. Scarface chose a man called Jonfré to lead them.

Jonfré was the sort of rogue Scarface found both likable and useful. He was from Donradé, just to the south of Gascolin, and his language was a dialect of Gasgoran. Like all the freemen of Donradé his face was marked with tattoos. Jonfré had lost his right eye in Nevenii service and wore a leather patch over the empty socket. He had curly black hair and beard, just turning gray, and an insolent manner that still, somehow charmed.

Scarface also had to learn the Cercan language, particularly the Dieri dialect. Mendarian spent some time helping him, sometimes in their lovemaking, teaching him the Hightongue, but it was necessary to learn the common language and to speak it like a native. The task was made more difficult because the Dieri were an insular people, and few of them spoke any language but their own. Orhan finally found another warrior who spoke Ghiblin and assigned him to Scarface as an aide.

Scarface had read about the Dieri; now he had to learn them, to know them as he knew his own fingernails. He was aware they were farmers and herdsmen, keeping sheep and goats, and learned what that meant to them as a people.

War, for them, had become a matter of grim survival, and they defended their own territory with ferocity but didn't raid their neighbors. The more aggressive Nevenii and Tuati in the east were both hungry for empire, constantly pushing against their borders, especially to the west. The Tuati were also a confederation of tribes, and they maintained an uneasy peace with the Nevenii, both groups salivating over Dieri plunder, both waiting for that last increment of power that would let them seize control.

The Senshenni, in the west, regarded war as a sport. They seldom raided Dieri land or into Gascolin, but fought ceaselessly with the smaller tribes in their area.

Scarface opened negotiations with the Senshenni, particularly the two bands nearest the Dieri. For streamers of bright cloth and ornate weapons, they agreed to keep their mountains clear of robber bands. The treaty did the Dieri little immediate good, but it signaled a beginning.

Most of Scarface's time was spent in preparation for the coming war. Defenses in the southeast had to be reinforced and second and third lines of defense prepared. Fortunately, the terrain was an ally, with cliffs and ridges that required only a little labor to turn them into formidable obstacles.

The men were drilled constantly, and he and Orhan took aside those who showed the greatest endurance and trained them to fight together. The Dieri had no cavalry and few horses. Their mounts, when they rode, were shaggy, jug-headed ponies whose sureness of foot and stamina were matched by their miserable dispositions. Ponies were gathered and given to the foreigners and the contingent on which Scarface and Orhan were concentrating the bulk of their time and hopes.

Late in the season, Scarface rode northwest to confer with the leaders of the Senshenni bands. A week after his return came the first snow flurries, and a pall of smoke could be seen in the north.

Messengers sped in all directions with the news the Senshenni had attacked the garrison at Hawk's-Talon fortress and had burned it. The special troops were mustered and, with Scarface and Mendarian leading them, rode north.

Chapter 6

They huddled together under the blanket they shared, shivering and wishing they could build a fire.

"There should be enough work to keep us warm in the next few days," Scarface said. "We turn east tomorrow."

"I still don't like it," Mendarian grumbled. "We're placing too much trust in surprise and the Senshenni. If they were to really attack now—"

"They haven't time to gather enough men to overrun the border garrison. Besides, they fear the eastern tribes, too. They've seen how our neighbors play at conquest and they'd rather keep a buffer between themselves and those voracious appetites. My conference with them was to let them know we were going to burn off the brush around Hawk's-Talon fort and use it as a pretext to move our army north for a raid on the Nevenii. Their headmen were hugely amused."

"Still, we're leaving ourselves vulnerable, bringing only a fraction of our army."

"We need the insurance of a strong defense. Besides, a large army would be difficult to move and impossible to conceal. With winter, most of the Nevenii tribes will have broken up into smaller bands, but if we were to bring in a massive force they'd quickly join together again. We'll fight a series of small, short battles instead of one or two major ones. The alternative was to sit in Crown Mountain while your borders and forces were nibbled into extinction."

She snuggled closer to him, her fingers wrapping around his. "I'm glad I've got you plotting for me."

~ * ~

For two days they fought their most bitter enemies—the cold and the snow and the mountains, losing men to all of them then they reached their first valley.

The Nevenii weren't mountain-dwellers like the Dieri. They lived in the valleys, raising crops and hunting and living in villages built on mounds, with wooden houses mounded around with soil, surrounded by palisades of sharpened logs.

The Dieri struck the first village just before dawn and broke their fast on warm Nevenii food. Scarface had worked with his troops to keep unnecessary violence and looting to a minimum. The tribes would be easier to reunite if no new grievances were born to keep old animosities fresh.

The Nevenii had kept a handful of slaves in the camp, most of them Cortelani, and he sent them back to their peoples with the message Father Wolf was coming to touch the hearts of the Nevenii, with reason or spears, as they chose.

Scarface let his men rest and warm themselves until noon, then they set out southward again. In the next ten days they fought as many battles. The smaller tribes sent men to guide them through the treacherous passes and to act as scouts, and some warriors, who fought with them against the Nevenii, while other tribes attacked local Nevenii outposts.

The war had bred revolution. At the end of ten days of little rest, rations eaten in the saddle or on the march, bitter cold and snow, and vicious combat, three of the Nevenii tribes called for parley.

They met in an otherwise deserted Nevenii village. One of their lords was newly invested, the old lord having died fighting. Mendarian had brought the staff and the crown and her robes, and she acted as regal as she appeared.

She gave them terms. They were to free all slaves, with compensation for their labor; they were to furnish hostages to ensure their peaceful intentions, and they were not to combine except for religious ceremonies or for council before the spring Great Council that would be held at Crown Mountain.

That evening Scarface and Mendarian enjoyed precious time alone with each other in one of the log houses. They slept, then their hands and mouths had rediscovered each other's bodies and they'd moved and sweated together. When, at last, they were both spent, Mendarian lit a candle and lay on a heap of furs, staring at Scarface. At last she broke the silence. "Ever the gambler, aren't you?"

"In what way?"

"In most ways. You've been at the head of the army in every battle. That arrow gash along your ribs could've come closer to your heart. I prefer to keep my advisors alive. And now you're gambling our enemies will stay beaten. We're here now, but we'll be gone tomorrow. What's to make them keep their words to me then?"

He glanced down at the bandage across his lower chest. "I bought something with that scratch. Our men no longer see me as just an outlander who's only the royal whore. I'm still not one of them, but now I've gained some small measure of acceptance—"

"Which you don't need. My commands are obeyed instantly, whether I say the words or speak through you."

"And how long do I live like this, being a concubine? I'd remind you that you went west facing the possibility of a state marriage. Do I have to worry my place will be taken by the first lord or power-monger you choose throw lots with? To be more than your whore and advisor, I must bring something to the match."

She hid behind her ice-mask again. "I value your advice. As for marriage, that's none of your concern."

He nodded. "We understand each other then. I'll stay at your side at battle, and I'll give you my advice for as long as you choose to take it. But I will still rule some place in my own name."

"Not in this empire."

"Not this empire," he agreed. "I'll take nothing from you, but I won't come to you like a beggar pleading for alms, either."

Studying her face, he tried to discover what subtle changes made it so cold. It was mostly in the eyes, although there were also other changes. When she finally relaxed he waited a dozen heartbeats, then said, "As for the rest, that was no gamble. I've studied these people and their word, once given, is stone. The hostages were only a formality. And if they did choose to break their word, the smaller tribes would have runners on their way to Crown before the council smoke had faded."

"Is that why you demanded they free their slaves? I was curious about that. Altruism isn't a virtue you wear well."

He snorted. "Altruism isn't a virtue, and I've never met anyone who wore it well. It's like a bird with gills; an impossible beast." He reached out and caught her ankle and began the lovemaking again. She was as eager as he, and they became locked in a passionate struggle that had nothing to do with battle.

Much later, as the candle guttered, almost gone, he held her in his arms and stroked her hair and softly called her name. When she didn't answer, he lay staring at the ceiling. "No, my love, don't believe in altruism." He paused to look at her face in shadow, partly out of affection, partly to see that she was, indeed, asleep."

"And, no, no slaves. Better to kill a man than rob him of his pride. He may give it away if he finds something he thinks is more important, he can sell it if money is so dear to him." He chuckled, a bitter sound. "That would be trading trash for trash. A soul that can be bought for money was never a soul worth the price. But pride is a thing that belongs to every man. Steal a man's pride and he'll be your deadliest enemy, because he has nothing left to lose and revenge to gain. Better for you—and better for him—to kill him." He lay staring upward for a long time, wondering if he hadn't traded away his own pride.

~ * ~

They set out again in a frigid gray dawn, with clouds scudding toward the bases of the mountains, and fought their way through a chill fog to their next battle.

They fought through the Nevenii mountains for twelve more days. Mendarian met separately with each of their other leaders and offered each the same terms of surrender.

Scarface had expected the southern Nevenii lords to ask aid of the Tuati and he'd also anticipated the Tuati response. They'd gathered their men and, assuming the entire Dieri army was locked in mortal combat with the Nevenii, attacked the Dieri outposts on their western borders. Later, they'd turn north and shatter an exhausted enemy, Nevenii or Dieri. Faced with unexpected opportunity, the Tuati reacted as Scarface had expected them to.

The forces he led south over the Tuati marches were larger than those with which he'd set out from Crown. The men they'd lost to the mountains and their other enemies were more than made good by other Cercans after Mendarian had promised all who joined her army a share of the booty from the conquest of the Tuati.

The Tuati had overwhelmed the line of Dieri forts on their border, not knowing Scarface had ordered the soldiers to offer only token resistance before retreating in good order to the next line of defense to join more warriors, still fresh.

Like an ocean wave, the Tuati had surged forward and hammered at the next line of defense. They were finally allowed to roll over that barrier, but they left behind more dead and far more wounded than they could afford. By the time they reached the third line of fortifications they were already both wary and weary. The wave had crested and had almost beaten itself out on the cliffs of stone and stone-hard men.

Then the Tuati discovered they were caught with Dieri both before them and behind them. Most of the other Cercans had gone to the Tuati towns, where they took their pay in plunder, but the Dieri and some vengeful Nevenii caught the bleeding remnants of the Tuati army between the second and third lines of defense.

The battle was bitter but brief. The Tuati had been assaulting the fortified ridges with little success, and then the army from the north, using the second line of ridges, released a flight of arrows. Men screamed and fell, darkening the snow. Another volley of arrows arched into the leaden sky and fell among men just turning to see a new enemy where none should be.

Arrows rained from both lines of fortifications, and every moment of indecision cost more Tuati blood, and then the cry for parley was raised. The arrows stopped and Scarface and Mendarian strode out onto the plain to dictate the same terms of surrender they'd given the Nevenii.

The band of warriors that had gone north returned to Crown Mountain after forty-five days, and the celebration lasted another two days.

Arv lat Paldisan had been left behind to serve as regent. His report to Mendarian held some items of interest. Forgren had sent Murtry and Ivo to act as the Union's ambassadors. Scarface's reaction was, "The worms have found the flour," and avoid contamination by treating the men with required courtesy when he couldn't avoid them altogether. Slightly more important was the news the Senshenni were becoming uneasy, now that the Dieri had settled the disputes on their eastern borders.

Scarface advised sending food to any western tribes found to be in need and keeping the border garrisons at their traditional strength rather than reinforcing them. To Arv's objections he pointed out that reinforced marches could, and almost certainly would, be perceived as preparations for war, while deliveries of food to the nomads, with no requests or demands for oaths of fealty, were less likely to be misconstrued.

Scarface and Mendarian spent every night together, sometimes in lovemaking, sometimes in conversation, and each inspired in Scarface its own sort of closeness. He learned to listen to what was unsaid but was never certain whether Mendarian was hiding from him or from herself.

One night he remarked she knew the warrior's trade well.

"I should," she replied. "My father was a mercenary who'd saved his pay until he could afford a hog farm. He had five daughters by my mother and two by his second wife. No sons. I was the oldest, so I was responsible for taking care of the farm when he was in his cups, which became more often as he grew older.

"He used to call me 'the princess of the pigsty.' I hated that and resolved to someday have a domain, and it wouldn't be strewn with pig shit.

"When I was fifteen, one of my father's old comrades visited with a friend of his. Estov was a very pretty young soldier, and I ran off with him."

Mendarian's eyes took a far-away look. "For three years I followed him. He fought in the border wars with Abaransa and, later, in the north against Bildesh. For three years I watched him decay. He took to drinking and beating me. Then, one night, he came in with his captain and told me he'd lost me to the captain in a game of knucklebones."

She chuckled. "Estov never seemed to understand the importance of timing. I was cutting meat for dinner, and I made sure he'd never again lure someone with that pretty face. The captain laughed as though someone had told a bawdy joke, then he beat me. I thought Estov was a brutal drunk, but the captain was sober and vicious. That's how I got my nose broken.

"It took a week before I managed to get away from the bastard. I couldn't go back to my family, even if I wanted to, so…it was hard."

His imagination could provide details. She'd been betrayed and used and had felt it deeply. She burned with memories, just as he did. And the paths she had taken for bare survival had left deep marks on her, a pain worse than old war wounds. If he could've taken away her buried pain, he would've, even at twice the cost in pain to him.

"Arv met me two paces from the gutter. He gave me back some of my pride. He treated me as though I was special, and he never asked anything of me."

Scarface felt a pang. What pained him most deeply was that Mendarian didn't realize she was truly special. It'd taken all her hawk-like ferocity to survive, but she'd survived, and for that he was grateful. He found himself opening to her until not the smallest piece of armor stood between her and his heart.

If they spent the nights together, they drifted apart during the days. He explored Crown Mountain, following passages that saw little use, becoming familiar with all the mountain's creatures, even the blind white rats of the caverns.

He also encountered passages and rooms unused for decades, perhaps for centuries, and rooms used more recently but considered best forgotten. Among the latter were the torture chambers, almost as the last ruler had kept them, with only the bodies taken out and interred in the catacombs. He also learned that had Mendarian not come when she had, Orhan's body would've been one of those burned and torn and wrenched apart. He'd been too popular with his troops and many of the people of Crown, and the emperor considered him a dangerous rival. This led to thoughts of differences between Mendarian and the last ruler, and some similarities as well. These dark thoughts he kept to himself.

He also spent much of his time with Jonfré, the one-eyed mercenary from Donradé, learning about the country and its neighbors. Donradé had been settled by the same peoples as Gascolin and Glangurra. Gascolin was, in many ways, the most advanced of the three, with a weak nobility and a strong king indebted to the merchants, so, commerce flowed and, with it, progress.

Glangurra was ruled by a king whose family could trace its lines farther than most would want to, but who was still only the first noble of the realm. Donradé had no king, only a collection of petty nobles, most of them engaged in polite or open war with each other. The country would've been overrun long ago despite the toughness of its farmers and woodsrunners, had it possessed anything worth taking.

The country was bounded by rivers, the Attré separating it from Gascolin and the southern branch of the river, called the Siscin, lay between it and Glangurra. To the east towered the bottom of the mountain range that sheltered Cerco and divided the continent, and which everyone called "The Spine." The Sazians occupied most of southern Donradé, keeping to the fertile River Bromron valley and the coastal plains, all the way to the borders of Shatilla. The Sazian empire thus blocked both Donradé and Glangurra from the sea.

Mild curiosity gave way to interest, which was replaced by intense interest. The king in Glangurrach was an old man whose only child was an unattractive daughter. Her suitors were few, and not particularly determined, since it was accepted the crown would go to the king's nephew.

Scarface smiled sardonically to himself. Donradé for challenge and Glangurra for dessert. Most of his work in Cerco would soon be done, and his crown—or crowns—called to him with a golden voice.

He stood and signed for Jonfré to follow him to his rooms, where he penned a quick note in Sinn.

Hadrian,

I suspect I'm doing clan business here in Cerco. Well and good. You may return the favor by taking the young man my messenger has brought you and cuffing some manners into him and seeing that his accent sounds more highborn than gutter-bred. If you have the time, you may also teach him a little of the practice of arms. I'll be sending you a brick and wanting a polished gem by spring.

Pausing, he considered other messages he wanted to send, decided against rubbing salt into open wounds, and signed the note with a scrawled "Morgan."

He rolled and sealed the parchment and handed it to Jonfré. "I have a mission for you. Pick me a son, and spare no expense. Choose him from one of the finest gutters or alleys in Glangurrach. Then I want you to take him to Gascolin, to a place called High Rage, and hand him over to a man with this note. The man's name is Hadrian. On your way through Donradé, try to find those places where the rulers can be purchased or leased for the smallest bribe. Let them know I want to hire mercenaries, and I'll take as many men as they'll let me rent. You might also let Hadrian know, discreetly, that I could use money and the services of an engraver."

Jonfré grinned and his eye twinkled. "I've always wanted to be 'Baron Jonfré.'"

"Do this mission well and you may be able to call yourself 'Duke Jonfré.'" He smiled at Jonfré's eagerness, then remembered the Great Council, now only a little more than two months away.

"Another thing. Tell Hadrian I need a wolf, the biggest he can trap. And someone who can cast the spell of transmigration. I need them both within," he counted, tapping fingertips on the stone table, "sixty days, so remember how long it takes to get to High Rage and tell Hadrian that many days less. The wolf should be sent to me in the most discreet manner possible, and preferably either drugged or under a spell of sleep."

After Jonfré hurried from the room, Scarface glanced with distaste at the other scraps of parchment littering the table. Arv seemed to want to build a court fueled by parchment, like that of Ghiblein, and Mendarian, too, seemed to constantly try to find some new way to complicate her rule or to change the Dieri into something they were not.

He preferred simplicity. The first step was to weld this collection of tribes into a nation—no easy task. The simplest and, probably, best way to accomplish this was to trade hostages, particularly children of leaders. There were no orphans in Cerco because the children in a tribe were the children *of* the tribe—the whole tribe, everyone taking equal responsibility for their upbringing.

By trading children, each tribe would gain knowledge of and respect for the customs of other tribes. Their own children would be the bond that tied them together as a people.

He was smiling into his steepled fingers when Mendarian entered the room.

"You look as though you've found a new toy," she said. "Not one that I like very much, I hope."

His smile broadened into a grin. "To be honest, I don't think you care about them at all." Occasionally, it was pleasant to be open and cryptic at the same time. He made some polite and distracting conversation, then, after a pause and making it seem as though the idea had just occurred to him, he suggested the trade of hostages, giving his reasons for the suggestion.

"It sounds very convincing. Bring it up tomorrow in council."

He nodded.

Mendarian dropped onto his couch and lounged. "There are some other matters of importance we need to discuss, such as how you intend to convince the leaders of the other tribes to place themselves under the Dieri."

"They won't. They'll place themselves under you. Cerco hasn't been a nation for a very long time, and it won't soon be one again. Too many forces keep the tribes apart. Reuniting them will take time, and some patience."

"And while I learn patience, the Senshenni will shred our borders."

He clicked his tongue. "You don't trust me yet. When have I failed you?"

For a moment the gray eyes were like frozen lakes, then she shrugged. "Not yet. Would you mind telling me what you've planned in that serpent's mind of yours for the Great Council? I'm not fond of surprises when there are lives in the balance, mine among them."

He brushed his fingertips against the wall and stared at his glowing fingers. "I'd really rather you didn't know exactly what I'm planning. If you know too much, your reaction may not be the proper response."

She stared at him with a basilisk's gaze and moved on the couch so her arms were above her head and her breasts strained the front of the robe. He stood, paced to the couch, sat on the edge, and began to put his arms around her.

"Not right now. I'm thinking, and I want no distractions."

He stared down at her, wanting her and still aware that she was the ruler, he the subject. "All right, if you must know—"

"I don't care. I'm thinking about something else."

Hurt and anger rose in him like bile but he pushed away the anger as soon as he recognized it. The games that were played.... Argument would gain nothing. It would, in fact, play into Mendarian's hands. He remembered how he'd earlier realized she would always have the advantage because he cared for her freedom, but she could walk away from him without the least hesitation or the slightest sense of loss. She still had the advantage. Not all his advice, nor his lovemaking, nor his courage in battle could cause her to give what she'd already chosen to withhold.

"Very well," He stood again. "I'll be at arms practice with your soldiers."

He'd almost reached the door when she said, "I saw that foreign rascal you've been drinking with leave your rooms, and he acted as though he were leaving on a matter of some urgency."

He bit off his answer before it reached his lips. Instead, he leaned against the door. "He took my measurements to be fitted for a crown."

Her cold-eyed nod reminded him of the bobbing movements of a snake's head. "Oh, I forgot to tell you, I've invited Hadrian for a visit. He should be here within the week."

He refused to show any reaction that could give her satisfaction. He simply continued his walk out into the corridor and to the armory.

Hadrian's visit became something to anticipate simply because everything else had become gray and tasteless. He sensed some change in Mendarian, a feeling she was tolerating him. Their lovemaking became less frequent and less satisfying, as her responses became almost habitual. His proposal about hostages foundered in council. Orhan gave the idea cautious approval. Arv opposed it for vague reasons which led Scarface to suspect he was fighting the idea because it wasn't his, and Mendarian delayed a decision on the matter until it could be reconsidered.

Again he held his anger in check. It'd accomplish nothing to point out he was supposedly an advisor and his advice had brought them every success they enjoyed.

Mendarian wasted no time on enjoyment of success. She wavered between worry about the Senshenni and the other tribes and fear the Dieri would slide back into obscurity. Conquest beyond the mountains of Cerco was, for the time, both impractical and impossible, although it would've ensured the Dieri army would find vigourous enough work.

The days filled with tensions and petty annoyances until Scarface came to look forward to Hadrian's visit as a relief from boredom and aggravation.

Six days after Mendarian had told him of the visit, riders arrived at the Ram's Gate of Crown, part of the escort Mendarian had sent to conduct Hadrian, Vornarei, and their twin daughters from the border of Gascolin to Crown. Scarface had just finished his evening arms practice and left immediately for the gate, where he met Mendarian, Arv, and Orhan. Mendarian herself held the stirrup for Hadrian when they halted, while Scarface helped Vornarei and the twins riding with her to dismount.

Hadrian seemed not to have changed at all, still wearing both swords and his black leather armor. Had Scarface not known better, he might almost believe Hadrian had been born in that armor, that it was a natural part of him, a carapace. Vornarei, too, was unchanged, still cool and distant, but the twins seemed more like real children, firing off, in their excitement, a volley of questions about the Dieri and their mountains.

Vornarei pleaded fatigue from the trip and Mendarian led her and the children to the suite of rooms she'd chosen for them, leaving Scarface to take Hadrian to the small council chamber.

They strode to the room in silence that Scarface didn't end until the door was closed behind them. He offered Hadrian a cup of wine, poured one for himself, and sat across the table from his clan brother. "Everyone is well, I hope," he said, in Sinn.

"Yes," Hadrian replied in the same language. "And both Poker and Martina wanted me to express their regards to you."

"I'm glad to hear that." The silence became awkward. "You'll be receiving a message from me, but I may as well ask you now." He told Hadrian what he needed.

Hadrian listened intently, stroking his beard. "The wolf will be difficult but I think I can manage something. You already have magi here with the power and the training. I'll ask Martina to have one of them reach you at the proper time. As for the money—I believe the clan has obligations to you for services rendered in the past. To what use were you thinking of putting the engraver? It seems the native artisans you have here are capable enough."

Scarface stared into Hadrian's opaque eyes. "I'm preparing to take up counterfeiting."

Hadrian's moustache and beard couldn't quite conceal a faint smile. "And whose coinage were you thinking of devaluing?"

"The Sazian empire's."

"You don't lack for ambition. Just remember, tired old lions are still lions."

Scarface expected Mendarian to return at any moment so he concentrated on the rivalry between Hadrian and himself, so when she entered she'd find two tigers, each trying to stare the other down.

As soon as she entered the room she slipped behind a mask Scarface hadn't seen her wear for a long time. "I'm very grateful for the friendship the clan has extended. You were my first and best allies, and I want you to know I rely upon your goodwill."

Hadrian had kept his faint air of amusement, so his answer revealed nothing. "We're pleased to hear we're so highly regarded. What you have done in Cerco is most impressive."

"That's one of the reasons I invited you here. I wanted to see what advice you could offer."

"Very little. I'm not familiar with the country or the people, but they seem largely self-sufficient. I did notice some very bright rugs and hangings your people make, probably during the winter. If you keep your mountains free of bandits, merchants will probably find the trip worthwhile."

"Thank you. I'll consider that." She stared at him for several long moments. "You really are a very handsome man."

Inwardly, Scarface laughed even as he hurt. He couldn't remember ever seeing Hadrian speechless, as he was now, but he also knew Mendarian had said what she had partly to sink a barb into his own soft parts, and she'd succeeded. He leaned toward her and, in Dieri, murmured, "Would you like to see some interesting scars on that face?"

"No!" Mendarian snapped, in the same language. "Back off."

He felt the draining of emotion from his own face and eyes as he fixed her with his gaze. With a cold and quiet voice, he said, "I don't believe I heard you say 'please.'"

Mendarian's control and self-assurance faltered. She glanced at her hands and her voice was unsteady. "Please," she finally murmured.

The tension in the air had become heavier than water. Scarface smiled at Hadrian and said, in Gasgoran, "You'll please forgive us, but your conversation reminded us of a matter carried over from council. Political differences seem so crucial at the moment and, after, they're decided, can be seen for the trivial things they are. It was, as always, a pleasure to see you again."

Mendarian gathered her dignity around her like skirts. "I'm sorry. I'm sure you're tired from the journey. I'll show you to your rooms. We'll have time to talk more tomorrow."

Scarface stalked to his own rooms and found a scroll plundered from the Tuati. He opened it and laid it on his table, almost wishing he could read the Abarsa in which it was written, when Mendarian entered the room.

"That was a fine little tantrum you threw," she said, her voice raspy with anger.

He glared at her. "If you're going to treat me and address me like a dog, you should expect me to show my fangs now and again."

She paced around the room, still not looking at him. "You embarrassed me in front of a man who holds more power—"

"I presume you did not intend to embarrass me with your remark." The anger he'd hidden and denied bubbled to the surface. "You may treat me, in private, in whatever way amuses you and I'll tolerate it but if you pit me against any other man, I'll tolerate him only because of you. And, if pressed, I'll have to think again whether my tolerance for your game exceeds my anger. Press me hard enough and I will kill.

"You're safe from me. You've crept into my armor and eaten away most of my guts, but any man who allows you to make of him a quirt, who slaps me across the face with my own pride, should be ready to have his throat torn out."

He looked down at the scroll again, unable to read it any better than he could before. He was aware Mendarian was standing across the table from him, staring at him, but he refused to lift his gaze from the parchment.

His emotions were being shredded and flung to the wind. Anger and hurt and desire and a deep caring all fought within him. Finally, without looking up from the scroll, he said, "It seems to be a cold night tonight."

"I'll have one of the women heat a brick for my feet."

He looked up. "Perhaps you should take the brick as an advisor. I'll leave a note on what I feel is the best way to deal with the Great Council."

In the silence that roared in his ears he searched the table and found a scrap of parchment, a quill, and an ink horn. Mendarian had moved around the room so he could no longer see her. He dipped the quill into the ink.

"Morgan, don't do this to me. For all that we do to each other, I still need you." She put her arms over his shoulders from behind, her hands resting on his chest. He stared down at the slender, tapering fingers. "I've been so involved with other things, feeling so trapped and bound, that I haven't had the time or energy to consider your feelings." Her hand moved to his arm, slid down to his hand, took the quill from his fingers and placed it in the ink horn.

He turned in his chair and looked at her. The icy mask was gone and the face was the one with which he'd fallen in love. All the annoyances and frustrations fell away and all he wanted was to be close to her again. He reached up and stroked her cheek, trying, with that touch, to express the tenderness he felt. Nothing really mattered but the moment and his feelings for her. The future was a dim thing, a shadow play, far out of reach, but the present moment was golden.

She sat sideways on the arm of his chair, leaving her arms around his neck. As she twisted toward him her robe spread open almost to the belt. Closeness and desire are kin to each other. He drew her closer and his hand slid inside her robe. For a time he savored the warmth and the anticipation that was spice to the meal, then he stood, picked her up, and carried her off to her rooms.

~ * ~

Mendarian rose and dressed early. After she'd put on slippers and robe and brushed her hair she sat on a cushioned bench and stared at Scarface, naked, still asleep. *Not yet do you escape, little captive.* When he left, it'd be on terms *she* chose. He was still too useful for her to discard. Last night still rankled, but it'd be foolish to let that disturb her at the moment. His male pride would, unfortunately, have to be catered to for a time yet. That was one of her handles on him, but when she no longer needed him she'd twist that handle until it broke.

No need to wake him. She stood and crept out of the room to the apartments to which she'd conducted Hadrian and his family. Like most of the rooms in Cerco, the door was an opening covered with a bright wool hanging. She scratched at the cloth and waited. Almost immediately Hadrian pushed the hanging aside. He already wore his armor and his swords.

She nodded a greeting. "I hoped we could finish our conversation of last night."

He stepped out into the corridor, followed her to the council room, and sat when she indicated a chair for him. She remained standing and, after he sat, began to pace.

"You spoke, last night, of trade and attracting merchants. Would it be possible for us to trade with High Rage until the merchants discover that Cerco is worth visiting?"

"Of course. I don't know that I can offer you what the merchants will pay for your goods, but we can make up the differences after the goods are sold."

"That's most generous." She turned and smoothed her hair. "Perhaps you could also suggest what I should seek in trade." She kept her face in profile to him, staring at the wall as though it was a window looking out over some picturesque vista.

"That'd be difficult for me to judge, as I don't yet know your people. Since your internal wars seem to have been resolved and wars with other countries aren't likely, you won't need arms or armor. At present, I'd suggest you take gold or silver, which is a decision deferred."

"Sound advice." Her hands rose again, almost absently, and her fingers toyed with her hair, arranging it strand by strand. Her earlier movements had loosened the front of her robe so that as she stood at an angle to him she revealed all but the pink tip of her right breast. She turned her head infinitesimally to glance at him. "It's really a pity you're married. We'd have been unbeatable together."

He came out of his chair like a cat rising, languidly, then moved toward the end of the table, his gaze locked with hers. She, too, moved toward the end of the table. It was strange to be looking down at him and, at the same time, be entranced by him.

Still staring into her eyes, he slipped his hand into her robe and gently held her breast as though weighing it then his hand slowly retreated and slipped between the folds of cloth below her belt. "What about Scarface?" he asked.

The tips of his fingers brushed her pubic hair, then lightly stroked her. She permitted herself a shudder and an in-drawn breath. "What about him?"

Hadrian stepped away from her. "Was that what you wanted?"

"I thought it was what you wanted."

"It was, at least, what you wanted me to want. Do you wish to continue playing games, or was this really to be a talk?"

Her laugh was a brittle sound that had not a nodding acquaintance with humor. "Your understanding is one of the qualities Scarface lacks. His usefulness to me is almost at an end."

"And what does he think of that? I doubt he'll give up his position as your advisor—or anything else to you—very easily."

Mendarian drew her robe tighter about her body, drawing it taut under the belt. "Are you afraid of him?"

He seemed to think deeply on the question, then, "No, not afraid, but I'd be reluctant to kill him."

"So, the feud between you and Scarface is—"

"Is between Scarface and I. You have no part to play in it."

His dismissal of her stung like a slap. She tried to find something that could crack his stone composure. "Why don't you call him by his true name—Morgan?"

"Because he's not yet Morgan. He's still Scarface."

She let another bitter laugh escape. "And he may never be." Hadrian simply nodded. "And what now? Does the clan scrap its treaty with me? Do we fight each other?"

"Why? What difference does my opinion of you make? It has nothing to do with clan policy. It's still in our interests that the people of Cerco be content."

Her laugh then was genuine. "You may be the coldest of us all."

"I just have larger wants and fewer hungers."

"Are you going to tell Scarface what I've told you?"

"That won't be necessary. He already knows the part that concerns him. You can read it in his eyes. Now, shall we go and have me acquaint myself with your people?"

For the next two days she showed Hadrian and his family Crown

Mountain and the Dieri, but treated them with distant courtesy She realized she'd never deceived Hadrian, and probably never could but, since his decisions were based on other than passions or emotions, she needn't concern herself with pleasing him.

When Scarface remarked upon her changed treatment of her guests she considered her answer carefully. She suspected telling him Hadrian had touched her, or had even tried to, wouldn't be believed and would raise more questions than answers. It might, if believed, precipitate a confrontation that could cost her Scarface before his usefulness was done. There was no way to turn the situation to her advantage so she simply stared balefully at him and said, "That's *my* concern."

On the morning Hadrian's party left for High Rage she again held his stirrup but with an air of formal courtesy.

As the group rode out the Ram's Gate she beckoned to Scarface. "We've been ignoring other allies. I'm going to invite Murtry and Ivo to dinner tonight. You will treat them with every courtesy. They're ambassadors of a very powerful organization, one which can build us or break us."

He frowned but said nothing.

She sent a messenger to Murtry and Ivo and received the reply they'd be delighted to take dinner with the ruler of the Dieri. She noticed they used the title "ruler of the Dieri" rather than "Empress of Cerco," but chose to ignore the implication. They would learn. For the rest of the day she busied herself with planning the meal and the direction of the conversation.

Scarface was withdrawn but polite at dinner and she was able to steer the talk toward the nations bordering on Cerco, and possible alliances.

Ivo suggested seeking an alliance with the Sazian Empire, since it had enough influence with Abaransa to effectively control that nation.

She looked an accusation at Scarface. "Why haven't you ever suggested that?"

He'd just finished eating and sipped his wine. "Because the empire is presently ruled by a council of two hundred. Even discounting those who are nonentities, there are still a score of men who might claim some power. It's far easier to wait until one man seizes power and deal with him. Also, the power of the empire is waning. Whoever takes control is going to face enough internal problems he'd be unlikely to look beyond his own borders, unless it's for help."

Ivo drained his cup and held it out to Mendarian, who'd picked up the flagon, then stared at Scarface. "Who'd you guess will be the man to declare himself Emperor of Sazia?"

"Barring assassination, a young man called Vesparin, who commands the army. Most of the empire's troops are rabble, but the Elites are still among the best soldiers I've ever seen. I'd guess there are already tensions between the army and the council. Weasels are always very wary of hounds, and the more the councilors try to control Vesparin or his army, the more quickly he's likely to lose patience and move to declare himself."

"So," Mendarian snapped, "we sit here and do nothing."

Scarface finished his cup of wine. "No, we work at making Cerco a nation again. And the most important single event in our future isn't forging a bond with a decaying empire but winning in the Great Council."

"That might well be," Murtry said, "but you can't ignore the world beyond Cerco. It should be easy enough to come to and understanding with Ghiblein."

Most of the rest of the evening's talk added only bits to what Mendarian already knew or had decided but she used the time to put Ivo and Murtry at their ease. After Scarface was gone she'd need other support for a time. The Union could be most helpful to her, and they'd probably be very willing to deal with her after Scarface was out of the way.

Actually, Murtry had a self-assurance about him that Scarface lacked. She'd thought Scarface a wolf, but he was only a housedog, one who, after the Great Council, would no longer be of use to her.

~ * ~

Scarface had invested a few hours in conversation with another mercenary from Donradé and learned about the religions of the place. A crown should have more than one point. When Murtry and Ivo had gone and Mendarian had dismissed him, he prepared for a visit to his future kingdom. He still had most of the gold he'd brought with him from High Rage. With a little of that, a week's rations, and his weapons, he needed only directions out of the mountains. He found Orhan in his rooms and was given a map of the safest route to Donradé. He also left orders for his horse to be saddled and ready before dawn. Sleep came easily for the first time since the border wars.

He was fully awake and dressed for traveling a full hour before dawn. He found quill, ink, and parchment, and penned a quick note.

Mendarian, I've gone to buy a god. Morgan.

~ * ~

The bitter cold nipped at his hands and face, worming its way into any opening in his clothing. Each day was an endless repetition of the day before—gray stone, gray sky, and snow that obscured the path so he feared for his mount each step of the way. Each night he dug a pit in the snow and sometimes, when he found wood, he nursed a small fire that couldn't quite coax the chill out of his bones.

The six days in the mountain were six slices of eternity, then for two more days he rode over rolling, heavily forested plains. His horse was almost dead when he finally reached the temple of Mordach, the Donradan war god.

The temple was part of a complex of wooden buildings, some no better than sheds. He stopped at a hut that, from the smell and the tracks in the snow, served as a stable. A young man dressed in the gray robes of an acolyte accepted the reins of his horse and a silver coin. The lad pointed out, when asked, the temple and the residence of the high priest, then led the animal out of the cold.

Scarface trudged through the snow to the porch of the long wooden temple, tried to stamp some feeling back into his feet, and clapped his hands together. Pushing open the door, he stepped inside.

Gradually, as his eyes adjusted to the dim, uncertain light of candles, he saw the entire building was one large room with painted walls and rafters. At the far end stood a large wooden statue, brightly painted, of a well-muscled man with eight arms, each hand gripping a different weapon. The statue's strong face was marked with red lightning bolts on each cheek, the points nearly meeting at the chin.

After inclining his head for a moment, Scarface strode toward the statue. A spear's length away he halted, drew his sword and dagger, placed them on the floor before the idol, and stood motionless, head bowed, for what he thought should be the proper length of time. When he felt he'd "prayed" long enough he picked up his weapons, sheathed them, left a gold coin on the floor where he'd laid the sword, and, as he turned to go, saw a movement in the shadows. *Good.* He'd have hated to have wasted either the gold or his performance.

He paced back to the door and outside, into the wind. Drawing his cloak tighter about himself, he set out for the residence of the high priest, almost as large as the temple and as elaborately painted.

Pulling open the door and stepping inside, he breathed on his cupped hands. In an alcove stood a man nearly as massive as the idol and with the same tattoos on cheeks and chin, but with only the usual two arms. The guard was, like a priest, robed in red, but the glint of metal at wrists and throat indicated he put at least as much faith in mail as in the protection of Mordach, and the spear he held was functional, not a simple staff of office.

"I've come to speak with the high priest," Scarface said.

"On what matter?" The man's voice was the rumble that could be expected of a man-mountain.

"Spreading the faith and building more temples."

"Stay where you are." The man ducked through a door and disappeared. Moments later he returned. "The master will see you. Leave your weapons for blessing at the shrine just inside the door."

Scarface removed his sword belt and slipped loose his knife and scabbard, stepped through the door, left the weapons before a smaller copy of the idol, and followed a corridor that ran only a few paces before making a turn, then another, to an open door.

Through a translucent patch in the ceiling enough sunlight was admitted to show a man, not quite as large as the guard, with iron-gray hair and eyes. He sat behind a table littered with scrolls and a very dependable-looking mace. His large hands were clasped before him as if in prayer but his attention was all on Scarface.

"Brother Michlis told me you're interested in helping spread the faith, and your manner tells me you're very devout."

Scarface knew it was the priest hidden in the shadows of the temple who'd seen his "devotions," not his manner, that had been convincing to the high priest. Still, it was easier to deal with a man who played games, as long as the rules could be discerned. He bowed. "My devotion is indeed very deep. I've observed that worship of Mordach is not total, even among warriors, and I've thought about this. I have several hundred men under my orders, and will have more. I think a tenth of each soldier's wages would be a fitting offering to the church."

The iron eyes glittered like nailheads. "Such reverence won't go unnoticed or unrewarded."

"That was my own thought. Eventually, as Mordach favors my cause, all Donradé will worship him, and all will give a tenth. Of course, blessings can sometimes be delayed, which would complicate matters both theological and secular. I prefer to simplify things. Simply, Mordach will favor unification of the baronies and war with the Sazian empire. And, as secular arm of the church, I'll accept half the offerings."

The iron gray eyes were like two knife blades, stabbing at his face. "Impossible! Offerings to Mordach are sacred, and their use for any profane purpose—"

"Excuse me," Scarface said smoothly, "but while I'm a novice with figures, I believe I learned somewhere that half of something is greater than all of nothing."

The cold eyes narrowed. "What, exactly, are you suggesting? Persecution?"

"Not at all. My devotion is much too strong for that. But if Mordach is unwilling to support my cause, then perhaps another god would be more gracious. And, of course, the rewards would be reciprocal."

The man behind the table leaned back. "You've ridden a long way. I'm sure you're tired and hungry, and I must pray for guidance. Rest, warm and refresh yourself, and we'll speak on this again tomorrow morning."

Scarface bowed and retraced his way to the alcove, reclaimed his weapons and, following the instructions of the guard, walked through the frigid wind to a building little better than a shed. At least smoke rose from a hole in the roof. Inside, the building was lined with pallets and had a fire pit in the center. He'd been given a place in the monks' quarters.

He smiled. This exposure to conspicuous poverty was a good sign. It meant Iron-eyes probably intended to haggle about the price.

Eight or ten men in yellow robes lay on the pallets or warmed themselves by the tiny fire. He slogged through the mud to join the circle of men around the fire, noticing that the thin pallets were kept almost dry by branches cut from evergreens and piled under them. The monks, whose faces bore only the lightning bolt tattoos, stared incuriously at him and he ignored them while he tried to work some feeling back into his fingers.

When his hands felt like parts of his body again he cast about for something to sit upon. Billets of wood lay stacked against the back wall. He gathered a couple of logs, dropped them by the fire, and sat on them, then tugged off his boots and let his feet and lower legs roast until the cold had left them.

He was just becoming comfortable when he heard the sound of metal striking metal. The monks lurched to their feet and filed out the door. Scarface pulled his boots back on and followed them outside, where a priest in red stood, holding a spear and with another spear thrust into the icy mud beside him. He went through a drill with the spear then invited one of the monks to take the other spear and attack him. The man stepped forward, tugged the weapon free, and lunged.

Of course the priests of a war god would be warriors, with arms practice for devotions. Scarface watched the men closely. It wasn't how he'd been taught to use a spear in the Marked Ones, but it was effective. Within the time it took to draw two deep breaths, the monk returned to the ranks holding his arm, while a red stain grew on the sleeve of his robe. Another man took his place and returned bleeding from a scalp wound.

The man in red practiced with each of the monks in turn, drawing blood or dispensing bruises. As the last of the monks tried to hide the pain of being struck in the ribs with the spear shaft, the priest gave them another lecture then ordered them to another, larger building.

This place already held perhaps fifty men, most of them sitting on pine-boughs, sipping from dirty clay bowls. The rest of the men stood in a line filing past the pot over the fire pit, dipping in their bowls and moving away to find a place to sit and eat.

The smell of the soup made his mouth water and he joined the line, took a bowl from a pile of crockery, and dipped it into the soup, which appeared to be a thin barley broth with a hint of meat. He raised the bowl to his mouth and drank. As nourishment or delicacy, the stew was a bitter disappointment, but at least the warmth in his belly was welcome.

As he drank what passed for dinner he glanced around the room. All the robes he saw were dirty yellow, the only red being stains from recent wounds. It was possible the priests were all fasting, but it seemed more likely they dined on something more substantial than watered horse fodder. When he finished his soup he copied the example of the men around him and carried his bowl back to the pile. After the last monk had finished his meager meal and taken back his bowl, the monks began to chant.

The chant seemed to be only sounds, the tones slipping past the thinking mind to the emotions below. The sound started as almost a dirge or lament. Gradually, the pitch and cadence changed, becoming less plaintive, more like a work-song, then the tempo increased again to make it sound like a triumphant battle-hymn. It ended with a war-cry. He stood when the others did and they trudged back to the barracks.

Lying on the pallet, covered with his cloak and a thin blanket, Scarface smiled bitterly into the darkness. The master had erred. The skimpy rations, privation and "devotions" obviously kept the monks from asking too many questions, kept them docile, and the high priest had probably hoped Scarface could be made more tractable the same way. The lesson would be an expensive one for Mordach. He'd been willing to accept a quarter of the offerings, and wouldn't have asked for warriors.

~ * ~

At dawn the men shuffled out into the cold. In other seasons, they'd probably have been kept busy farming, but in winter it was necessary to find some other activity. Morning devotions consisted of sword drill. Scarface watched as each monk, in turn, armed himself and faced the priest and each was dealt a superficial wound. He wondered if the priest would invite him to play, too, but he was ignored.

As the monks were sent to break their fast, the priest finally gestured for Scarface to follow and strode to the high priest's residence.

Scarface had learned to read the face markings. All those who served Mordach wore the red lightning pattern, and most of the priests he'd seen wore them over other designs. Apparently, the monks were slaves or little better than slaves, for every man in Donradé who was entitled to bear weapons bore some sort of pattern on his face before he was old enough to join the church. He was somewhat more impressed with the high priest when he remembered the man wore only the red lightning strokes. Still, a man who'd fought his way up from the bottom had weaknesses too. In fact, his very strength might be a weakness.

He again left his weapons at the shrine and walked to the high priest's room, to find the man apparently too absorbed in reading a scroll to look up, although Scarface had let his heels clatter on the plank floor.

At last the man stared up at Scarface. "After fasting and praying for guidance, I found inspiration and learned that your offer pleases Mordach. All but the amount. An eighth of the donations should be sufficient."

There was no place for Scarface to sit, so he leaned against the partition. "I've been meditating, too. I've seen the poverty of your order and decided that, for my needs, I'd require two-thirds of the offerings. I'll also need priests and monks to take up arms in my disputes with unbelievers."

"Impossible. The arm of Mordach serves only Mordach."

"That's exactly what I have in mind."

The hand resting beside the mace stirred. "You presume Mordach can be made to rattle his weapons to your tune."

"I presume nothing. I offer a plain business arrangement. If Mordach is above such mundane details, perhaps I can find some more earthy god. Maybe a fertility deity might be more appropriate for what I have in mind." He turned, as if to leave.

The fingers stirred again and touched the haft of the mace. "Beware. You try to push Mordach too far,"

Scarface stepped to the table, put his hands on its edge, and leaned toward the high priest. "I'm pushing no one. You can take or refuse the offer but if you wrap fingers around that mace, you'd best be a better warrior than the priests I've seen so far."

They glared at each other but the priest moved his hand away from the weapon. "A quarter of the offerings, two priests, and two score monks."

"Half, and ten priests, and two hundred men."

"A third. Five priests and a score of monks under each."

Scarface nodded. "Done. And I'll pay for the supplies for my ride home." He took out three gold coins. "For ten days' rations for my horse and myself. The rest is an offering to Mordach. We can consider it the seeds of a mighty tree."

"Leave your donation at the image of Mordach by the door. I'll give orders you are to be given everything you need."

~ * ~

Within the hour Scarface had eaten a good meal and was on his way back to Crown Mountain. By early afternoon the sky had cleared and the glare from the snow disguised the fact the way would become more treacherous from the thaw. After a time, however, he let riding become a thing his eyes and body did while his mind toyed with futures.

With four or five baronies under his control, and with the church supporting him, he should be able to enlist more lords in the war against Sazia. One successful battle should be enough to impress the nobles and, with the acceptance of his command by the soldiers, the army would be his, with or without the nobility. He kept watching the horizon and twice he saw smoke from a camp or farmstead, but he pressed on without stopping.

~ * ~

The sun had already set, eight days later, when he rode through the Wolf's Gate at Crown. He gave his horse to a soldier for care, went immediately to his rooms, and ordered food and a tub of hot water.

The food arrived first, and Mendarian with it. "I found your note. Did you manage to buy the god you wanted?"

"Yes, they're rather a bargain item in some places."

"Were you trying to make me worry, or did you just not think?"

He glanced up at her, surprised. "Worry? About what?"

"When my advisor leaves with only a short note and is gone for a fortnight, during which time he can't be consulted if there's trouble, I become concerned. And if you hadn't returned, what would I have done about the Council?"

"Why should you think I wouldn't be back? I gave you my word I'd see you through the Council, remember?"

"Words are cheap."

He fought back the temptation to ask whether she was speaking of his words or her own. He tore off a piece of bread, still warm, washed it down with wine, followed by meat and cheese and still more wine. "If I've done my work well, there were no problems requiring my opinions." He finished eating just as the servants brought a tub and buckets of steaming water. "We can talk more after I've bathed—unless you'd rather stay and watch me take a bath."

"Since nothing has happened here, there's nothing to talk about." She left the chamber.

The bath was a luxury after a fortnight of cold and mud, but contentment escaped him. The constant friction with Mendarian was like a file, wearing him down. He'd hoped that finding an equal, someone to whom he could share what he was and what he hoped to become would give him more than an ally. Now he felt more alone than ever. Other questions nagged him, just below the level of consciousness, so he buried them under a blanket of sleep.

Chapter 7

Crown Mountain was a beehive. Tribal leaders had begun to arrive with escorts of up to a score of warriors and as many family members. The lords and their families were settled in rooms normally occupied by Dieri families or in rooms that had been recently cleaned after a period of disuse that stretched back to the time of the loss of the crown and staff.

The warriors were given space in the barracks, and there were stony faces and sharp words that needed only the slightest spark to lead to sharp blades. Orhan finally solved the problem by starting competitions between the warriors with spears and bows and practice weapons, and contests of riding or wrestling.

Scarface watched the contests as often as he was able and he noted which of his mercenaries acquitted themselves well. He spent more time with Jonfré, who'd found five baronies near the Sazian border with lords willing to hire out their men. He'd also brought back a note from Hadrian saying the stone was flawed but would be ready for setting by midsummer.

The Council had become an immediate goal and it was with relief that he could count on his fingers the days before it opened. Another relief was provided by the arrival of a crate from Hadrian, one Scarface had taken deep into the mountain and left in unfinished caverns. Then he assembled the materials necessary to build a cage, and disappeared for almost a full day.

With the crate he'd received another note, advising him to find a woman named Topaz. Orhan knew of her and he gave Scarface directions to the room she shared with five other women while the Council was gathered.

Topaz was another unsettling surprise for Scarface. She was, like most of the Dieri women, blonde, but with eyes as green as emeralds, and the sight of her stirred buried memories. If anything, she was even more effeminate, but her resemblance to Martina was striking. He remarked upon the similarity.

"Perhaps it comes from our being sisters in power."

"I owe her a debt, or three."

"You'll pay when you can."

"Now, however, I have another debt to incur. I need a spell cast."

"No debt. You're doing this for someone other than yourself. I'll meet you here tomorrow morning, the second hour after dawn."

As he walked away he felt tension crawl into his belly and curl up to stay. He'd become aware of his growing dissatisfaction and a sense of impending disaster. Though all his plans were proceeding smoothly, the thing most important to him was slipping away. It was like trying to hold water in his hand—the harder he tried to grasp it, the more it slipped between his fingers.

Mendarian never visited him in his rooms and, when he went to hers, gave feeble excuses or found fault. He found his manhood being shaved away by a thousand tiny cuts and he knew that to resist was to lose everything. He strongly suspected Mendarian was sharing more than political confidences with Murtry, but he was too bound by his obligations to her to take any action to decide the issue.

More damaging, perhaps, than Mendarian's treatment was his own self-contempt at his acceptance of it. And now he'd seen a ghost from his past. He found himself looking forward to seeing Topaz again and, at the same time, dreading it, and for the same reasons. She was exciting, and she'd unchained feelings he'd thought securely bound.

Mead and wine were too weak to hold up to heavy brooding, he decided. He'd acquired a bottle of Ghiblin rye brandy, corrosive and with a wretched taste, but potent. He buried himself in his rooms with his mood and drank. Two hours later he'd smashed the empty bottle against the wall and stared morosely at the shards. Not even drink was an escape. He finally rose and went to bed, where he was disturbed by dreams that always fled from memory.

~ * ~

Two hours after dawn he stood before the hanging and scratched at the wool. Topaz appeared almost immediately and they walked together to the rough caverns in which he kept the wolf.

Topaz produced a glass rod similar to the one he'd been given by Martina, then she removed her slippers and robe, reminding him even more of his cousin. Although she was blonde and her skin was paler, they had almost the same body, and it required every vestige of strength he had to not reach out for her. His fingers seemed made of lead as he fumbled with buttons and buckles, then he was also sky-clad.

Topaz knelt on one knee on the rough floor, painting symbols on the rock and, at each sign he stopped and touched the pattern, letting power flow from his scars into the designs. The last pattern he touched was his own and he knelt, motionless, as she wove the forces they'd created into a bond between the wolf, the glass rod, and each other.

The ceremony was as long and arduous as the one performed by Martina, and the tension drained him as much as the magic. His back and legs became bars of agony, his vision dimmed and shimmered and, near the end of the rite, he had to bite his lower lip until it bled to keep from fainting. He wasn't even aware the casting had ended until Topaz stood before him, opening his pattern with a knife. He slumped forward to hands and knees and then forced his legs to take his weight. Lurching to his feet, he stumbled blindly as the world became a gray blanket thrown over his head, and his hand grazed a sweat-slick shoulder.

Arms were around him, holding him steady, and he was very aware of the body pressed against his. "Are you all right?" Her voice was weak from her own exertions.

He caught the shoulder and waited for the vertigo to subside and his vision to clear, then forced himself to draw away from her. At first, he could only nod then he rasped out, "Yes, I'm all right, thank you." He forced himself to walk, to pick up her robe and hold it for her. As he dressed as quickly as his lack of coordination would permit, he was struck by an almost overpowering feeling of *déjà vu*, and he remembered again that some noes are forever.

"I'll need your help one more time," he said, when his voice returned. "Tomorrow, three hours before the Council begins. Will you do this for me?"

She nodded.

He stared into her eyes and almost lost the struggle to try to kiss her. "Do you ever speak with my cousin?"

"Sometimes."

"I once did a very stupid thing—said a very foolish thing. I once suggested, at a dinner in Varish, that I didn't respect or care for her. I've often wished I could take those words back. Could you tell her that for me?"

Topaz flashed a grin. "That was a foolish thing to say—but one which was forgiven long ago. Now, forgive yourself. She knew you didn't mean the words and you'd regret having said them." She grinned again. "She thought your performance at that dinner was overdone but entertaining."

He summoned a weak smile. "She seems to know more about me than I would've guessed."

"Yes, and so do I, Morgan." Topaz left the cavern, leaving Scarface to stare after her but too weak to follow.

After a time he gathered enough strength to walk without staggering to his rooms and ordered a bath and a meal. After he'd bathed a guard brought his food and new problems. Two of the Senshenni lords wanted to speak with him.

Still, every problem could be a solution to another difficulty. He ate voraciously and told the guard to inform the Senshenni he'd speak with them if they came to his rooms.

Half an hour later he heard a scratching at his door hanging. He was already abed and decided not to rise. "Enter."

The Senshenni cautiously entered the room, their hands flying through what were probably wards against disease. Scarface chuckled, turned it into a cough, then grimaced. He turned the staged grimace into a transparently false grin. "My horse stumbled. I'll have to learn to pick more sure-footed mounts, learn to ride them better, or grow harder ribs." The tension leaked out of them like held breaths. They feared disease with a superstitious dread but were used to injuries. "But you didn't visit to talk about my horsemanship."

They glanced at each other, then the taller of the two nodded. "We have some doubts. If the tribes become one people again, what of our battles with other tribes? Our young men must become warriors. Iron must be tempered; wood must be seasoned, before either is fit to be used. So it is with young men. Before they may sit in our councils and have their words heard, they must first prove themselves as warriors. We don't fight for land, or to kill our enemies, but to add to our honor."

Scarface listened closely, showing respect for the speaker. Rather than answer immediately, he stared over their heads, gazing into some internal distance and, when he answered, he spoke slowly, choosing each word with great care. "This is a great difficulty. The empress and the Dieri want peace with their neighbors but, you're right, the tribes must also be strong. If the empress were assured your battles weren't acts of wanton killing and destruction. . . ." He lapsed into another apparently thoughtful silence.

"There's another answer, too. Your novices could be sent out to fight in other places. War's a common enough weed. I understand there's one brewing now in Donradé. If you sent your young men, they'd not only earn honor but booty besides, as well as warriors' wages, which would bring wealth to the tribes and trade with outsiders."

The nobles stared at each other. Best not to press the idea too strongly. Let them discuss it between themselves and with the other headmen. "Tell the empress or I what you decide. If difficulties remain, they can be dealt with."

The Senshenni drew themselves up and the taller one said, "Tell the empress we'll not only bury our lances at the Council, we'll break them as well."

The Senshenni had hardly gone before Mendarian came to his room and sat on the corner of his bed. "The guard told me you'd been hurt. Will you be able to attend the opening of the Council?"

"No and no. And yes." He grinned at her. "I'm not hurt, just tired from having helped cast a spell, but letting the nobles think I've hurt myself in a riding accident gives me a perfect excuse for not standing beside you at the Council—"

"And what's wrong with being with me at the Great Council?"

"The fact I can't be in two places at once. I'll be there at the proper time—and in the proper form. Orhan and Arv can deal with any minor matters that might crop up. The most important thing for you to remember is that you're not just the ruler of the Dieri, you're the Chosen One of Cerco."

"I won't forget, and I won't let them forget it either. Well, if you're all that tired, I'd best let you rest."

"I said tired, not dead. Oh, and I've guaranteed a couple of Senshenni lords that we have no intention of interfering with their war sports."

"I don't want war on our border."

"Then let them practice a little harmless predation on each other. You'll find the smaller tribes will also be opposed to a Dieri-imposed peace, especially if their young men have no other way to become warriors. The quickest but least profitable way to unite the western tribes is to give them a common enemy on their eastern marches. I don't believe you want that kind of unity. If it comes to that, the Dieri would probably win the war, but what would they win? Mostly, undying hatred, because the war would have to be fought against every family. As it stands now, the western peoples will keep your borders secure and, if you hire them out as mercenaries, they can provide you with a trade lever."

Mendarian paced the chamber. "I want a nation, not a collection of marauding bands cutting each others' throats."

"Nations take time to build, and common customs. If you decide to trade hostages with the other tribes you've made a beginning. Besides, what do you need a nation for? The mountains defend the people of Cerco against your most likely enemies. The Cercans will grow on their own terms."

"So now you're advising me to be empress in name only. Once, the Dieri and the rest spilled out onto the plains and were a real force. Now you want them to be content being shepherds and sheep."

"They're already content, as long as they don't have to fight for survival. As for spreading the empire, that was four hundred years ago. The world changes. The next empire won't be ruled by the Dieri, or the Sazians, either."

She glared at him with corrosive contempt. "Have you now taken up scrying?"

"No more than ever. Sometimes one must know something of the past before one can shape the future." He studied her face, trying to find in it the beauty that had once attracted him. The features hadn't changed but something behind them had. And yet he could still love her. "Don't worry; you'll still be ruler of more than Cerco."

"Words, always words. I'm becoming sick of your soothing syrup of words."

"I'm only free with my words when I'm willing to back them with action. And, speaking of action—" he patted the bed.

Mendarian stopped pacing and glared down at him. "Is that the trade you're offering? If I lay with you, you'll work your magic with the Council? You want me to whore for power?"

His blood suddenly felt like melting ice and the coldness reached into his eyes. "No, I don't bargain like that. Go to your bed alone, Mendarian. You've won your victory."

She stared into his eyes then sank onto the bed. "I'm sorry. Always there's this fear something will go wrong. I know you've planned well and carefully. You've done more for me than anyone else and I've been treating you worse than anyone else." Her hands closed over his and drew them together. She leaned toward him and her lips were moist and soft.

The ice in his breast melted with her words and the warmth in her eyes, and he drew her onto the bed beside him. His hands and lips were hungry for her as ever, but in some dark corner of his mind a small thought hid, waiting its chance to escape and later, although his body was content, a nagging uneasiness grew.

~ * ~

He didn't wake until almost noon and, when he finally rose, he took his meal in his rooms, maintaining the fiction that he was too badly injured to go out. When he did leave his rooms it was in the late afternoon, when most of the visiting nobility would be conferring with their allies and the Dieri were preparing the Council grounds at the base of Crown.

With him he took an extra cloak, used as a bag, full of patches of the glowing lichen carefully scraped from the walls of his rooms.

Topaz was waiting for him and together they strolled to the caverns where the wolf paced his cage. Scarface crouched beside the cage and examined the beast. He was large enough; larger than most wolves seen in these mountains and, with the spells lifted, he appeared to be healthy.

"What were you two saying to each other?" Topaz asked.

"Nothing, I was just being sure he was fit. What made you ask that?"

"There just seemed to be a sense of kinship between you two."

Scarface grinned at the wolf. "Perhaps we are kin." He remembered the last time he'd changed bodies and become a hawk—or had there always been some hawk in him? And now he was going to be a wolf. It seemed, somehow, fitting. Another thought occurred to him then. "I've done this once before, with a hawk. Do you know what happened to it?"

"Yes. It distressed Martina when the hawk died."

Scarface stared into the cage at golden eyes that regarded him with something like understanding. "I'm sorry." That death weighed more heavily on him than the deaths of a score of men he'd known or met. "We'll have to be certain our friend, here, survives." He looked from gold eyes to green ones. "The trigger to return to my own body is the glass rod itself?"

She nodded.

"Then let's get started. I want some time to become adjusted to this body, and I'll need you to rub this glowing stuff onto the wolf's body. By the time the Council begins, it should be full dark and I intend to make a strong impression.

"Are you sure you want to see your own body, like this?"

He nodded. Staring into the cage at his brother wolf, he took the glass rod from his pouch and snapped it.

He almost overbalanced until he landed on his paws, being careful not to touch the broken rod, then he backed away from the cage. Again the world became shades of gray, but the smells of the place almost overwhelmed him. What he'd lost in vision he'd more than gained in smell and hearing. The man in the cage, staring at him with panic-stricken eyes, reeked of fear-sweat and urine. He backed farther from the cage and turned to face Topaz. Her scent was a pleasing one of candles and work-sweat and some of the herbs with which she'd bathed and dressed her hair.

Strangely, he became more acutely aware of her sensuality. Had he been only a wolf, he might not have noticed, and as only a man he'd concealed it from himself, but now he was man/wolf, and he had to fight to keep strong feelings under firm control. He'd felt himself begin to react and immediately closed his mind to all but the necessity of his performance at the Council.

He probed with his nose at the cloak containing the plants, now smelling a sharp, acrid odor from them, and lay down on the floor, waiting for Topaz to cover him with phosphorescence. She drew out handsfull of the glowing stuff and rubbed it into his coat. Her hands were gentle and he discovered the sensation of her fingers rubbing his rough fur was a very pleasant one. He closed his eyes and experienced the world through senses and sounds and touchings.

Very soon he became aroused again but by that time Topaz had finished coating his back and sides with the glow from the lichen and, after she finished applying it to the fur of his tail, he rose.

He stared into her eyes, regretting he couldn't see them as green, then he gently nipped at her chin and stalked from the cavern.

He'd studied the ways out of these caves and followed the path he'd laid out for himself but soon realized the wolf senses were sharp enough to easily let him find his way outside. He was more aware of the movement of air through the passages, the subtle differences of pitch in the faint breeze, and the scents that made fresh air different from the musty odors of the closed tunnels.

Then he was outside the mountain, standing on a ledge.

The Council fire hadn't yet been lit and the sun, beyond the mountains, still cast a pale light. He crouched on the ledge, enjoying the warmth and the breeze that stroked his fur, drinking in odors.

He reveled in them, as he had in the sure, precise action of walking on four strong legs and in the power of the muscles that rippled under skin and fur. He felt as though he'd just been born, and the world was new, yet somehow familiar. He narrowed his eyes to slits and felt the pleasure of cool air and his own breath moving across his lolling tongue. For a time—not a long time or a short time, as he'd have marked it as a man—but just the right time, he rested, not thinking or remembering, just being.

When his breathing with the world turned into remembrance he found himself thinking of Topaz. She was, in a subtle way, a greater threat to him than Mendarian could ever be, and she was doubly dangerous because she'd become important to him.

Had he not decided he was responsible for the success of the Council, had he not decided his devotion to Mendarian must be at the core of his life, he might've asked Topaz to go questing with him. How many different forms could they have taken? How many different ways might they have desired each other?

With reluctance but finality, he put the troublesome thoughts away and studied his way down the mountain.

He waited until most of the light had seeped from the sky before he began his descent, and took a way down that would keep him out of sight of men. Snow had drifted across the ledges, here and there, and he feared it hid breaks in the stone and that it'd wipe away some of the pale glow. By the time he'd reached the base of the mountain he could smell the smoke of the Council fire and, on impulse, he stopped, threw back his head, and howled at the moonless sky.

His black-lipped mouth curled into a grin. The ones he wanted to impress would almost certainly take the howl to be an omen.

He followed the smell of men and smoke through the darkness until he could see a spark which, as he trotted toward it, became a blaze. He halted near enough to see light dance across cheekbones and brows and the ornaments worn by the nobles, while he was still only a little lighter shadow among dark pools.

Again he flung back his head and sang to the sky, then paced forward. As he drew closer to them he found the smell of men disturbing, warning of different dangers. He could smell their tension and fear and, in their voices, tight with controlled passion, he clearly heard their distrust of each other, and all his senses together let him feel their hostility.

He slowed as he approached a guard, then walked past the man, who eyed him with a mixture of reverence and fear. Other guards became aware of him, then one of them knelt on a knee, and his action was copied by others. Past the guards sat the nobles and their advisors, crouched on the ground or on robes of cloth or fur.

And there danced the fire.

It was his ancient enemy, unpredictable, its odors overpowering the scents around it, disguising dangers, occasionally snapping and shooting sparks to burn eyes or pelt. He then knew the flickering brightness in a new way—as a wolf. It was senses-stealer. Pain-bringer. Still, the fire and his fear of it were only obstacles, and he fought the wolf and won.

He paced a circle around the flickering light, walking between the men and the flames, learning each man by the scents that clung to him. When he'd completed his circuit of the lords he paced past a pit to where Mendarian sat on her jade throne, Orhan by her right hand, Arv to her left. Orhan stared at him with wide eyes, then slid the sword from its scabbard and placed it at his feet.

Arv's eyes had narrowed and his knuckles were pale as he gripped the hilt of his sword, but he didn't draw the weapon.

Mendarian had been almost as shocked as the rest by his arrival but now she relaxed in her chair, a smile playing about her lips.

He found it instructive to see her through other eyes. She, like Topaz, was enormously sensual, and there was another quality, one he couldn't quite wrap in words. This quality was dangerous, something brittle and couldn't be bound by custom or nature. A sort of hunger, it both attracted and repelled him.

He faced her in a silence that seemed to grow deeper as it lengthened. He'd have knelt before her to impress the lords but memory called back a voice saying, "Not for any reason." Instead, he paced toward Arv, pressing him back almost by force of will, never physically touching him, then lay down beside the throne and glowered at the men gathered around the fire.

Mendarian let the silence grow into a shapeless black presence looming over them all, then she spoke of the need for all of Father Wolf's children to join together as one family. Rivalries, she said, were part of a family, and so were disagreement, but a family needed a leader. Father Wolf had already chosen the leader of Cerco, first by giving her his staff and crown and, now, by appearing before them. Would the Children of the Wolf dispute this?

One of the Senshenni who'd visited Scarface in his rooms strode to the dark mouth of the pit, broke the haft of his lance over his knee, and tossed the pieces into the hole. One by one, the other leaders did the same, each breaking the symbolic weapon of his tribe.

Orhan watched impassively, then picked up his sword and used it to hack his hatchet in two, broke the sword, and tossed the pieces of both weapons into the pit. With a glance around the circle, he returned to his place beside the throne.

Beyond the circle of lords, Scarface knew, the power singers and memory keepers were committing to memory each sound, each flicker of light on eye or chin.

Scarface stood and walked in front of Mendarian then turned and faced her. He wondered if she could see the thoughts behind his eyes. Aware of the importance of each movement, he strode around the pit and through the circle of leaders, past the other watchers and the guards, and into the night.

Once he'd vanished into the cover of undergrowth he made his way back as he'd come, moving as swiftly as he dared in the darkness. The moon had risen and he used its wan light, with his nose and ears, to tell him what his eyes couldn't. It was easy enough to follow the trail of his own scent back up the side of the mountain and into the caverns.

Running with this tireless body was a pleasure, one that hadn't quite palled when he finally returned to the place of the cage.

Topaz waited for him, a large bowl of water steaming over a low fire. He trotted past it and stared into the cage at the poor, weak man-form that lay curled in a corner.

"He was afraid," Topaz said, "so I made him sleep."

He went to where she knelt by the fire and the clay bowl. She dipped a cloth into the water and washed the glow from him. Grateful for the warmth and perhaps even more grateful for the gentle attention, he lay, almost dozing, on the cavern floor. She washed him with the cloth and brushed his coat with a quill brush, and he both feared and doted on her closeness.

When she finished he rose again and, with a feeling akin to regret, placed his paw on the broken glass rod and collapsed on the floor.

Hands helped him roll onto his back and a face that was, to him, impossibly beautiful, gave his eyes a point on which to focus. He suffered the confusion and the weakness of a waking man, his will struggling with his physical and mental torpor. Temptation was stronger, and he reached up to her, drew her to him, and his lips found hers. After a moment's hesitation, her mouth opened to his probing tongue and, for some fractions of not long enough, he lived again in a place from which he thought he'd been banished.

At last she found the will to press her hands against his chest and pushed him away. Will and self-control finally returned to him and he released her. His lips twisted and tears coursed down his cheeks, and he turned away from her, battling an army of emotions he couldn't quite defeat.

Eventually, a truce was reached and the feelings withdrew to wait for another sortie. He wiped his face with the backs of his hands. Now that he was fully awake and conscious, he realized the wolf had, in his body, soiled itself.

Topaz stood a spear's length from him. He made his lips grin at her. "Running as a wolf seems to be a most powerful aphrodisiac. Please excuse my animal nature."

Her grin was genuine. "Under other circumstances, it might've been very pleasant, but not now."

"You'd better leave now. It seems I have some more cleaning to do, and I'll release our friend from his cage before I go. Again, thank you." He paused and groped for words. "Tell Martina, when you can, that I do love her. And tell her it was good to find kin here, in a strange place."

"Good night." Topaz went away.

He cleaned himself and his robe with the warm water and he opened the door to the cage. The wolf still slept and it was safer for both of them to let him wake and find his way outside.

With a last glance around the cave, he left for his own rooms.

~ * ~

Mendarian walked into the mountain at a steady pace until she reached the corridor near her own chambers, then she wheeled and caught Orhan by the arm. "We did it!"

"With the help of Father Wolf," he replied evenly, bowing at the name.

Mendarian almost laughed at him before she realized why Scarface had never spoken of the plan. Orhan was a believer. The idea he could be so naïve was almost inconceivable to her but his words were proof. "With the help of Father Wolf," she finally agreed, with a nod at the name.

Arv caught up with Mendarian and, with her, watched Orhan walk to his rooms. "He doesn't know, does he?" Arv asked.

"No, and he won't learn it, either." She caught Arv in a hug. "We did it! Cerco is mine. It's as much mine as my own hand." She raised her hand and curled the fingers into a fist.

"Yours and Scarface's."

"All mine. He may have shaken the tree but the fruit fell into *my* hand." She stared at him, surprised. "Why aren't you celebrating? All those years of selling your body to other men's armies, being a whore to war, and it's over! This country is yours, too."

"We have it," he replied, "now we have to keep it." He turned and trudged down the corridor.

Impatience burned in her. A victory and no one to share it with. The taste was already souring in her mouth. As she continued toward her rooms a figure detached itself from the shadow of a door. Her right hand went to her left wrist and the tips of her fingers touched the hilt of her dagger before she recognized Murtry.

He wore a smile. "Most impressive. Forgren will be proud of you—and very amused."

"Thank you. I presume you also found it amusing?"

"Yes, I did. You showed real ingenuity. Using religion, especially the way you did, was a very neat trick."

"Ah, but you have to give some credit to Scarface, who played his role so well. Now you know why I took him as an advisor. The Union will have to work doubly hard to show me it can replace him."

At the mention of Scarface's name, Murtry's face hardened but he snatched at the bone of the idea Mendarian had tossed to him. "How soon do you want the war ended between Ghiblein and Abaransa?"

"I've thought about it. Not soon. The longer they fight each other, the less energy they'll have for taking what's mine."

"Don't deceive yourself—" He broke off the words.

She knew the words he'd meant to say were important but she had no hope of hearing those unspoken thoughts at the present.

"Tell Forgren I may be casting about for a new advisor soon. One who can follow commands without hesitation, no matter what the orders might be."

"I may have a name or two to recommend to you," Murtry said. "Good night." He turned and vanished into the gloom.

She sauntered back to her rooms and replaced the staff on its rack and the crown on its pedestal, then threw herself down on a couch, wondering how long it'd take Scarface to return.

She considered visiting Murtry in his rooms but anything she said now would only detract from what she'd said moments ago. She shoved herself to her feet and paced the chamber.

Now that she had the authority, what treaties and alliances did she want or need? Gascolin would be a suitable ally, if a dull one and, probably, when she thought more deeply, a useless one. Why forge an alliance with someone who could be of no help and represented no particular danger? Donradé, to the south of Gascolin, was only a rabble of feuding baronies, from what Scarface and Murtry had said. Sazia bordered Cerco to the southeast but the Sazian court was overburdened with palms to grease.

Farther afield was Ianesk in the north, which might be some source of help should Ghiblein ever end its war with Abransansa, and, to the far east, Porcash and Doss. She wondered what Scarface would say to being made emissary to Doss. From what she'd been able to gather, his residence would probably be a rope dangling from the nearest tree.

Her reverie was interrupted by the sound of her door hanging being scratched. She spun to face the door. "Who's there?"

"My name is Topaz." The voice was the high-pitched voice of a young woman.

"Come in."

She amended her assessment of the voice from a woman to a girl. Still, there was something familiar about her, something that put Mendarian on her guard. She looked closely but couldn't recognize the face. She forced herself to relax. This girl was no possible threat to her. "What do you want, child?"

"I wish to leave Crown Mountain. I have kin in Stag Mountain, to the south, and I ask your permission to go there."

"Certainly." She'd almost forgotten these people couldn't move from one mountain to another without her permission. She considered asking the girl why she wished to leave and decided it was probably only another tale of young love gone wrong. She was still too excited by the night's victory to chance boredom and too pleased with the success to be sympathetic to someone else. "Have a pleasant journey."

The girl smiled, said "Thank you," and left the chamber.

That smile....

Mendarian paced again and tried to pick up her plans where she'd put them down, but something about the girl's smile nagged at her, made her uneasy. Finally she forced the half-memory from her mind.

Perhaps she should wait for Scarface in his rooms. And it'd be pleasant to have some wine. She found a bottle of Shannan plum wine and pushed through the hangings to his rooms. For a moment she was struck again by the stark simplicity of the place. Beyond a few scrolls and scraps of parchment on a table and the rumpled blanket lying in a heap in the middle of the bed, there was almost no sign anyone lived in these rooms.

She sat on the bed, facing the nearest door hanging, and waited. Finally the hanging twitched, then was swung aside and Scarface stepped into the room.

"We did it!" She threw herself at him, caught him around the waist, and buried her face in his hair.

He put his arm around her and hugged, then pushed her a little away. "I still need a bath, but, yes, we did it." He drew her close and kissed her. "I fully intend to make the rest of the night as interesting as the first part." He laughed. "Being a wolf gives one an appetite for flesh and, after I bathe, I intend to dine well." He caught her in another hug and kissed her again.

She returned the kiss, then drew away from him. She had the feeling he was somehow evading her. His kisses lacked the usual passion, even, lately, the desperation, and the grin and laughter never reached his eyes. "What's amiss?"

He looked away from her. "Nothing. Just tired and dirty." He tried a weak chuckle and failed.

"Horseshit, I know you better than that. What is it you're not telling me?"

He looked around the room. "I'm just tired. Spell-casting and shape-changing are hard work. Ah," he noticed the bottle on the bed, "good wine. In a very short time my night should be complete."

They both turned at the scratching on the door hanging. He winked at her, slipped into the bed, and pulled the blanket up to hide the robe he still wore. He motioned for her to sit on the bed and to hide the bottle. "Enter."

Servants brought a tub, filled it with water, and left the room.

As soon as the door hanging stopped swaying he was out of bed. "We mustn't forget," he said, as he pulled off the robe and flung it at the chest, "that I'm injured, practically choosing my saddle for the death-ride." He stepped into the tub, sat down in it, and leaned back, moaning with pleasure the whole time.

"You still haven't told me what's bothering you."

He scrubbed himself vigorously. "Nothing is bothering me that can't be cured by a bath, a frantic tumble, a good night's rest, and a ride." He grinned at her. "If you still think there's a problem we can try the rest and tumble again until we get it right."

She came up behind him, pressed her cheek against his, and ran her fingers down his hair to his shoulders. "Very well. You've earned any secrets you want to keep. As long as it's not another woman."

"Or she-wolf?"

She continued to stroke his hair. Something about his manner—something she couldn't put finger to—told her she hadn't been far from the mark. She watched as he stood and dried himself with an old blanket, and he put his arms around her.

"I'm dressed for what I have in mind," he said, "but you're still wearing too much clothing." He removed her belt, found the dagger up her sleeve and took the scabbard from her arm, then slid her robe down her shoulders. His eyes were hungry, so hungry she could almost feel them nibbling at her. He caught her up and carried her to his bed.

His hunger actually seemed to increase as they wrestled and sweated together on the bed, and Mendarian was exhausted when they were finally done. She lay on her back, her head resting on his chest, her legs drawn up, and she stared at her own alabaster thighs. With the way he'd made love to her, it wasn't another woman. What then? His excuses had been shallow. Did he know tonight was the last night he'd ever visit her bed? Or was it something else?

She slid one foot away and gazed at the leg still bent. Too many mysteries tonight—a night that had begun with such promise. First Murtry with his comment clipped short by caution or deviousness, then the girl—what was her name? Some sort of gemstone—who made her uneasy for no reason Mendarian could name, then Scarface and his strange mood. She slid the other foot forward and moved her head from his chest.

Tomorrow was soon enough for answers to the questions. She folded them up and put them away for the night.

~ * ~

She was still half-asleep when she opened her eyes and saw Scarface dressed for traveling and testing the east with which his sword slid from its scabbard.

"What—where are you going?"

"A place called Donradé." He sat on the corner of the bed. "I promised another crown to match yours, and I thought it best to leave while there's still shine on your victory at the Council."

"You're just going to abandon me?" Despite her intention to be rid of him, she felt an unexpected sense of loss.

"Your throne is safe here. Another's being built in Donradé, and I've a feeling it's being cut to my measure. You might want to keep up the illusion I'm still here, still hurt. It could give you another lever with which to bargain with the Union."

Her mind was still sleep-misted and questions seemed to hover, just out of reach. One finally ventured near enough to catch. "You lied to me! You planned this, and last night you knew you'd be leaving and you lied to me."

"No, I said what was bothering me was easily cured and it was. The bath, the time spent with you, the sleep, and this ride I'm going on are all things I needed."

"You're playing with words. You made the decision before you came through your door last night, and now you're reaching for a kingdom on my border. If you turn against me—"

"I made the decision to leave Cerco long before last night. I've told you before I wouldn't live in your shadow, that I'd take my own throne. And I'll never lead armies against you." He reached out to stroke her cheek.

Mendarian whipped her head away from his hand. "If I say the word, you'll never leave these mountains alive."

His face became bleak and his pale green eyes seemed feral. "Then say the word, but know the sound will be strong enough to shake your own throne." He turned away, then glanced back at her. "Oh, and don't go looking for your dagger. You had that chance in Varish." He ducked through the door flap, leaving her alone with her rage.

Fury almost blinded her. Her hands knotted into fists and she had to struggle to keep from screaming curses. She forced herself to sit on the bed until her mind began playing with possibilities. The first was to arrange an assassination, but that wouldn't be easy and it'd rob her of a measure of satisfaction. The second was to visit Murtry. The more she considered the idea, the greater her appreciation of it grew.

She dressed, then remembered the dagger. No matter. It wouldn't be needed.

Chapter 8

Mendarian allowed her resentment to simmer but kept secrets from boiling over. As much as she hated to admit it, even to herself, Scarface was right about keeping him, or the threat of him, as a weapon against the Union. When she reached the rooms in which Murtry and Ivo stayed, she paused before scratching the door hanging, unsure why she stopped, then she raked her nails against the wool.

Murtry shoved aside the curtain. "Good morning, Empress."

Was there a hint of irony in the title as he used it? She chose to ignore the perception and stepped into the room. Ivo was gone.

Murtry noticed her glance around the room. "He went to see the lords leaving Crown. Was it Ivo you came to see?"

"No." She sat on a stool. "No, I came to see you, to see what offers the Union would make me."

Murtry, arms crossed, leaned against the wall, and appraised her with a half-smile. "I'm not sure Forgren's original offer is still open. As for your domain, we'll respect your right to it in return for free passage across it to anyone who wears a green ring."

She glared at him. "If Forgren wants to make his original offer again, he may, just as I may decline or accept it. And I find your 'guarantee' insulting and shallow. I *do* rule in this place. I rule it because I'm blessed by Father Wolf himself." She made no attempt to keep a cynical cutting edge sheathed in soft tones. "It seems to me the Union offers nothing but it wants the convenience of using Cerco as a hiding-hole and quick-route for its agents in the east."

He finished the other half of the smile but all the humor had bled out. "Very astute. What do you want from us?"

"For a beginning, I want a treaty with Gascolin, one that assures me of a western boundary that includes all the mountains east of High Rage. And it'd amuse me to see the war between Ghiblein and Abaransa become a more spirited dispute. The more they hurl at each other, the less they'll have to use against me."

"That's impossible," he snapped. "You don't need to worry about them invading you, but Union interests are deeply involved in Ghiblein and, to a lesser extent, in Abaransa as well."

She stood. "Then let the Union make me an offer. Let them show their good faith by a strip of land five leagues wide along the eastern border with Ghiblein. If you want to discuss it further you may come to my rooms this evening. Come alone, but not with empty hands."

She stalked out of the room and strode to the Wolf's Gate, where most of the Cercan lords were gathered on their way out, and found Orhan talking with the leader of the Cortelani. She joined the conversation and heard Orhan repeat the assurance the Nevenii would no longer be allowed to claim more than a fair border around their towns. Mendarian rested a hand on Orhan's shoulder.

"Scarface is leaving the mountains for a time, to rest and meditate, but he thought you should know. No one else. To anyone else who asks, he's in his rooms."

"What about Arv?"

She realized, with a shock, that she'd forgotten about him. "Yes, Arv will know the truth, too, but I want it to go no farther." She paused. "Have you noticed the green rings Murtry and Ivo wear?"

"Yes, my lady."

"Quietly let your men and a few leaders we can trust know that if they see anyone but Ivo or Murtry wearing such a ring, I want the wearer brought to me, alive and well, but a prisoner."

Orhan bowed and strode away to carry out her orders. Why had she ever considered having him killed? He was so useful he was almost indispensable. His men were devoted to him and he was devoted to her—at least for so long as she had the staff and crown. And Arv was another useful man. She finally found him in his rooms, sunk on a couch, a bottle of Ghiblin rye brandy on the table before him, his eyes vacantly staring at the wall, or beyond it. He hadn't answered her scratch or the question called through the curtain, and she'd only gone into the room because he was Arv and she was the Empress.

"Why so grim?" She sat beside him and rested her hand on his knee.

His eyes flickered as his gaze moved from the wall to her and focused. "Because there's no use for me here. I'm just occupying these rooms. You have everything you need from someone else."

"You took care of me when I was useless—" She caught herself and fumbled for the right words with which to correct the truth. "I needed you before and I need you now. Scarface knows how to play power games and use whatever leverage he can get. Orhan knows the people, especially the men. But you know *me*.

"Scarface can tell me what can be done and how to do it, Orhan knows who to get to do it, and Murtry and Ivo know the effect it'll have on the Union, but only you can tell me if I *should* do what they propose. Without you, I'm all hunger."

He forced a weak grin. "So, they propose, you dispose, and I oppose."

She stood abruptly, her face rigid with anger. "If that's the way you see it, that's the way it'll be. You have your choices to make, and I can't make them for you. The small council will meet tomorrow morning. Be there, or not, at your pleasure." She stalked out of his room.

She spent the next several hours in a deep sulk and had to almost physically lift the mood to answer Murtry's scratch at her door hanging.

He stepped into the room and glanced about as if expecting to find Scarface hiding in one of the dim corners.

"He's been given a sleeping potion, so you needn't worry about being overheard." She dropped into a conspiratorial tone. "His health is very delicate. He may not survive the accident. There have been complications."

Hope and cunning briefly chased each other across his face. "Then the accident was real—or has he been given something to eat or drink that disagreed with him since he took to his bed?"

She assumed the mask of a superior smile. "Sometimes the cooking here leaves much to be desired." She sat on her bed and leaned back. "What have you brought for me?"

"I haven't yet had time to send a message to Forgren or receive one from him, but you're still looking for an advisor, aren't you? I know Forgren. I know how he thinks, what he wants, and what he might give for what he wants."

"You'd turn against the Union?"

"Didn't Scarface turn against the clan for you?"

The question still sometimes troubled her and Murtry's comparison made her doubly cautious. What was he really thinking? Still, there were ways of being sure. She raised and bent one leg so her knee thrust through the opening of the deep red robe she wore. "Are you offering me five leagues into Ghiblein?"

He licked his lips. His gaze was fixed on her knee, now gently swaying back and forth. "I think I can get Forgren to cede that much land."

"You *think?*"

He licked his lips again and rubbed his chin with the upper edge of his hand. "I can get it for you."

"Why don't you sit beside me and tell me how you propose to do this?"

He moved slowly toward the bed, his eyes feasting on her as she leaned back, supporting herself on her elbows. He unbuckled his belt and let it fall beside the bed. "It's bad manners to stand armed before an Empress."

"Were you going to stand? As for weapons, it's only bad form if it's a dagger. A sword is a different matter. But I won't have your boots touching this coverlet."

Catching the heel of one boot with the toe of the other, he lifted his foot free, did the same with the other boot, then unclasped the fastenings of his doublet. "While it might be permissible to wear a sword in the presence of a ruler, it's worse than discourteous to carry a concealed weapon." He stripped off the doublet and pulled off his tight-fitting breeches.

Towering over her, he seemed heavier than Scarface, more massive. She locked gazes with him while she reached down and untied the knot of the robe's belt and let the opening widen. "It's also improper to stand before an Empress with a naked blade. Shall we see if we can find a proper scabbard?"

~ * ~

When Murtry left, in the hour before dawn, she was satisfied with more than his loyalty. Scarface had treated her almost like a goddess. With his more direct lust, Murtry made her feel more like a woman. She stretched, cat-like, on the bed and grinned. Not all spells of binding were woven by magi.

She rescinded her order to Orhan to capture those wearing green rings. It was no longer necessary to worry about what messages they might carry when she controlled one of the sources.

~ * ~

Scarface leaned forward. It required an effort to lift his cup and move it to his mouth. He drank deeply, though the taste of the wine was flat, shoved the cup back onto the table, and used his arm, which seemed to have turned into a log, to wipe the spill from the beard he'd grown.

Perhaps he should've stayed a little longer in Cerco to celebrate but he knew time was fleeting. And the weariness that plagued him was a small thing. He might even consider it his reward for faithful service to Mordach.

Control of Donradé had been easy enough to assume, once he'd gotten the army and the hundred monks. One of the lords had challenged him and he had easily cut the man down. The "noble" was no loss; hated by his peasants and despised by his men-at-arms. Baron Jonfré was much more reliable.

Three northern lords still resisted him but the call for a Holy War had brought the rest of the lords, scenting plunder, scurrying to his black banner with its red sunburst eagle. Unfortunately the other lords of Donradé had brought with them their self-importance, their short-sightedness, and their endless petty squabbles. They'd come after spring planting, wanting to attack immediately, while he'd held them here, forcing some discipline and training on the half-wild farmers and gutter-sweepings mercenaries. With the best of his men-at-arms and the priests of Mordach, he'd spent long days turning raw meat into warriors while the nobles had stayed away because their peasants were being taught to use weapons.

Scarface had also had to learn. He was now proficient with the odd, light ax called the *doré* that was the favorite weapon of the men of Donradé. The head of the *doré* was mounted atop the haft like a thrusting weapon but curved outward into a flaring edge. It was usually thrown but could also be used for close combat.

He'd also had to learn the country and its people. The lords, for all their pretentions, were little better than robbers, armed men among farmers, jealous of their rule. Some few of them had limited ambitions but frittered away their strength on border disputes with each other. They'd resented his training their peasants to fight, just as they'd been angered by his recruiting the woodsrunners, mostly by the judicious use of conditional pardons. They'd also been distrustful of the mounted Senshenni he'd employed. Their ideas of armies and wars were of mounted charges by handsfull of household bullies and relatives.

He pressed the heels of his hands against his closed eyes and rubbed. When he found the energy, he'd stumble to his pallet. At least he now had an army three thousand strong, although his best troops—the Senshenni cavalry, the woodsrunners, the churchmen, and some of the mercenaries—amounted to no more than a fifth of that number.

He needed more archers. The woodsrunners and the Senshenni were good, and all the monks had some training with the bow, knowledge they could pass on to the farmers.

The two hundred pieces of gold and the thousand of silver he'd received from the clan were being well invested. As much as he could, he traded for Sazian coins, which he'd had shaved or plugged or, in some cases, copied in base metals and given a wash of gold or silver. These false Sazian coins had been used to double purpose—to buy arms and supplies for his army and, simultaneously, to damage the Sazians throught their trade.

He forced himself to his feet, walked loose-jointed the few paces, and collapsed onto his pallet to lie staring at the stained gray walls of his tent.

The King of Glangurra had sent no troops but was willing to join in the war against the Sazians by attacking Sazian settlements along his own coast after Scarface had struck south. This opportunism suited Scarface's own plans. Territory the Glangurrans took from the Sazians cost him and his army nothing, while it earned his allies the enmity of the Sazians and that, in turn, would make the Glangurrans more dependant upon him and Donradé.

Along with flattering words he'd also surreptitiously sent the King of Glangurra some mercenaries Jonfré trusted. If Glangurra went to war with the Sazians, the king's nephew would certainly lead the army and, in the confusion of battle, crown princes could quickly become dead bodies. The mercenaries had been sent to make that possibility a certainty.

~ * ~

Scarface's "son" arrived the next day, at midafternoon. As the "prince" rode into the camp, Scarface stared critically up at the young man. He was lean and handsome, green-eyed, black-haired, and hungry-faced, with a youth's fine moustache. He rode his horse well and, when he dismounted, he strode like a lord born. Scarface immediately saw the flaw Hadrian had mentioned—a coldness in the eyes and a curl to the lips that marked him a city-bred predator.

Scarface shammed a hug then led the boy into his tent, where they studied each other, both searching for weaknesses. It was best to establish an understanding immediately. "You know you're going to court at

Glangurrach to woo and marry the Princess Ukena. You will, by happy accident, be the next king of Glangurra. When that happens, you will well remember who your father is. You'll inherit both crowns someday, unless you really annoy me. So, you will wear the crown of Glangurra but I will hold the scepter."

The boy said nothing.

"What's your name?"

"Thienn."

"Well, Thienn, this afternoon they'll start the tattooing. You should be recoved and on your way to Glangurrach in two days. Have you any questions or doubts?"

The youth shook his head.

"I have a few doubts. I can read through your eyes, and it's not pleasant reading. You're very quick and keen, and you've probably already realized that your new-found charm can be a weapon. I'm putting you on the throne of Glangurra so I can rule there with a measure of legitimacy but, in a very short time, I'll have the power to take the place and hold it by force, if need be. If force isn't needed, we'll all be the happier.

"I can also read that you've thought of having me killed so your inheritance can be enjoyed while you're still young. The best advice I can give you is to never underestimate me and to not try to reach too soon, because if you fail to kill me on your first attempt, you won't live for a second try. And I can promise you that if that happens, you'll pray to whatever god you hold dear that you were back in your alley wrestling rats for garbage to eat."

Thienn sat on the corner of the table. "I've heard the princess is a homely wench."

Scarface sat in his chair, rested his heels on the edge of the table with his legs crossed. "Your morality, such as it is, is beyond my control. I don't demand your fidelity, only your discretion. Discretion and circumspection are two necessary qualities for a king, or a prince who wants to become one. And, upon, occasion, blunt honesty is also desirable. You have only one purpose to me. Fail that, and you're dead meat. How you succeed is your decision. I do hope you have the grace to be less transparent at the court in Glangurrach."

Thienn dropped his gaze and became a model of contrition. "I'm sorry, father." He let the curl find its way back to his lips. "Hadrian told me it was safer and wiser to play no parts with you."

"Very good." Scarface felt the stirring of a memory that was like a half-forgotten ache and leaned forward for a bottle of wine. "I'm giving you a choice. You know what you're here for. Do that, or take the horse you rode, the clothes on your back, and ten marks of gold, and you can ride away."

"Why?"

Scarface pulled the cork from the bottle and took a long drink of the sour wine, then tossed the bottle to Thienn, who caught it and drank. How to explain? He was unused to giving explanations. "I don't like keeping slaves, so you have a choice. If you go to Glangurrach wearing tattoos like these," he brushed at his scars with the tip of a finger, "then you'll be going for your own reasons. Perhaps it's to ease my conscience if ever I have to kill you."

Thienn took another drink, replaced the cork, and set the bottle on the table. "I've learned to like castles better than gutters."

"Then take your own, or ride to Glangurrach with fresh tattoos healing on your face."

"I've heard that being tattooed is painful. "One more drink first." He reached for the bottle and drained it.

Scarface swung his legs to the ground, walked to the tent-flap, and motioned for Jonfré and one of his men. "Take him," he said to the man-at-arms, with a gesture of his thumb at Thienn, "and get him marked." As soon as the mercenary and Scarface's "son" were gone he turned to Jonfré. "When you present him at court, carefully drop a few words into the right ears, words to the effect that a marriage between a princess who won't be a queen and the son of a man who'll someday be king in Donradé would be a cheap and easy way in which to build an alliance."

He strode to the table and picked up a pouch that had a pleasant weight and which jingled when he tossed and caught it. "Also, find an attractive young serving girl in the court who'll 'befriend' Thienn when he goes looking for excitement. I want to know everything he tells her or she can discover. If he finds other companionship, pay her for what she can learn."

"You don't trust him, then?"

"I trust him as I would myself," Scarface said, and laughed.

~ * ~

Two days later Thienn left for Glangurrach, and a fortnight later Jonfré returned with two important pieces of news. The first was that Princess Ukena was betrothed to Prince Thienn. The second was that the farmers in the Bromron River valley had enjoyed a rich harvest.

Scarface sent woodsrunners to scout the Sazian border defenses while he studied the maps he could find of the area. It was worse than useless to attack the Sazians in their forts. The hundred twenty good men they had in the northwestern garrison could hold a fortification by themselves against his entire army. With even minimal help from the rest of their troops, most from subject peoples, which amounted to another thousand men or so and which varied in quality from fair to poor, they could strangle his kingdom in its cradle. They'd have to be coaxed or threatened out of the safety of their fortifications and, if possible, forced to fight in places where their superior formations would be useless.

He'd made certain his archers were trained to fire in volleys and to work in teams to cover both advance and retreat. In some places, this tactic would more than make up for the Sazians' better equipment and discipline.

Scarface leaned over the best map. A strip of forest ran between the major Sazian outpost in the north and the river plains it protected, and the river and a good three days' quick-march stood between the outpost and the northeastern garrison. The northern outpost regularly dispatched patrols to follow the fringe of the Forest of Omaire that served as a border between the land claimed by the empire and Donradé. He pored over the map for almost an hour, then made his decisions.

~ * ~

An hour before dawn the army of Donradé broke camp and marched toward the Forest of Omaire, singing and clashing their weapons. By the end of the second day of march the men had settled into a grim silence, saving their energy for marching and carrying. At the end of the day Scarface ordered a halt and allowed them to build fires, eat well, and rest.

He kept his army in the forest the next day and, that night, chose sixty of the former outlaws and all two hundred Senshenni to be the first of his forces, besides the scouts he'd sent, to cross into Sazian territory.

In the darkness before dawn he left the greater part of his army to remain hidden while he rode to the border with the rest of the woodsrunners and a handful of mercenaries. After they reached the fringe of trees that marked the bounds of Donradé, they hid and waited.

The Sazian patrol, horsemen from the eastern edge of the empire, appeared at midmorning, almost dozing in their saddles. They wore brightly painted scale armor and tall, pointed helmets, and carried lances and crescent-shaped shields. He counted twenty men in the patrol, which carefully rode more than an arrow's flight from the trees.

He waited until one of them shouted and pointed to the tracks left by the men who'd crossed the day before and allowed the patrol a few moments to mill in concern, then waved a signal to his mercenaries. The mercenaries rode out of the forest at a trot, apparently unaware of the patrol. They'd ridden nearly a bow's shot from the trees before they seemed to see the easterners, then wheeled and raced back for the cover of the woods.

The patrol galloped after the fleeing mercenaries and Scarface waited until his men were almost in the forest before he gave the sign for the archers to release the first flight of arrows. Men and horses screamed and thrashed, and his mercenaries wheeled to attack. Caught in a double surprise, the patrol was cut to pieces. Only two of the easterners escaped, one of them wounded, and Scarface had to call back the mercenaries who'd started to chase them.

He didn't bother to watch his men finish the wounded or plunder the bodies. The survivors of the patrol would report they'd found tracks of a large body of men and they'd seen Donradans crossing the border. He could guess the size of his force would increase tenfold in the survivors' stories.

As soon as he'd returned to his own camp, Scarface dispatched another four hundred men, including most of the lords, under Baron Jonfré. Then he waited. He sent out more scouts and, from their reports, he could almost see the worried pacing of the Sazian commander.

The pacing would become more frantic tomorrow morning when the commander could see, from his own walls, an enormous cloud of dust beyond the woods to his east. The Sazian would have no way of knowing the dust was being raised by forty of the Senshenni, dragging blankets behind them.

The Sazian leader would then send out his own scouts and the woodsrunners would kill most of them, the few survivors being able to inform their commander only that Donradans had occupied the forest.

Next, the commander would dispatch his cavalry to go around the southern flank of the woods, where they'd be pounced upon by the

Senshenni. At that point, the pacing would falter, then cease, and orders would be shouted. The gates of the fort would swing open and the army would march. The soldiers would form up in their *seymanas*, their sixty-four man squares, and march until they'd reached the trees and the arrows.

When Scarface's scouts brought him word the army had left the fort he called his troops together and had the elder priest lead a prayer to Mordach, then sent the men to prepare for battle. He drew on chain mail that had been burnished until it shone like silver, a battle-helm, and carried a black shield with his red eagle blazon.

He and the priest led the army out of the forest and, with the screen of scouts ahead of his army and between them and the fortress, remained just out of sight of the Sazians.

His spies continued to bring in reports. The Sazians had halted by the eastern forest at sunset and pitched camp. They'd wait until the new day, to approach the trees just after first light.

Scarface halted his army and, despite grumbling from some of the lords, kept his camp quiet and dark.

At the dawn he could again almost see what was happening in the enemy camp. The lightly-armored mercenaries in the Sazian army would have to be prodded forward by the veterans, then men would die in the first flight of arrows, but the archers would then turn and run. The Sazians would dash forward into another flight of arrows then they'd take cover among the trees themselves and make a slow, cautious advance, constantly harried by arrows from bowmen who shot and ran.

As soon as the Sazians had advanced until they were out of sight among the trees, Scarface led his army into the woods after them but held his attack until they'd followed the Sazians through half the depth of the forest.

The Sazians had, by then, re-learned several important truths. It was impossible to keep a proper formation in heavy woods, their javelins and slings were almost useless but the arrows swarmed like deadly hornets and, finally, they could be attacked from both front and rear. They lost almost a quarter of their remaining men in the milling confusion of trying to defend against archers from both ahead and behind.

The Donradans forced a decision on the Sazians, then tempted them into disaster. The retreating Donradans held fast and even began a cautious advance, while the ones attacking their rear fell back.

The Sazians were unsure of what lay ahead of them but knew well the distance and the way they'd come. Still, as they retraced their steps, barely keeping their retreat from disintegrating into a rout, they were plagued by arrows from all around them. Of the twelve hundred soldiers the Sazian commander had led into the forest, less than two hundred lived to reach the fringe, where they were overwhelmed by fresh Donradan reserves.

Scarface had returned to the edge of the woods and watched the battle develop. When he saw the Sazians stumbling toward him he dismounted and drew his sword. The gesture might be a hollow one, but leading an army of barbarians required he get his blade wet.

He chose as opponent an unwounded man who wore the plate armor and carried the rectangular shield of a Sazian regular. The man saw him and approached, covering well with his large shield and pressing close to use his short stabbing sword. Scarface swung an overhand blow to the man's helmet to bring up his guard, slashed backhand to force him to keep the shield high, then swept his blade around in a low cut that took off the man's left foot. As the Sazian screamed and fell, Scarface cut again and caught him between the bottom of his helmet and his steel shoulder straps.

A Sazian militiaman was engaged with two of Scarface's farmers. Scarface sprang forward and cut the man down, then looked around and found the battle had ended.

He found a place to sit in the shade while most of his army reverted to rabble and plundered the bodies. They found the wine carried by the Sazians a greater treasure than the plundered armor or the odd bits of money or cheap jewelry. While most of his army drank or pulled on booty armor, he called the mercenaries aside and ordered them to dress in Sazian gear.

The fort still held a skeleton garrison and it'd be easier to take from the inside. He led the mercenaries in Sazian armor on a night march, leaving the rest of the army to recover, and Jonfré to follow his force as soon as he could find two hundred sober men.

The men with Scarface, in captured armor, halted just out of sight of the fortress and waited until noon the next day, when Jonfré and his men appeared behind them. Both groups moved toward the fort, the mercenaries apparently retreating from the Donradans. The garrison opened the gates to the false Sazians and, by midafternoon, the fort was in Scarface's hands.

He inventoried the booty. More weapons and armor, along with

Sazian money, amounting to eight hundred marks of silver and fifty of gold, and more wine.

The wine he carefully rationed, then buried himself in the commander's quarters with Jonfré. The Sazian leader had kept several excellent maps of Sazian territory but Scarface had to guess at garrison strengths. What letters he could find gave no figures and Scarface spoke little Sazian and read still less. Only two major Sazian garrisons remained—one in the northeast, the other at the mouth of the River Bromron.

The northeastern fort should have only a small garrison force. It stood near the base of The Spine, which was the natural border between Sazia and Donradé, protected still more from the west by the River Bromron, which divided southern Donradé. Jonfré and four hundred men should be enough to keep the place under siege and prevent the troops from attacking Scarface's main force from behind.

The fort at the mouth of the Bromron—forts, actually, because the Bromron was well over an arrow's flight wide at its mouth, and both sides of the river were fortified—protected the port city of Linistia as well as the nearby towns and villages, and so was certain to be well-manned.

~ * ~

They set out at dawn, leaving a garrison of their wounded. Jonfré and the men with him bound for the Sazian bridge over the northern Bromron, and the rest of the army following Scarface south through a series of hamlets and villages.

It was almost impossible to force his troops to act as saviors when their first impulse was to destroy anything they couldn't plunder or rape. They learned the lesson, somewhat, when he personally killed four men and had two of the nobles hanged. It was essential for his purposes that his men at least appear to be there to free their southern relatives from Sazian rule.

Still, refugees, most of them Sazian, fled his army, spreading panic, which did make it easier to keep his soldiers marching. The few small military outposts they found were either deserted or easily isolated and made impotent.

~ * ~

Six days of hard marching after the army had left the Sazian fortress and they came within sight of the walls of Linistia. Scarface had been concerned about the garrison there, which was large enough to beat his force in open battle and, if it remained behind its walls, would be invincible.

Glare and smoke were visible long before they saw the city's gray walls. He ordered a quick-march and, as they approached, it seemed his army had followed an even more rapacious horde. The fire had sunk, whether from having been fought or from having eaten everything it could consume, he was unable to guess. The gates stood open and he saw no heads at the wall. He squinted at the sun. Three hours remained before sundown.

He'd sent a hundred Senshenni with Jonfré. Now he called his other hundred to the head of the army. If he were going to ride through that gate, he wanted men with him who could shoot a bow from the back of a galloping horse.

With the priests and monks of Mordach behind the Senshenni, and the noble behind them, he led his forces toward the open gate, his eyes searching the gates and walls for any threat.

Nothing moved but the cloud of smoke, which curled and wavered like a dark plume in the breeze. He held his horse reined in to a walk but stayed ready to strike spurs and either dash forward or break to the right. He passed through the gaping gateway and saw only bodies and a furtive movement away.

Inside the walls, he halted and motioned for the Senshenni to spread out among the buildings and the wreckage of what had probably been a market. "Find me some people who can talk, and be sure they can still talk when I see them. Kill only if you have to."

While he waited he took a long drink from his wineskin, trying to cleanse his mouth of the taste and smell of the dense smoke and death.

The Senshenni soon returned with a grimy-faced urchin, a man in the rough clothing of a peasant, and an old woman. The woman and the boy spoke Gasgoran and, with them to interpret for the peasant, he learned the city's garrison had gone mad, fighting among themselves, then sacking and burning the city they were to have protected. With the boy leading, he took his men deeper into the tangle of buildings to a large, cleared area.

The men behind him stared in awe at the great walls and high buildings made of massive blocks and slabs of stone, and he knew the army had become more malleable. He drew off his helm and wheeled his horse to face them. "The Sazians have done our work for us. This is all the will of Mordach." He bowed his head long enough to hide the smirk. "This place is ours. Kill everyone who resists with weapons but spare the rest. I want anyone who can't speak Gasgoran brought to this square."

He waited another precious hour until he had enough prisoners to question. Again using the urchin and the hag as interpreters, he interrogated the Sazians. It was as he'd been told and had guessed. The Sazian army had employed mercenaries until they'd outnumbered the Sazian regulars and militia. He remembered that at the battle they'd fought, the Sazian regulars had made up only two *seymana*, the militia another three, and foreign troops and levies of varying quality had represented the other fifteen. The mercenaries here had caught the panic spread by the refugees and had rioted, battled the regulars and the militia, who'd grown soft in garrison duty, then sacked the city and fled in merchant ships.

The captured Sazians were escorted to the great fortified bridge that stood between the two halves of the city and sent across, then Scarface and his men pitched camp in the square.

In the morning he found the barracks and the quarters of the Sazian nobility. Everything of value had been stolen, burned, or smashed. Even the statues had been beheaded. He had the bodies of the dead gathered in the square near the barracks and, using a torch lit from a fire kindled by the rampaging mercenaries, burned them all in a common pyre.

About half the ballistae and catapults on the walls had escaped the fire but those were the only weapons he found, and he guessed they wouldn't have been left if the mercenaries had had time enough to steal them or destroy them.

He sent his men out again to look for the people of the city. The remaining Sazians were herded together and sent across the bridge to the other side of the river, where smoke still billowed, then he set about trying to organize the city for defense and to feed its population. This was *his* domain now, and it was his responsibility to keep plague and starvation from following war.

The priests of Mordach were given all the Sazian temples and, in return, accepted responsibility for feeding and sheltering the Gasgorans who'd begun to slink out of their hiding places. After a few inevitable clashes, his army and the locals learned how to live together within the same walls.

~ * ~

He spent the night on a pallet in a corner of a devastated Sazian temple dedicated to a goddess of wisdom. From where he lay he could see, in the moonlight, the head of the idol lying on the floor, facing him, and the marble face and blank stone eyes reminded him of Mendarian.

He wondered what she was doing now. The silence between them had grown too long. He should be returning to the north within the next eight or ten days and he'd sent a message with one of the Senshenni. He thought of the long, slender legs and the soft breasts as he'd seen them, touched them, in the dim light of her rooms, then he thought of Murtry caressing those same legs and breasts. He broke out in a sweat and twisted on that mattress as though it were a hot griddle.

Lately he'd taken little rest, driving himself until exhaustion forced him to sleep, but now he had time for regrets.

He rose and paced through the ruined temple, wanting to walk away from the belly-churning anxiety and dark thoughts but they followed him through the shadows and bars of moonlight.

How apt, he thought, that he was sipping regret in a temple of wisdom. No more wisdom now existed in his devotion to a woman with a heart of marble, just like the shattered statue, than there'd been when he'd ridden with her to Cerco or when he'd handed her a knife in Varish.

He walked until the ache in his legs sent him back to his pallet and there he stared up into the darkness. He could appreciate the irony of being a ruler of men while being ruled himself by some dark part of him that was mindless. He laughed bitterly at the incongruity of building an empire that might someday be greater than the Sazian empire in its old glory while he, the ruler, saw it only as a shadow-kingdom, only an offering to Mendarian; only a toy to please her for a time.

Closing his eyes, he tried to see her face, but the eyes he saw were green. At last he drifted into a fitful slumber.

~ * ~

Red-eyed and unrefreshed, he rode at the head of a column of men he'd chosen—the Senshenni, the nobles and their retainers, half the churchmen, and most of the peasant levies. Jonfré had taken all but twenty of the woodsrunners with him, and those twenty rode with Scarface across the bridge.

Crossing the bridge, Scarface glanced down at the waters of the

Bromron running between the bridge pillars that were like teeth in the mouth of the river.

He set an easy pace, to leave energy for greater effort when it was needed. From the smoke still rising from the port ahead he guessed the sacking might be continuing on the Sazian side of the river, but he saw no one on the bridge and he and his men entered eastern Linistia unopposed.

The mercenaries here had also fled but their destruction had been even more widespread. He and his troops marched through the shambles to a slaughter–pen. No mass pyre was needed here; he just ordered the bodies they found pitched into the fires that still raged. The few survivors they could find were gathered just outside the city walls and those that spoke Gasgoran were sent across the bridge while the Sazians were dispatched to nearby villages.

He pitched camp outside the walls, where he waited for two days for the fires to burn themselves out, then ordered the farmers with him to destroy this end of the bridge linking the two halves of Linistia.

Jonfré and his men arrived on the third day after the crossing of the Bromron, and the Donradans almost staggered under the weight of their booty. Jonfré's eye gleamed as he described how he'd take the northern fort.

The garrison, made up almost entirely of hirelings, hadn't kept the land cleared around the fort. Jonfré had observed that the wind always came from the sea during the day and had started a grass fire that reached the very walls of the fort and smoked out the men inside. The battle had been brief and he'd lost less than a hundred men. Then he'd left his wounded and fifty more of his peasants and brought the rest of his force south, looting all the way, until they'd practically had to throw away silver coins to carry gold.

Now they had only to wait for the Sazian Empire to send Vesparin and the Elites.

They faced a slight danger that Versparin would lead his army overland, across The Spine, although it'd wear down his men and cost more valuable time than passage by sea. He might also land the fleet in the north, although there were no natural bays there and the shoreline was a rock-toothed monster with a taste for wooden ships. Most likely, he'd try to land at the port of Linistia, which would've been expected to resist attack until the arrival of the Elites. Once he'd landed, his plan was probably to send his men out in two columns, pincers that would catch an enemy between iron jaws.

Scarface disliked waiting, especially if there were still treasures in the northeastern country to be carried off. He commandeered any carts or wagons and draft animals that could be found within a day's march and sent two hundred farmers and a few chosen mercenaries to gather everything of value they could carry across the northern bridge. They were to destroy nothing and kill only when forced to fight, but they were to leave as little of value behind them as possible.

The men who remained were trained to use the siege engines and practiced by sinking hulks in the harbor.

~ * ~

Two days later the Sazian fleet rode over the horizon with the morning sun. The fleeing mercenaries had burned the city's Sazian flag along with its standard. In its place Scarface had set up a rough wooden pole with a parley flag, a design of an open right hand on a field of red.

When he saw the ships, Scarface rode alone to the beach east of the city carrying another parley flag. He dismounted near the top of a dune, shoved and twisted the staff until it was secure, then stood, his hand on the pole, listening to the flapping of the cloth and the sound of waves rushing onto shore and retreating again.

The fleet halted, became an almost solid mass of ships, then one vessel broke from the formation and swept toward the beach. Well out of arrow-flight, the ship stopped and dropped anchor, its draft too deep to let it venture nearer. A boat was lowered and filled with a handful of men, one wearing gilded armor and a scarlet cloak.

Scarface paced down to the water's edge to wait for the commander of the Elites. The boat approached until its prow scraped sand and the man in gilded armor sprang over the side and waded ashore.

Vesparin was a younger man than Scarface, but with old eyes. He approached and spoke a phrase that Scarface, with his limited knowledge of Sazian, took to be, "Who are you?"

Scarface asked the same question in Gasgoran, received as an answer a shake of the head.

Vesparin repeated the question in Abarsa, Scarface responded by asking in Ghiblin.

Vesparin replied in Ghiblin, "Vesparin, General of the Elites. Who are you?"

"Daign, King of Donradé and caretaker of Sazian Linistia."

Vesparin wore a thin moustache and a carefully-trimmed beard that almost hid his sardonic smile. "I wasn't aware Donradé had a king, although I'd heard a man with black tattoos was putting together an army. As for Linistia, it's all Sazian and, from the looks of the place, your caretaking hasn't been to Sazian profit."

"The mercenaries in your own army did that. If I'd arrived here in time, I'd have hanged them for you. You and I are warriors fighting each other but I'm not your worst enemy. Your worst enemies are Sazians and Sazian hirelings."

The smile reappeared. "It's rather a surprise to be told who my enemies are by a man who led an army that invaded the empire."

Scarface grinned. "The truth is often heard in strange places and coming from strange mouths. Both sides of Linistia were ruined by your own army, and the center of your empire is sagging under the weight of two hundred vultures, most of whom would like to pick your bones. In a way, I may be your best ally, because I'm going to give you a victory—for a price."

Vesparin's lips and his pale blue eyes narrowed. "Name your victory, and its price."

"The empire has lost all its holdings here in Donradé. I'll give you back half. Everything east of the River Bromron. Considering what's been lost, regaining that much will seem like a victory to the people of Sazia. That should give you the support you need to dissolve the Council and make yourself emperor."

Vesparin laughed loudly. "I can easily take more than you're offering to give. I have two thousand Elites in those ships, and cavalry as well."

"You may be able to take it, but not easily." Scarface gestured at the fleet. "How many of those troops do you think will live to land? Most will, but not all. My army is no match for your Elites, but we'll still cost you men when we fight our way out, and if we have to fight to the death, I'll leave behind a wasteland that'll stay barren for fifty years. What I can't take or burn I'll trap or poison; and I'll do it on both sides of the river if I'm forced to.

"Further, if I can get away, as I'm sure I can, you'll have to garrison the country, an expensive waste of men to watch over a desert, for as long as I'm alive. If we can come to terms, I'll respect Sazian rule on this side of the river."

"That leaves me in the difficult position of having to gamble on your word and your future," Vesparin said. "There's another, safer gamble for me. I can take back what you've invaded and add all of Donradé to the empire. If I follow you long enough, I'll run you to ground, then your future will be something on which neither of us will have to wager."

Scarface allowed his annoyance to creep into his voice. "And gain what? Does your army eat ashes? You're here in Donradé because it's a buffer—part of which I'm willing to let you keep. But you're also here because the place brings more gold into the empire's coffers than it costs you to defend it. But if I have to fight you, I'll make certain the cost in gold and men will drain you, and what you get out of the place won't be fit for ships' ballast.

"Take Donradé if you think you can—then try to hold it while the Council screams to the people about what you've cost the empire for a hollow victory. The only real victory for you will be over the Council. It doesn't matter how much territory the empire holds, if it's being badly governed."

Vesparin stroked his beard in a manner that reminded Scarface of Hadrian, then glanced at the ships riding at anchor. "How do we seal the bargain? And how do we know we can trust one another?"

"We'll trust each other because we must, because we can both make good our threats. You have the power to take what you claim, while I have the power to destroy what you take. There's a bridge in the north to which we can bring treaties."

"I'll meet you again on the bridge in the north." Vesparin turned to go.

"Remember," Scarface said, "we confine our battles to this side of the river. The men in Donradan Linistia won't attack your ships unless you try to land at that port."

Vesparin nodded and waded back to the boat, and returned to his ship. Scarface reached the walls of the port in time to see the single ship rejoin the fleet. From late morning until early afternoon he saw the ships clustered together and he tried to guess at Vesparin's plans.

He might wait until dark to try to cut his losses from the heavy defenses but ships on open water, particularly a fleet as vast as the one outside Linistia, could still be seen, and darkness added to the danger of the landing soldiers. He might try to land at one of the beaches and avoid the port entirely, attacking it from overland, but the shoreline was shallow and this meant that only a handful of men could be landed at a time, making them vulnerable to attack from shore.

As he watched and waited, the vessels advanced into the harbor. Vesparin had decided, as Scarface would have, to take the losses from the defenses and lose no more time to attack. On this side of Linistia, only one catapult and two ballistae had survived the fires. With the creak of timbers and skeins and the crash of the arm against the padded crosspiece, the catapult launched a stone. It seemed impossible the missile could miss striking a vessel in that dense mass of ships, but a geyser of white water rose and collapsed.

The second stone loaded onto the arm had been wrapped with pitch-soaked rags. A soldier touched the cloth with a torch, then the arm swung up and forward again.

A ship shuddered and, within moments, burned and sank. Another flaming rag-bound stone arched out and struck clear water deep in the armada's formation. The fourth stone set another ship afire and, instants later, the ballistae crashed and cast their great spears at the nearest vessels. One struck a ship and the sea sprang up through the rent in the ship's hull like a conjured demon.

The Sazians called themselves "the children of the sea," and Scarface wondered how many of them were going to return to their mother's arms today.

His men worked frantically to reload the heavy weapons. The ballistae were quicker and more accurate than the catapult but Scarface knew the ships also carried ballistae and he would, before long, have to abandon the walls.

Six more ships were crippled or sunk, two of them snagged by the sunken hulks in the bay, before the Sazian ballistae had reached their effective range. One of their huge javelins struck the wall near a catapult and a man dropped, nearly decapitated by a large stone chip.

Scarface ordered the siege machines put to the torch then he led a dash down the stairs. At the quays his archers were already creating a storm of arrows, many of them flame-tipped, at the oncoming ships. Two or three of the biremes, their sails afire, fell out of the formation and another heeled with a groan of timbers as it was ripped up the belly by another sunken hulk. The crew swarmed frantically on the deck but the mortally stricken vessel went down in moments.

The missiles from the Sazian ballistae fell thick on the docks and when Scarface called for a retreat he had to shout over the screams of the wounded. His men fell back, sending a last shower of arrows at the ships, then scrambled through the dead city, trying to gain as much of a lead on the Elites as possible. Within half an hour the Sazians had landed and began to form their ranks.

Scarface left a rearguard of Senshenni to harry the Sazians while he withdrew the rest of his men, clearing the city of all but the rearguard by early evening. The Elites were slowed in the city, where their formations were largely ineffective against the fast-moving Senshenni, who sent flights of arrows into the neat lines, then were gone, and the darkness hampered the Elites even more.

The Donradans who'd left at dusk marched until late into the night, snatched a few hours of restless sleep, and resumed their retreat before first light.

~ * ~

The contest between Scarface and Vesparin became a deadly game, with living soldiers as the pawns. The Sazian cavalry, over four hundred of the easterners, rode out the city gates at dawn, followed by the Elites.

Vesparin sent his cavalry ahead to reconnoiter and pick at the Donradans but the Senshenni, with their arrows, kept the easterners at a respectful distance. On the second day the Sazian cavalry attempted a sortie against the retreating Donradans but many of them reeled back as arrows killed horses or emptied saddles, and those who pressed the attack were met, not with panic, but with planted spears and hurled *dorés*.

What was left of the Sazian cavalry, perhaps a quarter of their original number, fell back to the Sazian ranks, where they rode behind a screen of the Elites.

Vesparin had experience in other battles and he learned quickly. Scarface knew no tactic could be used against him twice.

The days and much of the nights became an unending ordeal of retreat and what little plunder could still be gleaned had to be taken on the march, within sight of the Sazian army or the dust it raised. The Donradans grumbled, even as they stole, especially the nobles, who clamored for a chance to mount a charge against the Sazian line. Scarface kept them retreating, with only enough combat to slow the pursuit and cost Vesparin token soldiers.

Vesparin had divided his army into two forces; the larger, slower left flank followed the edge of the riverbank while the quicker-moving right wing marched well to the east of the river.

Scarface used the Senshenni to keep the right wing busy defending itself while occasionally leaving a few groups of woodsrunners with bows to release a flight or two of arrows at the column marching along the river before falling back again.

Once, Scarface scratched a handful of signs into the dirt along the riverbank trail and had the faint satisfaction of seeing several marchers burn, but it didn't noticeably slow the advance of the stoic Elites, and he couldn't make enough fire-signs quickly enough to have any real effect, so the Donradans continued to rob and run.

Their greatest remaining danger was at the bridge which, after what seemed a decade of retreat, was finally in sight. The flood of Donradan troops was dammed, with only a stream of soldiers able to cross the River Bromron.

Scarface ordered his infantry to fan out in a semi-circle to protect those crossing, and the arc gradually shrank as more men got across, but not as rapidly as the Sazians advanced. Then he sent the Senshenni out in one last sortie to give the Sazians pause before ordering the Cercans across the river.

He observed again there were no problems without solutions, and the best solutions ended other problems as well. He ordered the nobles, their retainers, and most of their men-at-arms into the protective arc of footmen. Now, he told them, was the proper moment for them to mount their charge, for if they could break the Sazian right flank they could wheel and smash the main body of the Sazian army against the river.

Bright banners flying, the nobles pressed their horses through the mass of foot soldiers and formed up in a ragged line facing the right flank of the Sazians.

Scarface watched from among his infantry as the nobles urged their horses toward the wall of shields and points, first at a walk, then at a trot, then they struck spurs to their mounts and charged at a gallop.

The arrows launched by the bowmen raced upward, slowed, seemed to hover as though choosing their own targets, then fell like striking hawks into the lines of the Elites.

The battle was finished within a dozen heartbeats. Most of the arrows glanced from the large, curved shields of the Elites, the rest claiming only a handful of prey, then the Sazians in the rear ranks cast their light javelins at the charging Donradans while the front ranks planted their heavier spears. The lords of Donradé and their horses became a screaming mass of struggling forms, then the Sazian line swept forward, short stabbing swords did their work, and it was done.

The futile charge had, however, served its purpose. It'd momentarily halted the Sazian advance and the last of Scarface's men dashed across the bridge, leaving their leader alone, facing the Elites. Still out of range of javelins and sling bullets, he wheeled his mount and rode at a walk across the bridge into Donradé.

The Elites halted just beyond the reach of Donradan arrows and Scarface ordered his men to fall back a like distance from the bridge while he dismounted and stood under a parley banner. A flash of gold in the line of iron was Vesparin, riding toward the truce. He rode to the bridge, dismounted, and both leaders strode to the center of the span.

"Did you bring a treaty?" Scarface asked.

"None will be needed. Couriers have brought me word there are riots within the walls of the capitol. I doubt your barbarians need a scrap of parchment, and neither does an emperor."

Scarface inclined his head, almost a nod, almost a bow. "Good fortune, then."

Vesparin returned the gesture then waved his hand at the bridge. "Shall we have this broken up?"

Scarface placed his hand on the stone of the railing. "Maybe it's better to leave a bridge. It can be watched by both sides. And you never know when Sazians and Donradans might need each other—and a bridge."

Vesparin smiled. "I find myself wishing you'd been born Sazian."

"Strange," Scarface replied. "I was just regretting you had been."

They turned, walked back to their horses, and rode to their armies then soldiers shouldered their weapons and marched away, each army leaving a handful of men to watch the bridge

~ * ~

Scarface led his men back to the Sazian fort and gave his soldiers two days in which to rest while he tallied his losses and gains. With the garrison Jonfré had left at the fort he'd taken straggling back from the border, of the three thousand men with which he'd begun the war, twenty-four hundred remained, both at the fortress and in Donradan Linistia. Of the six hundred dead, most were contentious nobles or their followers, which actually represented a gain rather than a loss.

Jonfré and a hundred fifty men were sent south to Linistia, Duke

Jonfré to rule the conquered—no, "liberated"—territory in the name of King Daign.

While the men relaxed, one of them created a ballad about the gallantry of the last charge of the lords of Donradé, who grew in stature when they were no longer present to tarnish their own images. Scarface saw the danger of allowing antagonists to become heroes but his sense of irony let him appreciate the grim humor. The stupidity of the nobles had done more than buy time for the evacuation of the better part of his army, it'd also given him lands and titles to award to men who were, if not personally loyal to him, dependent upon him, for they'd know that what a king had given he could also take.

He chose the new lords carefully, selecting the mercenaries and even some men-at-arms who'd served most closely with the peasant levies, and even two former bandit leaders were elevated to the nobility.

Half the siege weapons of the fort were dismantled for transport, then, leaving a signal garrison of a hundred men, he led the rest of the soldiers north, his army dwindling as most of them dispersed to their homes or to their new holdings.

Now there were debts to be paid, and the three lords in the north who'd defied him would find the currency in which those debts were paid to be harder and sharper than gold coins.

He still had over five hundred men with him when he reached the holding of the southernmost rebel lord. The fortification was an earthwork moat and a wall, wooden stakes pointed outward, and a cluster of log buildings, as were most of the holdings in Donradé. He drew the warriors, now all veterans, together and raised his arm.

When he swung down his arm the first flight of arrows sent the defenders who could still run scurrying for cover and his foot soldiers dashed forward under cover of the second flight. The fight was vicious and brief, and Scarface left most of the body of the former lord dangling from the crossbar of the main gate.

One item of plunder Scarface had kept for himself was a lap-desk with compartments for parchment, ink, and quills. That afternoon he sat in the dining hall with the desk across his knees. He tickled his lips with the plume of the quill and stared with eyes as blank as the parchment before him, searching for words.

He glanced up at the monk of Mordach who'd deliver the message and whose face was still healing from the recent tattooing. The man resembled Scarface in face and body, with black hair and greenish eyes, and the fresh tattoos were black, clawed fingertips.

Leaning forward, he dipped the quill into the ink, and wrote.

Mendarian, Empress of Cerco,

You are invited to the west to discuss terms of treaty with king Daign of Donradé. As proof of his high regard, he sends you an advisor who will not disturb you with advice.

Morgan

He rolled the sheet of parchment, bound it with a strip of black cloth, and handed it to the monk. "The Senshenni will see to it you see Mendarian. Give this message to no one but her, and remember to keep your face well hidden in your cowl until Mendarian tells you that you may be seen."

He watched the man leave the hall. Devotion to a cause could be a good thing. At least it was useful to those who created the cause. He picked up the green ring he'd taken from the hand of one of the rebel lord's men.

Apparently, Forgren had decided having a kingdom in the south rather than a clutch of impotent little baronies constituted a threat to the Union. He'd consider it even more of a threat if he knew who was king. Interesting. He'd almost forgotten the Union, although Gain was within easy reach of his army—if he wanted a war with Gascolin. That was a fool's thought, and he dismissed it.

The march north to the second rebel holding was more difficult, now that the plains and the marginal woodlands were behind them, and now they struggled through heavy forest, following game trails and an occasional path. They'd been forced to move slower and clear a trail for the siege engines. Scarface remembered the Sazian roads in southern Donradé with fondness. Something like them would be needed here, particularly if the way could be made secure enough to attract merchants.

Five days were required to reach the second holding, and less than an hour to reduce it. Scarface then tossed and caught a pair of green rings.

The third fortress had squat walls of stone and the ballistae and catapults were needed. A breach was finally made in the wall and a portable bridge let his men across the moat. Scarface led the attack into the castle and by the end of the day he had a third ring.

That night he wrote another message which, with a small chest, he gave to a mercenary to deliver to a place in the north, a castle called Gain.

He leaned back in his chair, smiling. He couldn't confuse Forgren forever, but he could provide an interesting puzzle and a degree of annoyance. As he rested, his back against the rough wood, he was struck by the knowledge that his victories had been bought, not won, and the price had been his freedom. If he were going to keep the kingdom he'd built he'd pay a price in labor and desires that could probably never be fulfilled. To make a kingdom of Donradé, he'd have to establish a capitol, create a system of roads, and limit the rapacity of the lords who ruled in his name.

After shoving himself to his feet he trudged toward the stairs to the sleeping loft. He'd almost reached the stairs when he heard his name called and a man in Glangurran livery handed him a scroll bound with a ribbon and secured with a wax seal.

He returned to the hall with its torches and, keeping his features impassive, read. The message was from King Terralyn, congratulating him on his victories, announcing the brave but unfortunate death of Crown Prince Dhian, and asking his blessings on and presence at the wedding of Prince Thienn and Crown Princess Ukena, which would be held on the second day after his arrival in Glangurrach.

"How did the crown prince die?"

"He was killed on a scaling ladder, leading the attack on the Sazian port."

"Regrettable. How many men died with him?"

The man looked infinitely weary. "We lost almost two thousand men."

"Did you take the port?"

"Yes, finally."

Scarface stood and trod to a torch, where he rolled the message and fed it to the fire. "Eat and rest. I'll give you a reply in the morning." He turned and trudged up the stairs to his pallet.

It hadn't been necessary to send the mercenaries. Any leader so stupid he died on a scaling ladder was best a dead hero, more useful rotting in his grave and growing in legend than leading doomed armies or ruling. Dhian had done more for Scarface than he could ever have accomplished for Glangurra. He'd weakened the country until Terralyn or his advisors considered the sudden marriage a lesser evil, meaning they'd been hurt badly enough they'd depend upon Donradan arms and goodwill.

~ * ~

In the morning he composed a reply, offering condolences on the early death of the crown prince and announcing he'd attend the wedding with fifty of his retainers.

His ride to Glangurrach led through an uplands region of western central Donradé, and among crags and evergreen woods he found a place where a river forked. He left most of the men who'd ridden with him at the fork to bridge the branches of the river and to raise buildings on the spit of land between them.

Then, taking fifty men, he set out for Glangurrach.

~ * ~

Forgren didn't look up from the message he was writing when he heard the knock at his door. "Enter."

Valdemar stepped into the room and walked to the table. "You wanted to see me?"

Forgren signed the parchment with a flourish and finally looked up. "Yes. How would you like to perhaps finish what you started at a dinner in Varish?"

Valdemar frowned. "I don't know what—"

"I'm not certain myself. Murtry and Ivo are supposed to be watching Cerco for us and, according to them, Scarface is still recovering from an injury, although they haven't seen him in months, and that seems a suspiciously slow recovery to me."

He stood and paced. "Another problem arose at about the same time, one that bore certain suspicious marks. A man appeared in Donradé and, with the blessing of the high priest of Mordach, united most of the petty lordlings and began to train their men. According to reports, the man's about the right height, black-haired and green-eyed, and he has five black tattoos on his upper face and his banner is a red eagle on black. Does that remind you of anyone?"

Valdemar's hand went to his waist and his fingers curled as though gripping a dagger. "Now I remember what was started in Varish and, yes, I'd be happy to finish what was begun there."

Forgren returned to the table and lowered himself into his chair. "Good. I'll finish telling you what I know. It may be useful to you. The man, who calls himself Daign, raided south into the Sazian Empire and was thrown back out but apparently made a deal with Vesparin." He frowned at a thought. "He seems to have become strong enough to consolidate his rule in the north."

After considering for a moment how much he wanted to tell, he decided the past was dead and, so, harmless. "We had three men in the north of Donradé. Daign killed them and sent me their rings, which means he had to know about the Union. Unless someone has been talking too much, which is very unlikely, he's either being helped by or is, himself, a former member. I know of only one living."

Valdemar licked his lips. "A temporary situation. How much help can I count on?"

"Take all the money you need, and Harma will provide any spells you find necessary. How you do it is your concern, but I want that man dead."

Valdemar nodded and strutted from the room. Forgren watched him go, then looked down at the message he was sending Murtry. Maybe the devil had learned to be in two places at once. Or maybe it was coincidence, but he'd sooner bet wolves had taken up eating wheat. Better to try to find out if Scarface were really in Cerco, and nothing less than the sight of him would be proof.

If Scarface wasn't in Cerco it meant Mendarian couldn't be trusted. Forgren sighed. She was a woman worth the having, and it'd be a pity to find out she'd have to be dealt with. Like Vesparin. Too much Union gold had gone into Sazia to allow one man to upset all his gains there. He'd had the Council in his purse, and now everything he'd won was gone. Versparin would hold the empire together for another generation, and Vesparin had no price Forgren could pay. If he weren't so well-guarded....

One or two well-placed spies would help. There was a situation that could be dealt with in time, while an enemy within reach of Gain was a far more immediate danger. He should've seen the possibilities for Donradé and taken control of the place for himself long ago, but it seemed far more trouble than it would've been worth to him. Now it had a leader who was a threat. And an annoyance.

He picked up and read again the message he'd received from Donradé.

Forgren,

You've paid well for the ears of my northern nobles, and I
believe everyone should get what he pays for.

Daign, King of Donradé

Forgren crumpled the parchment and threw it into the fire. He'd have done the same with the chest but for the stench the ears would make when they burned.

Chapter 9

King Daign ate little and only sipped at his wine. A faint smile hid under his new beard and he saw but didn't watch and heard but did not listen to his men seated along the table. For the moment, at least, he was satisfied. His plans were an orchard and almost all the trees were bearing sweet fruit. The sensation was an uncommon one and he was afraid to disturb its delicate balance.

Duke Jonfré, sitting at his left, leaned toward him. "I hope your son's wedding was impressive."

The smile broadened. "Yes. It was my first visit to Glangurra and I didn't know the men aren't tattooed but paint their faces for important occasions."

Jonfré scratched at his beard. "I knew a mercenary from there once. He always painted his face before a fight. Maybe he considered them special occasions. I know you signed a treaty with them. What did we get out of it?"

"More influence. And while I was in the city I hired some stonemasons to build us a proper castle here. Also—you've noticed the urchins at the foot of the table?"

Jonfré nodded. "More of the royal family?"

Scarface almost choked on a sip of wine. "No. At least, not formally, but in a few years they and some of our own will be stonemasons, armorers, scribes, and our best soldiers. They've proved their toughness by surviving Glangurrach's alleys. They had nothing there and they'll be grateful for a future here." He leaned toward the high priest of Mordach, seated at his right. "Glangurra is also waiting for the words of Mordach, and his priests. I'm sure Mordach favors the greatest possible closeness between his chosen peoples."

The iron priest folded his hands. "I assume the King of Glangurra is as deeply devout as you are?"

"King Terralyn is an old man who seems to have aged even more since the tragic death of his nephew, the crown prince. Prince Thienn rules in fact if not in name." He managed to keep most of the sarcasm out of his voice.

His earlier mood had passed and now he felt an intense loneliness. Besides the urchins at the foot of the table, the hall held only men. That would change when the many widows of Donradé and Glangurra made their way to the city he was building, but he felt the need to have a certain woman with him. Or did he? His present mood was so deep that almost any closeness would be a relief.

His message to Mendarian had been gone long enough he could expect a reply, or even a visit, at any time. If she cared enough to reply. While his mood turned dark, the others at the table deserved their merriment. He made a smiling mask of his face and retreated deeper within himself, peering out only often enough to see when the others at the table walked or stumbled off to sleep.

When less than ten of the men remained—half of them slumped over the table—he stood and walked from the room

In the dimness of the corridor he saw a glint and threw up his left arm, then ground his teeth together to keep from crying out. A thrown dagger had taken him in the forearm and was stuck between the bones. He heard the sound of running footsteps.

His shout, "To me!" rang in the building and other footsteps pounded toward him. By the light of a torch at the other end of the passage he could see Jonfré turn the corner, his sword drawn.

For a moment he was able to forget the pain in his arm to recall a spell and cast it, drawing power from his scars. A gesture required by the spell brought a wince and an in-drawn breath.

Valdemar could be seen creeping down the passage, more than halfway to where Jonfré waited. "I want that one alive," Scarface shouted.

A man with a spear had also reached the far end of the passage. Jonfré snatched the weapon and, as Valdemar charged toward Scarface, reversed it and hurled it butt-first. It hit the little man in the back of the head and he sprawled face-down.

Some of the other men at the table had finally reached Scarface, and Jonfré and the guard with him dragged Valdemar, stunned and bleeding from the head, to him. He wanted to shake the knife from his arm but, with his men watching, forced himself to slowly reach for it, carefully grip the hilt, and draw it free.

The wound throbbed and burned, and he looked closely at the blade.

Besides his own fresh blood, a dried gray-brown stain marred the steel. Another spell, one Hadrian had once taught him, teased him by hiding in old memories. He recited what he could remember and felt a weak current flow from his scars to the arm, but the pain increased. Now his hand and arm felt as though they'd been thrust into a boiling cauldron. He could see his fingers beginning to swell and he could hardly move them.

He forced himself to keep his voice quiet and steady. "I need a new battle-flag. If you start the tattoo under his right arm, the head of the eagle should be under his left arm,"

A wave of dizziness rolled over him, receded, surged back, stronger, carrying nausea in its wake, and he could feel the strength seeping from his muscles. His mouth filled with the taste of bile and his vision dimmed and blurred.

No! Not death like this! He staggered a step forward and bumped against the door frame. Despite his fierce will to stand erect, his body failed him and he sagged against the frame. His hands clutched at the wood and he tried to hold himself up but his muscles rebelled, knotting and turning limp. He was aware of falling to the dirt floor, of the bile rising from his belly, and the wrenching of his bowels and bladder. He smelled vomit and excrement and, from very far away, heard voices he no longer recognized.

~ * ~

Mendarian had learned that whenever Murtry grew hesitant, or she wanted time to herself, she needed only invoke Scarface's use-name, which worked as well as any incantation. After a time, however, she sensed evasion in his manner. The land she wanted was still Ghiblin, and Murtry's excuses about Forgren's intransigence were becoming repetitious.

She knew she'd been right before, not to deal with underlings, but the error could be made right easily enough. Murtry would hardly be eager to tell Forgren that other men than Scarface had spent the night with her. As for Ivo, Murtry had convinced her the man knew nothing, that Murtry had been most ingenious in planting a number of blind trails.

She was preparing to make a final demand of Murtry, who'd been allowed to visit her less often, letting him know her chambers would be enemy territory unless other territory changed rulers, when she received the message from Scarface.

The note changed matters, complicated them. The Donradans were mere barbarians, but the Senshenni who'd brought the message claimed to have fought Sazians and King Daign, who was Scarface, had wrested land from the Sazian empire. The Senshenni were known to boast, but not to lie. Suddenly, a five league strip of battleground along her eastern border seemed a very small thing.

If Scarface had actually pounced on and eaten part of the oldest and strongest empire in the west, she might do well to join the feast. Clearly, the message was an invitation to dine, one she could find worthy of accepting. Still, too much haste was unseemly.

She installed the mock Scarface in the real one's old rooms but firmly established the borders. Still, it was useful to have him in the shadows.

While nothing actually demanded her attention in Cerco, she stalled for a time before announcing her decision to Arv and Orhan to ride to Donradé and perhaps make an alliance.

Her conversation with Murtry was brief and pointed. She'd been invited to attend the coronation of Donradé's king and to sign a treaty with that country. When she returned, she expected to find the eastern border of Cerco had grown by five leagues; otherwise she'd perhaps need to discuss the matter with Forgren himself, rather than a lackey.

The Senshenni who brought the message acted as a guide for her and the ten Dieri Orhan had chosen to ride with her, and she left the empire in the hands of Orhan and Arv.

It was with a sense of real relief she rode away from Crown Mountain. Arv's drinking, and his mood—always gray shading to black—had begun to affect her. He was slowly destroying himself. Why should it matter to her? He'd been right—he was useless. He lacked foresight, initiative, and courage. So why should it matter to her if he drank himself to death? The question had no answer she wanted to examine.

Then there was Murtry, who'd obviously been using her. That demanded retribution. Nobody used her. She would not permit it. But for now, it was enough just to be away from him, giving herself distance and time to devise a proper revenge.

Finally, there were the restrictions of rule. She had little enough governing to do, being ruler of a collection of sheepherders and farmers and half-nomads, but there was still the responsibility of being their living goddess.

She twisted in the saddle and looked back at Crown, half-expecting to see it shrouded in a heavy fog of visible doubts and frustrations, and then she looked up at the cerulean sky overhead and the road before her. This was something like the old days, when she was free, but better now because she knew where her next meal would come from. She breathed deeply of the cool, clean breeze that stroked her face and played in her hair, taking the fresh air into her chest, cleansing herself.

She could easily enough discover where Scarface had been. The Senshenni knew the location of the last of the three holdings Scarface had planned to attack and led them to a fortress with low stone walls and the rotting remains of its previous lord dangling above the gate. The new lord, a foreign mercenary, told them Scarface had gone southwest with his men at the new of the moon.

Mendarian considered the man ignorant and insolent and felt he should've been elevated to the nobility the way the holding's last lord had been—by a rope. She calculated quickly and decided Scarface had been gone from here for almost twenty-five days. As she climbed back into the saddle she decided Scarface was either unconcerned about the quality of the men to whom he entrusted holdings, or he was becoming desperate.

On her way southwest, Mendarian wondered whether it was worthwhile allying herself with a country so backward it lacked a fixed capitol. She was having to chase Scarface all over the country.

Then she laughed with sudden insight and real pleasure. The country was beautiful, its foliage already wearing bright fall colors, and the ride was pleasant. Even the weather was agreeable. Scarface would probably build a capitol to which everyone would know the way but, for now, she'd find him. She took pleasure in the ride and nothing, at the moment, drew her back to Cerco and much to make her want to stay away.

Six days out of the mercenary's holding she saw a few mounted men, most likely a patrol, and she expected them to stop her party but they only waved their cloaks and rode on.

Within an hour her group reached a narrow border of water-scrubbed rock and a deep, fast-moving river. From this clearer vantage she could see, far down-river a man standing atop a stone tower. From his attitude she guessed she and her men had already been seen, a report had already been given, and the figure watched with idle curiosity.

The Senshenni led them in the direction of the tower and soon she could see a spit of land cutting the river in two, like the prow of a boat, and the land, which could only be reached by a rude bridge, was crowned with a palisade of logs. Apparently, Scarface had chosen this place on which to build his capitol. She urged her horse into a trot.

A sense of wrongness nagged at her as she stared at the walls. Her roan clattered and boomed across the bridge, which stood between two towers and, once within the walls the pressure of premonition increased. Her guess became a certainty when she saw the mercenary with the eye-patch waiting outside the crude wooden hall. She stopped before him and, as he stepped forward to hold her stirrup, she saw an unaccustomed grimness on his face. ""What's amiss?"

"Scarface is down, maybe dying." He held the stirrup and, after she'd dismounted, tossed the reins to a boy.

Mendarian felt something like panic, a coldness in her hands and feet and a hollowness in her belly. "What happened?"

He led her into the hall. "An assassin. Scarface took a dagger in the arm and the blade had been dipped in some kind of poison." He trod to a corner and lit a torch from one blazing nearby.

As he held the fire above the figure on the pallet, Mendarian gasped, both at the sight and the smell. A sickly odor hung over the body and the sweat-soaked cloth clinging to the form. His face was puffy and livid, with rivulets of sweat flowing from pools in every depression in the skin, and when she reached out to touch him she felt the heat of his fever.

"Can I see the wound?"

Jonfré said nothing but peeled back the blanket over Scarface's left arm, which was dark and swollen and loosely wrapped with a strip of stained rag. She gently tugged the scrap free and saw the area around the puncture was crusted. "Get me some tuber roots. I want several of them, one cut in half, lengthways."

While the man jumped to follow or delegate her orders, she again stared down at Scarface, suddenly protective of him. She might avenge herself on him, but no one else had the right to cause him so much pain or make him die such an ugly straw death. They had a bond between them that, for good or bad, transcended the normal rules, but by the normal rules he should be allowed to die on his feet, his weapons bare in his hands.

She found a soft cloth and ran it across his face to remove some of the sweat and he winced and moaned at the touch. She bathed his face to bring down his fever, afraid that this, too, would cause him pain, but he was again unconscious, with breathing so shallow she was afraid it'd stopped.

When they had, at last, brought her the roots she'd ordered she drew her dagger and reopened the wound. The blood didn't flow and she overcame her revulsion and fear of causing pain to squeeze his arm. Thick, dark blood and pale yellow matter oozed out of the wound and she had to cut again to drain more of the death from his arm, then she washed the skin and bound half a root against the gashes to draw the infection and the poison out.

"I want a pallet brought here," she said. "For now, this is all I can do."

She refused dinner, knowing the thick, cloying stench in the corner would make it impossible to keep a meal down. As she lay on her own pallet beside Scarface's she tried to understand the feelings at war inside her. Why should she care what happened to him? He might die anyway, so what was the good of giving her feelings? And somewhere, from even deeper, came the dark answer that she hoped he'd die so she could throw away feelings on a corpse rather than have to give them to a living man.

The next day, early, she changed the root on his arm, the old one having turned vivid purple and yellow-green. She stroked his face, noticing it had lost some of its puffiness, then opened one of his eyelids. He moaned and his pupil shrank rapidly. She gave him water and, when he slipped away, looked at the arm. Some of its bloated appearance was gone and it seemed to be lighter, with some of the putrid color leeched out.

She'd worked on Arv and some of his friends often enough to be familiar with infected wounds, and this one seemed to be similar. If the fever didn't burn the good sense—such as it was—out of him, he should be showing signs of recovery before long.

His mending was slow, slower than a normal wound, even an infected one, and she wondered what sort of poison had been used and why it hadn't killed him. She asked Jonfré, who shrugged.

"I don't know anything about poisons. An honest warrior has nothing to do with them. As for why he didn't die, I think maybe he cast a spell."

She looked at the body on the pallet. It would've been better for him had he known the spell better, and it might've been better for him if he hadn't known it at all. These thoughts she kept to herself as she watched him regain what he'd lost, including a stirring in her own feelings.

~ * ~

For a time he didn't exist. Then, pain. A dark world of agony, black laced with red. Pain! At least he could feel that much, then the thoughts whirled away in another whirlpool of anguish.

He fought the pain and it slowly receded to become a more refined anguish. He heard voices and some sensation returned. He still burned, although he lay on a wet pallet and was covered with a damp cloth. Sweat ran from his face, pooled in his eyes and ran into his ears.

Something grated across his skin and took away the sweat. He tried to force a word out of the cauldron of his lungs, up his aching throat, out his burning mouth, but he could hear no sound he made. He gave himself up to the fire and forgot voices and light.

For an eternity he struggled and drowned in a sea of flame, wanting the peace of surrender but unable to take it.

The sounds returned. Had there been sounds before? He still struggled in the fire, pushed it away with all the power that hid in him. He heard voices and one of them, a slightly harsh one, drew him to it. He felt the pallet under him, the ache in all his bones and joints, the dampness that gave no relief. He drew a breath of fire into his chest and forced a burning coal with sharp edges upward and through his mouth, and he heard the sound of it.

Something hard and coarse was dragged across his face and touched an eyelid. More agony as the lid was lifted and a bright, searing light stabbed through his eye and into his head.

The harsh voice he wanted to hear again said, "Give him water."

Something wet but abrasive touched his lips and he felt moisture in his mouth. It seemed to turn to steam there and went away, and he went away, too.

Years later he struggled again to the surface of the lake of fire and was given more water. At last he could feel it as a liquid, as most of the fires had burned down to sullen coals. His eyes were opened but the room was dark and the touch of the cool hand was less unpleasant. He again heard the voice and he remembered then that it was Mendarian's.

He tried to say her name but his body was still a poor servant. A sound did escape, though, and he felt his head and shoulders lifted. He fought vertigo and dull-knife anguish, then something was pressed against his mouth and he swallowed a mouthful of water. It quenched the coals for an instant.

"I'm here," he heard her say.

The thought was something to cling to, and he held it tenaciously, and found another thought to tie it to. Life. Alive. He was still alive. Astonishment escorted another thought. No one had shoved another knife into him as he convulsed in his own shit and puke.

Then he had another fire kindled, and its name was shame. He'd been humiliated before his men, and a high and terrible price would be paid for that. Anger reached down to the place to which he'd fallen and lifted him up.

When he was able to open his eyes again the room was dim but light enough to see he was staring at ceiling beams and rafters. He turned his head and made out a shape beside him. When he'd rested from the exertion of turning his head he tried to say her name but heard only a hoarse mumble. He tried it again and it was nearer the proper sound, although it was still a rasp.

She stirred. "Morgan?"

A grunt was sufficient for "yes."

He felt something cool touch his cheek and knew it was her hand. He moved his head so he stared upward. She understood, and he gulped at the water she poured into his mouth. After a time she gave him another drink and he could form words. "I'm sorry."

"For what?" How could a harsh voice sound so gentle?

"For almost dying before telling you that I love you."

"I'm sorry you almost died before I told you that I love you."

Suddenly, pain was unimportant, a trifle, as another pain, one so constant he'd almost forgotten it existed until he felt the relief of it, lifted from him. He felt a tightness in his face and throat and his eyes stung. He knew he couldn't control his voice, so he simply waited. When the tide of emotion ebbed, he forced the words out. "Will the Empress of Cerco wed the King of Donradé?"

She laughed. "Why doesn't Morgan marry Mendarian?"

"He will, if she'll have him."

"Always and forever." He felt as though the rough pallet, wet with his own sweat, was a cloud. "How soon?" His own voice seemed to come from far away.

"As soon as you're able."

"Then send messages to those you choose to invite."

"And the Crown Prince and Princess of Glangurra?"

"Yes, them too."

He fell asleep, woke to daylight, sipped broth and wine, and slept again.

By the next day he could remain awake longer. He endured the agony of being moved to a fresh pallet. When Mendarian finally slept he spoke quietly with Jonfré. He'd been unconscious for four days and Mendarian had arrived on the second day.

"Does she know who it was who tried to kill me?"

Jonfré's eye gleamed and his face formed a ferocious smile. "I thought it better not to bother her with some details. She might be squeamish."

"She isn't, but I'd still prefer she not know. Tomorrow, get her out of this place. Show her around, anything, but get her away from here."

When he woke again Mendarian was gone and Jonfré was standing beside his pallet. Scarface drank a cup of water and chewed on a piece of venison, his first solid food, then he nodded to Jonfré. "Prop me up with pillows and have our guest brought in."

After suffering the rasping on his still-sensitive skin and the vertigo, he stared down at his left arm. It was still discolored, the fingers were still stiff, and the wound was going to leave an ugly scar but apparently he'd keep the hand and arm.

Valdemar was dragged into the hall, chains rattling. He seemed unsteady, hardly resisting his two guards, and Scarface remembered tattoos were painfully acquired. The little man was naked, and the skin from just below the arms to his lower abdomen was black and red, the royal pattern.

"Turn around," Scarface grated in his hoarse voice, "so I can admire the work."

Valdemar spat toward him.

"Turn him around," Scarface said to the guards. They jerked at the chains, forcing his arms up and making him turn around. He almost fell.

"Very good," Scarface said, in his hoarse whisper. "Now, take him away and take that off him—carefully. I want him to appreciate the artistry, so don't let him bleed to death. Be sure to use enough salt."

Valdemar paled and screamed curses and one of the guards knocked him to the floor.

"Take him out of here, but don't strike him again. I want him able to feel the knife-work. Oh, and do it far from here. While I'd like to be able to enjoy his dancing and singing, I'd hate to have the Lady Mendarian's sleep disturbed by his boisterous appreciation.

The guards half-dragged, half-carried Valdemar outside.

When Mendarian returned to the hall Scarface was eating more venison and sipping watered wine.

"What are you smiling about?" she asked.

"A wedding to come, and an amusing conversation."

~ * ~

The day after ordering Valdemar flayed, Scarface had his pallet taken outside. The stonemasons from Glangurra had begun to build a stone wall to replace the wooden palisades, and the ballistae had been reassembled atop stone towers. He gestured around at the rough pole buildings, the raw and scarred dirt, and the signs of construction. "This isn't a fit place for a wedding, much less a royal wedding." He pointed across the western branch of the river. "Let's have it there, among the trees."

Mendarian glanced at the forest. "Whatever you wish." She looked down at Scarface on his mattress. "I hope you don't mind that I've invited the clan. I've even asked Poker to hear our vows."

He laughed. "That won't please old Cruach, the high priest of Mordach, but we'd probably have trouble dragging him out of the church treasury to attend anyway."

He wondered which members of the clan would come. Hadrian, almost certainly, and it'd be good to have his rival here to observe Scarface's triumph. And it'd be good to see Poker again. Strange, there still remained such a feeling of closeness despite their differences. Martina? He found himself hoping she wouldn't come here. If she hadn't been a cousin....

The rest of them didn't matter. They were kin but they weren't kin he'd chosen. He'd rather have a drink and a laugh with Jonfré, or a conversation with Orhan, than to spend time with Travesty or any of the rest.

Mendarian put a hand on his shoulder. "Why so grim now?"

"Just tired." The sunlight was making him uncomfortably warm and he knew he should go back inside. "Time for me to rest again."

~ * ~

The next day he hauled himself, unaided, to a sitting position and, by clenching his teeth and fighting off the darkness creeping in from the corners of his vision, managed to struggle to his feet. His joints were all afire and he was afraid to move, afraid he'd fall, but he was standing again.

Sweat ran down his face, stung his eyes, and he was breathing as heavily as if he'd just fought a battle, but he was on his feet and, after he'd recovered most of his strength, he took a single step.

His knee almost folded and the muscles in his thighs trembled, but he made the first step. "Bring the pallet here." He was afraid to walk further. When the pallet was placed before him he sank back onto it with a sigh.

"Be wearing the clothing in which you want to be married five days from tomorrow," he told Mendarian.

~ * ~

On the following day he rose four times, the last time for almost an hour, and he walked a triple score of paces, although it drained him. He and Mendarian talked deep into the night and he rose late the next morning. Mendarian had already gone for a ride while he slept.

He had Valdemar brought to him again, along with the new battle-flag, which was mounted a hand's length from the top of a pikestaff.

As Valdemar was shoved into the room Scarface observed with satisfaction he could hardly stand erect and his face was deeply lined. His body was a mass of salt and bare, festering tissue, and an odor of sickness hung about him. Obviously, he was ill, perhaps dying. Scarface smiled at him and gestured at the flag. "I think my artisans have done a magnificent job, don't you?"

Valdemar seemed only able to breathe a bit more deeply.

"Still, it's missing something. Every worthy battle standard needs something at the top of the pole. I'm partial to skulls." He motioned to the guards. "His will do nicely. Peel me his head."

Valdemar struggled with a strength born of panic but he was thrown to the floor and held down as one of the Donradans whipped out his knife, cut an "X" across the top of his head, then drew and trimmed the skin away. His hoarse cries quickly weakened to sobbing gasps. The sounds stopped before they'd skinned him down to the upper jaw.

"You can finish your work elsewhere," Scarface said, staring at Valdemar's green ring. "Oh, and you might wipe up the blood."

He improved more quickly than before and when Thienn and Princess Ukena arrived he insisted upon holding Thienn's stirrup. Mendarian insisted, just as vehemently and with more success, that it was enough he be present for their arrival, and she and Jonfré could perform the honors.

Thienn swung down from his saddle, almost entirely ignoring Jonfré, tossed him his reins as though he were a servant, and strode toward Scarface, slapping at the tops of his high boots with his gloves, his cold eyes smiling. "Hello, father. I was distressed to learn of your—uh—illness."

Scarface stood and embraced Thienn, used it as an excuse to slip the green ring into the young man's hand. "The ones who wear these may try to deal with you," he murmured. "Just remember, they die as easily and noisily as anyone else. They take with them neither dignity nor secrets." He caught Thienn by the shoulders and held him at arm's length. "It's ever a pleasure to see you again," he said loudly.

"I'm eager to see my new mother," Thienn said.

"Mendarian, have you met my son, Thienn?"

Mendarian had been speaking with the princess. Now she whirled, eyebrows arched. "Not yet." She took Ukena's arm and they walked together to the two men.

As they waited for the women, Scarface inclined his head toward Thienn's retinue of fifty men, all well-armed. "I regret this isn't a city, like Glangurrach, and there are no beds with silken sheets. In fact, we haven't the room to shelter your honor guard within the walls. My men will give them tents, which they can set up among the trees. I'll have an equal number of my own men quartered with them so they won't feel slighted."

"You always were the proper host, father," Thienn said dryly.

Mendarian granted Thienn a nod of the head that neatly missed being a bow. "You'll forgive my lack of greeting to a future kinsman. Your father has neglected to tell me some details." She glared at Scarface. "You never, for instance, told me what a striking man your son is."

"Father's always been taciturn." Thienn bowed to Mendarian. "He also never told me how lovely his future bride is." His cold green eyes were almost laughing. "May I present my darling wife, Ukena?"

Scarface bowed to Ukena, who was staring at the three of them with the frightened eyes of a doe caught in a circle of wolves. Her plainness and her anxiety made him suddenly ill at ease. He smiled and held out his hand to her. "Yes, I've met my royal daughter-in-law." He gently pressed her hand and saw that she relaxed a bit. "Is Thienn treating you well?"

"Oh, yes."

"I'm glad. You deserve it." His glance at his "son" was a warning. "You must be tired and hungry, and it's time for the noon meal." He turned to Jonfré. "See that the Crown Prince's retainers are fed and cared for." He placed particular emphasis on the last two words.

"Have you chosen a name for your castle yet?" Thienn asked.

"I think it will be 'Hope.'"

The princess was weary from the unaccustomed riding and after an afternoon of following Thienn around as he studied the fortifications, and an evening meal more filling than delectable, she went to the corner of the sleeping loft Scarface had ordered partitioned with blankets. Soon after, Scarface had to go to his own pallet. As Mendarian sat beside him she stroked his hair.

"Sleep well. I'm going down to talk to the son you never told me you had. Don't you think it's a rather large omission to keep from the woman you're marrying?"

"He's only my son because I needed one to sit on a throne in Glangurrach. He's a tool, like a sword, nothing more."

"I'm not so sure of that. He seems to have his father's ethics—or lack of them."

His eyelids were lead and ideas faded as he reached for them. He heard his own voice say, "Watch him well. You can tell when he's lying. He moves his lips." Then warm darkness spread over him like a blanket.

~ * ~

Mendarian walked along the stone wall with Thienn, Scarface's warning still in her ears. They reached a section of wall that was still only waist-high and sat on the stones, Mendarian with her back against a taller rock. She decided to draw his fangs at once. "Your father tells me you're not truly his son, and that you'd try to lie to me."

He looked down at his hands. "I'm not his son. I don't know whose son I am." He looked up and stared into Mendarian's eyes. "I never knew either of my parents. I grew up in alleys, shivering in the winter, living under rags, and eating what I could find or steal. I've fought rats for what I ate, and sometimes I ate the rats.

"The only friend I had was a girl, a little older than I was. I thought I'd made myself forget her, but you remind me very much of her."

In the moonlight Mendarian could see tears glistening on his cheeks.

"I suppose I should be grateful to be out of the gutters and in a royal castle, but a part of me is still in those alleys. I can't search for her. I'm afraid if Scarface knew of her, he'd use her to control me. He's already played with my life to suit his own ends, and he's threatened me with death if I err in the slightest to upset his schemes. I can't imagine a man who uses people as he does hesitating to threaten, or even kill, one more urchin."

She'd wondered why Scarface had children in the camp. Now she wondered if he'd guessed Thienn's weakness and had taken as many as he could find, hoping one of them was Thienn's lover.

Thienn reached toward her as though to touch her face, then he seemed to realize what he was doing and placed his hand on hers instead. "I'm sorry. For a moment I forgot myself. Especially in this light, you really do remind me of her."

A flood of emotions washed over her as she stroked his face, brushing away the tears. "It's all right." She forced a grin. "If we're to be kin, you should think of me as your mother, not as an empress."

His voice was unsteady. "I'm sorry my lady, but it's hard to think of you as my mother." The hand over hers trembled, then rose to touch her forehead, her eyelids, her cheeks, and lingered around her lips. "It's very hard to think of you that way. The resemblance is so strong." His fingers caressed her chin, the line of her jaw, then down the side of her neck. "So like her, and I miss her so much."

He leaned toward her, then drew back. "Your pardon, lady. I almost forgot myself. I'd best go in before—" He appeared confused and embarrassed.

Mendarian laughed. "Don't be afraid. I understand your feelings. I'll do what I can to get Scarface to allow you—"

"On, no, please don't say anything to him. It could mean my life—or someone else's. I don't even hope to learn who in the court is spying on me. Please forget everything I've told you. If Scarface learns—"

Something rang false in her ears but she couldn't decide exactly what had suddenly made her cautious.

He looked away from her. "I'm sorry, my lady. He's the man you love, the man you're going to wed, and I've been telling you things about him that—that you'd rather not hear, I'm sure. I was a fool, taking a chance on your happiness just because of—"

"Because of your own unhappiness? Isn't that what you'd have said? You've a right to be happy, too." She caught his head in her hands and gently turned her face toward her. "You do have a right to be happy, too. Don't forget that. I'll do what I can, without giving you away, to have

Scarface leave you alone." She was struck by the beautiful young face, so drawn by sadness. Impulsively, she leaned forward and touched his lips with hers.

He almost drew away from her, then he responded and his tongue slipped between his lips and touched hers and his hand rested on her shoulder. Suddenly he drew back. "The resemblance is so strong, my lady—" He jumped from the wall and almost dashed back to the hall and the loft.

As Mendarian lay down beside Scarface she tried to understand what had made her suddenly suspicious of Thienn. She also mused about what sort of bedmate he'd be, with his slender, supple, hairless body. She glanced at Scarface, his features drawn, unable to hide the pain in his sleeping face.

~ * ~

When Scarface opened his eyes the next morning he found Mendarian staring at him. "You're being very harsh with the boy. First you dragged him away from the girl he loves, just to suit your own ends, then you keep him under your thumb, afraid for his life."

Scarface blinked, puzzled, then understood and laughed. "Thienn must've been most inventive. At the time of his marriage he had two mistresses, and I haven't received a report lately. As for his fear, which I suspect is mostly sham, it's the only form of instruction he'll take. Sometimes I regret forging that tool. He's too willing to cut whatever or whomever he touches."

"Then he lied to me!" Mendarian's voice was a blade, sharp-edged and threatening.

"Of course he did. Expecting the truth from him, unless it suits his purposes, is like expecting water to burn."

"And what are you going to do about it?"

"Warn you again that he's a skillful liar and continue to watch him."

~ * ~

The outriders had seen more visitors approaching and they signaled the men in the towers, so Scarface was waiting when Hadrian, Poker, Raven, and half a score of men rode into the camp late in the morning. Scarface was in his chair while Mendarian, Jonfré, and Thienn held the stirrups.

Thienn was chosen to extend the courtesy to Hadrian and it was an office he performed reluctantly. When Hadrian reached the ground he stared up at the Crown Prince with an enigmatic smile. "You've prospered, nephew."

Poker had hugged Mendarian then walked within several paces of Scarface's chair and bowed. "Our leader suggested I be courteous but distant," he said, in Sinn, then, in Gasgoran, "Greetings…King Daign."

"Good advice," Scarface replied, also in Sinn. "I doubt our clan sister needed it." Raven appeared as quiet and aloof as ever. "I welcome you all," he said, in Gasgoran.

At dinner that evening Poker raised his cup. "To Mendarian and Daign." After they'd all sipped their wine he raised one slanted eyebrow at Scarface. "Do you remember that theological argument we had?" He lapsed into Sinn. "I gather you don't completely trust the woman, brother. Is that the proper way to approach a marriage?"

Scarface dipped a finger into his wine and drew patterns on the board before him. He replied in the same language. "It's a thing I've wanted almost since I met her. I've finally won my heart's desire."

"Be careful, brother. I like your lady, and I love her as I do all Ianno's creations, but I'd trust her no more than you do. Do you really think she'll be bound by a vow, should she change her mind? She and I once spoke of snakes. I'd say a snake may be safely admired from a distance, but if you reach out and touch it you may lose a hand—or worse."

Scarface changed back to Gasgoran. "It's a fine point, one I'll keep in mind, but perhaps the gods themselves change and grow. Couldn't it be possible my service to Mordach also pleases Ianno?"

"No, Ianno is never pleased by conflict. It represents an absence of His spirit."

"But if a war is just, or serves a people—"

"War may be necessary. Rarely, it may even be just. But it's never a sign or source of good. It can never be sanctified. If you look into your heart, beneath the passions of the moment, you'll see the truth, and all the passions, all the words, are merely attempts to hide the truth deeper."

This began, as Scarface had intended, a wider argument at the table, one in which all but Hadrian, Raven, and himself became involved. Scarface saw Hadrian staring at him with a trace of amusement and wondered if the other man had been tempted to say something "theological." He was still wondering that when the evening was done and they'd all finally gone to their pallets.

As Mendarian sank onto her mattress, next to his, she said, "I was surprised by Poker's rudeness, speaking in a language foreign to most of us."

He was too tired to elaborate, or to lie elaborately. "Some concepts are foreign, too, and the ideas don't bear translation well." He waited but there was no answer from her and so he let himself down sleep's well.

~ * ~

He rose feeling renewed but hoarded his strength for the afternoon, when he and Mendarian would say their vows. He was carried to the forest, dressed all in black but for the ermine-trimmed red cloak and a simple golden circlet on his head. Mendarian wore an exquisitely decorated dress of blue and the sunburst crown of Cerco.

For the first time Scarface could remember since boyhood, Hadrian was dressed, not in his black armor and weapons but it a doublet of silvery gray, with only a single dagger at his side.

Scarface rose from his pallet, took Mendarian's arm and, together, they walked to the glade where Poker and the others waited.

When they stood before Poker, Scarface turned to Mendarian. "I take thee, Mendarian, to be my wife, my lover, my friend, my earth and sky. I will be thine always whether thou be empress of all or only the queen of my heart. My eyes are thy eyes, my breath is thy breath, my heart is thine. This I swear, for as long as earth rests under heaven's high vault." From his little finger he took a ring of silver and set it on her middle finger.

She listened to his vow with downcast eyes then awarded him a smile that almost made him giddy. "I choose thee," she leaned forward and into his ear, murmured, "Morgan." Her voice rose as she continued, "to be my husband and lover, my boon companion and guide. I will love thee and be with thee always when thou hast need of me." From her sleeve she took a ring of silver and placed it on his middle finger.

He motioned to Jonfré, who held a cushion on which lay a doré, its haft of ivory, its head polished and engraved and inlaid with gold. "As I wed thee, Mendarian, I also make thou Queen of Donradé. By this sign is the kingdom wed." He handed her the ax, then placed his arm through the crook of hers and they returned to the pallet, on which he was carried back to the great hall and the feast.

During the long dinner his weariness returned, weighing on him heavier than the royal cloak.

Mendarian noticed his increasing weakness. "Shall we go to rest?"

He grinned. "Perhaps rest is all that can be hoped for tonight, but later—"

"There'll be time for that; all our tomorrows. But you need your rest. I'll come up with you and we can talk."

Scarface started to stand but his legs failed him and he dropped back into his chair.

"Hadrian," Mendarian said, fear in her voice, "will you help –?"

"No," Scarface snarled. Hadrian was already on his feet offering an arm's assistance. Scarface ignored it. Concentrating on his scars, drawing strength from them to lend to his body, Scarface shook his head. "No, I'll walk and climb on my own." He felt the power gather and flow and he forced his legs to work, to make him stand, to carry him from the room and up the stairs, to take him to the pallet on which he sank gratefully.

Mendarian had followed him. "That was foolish pride."

"But it was *my* foolish pride," he replied.

She laughed. "You can really be rather obnoxious. Maybe that's why I find you so appealing."

He put his arm around her. "Let's look for some more reasons."

Chapter 10

Mendarian breathed deeply of the colder, thinner mountain air. The ride back to Cerco with her escort of Dieri and an equal number of Donradans, had been uneventful but pleasant. The time had come for her to return to Crown Mountain, to be ruler again. She found less pleasure in that than once she had. Perhaps she'd give up this "empire" of tribes and spend her time as Queen of Donradé, at least, as soon as the castle was built. Donradé had its own charms, rustic as most of them were.

Now she knew why Murtry had smirked and been so ready to insure Cerco's survival. If the Ghiblins attacked Cerco, it'd only be because it was on their route to somewhere weaker but more worth the taking, like Gascolin.

The coming of winter, earlier in the mountains, was announced by the first flakes falling from a silver gray sky. She watched her roan carefully pick its way over a jumble of damp, slick rocks and she looked forward to Scarface's coming when winter reached Donradé and no king but the sun would be needed.

The chill in the air, the dim half-light of an overcast afternoon, fitted her mood, making her feel alone and yearning for simple comforts, like a cup of hot mulled wine and a warm bed.

Crown Mountain loomed much closer than when she'd picked it out from the other peaks that morning, and she hoped they'd reach its light and warmth before nightfall. She and her escort rode on with a mixture of hope and grim endurance. As daylight bled from the sky they neared, and finally reached, the Wolf's Gate.

Orhan and most of the people of Crown stood waiting for her when she rode into the mountain but Arv wasn't among them. Orhan held her stirrup, and her first words were "Where's Arv?"

Orhan seemed terribly concerned that her horse's reins be folded just so. "He's ill, my lady."

"Ill? Is it serious?"

Orhan glanced around at the men with her, nodded. "The problem he had when you left became worse." He kept his face expressionless. "Some old war wounds are like that."

She felt a brief but very real surge of affection for Orhan, who was so concerned with Arv's standing he wouldn't admit to the men Arv was almost certainly in a drunken stupor.

"I'll see to him right away." As she left she saw the leader of the Donradan escort greet Orhan. The man had been one of the mercenaries Scarface had found in Cerco, and so Orhan had been both captor and captain to the man.

She didn't stop to change out of her rough traveling clothes, or even to take off her cloak, which was stifling in the warmth of Crown, but hurried to Arv's room and scratched on the door. When she heard no answer she pushed the hanging aside and stepped into the room.

The place reeked of stale wine and brandy. Her eyes had adjusted to the dimness of the dim fluorescence, and in the room's near-darkness she could barely discern vague shapes. She advanced cautiously, moving each foot slowly and close to the floor, afraid of falling over something unseen. Her foot touched something heavy that rolled in a half-circle and she reached down and, with her fingers, identified it as Arv's helmet. She could feel the rust on it.

"Arv, where are you?"

She heard a muttered answer from the shape by the wall that could be his couch and she crept toward it. Her foot touched something else, which tipped over on the carpet and she heard liquid running out of a bottle. From the fresh smell added to the background stench she guessed it was wine. She reached the couch and the odor was far worse, for the smell of stale liquor was mixed with the stink of drunk-sweat and despair. "Arv?"

Again the muffled answer that might have been, "I'm here." She lowered herself to the couch and reached out to the figure she could just perceive. He was naked and covered with sweat.

"I'm here, too," she said, and sat beside him, stroking his damp hair until he finally fell into a sleep that was partly stupor.

When she was sure he was asleep she crept out of his room and went to her apartments. They were, as she'd left them—lonely. She missed Scarface and, in this place they'd been together and apart so often, she felt a deep aloneness. In her aloneness she undressed and went, alone, to bed.

~ * ~

Morning was a stronger time. She informed Orhan she'd hold an audience with the people at noon to announce her marriage to King Daign of Donradé then she found and lit a candle and returned to Arv's room. He was still snoring when she flung open the curtain and stalked into the apartment.

Suddenly she halted. It was disturbing to see him naked. She set the candle on a table, picked up a blanket from the floor, and threw it over Arv, then sat down on the couch beside his head and shook his shoulder. "Time to be up and about! Your empress commands!"

He woke slowly, his voice and movements still clumsy with sleep and drink.

She allowed him a few moments to realize where he was and that it was she who was pummeling him awake, then she shoved him into a sitting position. "Up! I want you up, and I want you up *now!*"

Again a furry, mumbling response in which the words were indistinct but the tone was one of entreaty. Pity and a sort of desperation struggled within her, and her pity was transmuted. "I want you up. I want your armor gleaming and you bathed and in clothes that don't stink, and I want this done before noon. I'm holding court then and I want you by the dais—no, I want you and Orhan standing beside my throne. If you haven't any pride in yourself, try to show a little pride for me."

Arv stared at her, his dirty and unshaven face dazed and empty.

She suddenly realized she hadn't yet told him. "I'm going to announce that I've married King Daign of Danradé."

"Who?"

She laughed. "Scarface with a crown. Or a crown and a half. Now, I want you ready for court before noon, and you have much to do."

She left him still struggling up out of sleep and ordered the first two women she saw to take a tub and unheated water to his room. The shock of cold water would be good for his soul as well as his body, she decided, and he needed the shock of cold reality even more. Some arms practice with Orhan or one of his more capable warriors should prove to Arv his strength and reflexes were as rusty as his armor.

Why care? If he wanted to destroy himself, perhaps it was best to allow it, but she couldn't force herself to give up so easily. If he broke now, he'd break while being re-tempered, and she'd at least have tried.

She then walked to Murtry's and Ivo's rooms. They were speaking in undertones she could barely hear through the curtain and, from the sounds of the odd word she could identify, they were speaking Porcashian. She was tempted to eavesdrop but, since she could only hear a few words, she scratched at the door.

The voices stopped and footsteps moved across the room to the hanging. Murtry opened the curtain and stared coolly at her. "Welcome back. We just heard of your return this morning."

She nodded. "I presume you've heard the other news as well?"

"That you married the King of Donradé? Yes."

"Good. Then I won't need to worry about surprising you when I announce it in court at noon." She wanted to tear the superior smile off his face, hurl it at his feet, and stamp on it.

"No, no surprise. How does this affect your relations with the Union?"

"That's for the Union to decide, isn't it? Does Forgren still wish to deal with me, knowing I'm not about to climb into bed with him?"

"There are all sorts of power. I suspect he was more annoyed that you married for political reasons without consulting him than that you married someone besides him. He might now believe your interests no longer coincide with ours."

She gave him a sardonic smile to match his own. "Do the interests of people seeking power ever really coincide? I choose not to be a beggar or a servant. I don't give, I trade. If Forgren wants anything more of me, including the use of Cerco, he's going to have to make me an offer."

She turned to leave then looked back at Murtry. "If you'd like, you may come to dinner in my rooms this evening, but bring Ivo. If we're to reach a new understanding, I want all the terms clearly understood. I'll see you at court."

Another servant found Orhan for her and he scratched at her door soon after.

Mendarian sat in a chair, a smaller, lighter copy of her throne, and watched Orhan closely for any reactions to her words. "We have important matters to deal with. For a time, I'll continue the charade that the man in the rooms next to mine is Scarface." When playing Gods and Kings she'd noticed it was best to keep one piece hidden.

"At the moment, though, the most pressing difficulty I have is with Arv. I want you to work him. I want you to treat him like a recruit. You or one of your better men are to make sure he has fresh practice bruises every day."

He nodded.

"Has anything of importance happened while I was gone?"

"Two or three messages were sent by Ivo and Murtry, and they received two, one of them with a small package. Other than that, no."

"You don't like them, do you?"

"No."

"But you'd work with them if I ordered it?"

"Yes, my lady, but one need not like orders." He relaxed a bit from his rigid stance. "If you ordered it, I'd chop off either of my hands, but I wouldn't have to like the order. Pleasure has nothing to do with duty."

Another question occurred to her. "Why don't you like them?"

"Because they care nothing for the Dieri. What they do, they do only for themselves. They have no loyalties outside themselves and the other wearers of the green rings."

Her laugh was sharp and brittle. "And you think Scarface has?"

His grin was an uncertain thing, flickering across his face like torchlight. "He might not admit it, and he enjoys using power but, yes, he does care for things outside himself. Otherwise, Father Wolf would never have chosen him to be his instrument."

She was unable to keep the astonishment out of her eyes.

The uncertain smile returned and vanished again. "Yes, I knew the wolf at the Great Council was Scarface, but it was also Father Wolf. That was the part I respected enough to offer my weapons to. It was by the will of Father Wolf that it was done. It doesn't matter, in the end, why Scarface did the will of Father Wolf. Whatever his reasons, what he did ensured the survival of the Dieri and made Cerco a nation free of Ghiblein or Abaransa. Do you believe this couldn't be the will of Father Wolf? And now, to some degree, Scarface has been sanctified, doing the will of our god."

Mendarian's laugh changed to one of amusement and then pleasure. "You're very convincing. Somehow, it sounds plausible as you say it. Do you think Father Wolf approves of my marriage?"

"It has nothing to do with him. Cerco has nothing to offer Donradé but peace and trade, or they us."

"You're more astute than you appear at first glance. You'd make a worthy emperor."

"It's not a thing I want."

"But, if it were the will of Father Wolf?"

"Then His will be done, but, again, duty isn't necessarily pleasant."

She smiled. Her affection for him had just grown again. Perhaps, in a while, it'd be the will of Father Wolf that Orhan wear the crown and carry the staff. Both were becoming weights on her. "We must talk more, soon. Tomorrow, in the practice caverns."

He bowed and left.

She put on again the dress she'd worn for the wedding. The use of Forgren's gift for her wedding to Scarface and for this occasion seemed a fitting insult. She then put on the crown, took up her staff, and walked to the throne room.

On the way she passed a knot of three or four women exchanging recipes and gossip, and a dozen paces later walked past a couple of men, probably planning to provide some new gossip. It was all about reputations.

In some ways, she decided, a rustic empire or kingdom was best. In places more urbane, half a dozen people would've helped her dress and a score or more would've walked to the throne room with her, all babbling so loudly she'd be unable to think, or remember she was still human, like her subjects.

People were already gathering in the throne room, mothers hushing infants and children, the children trying to slip away to find a better place to see and be seen, the men trying to look like the dour warriors they were. For the Dieri, an audience was like a village fair capped with awe.

The people drew away from her as she walked through the crowed to the dais and sat on the throne of jade. Orhan arrived moments later and, much later, just when she'd begun to worry, Arv appeared at the door and made his way to her side. His walk betrayed a slight unsteadiness and he seemed uncomfortable with even small sounds, but his armor was polished, his clothing under it was clean, and the stubble had been cleared away with a razor.

As he trod across the dais she motioned for him to approach and leaned toward him. "Come to my room for dinner tonight. It'll be an occasion when I'll need your wit and nerve."

He nodded then grimaced at the pain the movement caused.

Arv took his place beside her and Mendarian tapped the end of her staff on the stone slab. In the stillness creeping toward silence, she looked at the faces in the crowd. Yes, both Murtry and Ivo were there, and the Donradans. She recognized dress and hair styles of several of the tribes of Cerco; Nevenii, Cortelani, Tocsan, Senshenni, Eripo, and even Tuati. It had once rankled her that other nations hadn't sent envoys but that dissatisfaction was gone now.

"I have been away from you, my people," she said, "and I have returned with a treaty of peace with Donradé, sealed by my marriage to their king. I remain your empress and you are still my first concern.

"This treaty changes nothing except that another border has become more secure. Father Wolf looks with favor upon His people—all his people," she added, directing her gaze at the men and women from the other tribes. She smiled. "It's good to be back among you."

She tapped the staff on the dais and stood. All the adults and even most of the children bowed as she walked through the crowd and through the doorway. Once out of the Great Hall she relaxed and strolled to her rooms.

Later, when life and movement had returned to the corridors she stopped a soldier and sent him for the Teller. The rest of the afternoon she spent at ease, listening to the history and legends of Cerco, taking special pleasure in the tale of the Great Council Father Wolf Himself had visited.

Arv scratched at her door in the early evening and she dismissed the Teller. Arv entered, limping, and his left arm occasionally trembled with strain from having held a shield for an unaccustomed length of time, but he seemed fitter than she'd seen him since she'd brought Scarface to Crown. She directed him to a stool with a wave of her index finger. "How's the leg?"

"It should be several interesting colors by tomorrow but nothing really the matter with it." He glanced around the room and she wondered if he were looking for a bottle. "It's been a long time since I've been here. It hasn't changed much." He focused his attention on her. "You said you needed me."

"Yes, we're going to come to terms with the Union tonight. I'll want your advice and your support."

"What about him?" He nodded toward the room next to hers.

She stood and paced to the door and scratched on the hanging. Moments later the Donradan who looked like Scarface stepped into her room. He wore a simple black robe and, in a way, his resemblance to Scarface had grown stronger. His face was largely hidden under a long, full beard now, and he'd become gaunt and pale, with dark borders around his eyes. Apparently the inactivity had poisoned him just as some concoction had poisoned Scarface.

"I want you to eat dinner with us," she said to the man, in Gasgoran, "but say nothing and answer all questions with a shrug or a grunt. In another week you can return to Donradé."

The man's relief and gratitude were obvious. "Thank you, my lady."

She gestured toward the man and said, in Ghiblin, "I think he looks enough like Scarface to eat with us. I don't expect Murtry or Ivo to have many chances to study him. Besides, within a short time the game will be over. When 'King Daign' arrives, I expect them to recognize him instantly."

"Then why play the game any longer than you must?"

"Amusement strikes me as ample reason. I want to see their smug faces when they learn they've been gulled."

She began to tell him of her trip and almost reached her arrival at Hope when Murtry and Ivo arrived. Mendarian stayed in her chair and kept Arv on his stool with a cough and a glare when he'd have risen.

Murtry carried a bottle and, with a grin, waved it at Arv. "Would you care for some Shannan plum wine?"

Arv stared hard at the bottle and ran his tongue along lips that suddenly seemed very dry but another scowl from Mendarian reinforced him. He shook his head. "No."

"And you?" Murtry turned his grin on Mendarian.

"I'm becoming careful of who I drink with. I prefer to drink only with friends, and we're yet to be sure that's what you are."

Servants entered carrying platters of food and flagons. Mendarian had directed that the flagons contain only water. The clatter of dinnerware on the table drew the false Scarface from his rooms and the five of them gathered at the table. Murtry seemed to be trying to make amends, gesturing expansively as he spoke of what the Union could accomplish.

"All very well," Mendarian snapped. "Fine tales, but what are you willing to give us here? I think Cerco should see something for being a safe haven for your gallows-fruit, and I'd like to see something more substantial than promises. Gold has an agreeable ring to it."

Murtry cocked an eyebrow. "What do you think, Arv?" His smile was an unpleasant thing.

Arv washed down a mouthful of mutton and bread with a long drink of water and turned the point of his dagger toward Murtry. "I think

Mendarian is right. After a handful of bright words and an occasional fresh supply of more words, we're received nothing from the Union."

His voice faltered and he blanched and clutched at his stomach. He clamped his teeth together; the muscles in his cheeks standing out, and waited for the spasms to pass. "You've used Cerco and given it nothing but your pres—" His eyes glazed with pain, one arm covered his belly, his other hand clutched the edge of the stone table.

Ivo shot to his feet. "Arv, are you ill?" He moved around the table until he stood by Arv's elbow then, snake-quick, he snatched up Arv's knife and, with his unusually long reach, drove the blade into the false Scarface's chest.

The Donradan had been leaning forward, staring at Arv with frightened eyes. He gaped down at the weapon that had killed him, his hand feebly trying to brush away Ivo's hand then, with a hideous gurgling; he slumped forward and fell to the floor.

Mendarian had felt first concern, then panic, at Arv's pain. When Ivo struck, she was too stunned to move.

Murtry sprang to his feet. He snatched up the knife from beside the dead man's platter and side-stepped around the table.

Arv's hand had slipped from the edge of the table and he collapsed, sprawled across the floor. With a last effort he rose to one knee and lurched to a half-kneeling position but was unable to defend himself as Murtry slashed at his throat. The last sound he made was the rattling of blood and air escaping his torn throat. Blood sprayed from his slashed artery, his eyes rolled up until only the whites could be seen, then he fell.

Ivo had moved as soon as he was sure his victim was dead and, before Mendarian could scream, had clamped a hand over her mouth.

Murtry tossed the knife he'd used to kill Arv beside the other body and, left-handed, swept Mendarian's knife well out of her reach.

She clawed at Ivo's hand, trying to push it away from her face but his arm resisted like an iron bar.

Murtry bestowed a poisonous smile on her as he poured water from a flagon over his hand, washing away the blood and letting it run into a cup. "You're going to describe to the guards how Arv and Scarface argued and killed each other." He ignored her frantic attempts to shake her head or free herself from Ivo's grip. "Oh, yes, you're going to do just as you're told. And when your husband comes here, you're going to help us take him, too." He reached into his pouch and drew out something small and dark.

"Do you recognize this? A button you lost from a blouse. With it and your name, Harma was able to cast a spell, and I need only set the trigger." He dipped the button into the cup. "Blood and water seemed appropriate. I suppose I should thank you. You've brought us three kingdoms." He held up the button. "As soon as the blood-water dries on it..." He stared intently into her eyes and she felt the strength leave her arms. "I think you can let her go now, Ivo."

She tried to open her mouth to scream but her jaw wouldn't move, and she couldn't even raise a sound in her throat.

"Excellent." Murtry might've been commenting on a horse-race on which he hadn't wagered. "Stand up."

She tried to force herself to remain seated but her legs moved her feet back under her chair, then straightened, pushed the chair away with the backs of her knees.

"Now, imperious woman," Murtry's voice seemed like an echo, "Empress of Cerco, kneel before us."

The last thing she remembered as her legs bent again was that she couldn't even cry.

~ * ~

Scarface stood atop a newly completed section of wall, surveying the scene below him. He stood, legs apart, hands on hips, knowing he presented an easy mark for anyone with a bow or spear who wished him dead, but knowing, too, that living in constant fear was the worst death.

The walls, all built with a slight outward curve and interrupted at intervals by what would become towers, were on their way to completion, and laborers dug out the foundations of the keep. He'd decided to keep alive what greens still grew in the bailey until the work was done, then the workers would use the stone chips mixed with gravel from the river to fireproof the area between buildings and walls.

Other holes, much smaller than the foundation, were scattered about the area. They were only holes now, but with windlasses over them they'd be wells. They were even more impressive than they looked; for even small wells were difficult to dig in the rocky tongue of land one which the castle grew.

A thousand things needed yet be done but a grand castle would stand here. A stray thought brushed him with its wings as it fluttered through his memory. He'd once thought that with ten years' grace he could build a stone fortress that would weather any storm. He laughed at the time now. He'd do it in less than half the time.

He made his way down, dropping from one wall to the next lower level until his final leap found him standing on the churned ground. He'd just taken two steps toward the hall when a man rode clattering across the bridge and half-sprang, half-fell from a well-lathered horse. From the man's hair and garb, he was a Senshenni.

Scarface turned and strode toward the man, who was arguing with a guard. A dozen paces away, Scarface recognized the Senshenni as one of the mercenaries who'd fought in Sazian Donradé.

The Senshenni recognized him at the same time and held out a roll of parchment. The guard reached for it, the Senshenni snatched it away from him, and another argument started in two languages. Scarface reached the pair before knives were drawn and he sent the guard back up onto the wall and unrolled the sweat-damp message.

It was written in Ghiblin and he glanced at the name at the bottom. Orhan had sent it. Scarface spoke Ghiblin well enough, but reading it was as difficult for him as writing it probably had been for Orhan.

Come soonest. False Scarface died by Arv. Died Arv. Mendarian Forgets. She is anothers. Murtry and Ivo rule her and Cerco. Come soonest but secret. Take Wolf's way. Orhan

Even with the words making little sense, the urgency of the message was obvious. He glanced around the bailey, bellowed for Anjular, waited for the echoes to stop, and called out again.

The man had been arguing with a mason—damn the penchant these Donradans had for arguing with anyone about anything—but at the second call he dashed toward Scarface, who felt a moment's regret he'd sent Jonfré south a score of days ago, but Anjular could be trusted to carry out orders.

"Get me a horse." He looked up at the sky. "And some warm traveling clothing. I want all this done before this man's horse is ready to be fed."

His Dieri, quickly learned and now in danger of being as quickly forgotten, was still sufficient to offer the messenger wine and a place to rest. When Anjular returned, Scarface clapped the Senshenni on the shoulder. "See this man is well-fed, given a place to rest, and pay him well. Give him anything he wants that isn't another person or the castle itself."

Anjular's stolid, blocky face, with its pattern of blue horseshoe-shaped patterns on forehead and chin, showed no surprise. "I've given orders about your horse and supplies. They're getting them ready now."

"Good. You're leader here until I return. Keep everyone working, and with as few discussions as possible." He turned and trotted back to the hall, to a place where he kept the scepter and a ready purse of gold and silver. The best mounts and provisions were those bought on the way.

When he emerged from the hall Anjular was waiting for him. "The horse is almost ready."

"Good. Now, send a message to Jonfré. Tell him I've had to go to Cerco but I expect to be back before too long. Whatever orders he gives you, carry them out."

He wheeled to face the stables and strode, cursing, toward the building. As he reached the door, two men brought out his horse, saddled and ready, with clothing and supplies in bulging saddle pouches. Scarface snatched the reins, sprang into the saddle, then kicked the animal into a gallop.

He was outside the walls in moments and urging the horse to even greater speed. Orhan's message and the fatal words had tied his stomach into a knot.

The horse was almost ready to drop when he approached another holding. He gnawed a piece of dried meat that chewed and tasted like old leather and washed it down with the wretched local wine while he waited for them to prepare a fresh mount. For two days he rode from one holding to the next, leaving a trail of lathered horses, then he rode out of Donradé and into the mountains, leading a pack-horse.

On the second day in the mountains he lost his pack animal when the horse slipped into a crevasse hidden by snow. Scarface doubly regretted the loss but kept to the killing pace he'd set.

An hour after losing the pack animal he encountered a party of Senshenni and traded his winded mount for a fresher and hardier animal. They gave him a share of their trail rations and offered to ride with him, but he knew now what Orhan's note had meant, and he knew he had to ride alone.

He left the tribesmen, urging the shaggy pony to the limits of its endurance and the fading light then made a cold camp. The night was bitterly cold and the heavy cloak he wore damp with snow, but he laid down beside the horse and tried to sleep.

Orhan had tried to tell him that somehow Murtry and Ivo had gained control over Mendarian and had killed Arv and the false Scarface, probably making it look as though they'd killed each other. So, he'd have to avoid Dieri patrols, which would hardly be searching diligently for him. The words of the message were unsettling; for Orhan obviously knew he'd been the wolf at the Council and was advising him to slip into Crown by the same route he'd taken then.

He shivered in the damp, frigid cloak and wondered whether it was cold or tension that kept him awake. He finally fell into an exhausted sleep, still wondering.

~ * ~

He was awake and leading the pony toward Crown before dawn. When a dim sunrise finally gave the pony enough light to see his way, Scarface clambered into the saddle and rode. When the light was strong enough, he spurred the animal for all the speed it could muster, though exhaustion and hunger began to wear on him and eat into his too-recent recovery. His left arm ached and he battled waves of dizziness, some so bad he had to slow his mount to a walk and cling to the saddle with both hands, or almost lie down on the horse.

He saw Crown Mountain before the pony faltered. Despite the cold, the beast was covered with lather and its breathing was ragged. He urged it on although he could feel it trembling with fatigue and it sometimes stumbled.

At last it went down and he threw himself from the saddle. Blood poured from its nostrils and it couldn't struggle to its feet. He stroked its neck as it labored to breathe, taking in whistling gasps and exhaling a pink foam.

"I'm sorry," he said softly. "You were a gallant animal and I had to use you badly. Every moment lost now…" He whipped out his sword and slashed the pony's throat. Better a quick death. He drank a double handful of the animal's blood, feeling some warmth and strength flow back into him, then he set out, afoot, for the mountain.

He knew he was in a desperate race with the sun and trotted, slowing to a walk only when the footing was treacherous. Once he had to halt and remain immobile for precious time as a Dieri patrol passed within a spear's cast of his trail, and broke into a lung-searing run when the way was clear.

The trail he'd taken as a wolf was hard to find, with the early snow of another season obscuring the way and, while it'd been easy to travel that way on four strong legs, it was more difficult on two unsure ones.

At last he reached the opening into Crown and, after following the twisting way into the mountain, sure his memory had lied to him and he'd be forever lost in the caverns, he found the rusting cage in which he'd kept the wolf.

Now he was sure of his way, but less certain how he'd deal with Ivo and Murtry. He wanted them dead but killing them might leave Mendarian dead, or as bad as dead, if they were controlling her. At the thought of that refined slavery, which even the most independent spirit couldn't resist, he gave himself over to a cold fury that cleared his mind and lent strength to his fatigued body.

He reviewed his scanty knowledge of poisons and potions. The Dieri used a particular root, ground up, as a sleep-draught. Some of it should be in the barracks, in the small room where the sick and wounded were tended.

To get to the barracks he'd need to use a spell he hadn't cast for a time, and he meditated to draw up all the words and gestures in their proper order, then he chanted the spell, dampened his forehead, and became less than a shadow.

The corridors were nearly empty, he noticed, as he trudged to the barracks and the infirmary. Once in the room, he quickly found the correct jar, the Dieri pictographs serving better than any writing to mark the drugs used here. He took a handful of the powdered root and made his way to Mendarian's rooms.

He slowed as he neared her rooms and halted beside the door curtain, straining to catch even the slightest sound. It was time for dinner. If they were already eating—no, after he'd waited a short time he saw servants approach, bearing platters for an evening meal for three. As the men and women filed past him he dropped the powder into the flagons, then followed the servants through the door covering.

Mendarian sat at the table, her hands resting on the stone, her eyes dull, her face expressionless. Ivo and Murtry dismissed the servers then Murtry glanced at Mendarian. "Eat and drink." With no change to her blank face, she did as she was told.

The rage burned cold in Scarface's veins. He doubted the sleep-draught would affect Mendarian but closely watched the two men. He'd already decided Ivo was dispensable. It was Murtry who gave the orders and who was the spell-caster. And it was Murtry who was the first to nod and catch himself, to try to fight the sudden weariness that slid him toward the trap of sleep. He glared at his cup and opened his mouth, then slumped forward, snoring.

Ivo regarded Murtry with the owl-eyes of a man laboring to keep those eyes open. Scarface let the spell of concealment dissipate.

Ivo gaped up at him as Scarface drew his sword and hacked down at the man. It was a pity to let such a creature die a relatively clean and easy death, but dealing with Murtry would demand all his attention.

He opened the door hanging and glanced down the corridor. Nothing moved. He caught Murtry under the arms and dragged him out into the hallway and down to the chamber he'd so long ago ordered cleared and cleaned.

Preparations cost more time than he thought they should have, but he was still able to steal a short nap before Murtry came awake.

~ * ~

When he heard the moan, Scarface straightened, sat erect on the small throne on which the emperors of Cerco had sat while watching the torments of their enemies. He smiled at Murtry, who was just realizing he was naked and bound to a wheel, secured by thongs attached to each finger, holding him so only his toes touched the floor. The strain was tremendous and, after a time, a man would die, suffocated by the expansion of his own chest and back muscles. Murtry wouldn't die that easily but the thongs around his fingers made it impossible for him to cast spells.

Murtry glared down at him. "So, hell wouldn't have you either."

Scarface chuckled. "Most flattering, but I wasn't expecting pleasantries, only answers. What did you do to Mendarian, and how can the spell be lifted?"

"If I weren't bound and I had a sword in my hand—"

"Judging by your past behavior, you still wouldn't have the guts to do anything. You've had your chances before and tossed them away because you feared to risk. Now it's my game. I suggest you answer my questions and save yourself some discomfort."

"If I tell you what you want to know, will you let me live?"

Scarface tilted his head back and his laughter echoed through the room. "Do you expect me to lie? No, no such weak comfort for you. But

I will give you my word about a thing. If you tell me how to lift the spell on Mendarian, I promise it won't take you more than twenty-four hours to die."

Murtry paled but twisted his mouth into an attempt at a grin. "You're forgetting, I have the answers you need. To get them, you'll have to make me an offer."

"I've already promised you a quicker death than you deserve, but that's enough idle conversation." He stood and strolled behind Murtry, secured manacles to the man's wrists, making certain they had enough play that they gave no relief to his fingers, then walked around to face his enemy. He carried a pair of long-handled tongs with flat ends. Slowly and deliberately he captured the first joint of Murtry's right index finger between the flat jaws of the tongs and pressed on the handles.

Murtry screamed as he felt the bone being slowly crushed.

Scarface smiled and lowered the tongs. "You see, there are still at least thirteen more bones in that hand alone that I can easily reach, and even after the hand is useless to you, it can still be a source of amusement for me. For instance, after I smash the bones, I can cause almost as much pain just by flicking your fingers with a fingertip. Now, would you like to make this less unpleasant for yourself by telling me how to free Mendarian."

Murtry clamped his teeth together, shook his head violently.

Scarface took a long time to crush the first bone of the middle finger. "Eventually, I won't have to worry about your fingers not being bound. Let's see, there are now twelve bones in that hand needing attention. I think...the little finger next and—"

Murtry took a deep breath. "In my purse you'll find a button. Cast a spell of release using Mendarian's name, then burn the button. That should suffice."

Scarface set down the tongs. "I hope you've told me the truth, because if you're lying to me you'll see next spring with at least one eye, and you'll hate every moment of it." He dug into the purse, found the button, and left Murtry to anticipate his return.

~ * ~

Mendarian still sat at the table in her room. Scarface carefully recited the spell of release, drawing enough power from his scars to lift Murtry's spell. The sensation of draining was stronger than he'd expected, and he guessed it must've been Harma who'd cast the spell. When his chanting and gesturing were done he placed the button on the table, took one of the guttering torches, and held it to the piece of horn.

The odor of burning horn, which smelled like burning hair, seemed to revive Mendarian. She swayed in her chair and blinked, then her eyes focused on him. For a long moment he watched a series of expressions, most of which he couldn't read, flicker across her features, then she stared at him through her ice-mask.

"How long was I dead?"

He replaced the flambeau in its sconce. He ached to hold her but the expression in her eyes, or rather the lack of expression, made him afraid to approach her. "Longer than you should have. At least ten days. I'm not certain. I haven't talked with Orhan yet." He looked down at the table and leaned on its edge. "I've missed you. I'm sorry I wasn't here when you needed me."

She shrugged. The lack of emotion that accompanied the movement dismissed him and his feelings as unimportant, as though she neither wanted nor needed comforting.

Had the spell of release worked, or was she still less than alive? He held out his hand to her. "Let me take you to your bed. You need rest."

Her voice was as devoid of feeling as her face. "I have some thinking to do, and I'd rather do it alone." He tried to put his arm around her but she avoided him and went to her room with her bed.

As he left the room he regretted he'd given his word to Murtry. He stalked to the barracks, where he took a long-duty candle, then returned to the torture chamber and lit the candle from a torch. He glowered at Murtry. "This'll burn for twenty-four hours. You'll go out before it does."

"Mendarian is very accomplished in bed," Murtry said. "I'm glad I had her before we cast the spell on her. She was much more lively before."

Scarface strode to the back of the room, returned with a cage holding four of the cave rats. They were hungry enough to fight among themselves.

Murtry struggled to keep his voice low and firm, almost succeeded. "She seemed to think you were an indifferent bedpartner. She told me, several times, how much better I was. According to her, everyone from Orhan to the stable boys were better lovers than you."

Scarface drew his knife and held its point near Murtry's belly. "Don't waste your short time. You're managing to annoy me, so that's a victory of sorts for you, but you can't make me so angry I'll kill you quickly."

He made a precise incision in the lower left side of Murtry's belly. When he thrust his fingers into the cut, Murtry gasped, and as he searched to find and tear loose the bottom end of the intestines, Murtry screeched and gave a quavering moan. Scarface finally held a string of guts and dangled it over the cage, driving the rats into a frenzy.

He watched as they fought over the entrails and dragged at them, eating what they could reach. Scarface resisted the temptation to moralize. What he was doing was not moral, nor just, but revenge; and he preferred ugly truth to self-deceit. When the string of gut from Murtry to the cage was drawn taut he cut it off near the body and tossed the end into the cage.

Murtry whimpered and blood ran down his chin from where he'd bitten through his lip.

Scarface drew his knife again and lengthened the cut in Murtry's belly, then drew on a pair of mailed gauntlets. He opened the top of the cage, caught the first rat to spring up, and slammed the lid down. With one hand he drew the slash open. "I'd like to make an introduction," he said, and shoved the rat into Murtry's belly.

He pulled off the gloves and sat on the throne, not quite listening to Murtry's hoarse screams as his belly throbbed and fluttered with the movements of the rat inside.

When the rat no longer moved he put on the gloves again, took out the rat's body, and replaced it with another. Murtry died before the third rat had gorged itself.

Scarface glanced at the candle, which hadn't yet burned half down, then stared at the corpse hanging from the wheel.

There seemed to have been little satisfaction derived from exacting pain from Murtry, perhaps because it made no amends, relieved no one else's pain. Worse, he felt soiled—a feeling he hadn't anticipated. His rage had been an irresistible force directing him, sustaining him, but it was spent now and he was alone, tasting the ashes of burned-out fury. He felt no regret for Murtry, who'd received only what he deserved, or less, but he knew he'd never boast of what he'd done here. Like Mendarian, and like Murtry, he'd lost something in the last few hours.

The thoughts were unpleasant ones on which to dwell, and he had the sense Mendarian needed him now. He levered himself to his feet, suddenly aware of his weariness, and limped to where the body hung. With a few slashes he cut the thongs and, when he opened the manacles, the dead thing fell to the floor. He'd have to ask Orhan to clean the room again.

Soreness in his back, legs and left arm made him hobble like an old man to Orhan's quarters. Orhan was gone but he told the lady Marikaa he'd be in his own apartments, waiting. She seemed not too surprised to see him and he wondered whether Orhan had told everyone that he'd returned.

Still, he saw few people on his way to his rooms. When he pushed open the hanging to what had been his rooms he saw that it must've been taken over by Murtry, or perhaps both Murtry and Ivo—a second bed stood against the wall opposite the doorway. Several rolls of parchment lay on the table and he decided they'd probably be interesting to read, but they could wait. With a grunt at having to lean over, he laid the scepter by the bed that had been his, pulled off his boots, took off his weapons, and sprawled across the bed.

~ * ~

The sound that woke him was that of a mailed arm slamming against stone. He tried to clear the sleep from his eyes and mind, noted the scepter and sword were within reach, then dragged himself from the bed and staggered to the door.

The grim lines in Orhan's face were deeply drawn. Scarface nodded, motioned for the other man to enter, and stumbled back to the bed and sat down. Words and feelings all seemed beyond his reach. Finally, he said, "It's good to see you again."

Orhan nodded. "And you. I hadn't expected you quite so soon."

The silence became awkward. "I left some trash for you in Mendarian's room and in the torture chamber," Scarface said. "It's not worth burying in the catacombs, and I wouldn't show contempt for the wolves by leaving it for them to find. Burn it."

"The Empress has already ordered Ivo's body burned." Orhan looked down at his hands as though surprised to see that he was rubbing them together. "Have you spoken to her yet? She almost seems to still be under the spell."

"Only briefly. I'll see her again as soon as I've recovered my wits."

Orhan leaned against the wall and looked down at the floor as though reading the pattern in the rug. "I'm sorry. I hope that…." His voice trailed away into another awkward silence, then he left.

Scarface knew he should see Mendarian, speak with her, draw out the poison in her feelings as she'd drawn out the poison in his arm with a poultice, but he also knew he desperately needed sleep, that the last few days had robbed him of his last reserves. He tried to get to his feet and his body made the decision for him. He collapsed on the bed.

~ * ~

He was visited by fetches and fears, creeping toward him in the fog of his sleep, then springing out at him, leaving him sweating and shaking. Murtry and Mendarian made love before him. He could clearly see Murtry thrusting into her and the angle of Mendarian's long legs, then they shouted and laughed at him. Murtry's face changed to that of a huge rat, and his laughter sounded like a scream.

Scarface smashed them both with stones conjured from the air but they continued to laugh and mock him. Hadrian stood at his door and stared at him with an expression Scarface had never seen on that mask-like face—utter contempt.

Poker, tears coursing down his cheeks, stood over him and intoned a prayer for the dead. Martina approached, as though to comfort him, but turned away, horrified. As she turned, her skin became fairer and her hair paled from black to blond, and he knew her eyes were now green.

He wanted a mirror to see what had caused such shock and disgust.

Mendarian, with a frost-smile, handed him a sheet of silver. He studied his reflection; saw nothing that hadn't been there before. Except his eyes. Why hadn't he noticed it earlier? His eyes were enormous and hungry. And his teeth were sharp; sharp and jagged and framed by a grin that would've wrung a shudder from Mordach's wooden statue, but the greatest horror were the eyes, those pits into the void.

Topaz regarded him with an expression that seemed infinitely sad. She wanted to ease his pain but couldn't bear to approach what he was; what he'd become; what he'd made of himself. She couldn't face that frantic, soul-devouring hunger.

~ * ~

When he woke he had to wipe tears from his face.

He rose and walked to the corridor, where he paced until he found a woman and asked that a tub and hot water be brought to his room, then he returned to the room and dug through the chest of Murtry's clothing until he found something suitable and tossed it on the bed.

He must see Mendarian and he must do it now. The bath was a delay, and after that he'd find another excuse. No more delays. He stood and walked to her room.

Mendarian sat on her wooden throne, staring at nothing or at something only she could see. His movement toward her was a cautious, tentative advance toward an enemy he couldn't fight. When he stood beside her he placed a hand on her shoulder. She shrugged it away.

He cleared his throat. "How long can you hate me for not being here?"

Her glance at him was like a physical blow. Her face was set, expressionless as stone and her eyes were wells of contempt and frigid hatred. "How long have you got?"

He tried a laugh that didn't even come close to the mark. "Less time than I'd like. Getting less all the time." He turned his back to her. "I'm sorry. That's nothing you want, but it's true." He saw the unopened bottle on the table. "May I?"

"Please yourself."

He poured the rich purple wine into a silver cup and drained it, hardly noticing the taste but grateful for the moisture it brought to his mouth and throat. "Mendarian, I love you. I'd give anything to change what happened, but I can't There's no market for past mistakes. Will you come with me and be my queen? Or I'll renounce my throne and stay here. Or we can both walk away from what ties us to past grief and go roaming."

He waited for an answer in the petrified silence and finally walked slowly from the room.

The wine had made him tipsy enough to make his movements careless but not drunk enough to numb him. He returned to his rooms, stripped, and stepped into the tub that had been brought in his absence. The smells of man-sweat and horse-sweat he scrubbed away, but the stench of death seemed to cling to him.

After he'd bathed and dressed in fresh clothing he read as many of the parchment scrolls on the table as he could. One was a direction to bribe one of the Sazian generals plotting against Vesparin. He could send that by messenger to Vesparin. Other orders seemed to be for an advisor of the Ghiblin warlord, yet others were in Abarsa. He guessed the Union was trying to end the war between Ghiblein and Abaransa and, from what he could understand, have Ghiblein attack northern Gascolin through a part of Cerco where agreements for passage had been ordered by Mendarian. He'd dispatch those letters, too. Hadrian should be able to see they were put to their best service.

For a score of days he battered himself against the wall of Mendarian's silence, hoping to scale the barricades of her loathing and, each day, he ate another helping of her contempt, until fighting on became too painful to bear. He wanted to be near her, to share what he was and what he had with her—although that seemed more curse than gift, but he knew each assault on her disdain was not only another loss but a source of more stone for the wall she was building between them. He could do nothing, reach nothing.

When the price became impossible he dressed again in the garb he'd worn on the ride from Donradé and went to her rooms. She was in her chair, listening to the Teller recite ancient legends. Scarface gestured at the man, who excused himself and hurried from the room.

"You had no reason to do that."

"Yes, I did. I need to speak with you."

"There's nothing new to be said. Everything you've got to say you've already said in a hundred different ways. It's past tiresome."

"I'm returning to Donradé. There are things I need to do there."

"Then you'd better go and do them. Have a pleasant journey." Her tone made it an open lie.

"I wish you could shed those tears," he said. "Not for me, not even for Arv, but for yourself." He reached out to touch her cheek but she shoved his hand away.

"If that's what you came to say, you've said it. You may leave."

"I do love you." He waited for a response, and left unsatisfied. The ride back to Donradé was much longer than the ride to Cerco had been.

~ * ~

The odor of burning hair reached Mendarian in her far place and brought her back. Morgan stood before her, holding a torch, and she could see Ivo's head and shoulders and a dark puddle of blood on the floor, and she almost remembered what had happened, as though she'd dreamed it.

Overwhelming powerlessness caught her, held her, seemed to try to crush her in an iron grip. Arv was dead, she'd been a slave, and there'd been no way to prevent it. Humiliation burned her like a red-hot iron, branded her with shame.

Life had no meaning; it was only a series of interlocking designs, her own and those of everyone else, and there was no one to turn to, no one who didn't have their own designs to carry out. Scarface had been too busy building his own power to protect her. He'd been gone when she needed him most. She was completely alone in a world of ravening beasts who only wanted to eat her and pick their teeth with her bones.

Rage, contempt, and self-contempt were the witches' brew she drank to build her strength anew. If there were no one she could trust, then no one could trust her, either, or did so at their own risk. If everyone around her pursued their own interests, she'd do the same, and her greatest interest was in destroying anyone who could be a threat to her.

She was dimly aware of what Scarface said, and not sure of her answers, but she understood completely she was rejecting his solicitude which was, at best, insulting because it suggested she was too weak to take care of herself and, at worst, a mask behind which he hid his motives.

Then he was gone, off building his power again, but she'd had the satisfaction of seeing him leave nursing a hundred little wounds she'd inflicted without his ever being able to strike back.

During the winter Mendarian brooded and marked her enemies. Both the Union and the clan had to be shattered. She could trust neither group because she couldn't control or manipulate them. Of the two, her resentment at the Union ran deeper, but the clan was more dangerous because its members were subtler. And hurting the clan would wound Scarface more than anything she could do to him.

It was essential for her purposes that Scarface hate her. Some weaker part of her had responded to his concern and her own best protection lay in destroying his caring, so when the time came to destroy him utterly, neither her hand nor her will would waver.

She waited until spring, when the passes were open, then sent a message to Forgren, telling him Scarface had contacted both Vesparin and the clan, and he was preparing, himself, to launch an assault on Gain from Donradé. And she asked him to visit her at Crown Mountain.

Rather to her surprise, the messenger returned with a note from Forgren advising her that he'd visit Crown and would leave for there no later than ten days after he'd sent his message.

~ * ~

Twelve days after she read his words, she held Forgren's stirrup while he dismounted. He moved stiffly, as though in discomfort, and she guessed he hadn't ridden so far from Gain in many years. She offered him the rooms adjoining hers and took dinner with him in her chambers.

She dismissed Murtry's enslavement of her as the man's own idea, for which Forgren couldn't be held responsible, and Arv's killing as a necessary minor inconvenience. She elaborated on Scarface's killings of Ivo and Murtry and mentioned again that he'd sent messages to Vesparin and the clan after reading the documents Murtry had left. And she described Scarface's plot to attack Gain sometime after spring planting in Donradé, with the clan to distract the king at Gascoyne. Obviously, Scarface had never actually left the clan. That had simply been a ruse to deceive both her and the Union.

Forgren seemed unlike himself, more silent and watchful. He spoke little and listened intently, as though memorizing everything she said. He went alone to an early bed and left for Gain shortly after dawn the next day.

It wasn't until he'd ridden out the Horse's Gate that it occurred to her that it might've been someone other than Forgren, that the leader of the Union might be as suspicious of her hospitality as she would've been of his.

Still, the seeds she'd planted would grow when the man returned to Gain, and more seeds would take root when one of the Donradans took the news to Scarface that Forgren had visited her. Her plan was subjected to an unforeseen complication when two Donradans disappeared, and her crown with at least one of them. Beside the crown's pedestal she found a note, written in Gasgoran.

Even palmers have friends. Ragne

After her first outburst of rage she puzzled over the reference to palmers, then realized he must've been a friend of the palmer she'd met on the road to Gain so long ago. She immediately sent messages to the Union, the clan, and even to Scarface, telling them to watch for a man who called himself Ragne and, if he were found, he was to be returned to Cerco dead or in chains. Even as she composed the messages, she wondered if those who were to receive them hadn't been the ones who'd paid Ragne for his work.

Chapter 11

The peddler's wagon groaned and rattled, and creaked a final complaint as it stopped beside the band of armed men. The driver grinned nervously at the soldiers, displaying the gap where his front teeth had been, and bowed toward them from his seat at the front of the wagon.

One of the soldiers loosened the rope that tied down the heavy cloth protecting the goods from dust and weather. He lifted the canvas and examined the merchandise, then studied the merchant. He saw a man of late middle age with a fringe of graying hair falling to his shoulders, pale, watery eyes, a broken nose, missing teeth, and a scanty beard paler than his hair.

"What are you doing, traveling alone?"

"I was in Gascoyne when I heard the news. It'll be a month before those fools can get a caravan together, and I decided it was worth the risk to get here first. I want to get as much Shannan wine and brandy as I can, now that it's not going to be made anymore."

The soldier laughed. "Then you made your trip for nothing, haggler. We took the orchards and vineyards without damaging them, and we captured the distillery, too. We'll be able to bottle as much as they ever did before." He laughed louder as the merchant's expression settled into deep gloom, then brightened with a craft smile.

"Ah, you know that, and now I know it, but bad news travels faster than good by three-to-one. So if I can buy up wines and brandies, I can still show a fine profit before other outlanders learn it's still being bottled."

"What have you brought to trade for it?"

"Bright, soft fabrics from Shatilla and bars of iron from Bildesh. That's the real secret of their fine blades, you know, their iron. And perfume from eastern Gascolin. You know what most women'd give to have a bottle of Gascoyne perfume, don't you?" He nudged the soldier with the tone of his voice and the glance of his eye.

"No money?"

"Would I carry money without a caravan? Do I look to be that sort of fool?"

"Fools come wearing all sorts of faces, and not all of them wearing motley." The soldier, who seemed to be the leader, drew a nugget of chalk from his pouch and marked the wagon with a circle and a wavy line, then gestured for the peddler to move on.

The trader shook the reins and tapped the donkey with a long switch, and the wagon rolled forward with the outraged shriek of axles demanding to be oiled. The donkey slowed when it reached the uphill section of the road through the pass, and its ears flicked with agitation as it followed the trail between steep banks of stone. The beast slowed even more when it left the mountains behind it and started down into the valley. The valley, to the merchant's eyes, was green, with a dark brown slash running from the mountain wall to where everything was an indistinguishable blur.

A clump of trees huddled beside the road, some of them leaning over the trail as if to look along the track, and more soldiers lounged in the shade. As he approached, most of them sprang to their feet and crowded into the road, shouting for him to halt.

The trader stopped the wagon, climbed down, and submitted to the search of himself and his wagon. One of the men took his knife and seemed to be dubious about returning it, although it was used mostly for cutting bread and cheese. At last the man tired of his game and handed the knife back. The merchant, obviously nervous, bowed to each of the four men in the road, grinning furiously. One of the soldiers marked the wagon with another pattern over the first then waved him on into the valley.

The merchant's weak eyes detected nothing wrong with the castle until he was stopped by a third patrol in the streets of the town. He glanced at the structure, then squinted. The keep was a pile of rubble from its foundation to the north wall, and the fall of the tower had caused the collapse of a section of the wall. He could also dimly perceive objects over the castle gate.

He asked the guards about them and one of the men grinned. "Follow me." They walked through the streets of High Rage, much quieter now than they'd been in the past, with an air of grim endurance rather than the bustle and enterprise that had so marked the town before.

When the merchant was almost under the wall he could finally see the objects. They were heads, mounted on pikes. One still wore a green cloth over its eyes. One's gaping mouth revealed long, sharp teeth. The hair of the women's heads waved like dark banners in the wind. The guard thrust upward with his thumb. "The previous owners. See anybody you knew?"

The peddler squinted at each head in turn, the spat between the gap in his teeth. "No. Do you know an inn in the town worth the name?"

The guard shook his head. "We're quartered in both the inns and some of the houses. You might go asking shopkeepers, if you can get any of them to come to their doors. If worse comes to worst, you can bed down with your donkey tonight at the stable." Together they walked back to where the donkey and wagon stood waiting.

Travesty's head hadn't been on the wall. It must've been he who'd activated the spell in the dungeon that had brought down the tower. Hadrian led the donkey down the street, tapping on several doors until he'd reached the one he'd intended to visit.

Zeisenis had been with their army in Doss. When he opened his door, Hadrian gestured, using the fingertalk then, after apparently reaching agreement with the baker, he led the donkey and wagon into the stable. He trudged back to the bakery, giving soldiers and the few townspeople who were outside wide berths.

When he went into the baker's shop he disappeared into it like a rabbit into its warren. Inside, he observed the ovens were cold and there was no sign Zeisenis was preparing to make bread. Zeisenis was grim and anxious, his treatment of and manner toward Hadrian resembling that of a faithful hound afraid he'd be kicked.

Once the door was closed, Hadrian gripped the man's forearm. "If the clan couldn't defend itself, it could hardly ask all its friends to die with it. Your life wouldn't have bought anyone else's." He found a bottle of wine. "Will you drink with me and tell me everything you saw and know?"

He listened closely to Zeisenis' account, asked a few questions, then leaned back and made a few guesses.

Forgren had sent his men into the valley disguised and in small groups so no alarm would be raised, then several of the groups united to overwhelm the defenders at the pass. With the mountain breached, the lord of Gain had sent in an army of mercenaries and men wearing the livery of Gascoyne, under the command of Lidhyar and men wearing green rings.

Travesty had spent the clan and the garrison in harrying attacks on the army so when Forgren's army reached the walls the defenders could only surrender. When the last of the townspeople had left the gate and the soldiers of Gain entered, Travesty had caused the collapse of the keep.

The price to the clan had been steep and bitter; the elders had been killed after the surrender and Travesty had buried himself under High Rage. Every other member of the clan at High Rage had died fighting. At least Travesty had saved the people of the town from a battle and Gain had lost as heavily as the clan, or almost as heavily. Martina had, during the brief, bitter struggle, killed Lidhyar and she and the rest of the clan and the garrison had taken over two hundred invaders along on the way to death. Now, the Union occupied the valley and allowed free entry but made it all but impossible to leave.

Hadrian stroked the skimpy beard of the face he wore. "I'd like a place to sleep for a while."

Zeisenis gestured at his pallet. "Sleep there. I'll be in the shop if you need anything."

Hadrian waited until the other man had gone before he lay down on the pallet, turned his face to the wall, and wept. There'd be time enough for revenge—there was always time enough for that—but now was a time for mourning.

It was small relief that he'd sent Vornarei and their daughters to Sin Garlef when he'd gone to Sazia to recover the crown of Cerco. While his wife and daughters were safe, he'd lost Poker and Martina and many other brothers and sisters, and he'd had to look upon their lifeless faces and deny them.

He'd already begun the revenge. Before he'd changed into the body he now wore, he'd left a corpse in the royal bedchamber in Gascoyne. Kings were responsible to and for their subjects.

He wouldn't kill here, in the valley. Travesty had sacrificed to save their own subjects a war, and he wouldn't throw away that sacrifice by inviting reprisals here.

To begin his campaign against the Union he needed first to marshal his forces. He needed to know how many of the clan were still alive and which strongholds had been attacked. He didn't know if his son, Damon, was still alive in the Empire of the Book. He'd have to find out, contact Gisli in Ianesk and Eagle in Bildesh. But all these were only plans and hopes; smoke in the wind. His first task was to escape from Valé Shanna, and for that he needed rest. He cleared his mind and gave himself to sleep.

~ * ~

He woke three hours after sunset then rose, opened his pouch, and touched the stone in a smaller bag. The change was a relief. He threw back his shoulders and stretched, grateful to have the use of his own body again. He called for Zeisenis and, when the man appeared at the doorway, picked up the bottle again and waved it at him. "One last drink together before I go."

Zeisenis sat at the table in the center of the room and touched cups with Hadrian before drinking. Hadrian gestured with his cup. "I'm going to strike you on the head on my way out of here—not hard enough to really hurt you but hard enough to look serious. The lump may save the head. I'll want you, well after I'm gone, to go running to the soldiers claiming you recognized me and I attacked you."

"No need for that."

"The only way out of this valley is to sneak out, and the merchant will, of course, have disappeared. Forgren's men aren't too stupid to guess what happened. They probably already know you're letting me stay here, so this would seem to be the only way for me to escape and let you keep your head at one end of your neck and your body at the other."

Hadrian took off his swords and secured them to his back so they wouldn't interfere with running or climbing, then again caught Zeisenis by the forearm. "The best advice I can offer you is: endure. The Union won't last forever, and they'll crawl back out of Valé Shanna sooner yet. Until then, survive." With a fluid motion he swept up a roller and struck the baker hard enough to stun him and draw blood.

"Fall," Hadrian said. "They'll expect to see dirt on your clothing. Stay on the floor half as long as it'd take you to make a loaf of bread, then run shouting for the guards as though your life depended upon it as, in a way, it does." Then he was through the door and gone.

~ * ~

Forgren learned later that Hadrian had slipped through the fields and mountains as though he had no more substance than a wisp of smoke. And for nearly twenty days, nothing was heard of him.

~ * ~

Mendarian woke, nervous, unable to guess whether she'd been roused by an unusual sound or by the sudden cessation of some accustomed noise. A shape by her bed moved. Hadrian pushed back the cowl of his cloak to show his face then held up the sunburst crown of Cerco.

"I got this back for you, but don't try to thank me. I've taken your voice for a time." He carefully placed the crown on its pedestal. "I'm trading the crown for, a little while, your voice, and am giving you a gift of memories to sweeten the bargain." He leaned nearer. She tried to move away, to avoid his stare, but she felt like a bird fascinated by the eyes of a snake.

"I'm not going to kill you. The one you've hurt most is Morgan, and so your life is his to give or take, but the gift of memory I can give you."

She saw Martina, eating a meal after a long fast. The vision was so vivid she could almost feel the other woman's hunger. That illusion faded and was replaced by a scene of Martina in her rooms, playing with a kitten, and the warmth and affection were almost palpable. Then she saw Martina's head on a pike, rotting and weather-eaten.

She was shown each of the clan who'd died at High Rage then saw their heads displayed on pikes, all but Travesty. She saw him brushing his hair back from his face with his hand, that characteristic gesture that meant he was thinking then she saw the hand, bloody and broken, protruding from a heap of rubble.

Hadrian had saved Poker for last, and Mendarian writhed on the bed as she heard again his gentle voice. Though her own eyes were closed, she saw his eyes, always so alive and gentle, vacant and glazed.

She'd have screamed at Hadrian to take the images away but he had, as he'd said, stolen her voice.

"You have your crown back. I can't return the courage you've never had, but I can make you see the deaths you've caused. Accepting responsibility is much easier when it's only words being mumbled and doesn't really touch you. That form of cowardice I'm taking from you, and the comfort that goes with it. Now sleep, but not soundly or well."

Mendarian struggled against the weights on her eyelids but lost. When she woke, early the next morning, she was still tired and irritable. She wanted to dismiss the visitation as a bad dream or an illusion. Then she glanced at the pedestal and wished she hadn't looked. The crown rested there.

~ * ~

Forgren glared at the nervous soldier who'd entered and laid two more green rings on his table. "Now who's dead?"

"Shamasko and Sarkis."

"Get out." He watched the man shuffle out the door. The soldier had obviously been relieved to be bringing in other men's rings rather than having his own laid on the table, unsure of the time he had left between the clan's vengeance and Forgren's uncertain temper, and feeling the strain of a man caught between a fire and a cliff.

Forgren cursed as he swept up the rings and held them in a clenched fist. The members of the Union were beginning to refuse to wear them except inside Gain itself, and this was creating difficulties. Now he had to tell his agents who they were supposed to meet when, before, he could keep the contacts secret, even from the men who met them. It also increased the risk of having part of his network discovered, and it left messy tracks.

He cursed again. The one member of the clan he'd most wanted dead—besides Scarface—and Hadrian hadn't been at High Rage when the place had fallen. Of all of them, he was the one most likely to hurt the Union. Forgren picked up the parchment and read it again

This is the first.

It was signed with the first sigil of "Hadrian" and marked with the winged dagger. It'd been tied to the arrow that had struck one of his men in the eye. When the rest of the party had searched the small patch of trees and brush from which the arrow had come, they'd found nothing. Of course.

From that time on, Hadrian had become a phantom riding a nightmare, leaving as his only trail a series of bodies, each with a scrap of parchment nailed to his forehead. The signs were always the same; the mark of the winged dagger.

There should be some spell that could be laid to an enemy through his handwriting, but Harma had tried to find it and failed.

It'd be easier if Hadrian were to raise an army and fight the Union in the field. Forgren was confident of his army, his tactics, and his own personal power, but it was almost impossible to defend against Hadrian working alone. To defend himself, Forgren needed take a thousand precautions, almost all of them wasted effort, none of which might cover the particular scheme developed by the assassin's devious mind.

Not only common soldiers but even his lieutenants, men he'd come to rely upon, constantly saw murderous shadows lurking at the edges of their vision. Harma was preparing to move out of Gain to a lone tower a quarter of a league from the castle. He'd ordered the land around it cleared, so an enemy couldn't approach to within well over a bow-shot without being seen.

Forgren hoped Hadrian would try to kill Harma in his tower. Harma hadn't even told Forgren of all the defenses, but he knew they were formidable. The place was to be surrounded by men personally loyal to Harma, and all the men would always work in groups of three. Only three men, all of them close to Harma, would be permitted into the base of the tower. They'd prepare his meals and taste each meal they carried in, and they'd deliver the food by means of an ingenious pulley-system Harma had devised.

This would be needed, for Harma planned to have the only stairs leading to the tower sealed after he'd entered the place. Anyone trying to scale the tower would be seen by the guards and, even if they were invisible, Forgren was sure the wall, the top of the tower, and the pulley cage would be protected by alarms and spells to kill an intruder coming in any form.

He chuckled. That meant there'd be dead pigeons knee-deep all around the place, which would probably mean dead hawks and kites, too.

If Harma were making himself safe from magic and assassination, he was also moving himself away from the armed protection when Scarface attacked. *If* he attacked. Why hadn't he struck by now? Open war was preferable to uncertainty.

The possibility that Mendarian had begun this struggle for reasons of her own had haunted him. He should've scouted more, but if Scarface had planned an invasion, any delay could've been fatal. Now, with the king dead in Gascoyne and no clear claimant to the throne, an invasion from Donradé was almost inevitable. He couldn't believe that with Scarface's opportunism and appetite for power, the man wouldn't take advantage of an empty throne and a possible civil war.

Perhaps the appearance the Union controlled Gascolin was sufficient to keep him at bay, although he'd never before been afraid to walk boldly where he wasn't wanted.

Forgren considered leaving Gain. High Rage was more defensible, given a measure of ruthlessness, but the clan had left the place a ruins. Damn them!

~ * ~

Hadrian watched them prepare their camp for the evening, deriving a sardonic satisfaction from the precautions they took. They had no reason to suspect he'd been stalking them and still they were afraid. He accepted it as a compliment. He observed carefully as they staked out the black thread with the bells, and he chose his way through that defense while it was still light. After he'd noted where the men had chosen to lie down and where the guards would stand, he slid deeper back into the knee-high grass.

In denser cover he waited and remembered. The Shield of the Saint in the Empire of the Book had withstood an attack and Damon had killed Runa, although he'd been wounded himself. The attack had cost the Union far more than they could've achieved, even had it succeeded. It'd almost precipitated a holy war and had resulted in the outlawing of anyone found wearing a green ring. Not all the followers of Ianno were as pacific as Poker had been, and Poker had been a favorite of The Voice of the Faith.

Gisli had reported the Union hadn't attacked Northhome in Ianesk and Hadrian suspected the stronghold was one Forgren hadn't learned about. In Bildesh, Eagle had taken heavy losses but had avenged his brothers, Hawk and Wolf, and still held Eyrie. He was sure help from Gisli would be enough to break the siege and the besiegers. In the east, the clan had no strongholds in Porcash, where the Union had been strong—had been—he'd noticed Forgren was having to draw more men from there—and the Union had few, if any, agents in Sin Garlef.

Perhaps after he'd killed a few more Unionists he'd contact Morgan. He wondered if Morgan even knew the Union had attacked the clan. It was common knowledge here in the north but gossip traveled slowly, and he knew of no one else in the clan who might've tried to send him a message.

He couldn't envy Morgan, who'd be torn between the clan and his woman. Despite his impatience and even his disavowal, he was still one of the clan, and some of the deaths would cut him deeply.

Hadrian lay on his back and watched the sky darken and become more vivid. He was no longer thinking, simply existing, like the grass around him, and waiting for the night to be his cloak. When it was dark enough that each star was a brilliant point of light, he crept toward the camp.

He halted a horse's length from a man with a bow. The starlight was enough to let him clearly see all the sentries. Alert to any traps that might've been set after he'd crept away, he slipped into the camp. The man he'd chosen was a reinforcement from Porcash and apparently the leader of this group. He reached his quarry where he lay and drove his poniard into the base of the man's skull, then waited for any sound that would tell him the guards had heard the death; heard none.

He slipped a nail out of his pouch, along with a scrap of parchment, and drove the mail into the man's forehead with a stiffened palm. He waited. No one appeared to have seen the movement or heard the faint noise.

On his way out of the camp he heard one of the sentries talking. Whether from vanity or just the need for company, the guard told the next nearest sentry he'd been among those chosen to guard Harma in his tower.

Hadrian listened closely to the little information the man could or chose to give then continued out of the camp. By dawn he was in a fox's den, carefully cleaning the blood from his dagger.

It'd be absurd to go after Harma who, by withdrawing to hide, was effectively dead to the Union already. The tower would have all the usual traps, wards, and spells of protection in addition to anything special Harma could devise, and Harma was probably the most accomplished magus Hadrian had met.

That reason alone was enough for the assassination: to kill the most powerful man in the Union, and in the most impregnable place. If he could leave the mark of the winged dagger nailed to Harma's head and escape, he'd turn the Union's fear to panic and despair.

He considered places impossible to attack then went to sleep; letting that part of his mind that never slept deal with the question.

~ * ~

Winter had been long and tasteless, as flat as stale beer. The company of his men had become something to endure rather than enjoy. Women had begun to arrive at Hope, giving new meaning to the name, but Scarface remained solitary, becoming more taciturn, grinning only when he needed a social lie. His only sources of relief were the evenings he spent with the children from the alleys of Glangurrach. If he'd saved them from hardship, they were repaying him with company that saved him from another sort of hunger—the need to trust and be trusted.

Still, the melancholy was too deep to be completely dispelled and some evenings he sat motionless in his chair, staring at the fire as though looking for answers in the shapes of the flames.

During the days, he had little to do but stay warm. He did practice with his weapons and studied and re-remembered the few spells he knew. The high priest of Mordach had come to see the beginning of the capitol and the temple of Mordach being raised by the monks and priests, although work on that, too, had been halted by the weather.

Jonfré had pronounced the northern winters too inhospitable and had gone back to his city of Linistia.

All the other men of Hope were too limited, trapped in reliving past victories or pinning themselves with their hopes on some limited future goal. Fortunately, the place was too bucolic to produce fawning courtiers.

And so Scarface had sunk deeper into his mood. Loneliness had grown from a persistent and accustomed ache to a ravenous hunger. He'd give a holding to sit with Travesty and listen to the other's advice, even as he planned how to disregard it. He'd give all southern Donradé to talk again with Poker or laugh again with Martina.

His head snapped up at the sound of a man stamping his boots and asking for King Daign. Suddenly nervous, he stood and strode to the vestibule. The messenger looked up as he approached and, from the studied passivity of the Dieri's face, he didn't want to read the message, but he must. The wax bore the imperial seal of Cerco. He broke the seal and stared at the lines of writing, then stepped closer to the fireplace, the easier to read the bad news. He recognized Mendarian's handwriting.

Scarface,

You could no more protect your family from me than you could protect me from the Union. If you are fool enough to return to Crown you do so at your peril. You've been replaced. Your advice was as insipid as your lovemaking.

Mendarian

Shock and outrage tore at him as wind tears the sails of a ship. The final taunts stung, but his mind finally deciphered the first part of the message. He felt as though he were made of ice, that the words on the parchment had done to him what the winter could not. His face became a mask of cold iron. He crumpled the note, tossed it into the fire, and planted his fists on his hips to hide the shaking of his hands.

He desperately wanted to scream curses, to give voice to his hurt and rage, to draw his sword and destroy everything within reach. Instead, a colder part of his mind, a part that forgot nothing, especially consequences, formed the words he spoke. He stared at Anjular. "Get me two men for messengers. Tell them I want them ready to leave immediately."

Anjular jumped to his feet and sped from the hall.

While Anjular was gone Scarface considered the message he'd send. He'd already fought and beaten his first impulse, to lead an army against Crown Mountain and turn it into a valley. He'd once given his word he'd never do that.

A second desire was to lay waste to Gain, but the approaches to the place were well-watched and it was bootless to attack an enemy who'd never stand and fight if they saw a chance of losing a battle. Riding alone to Gain wouldn't draw them outside their walls, either. Forgren and his hirelings would only laugh and bury him under an avalanche of mercenaries. And that'd leave Mendarian to gloat over his corpse.

He remembered having heard a voice, weeks ago, a voice that sounded like Martina's, calling out his true name. He knew, in that moment, the voice had indeed been Martina's and he'd heard her die.

He collapsed on his chair, his face still immobile, his body almost shattering itself with suppressed grief and rage.

When the messengers trod into the hall he stared balefully at them. They looked at the floor. "You," he pointed at the shorter, slighter man. "I want you to go to Duke Jonfré. And you," he nodded at the other messenger, "are to go to Prince Thienn. Tell them I want them here as quickly as horses can bring them. And I want you to go to them just as quickly."

Both men rushed from the hall and some unreachable part of him was amused by their fear.

Glancing around the room, Scarface was surprised to see the Dieri messenger still standing, as though waiting for a reply. For a moment he was tempted to cut the man down, but shame and reason stayed him. To kill the man simply for doing his duty was unworthy, doubly so because the man showed courage. And his killing the messenger would probably provide amusement for Mendarian.

He looked more closely at the man and vaguely recalled him as one of Orhan's lieutenants. If his memory was correct, the man had a wife and a daughter.

"Eat," he said, "and rest. Tomorrow you may return to Crown. Inform Mendarian I have nothing to say to her."

He saw Anjular at the back of the hall. "Get me a horse, saddled and ready." Anjular darted out the door.

There were a few soldiers and workers in the hall and he couldn't reveal his feelings to them. He rose and climbed the stairs to the loft, where he chose a heavy cloak, and then stared at it as though he'd forgotten why he'd picked it up. Instead of heavy gray cloth he saw brown eyes and an impudent grin that reached to his heart.

He could never, now, return the favors she'd done him. The sensation of impotence shook him so hard he actually stumbled. Nothing he could do; no way to raise the dead or even tell them what he felt. After all the power he'd claimed and taken, the world still continued, uncaring, and the fates weren't ruled by scepter or crown.

He tossed the cloak about his shoulders and hurried down and out into the list. The snow was gone, except for patches left in shadow, and the men were again at work on the walls and keep. Across the river, the woods turned green. The winter in which he'd been living had been in his own soul.

He'd become so deeply sunken inside himself he hadn't known the men were working again. Although his power was only an illusion, it was enough to keep him in the illusion of winter, as his own men were so afraid of his dark mood that they hadn't even told him of the end of winter outside.

He hurried to the stable and took the reins of a rangy gray and threw himself into the saddle. He ducked to avoid the low door and kicked the horse into a gallop, across the list and the bridge, and urged the animal into a dead run into the woods.

Crouching low in the saddle, burying his face in the mane that whipped at his eyes and cheeks, he tried to put his feelings of desolation behind him with all the speed he could coax or demand from his mount.

He hadn't ridden for months, and it seemed a release he'd needed without realizing he'd needed it. He gave himself over to the headlong race through the trees, guiding the horse in a great circle to bring him back to Hope.

Hope.

What bitter irony that name had become in the time it'd taken him to read a message.

When he returned to the stable he handed the reins of the lathered animal to a boy, told him to tend it well, and returned to the hall where he dressed in armor.

Again in the list, he found several men with whom to practice. He'd neglected serious arms drill for at least the last month, and he tired quickly but forced himself to continue until even the practice sword was heavy in his hand. With the sword alone he'd beaten men with sword and shield, ax, mace and shield, and sword. When his strength had been insufficient, he'd used skill, and when his opponents matched skill with endurance, he'd fought on sheer will.

When at last he was so exhausted he was unable to raise his arm or stand without stumbling, he called a halt, not sure he'd have won all the matches had he not been king. The memory of Hadrian and his deadly blades gave him another taste of humility.

After returning to the hall he took the bottle of wine up into the loft and drank until weariness and the wine carried him away from a world without Martina or Poker but in which Mendarian and Forgren thrived.

~ * ~

He was unsure whether it was night or early evening when he woke, memory gnawing at his heart and belly. Strange, how his torment of Murtry was being visited on himself, although his regrets had sharper teeth than any rats, and would take far longer than a few hours to kill him.

He re-lived his first meeting with Martina, before he'd learned she was a clan-sister. The army of Das had been more cosmopolitan than most armies because the Union had been deeply involved and, through them, the clan, which was just beginning to re-gather.

The camp had reflected the polycultural character of its inhabitants, with orders bawled out in seven or eight languages, strange odors of foreign cooking and even more foreign drugs, drab peasant garb contrasting with bright robes worn by nobles and furs and bare skins of barbarians—all emphasizing the uneasy collision of cultures and customs.

He'd seen her talking with Murtry. She hadn't been wearing much more than body-paint. Scarface had heard of a nomadic people south and east of Sin Garlef who painted their bodies, but had never met one of them, although he suddenly wanted to.

From her dress, or lack of it, he hadn't been able to guess whether she'd joined the army as an amazon warrior, a mage, a healer, or a camp-follower. Feeling more self-conscious than he'd admit, he'd approached her, glad that Murtry had stalked away, apparently not pleased. He stopped before her, trying not to be too obvious in his admiration of her body. "I'm called Scarface. And you're beautiful."

"I can see why you're called that, and we both know you're quite observant." She grinned at him. "Did you have anything to say to me that wasn't already obvious?"

He looked down at her. "I never thought I'd envy a coat of paint."

Her grin broadened. "I'd be tempted to see if you couldn't get closer than the paint, but I never partner with kin."

As he lay on the pallet he felt again the mixture of disappointment and deep affection, then the present carried in its load of grief and anger. Tears welled in his eyes and ran down the sides of his head. For a time he let himself mourn a loss that was as deep as the heart could reach.

Other memories crowded around him and demanded his attention: Mendarian's ice mask, the sharp words she'd used to cut him. He heard all those bitter words again, and the other words, the lies, when she'd said she loved him, and those lies were a greater torture than the insults. She'd used him, humiliated him, and discarded him, and then she'd killed the few other people for whom he cared deeply. He hadn't known, himself, how much or how deeply he'd cared until now, when it was too late for anything but remorse.

He imagined a thousand different tortures and humiliations to which he wanted to subject her, to tear at her calm contempt and frigid hatred until she screamed and pleaded for death. He visualized all the ways she could be hurt and used and beaten, as his pride had been hurt and used and beaten.

The images brought no relief, did nothing to lessen his pain or anger.

He rose and lurched out into the night, trying to walk away his feelings but they were leeches, clinging to him, draining him. He strode along the walkway built into the walls until he heard pre-dawn birdcalls, then he trudged back to his pallet and lay down, utterly empty but still unable to sleep.

Unrefreshed, he rose an hour later and drove himself to near-collapse, riding, practicing at arms, ignoring most meals, drinking to coax nearer dreamless sleep, but unable to let go of the demon feelings that gave him no quarter. Again the next night he prowled along the battlements, wrapped in a dark cloak and a darker mood, and the sentries learned to ignore his presence.

Chapter 12

The days passed, uncounted and almost unnoticed. Martina's face became blurred in his memory and grief's sharp edge was somewhat dulled, although the sense of loss and the affection was a strong as ever.

Mendarian's face became ever clearer in his mind. He tossed and twisted on his pallet, and in the shadowy halls of his heart he cursed her, called on every god and every demon to keep her from rest and to inflict on her even a portion of the agony that wracked him. The days were ordeals of forcing exhausted muscles into frantic action and the nights were demon-haunted periods of anguish or death-like sleep that gave no rest.

When Thienn rode into Hope with an escort of ten men, Scarface waited in the hall, leaving the greetings to Anjular. Thienn swaggered into the dim hall and glanced disdainfully around at the rough wooden interior.

"You needn't worry about contamination," Scarface said from the throne, not rising. "You won't be here long. Jonfré should arrive soon. I'll announce my abdication then. You'll gain the two thrones sooner than either of us had expected."

Thienn's lower jaw had sagged when Scarface had said "abdication." He managed to close his mouth and drop onto a bench.

Scarface pinned him where he sat with a cold stare. "I'm going to give you some advice as a going-away gift. The abdication is total and final, and I strongly suggest you leave me and mine alone. Listen to Jonfré and your other advisors. They're the conscience you were born without. And if you exercise your power too harshly, you won't be the first king not to die of old age. Care for your people and they'll do the same for you."

He stood and stalked from the hall to the list and more weapons-practice. For a while he watched some of the older boys, whom he'd intended to make leaders in his army, being trained. He wouldn't practice with them. His patience was too short to make him an adequate teacher and he saw the futility of beating someone without explaining to them how to avoid it.

He'd chosen men for the boys' early training very carefully, selecting patient men who still demanded the best of their students, those qualities being more important to novices than having skilled practice opponents. Later, when they'd learned the basic skills, they'd be able to learn from their mistakes without instruction, but too many losses without learning led to disappointment.

When one of the more experienced trainers was free, Scarface practiced with him. When that soldier was too tired to continue, he chose another. He fought on until he dripped sweat and his entire body trembled with fatigue.

He dropped onto a bench, pulling air into his aching lungs. Immediately, he regretted the pause. Every opponent had been a substitute for Forgren and he had, only with difficulty, refrained from killing strokes that, even with practice swords, would've broken bones.

But when he stopped moving he was left with memories of his own failures, his own guilt. All the noise, all the frantic activity, only temporarily eased the burden. He'd burned the letter from Mendarian but every time he closed his eyes it was as though the words had been burned into his eyelids, and every silence brought the sound of her voice.

Sometimes he heard her cold rejection, at other times, more painfully, her professions of love, and they were harder to bear. The worst times were when the voices came together in a sort of crowd in his mind in an almost deafening babble.

The decision to abdicate came when he realized he wasn't ruling, he couldn't rule, that it had become, for him, an empty, hollow joke. He wanted nothing but to stay on his pallet until he died, or even to hurry the death, to slash his own throat or, perhaps, to ride away to some secret place and use the scepter on himself, to end all the hurting. Now he had nothing left but the thirst for revenge.

He'd probably still be on the pallet, he reflected, but for his sense of indebtedness. Forgren had forgotten that Scarface believed in value given for value received, and that he always paid his debts. But first, he'd see Mendarian.

He bore two more days of waiting before Jonfré arrived. Scarface had made his preparations for departure, needing only a final meeting before he could mount the waiting horse. When Jonfré dismounted, Scarface whispered, "I'm abdicating," into the man's ear.

Jonfré's face revealed nothing of what he thought or felt. "Have you really considered this?"

Scarface nodded to Jonfré, and gestured to the man with the bull's horn, who relayed commands. The single eerie flat note rose and fell, and the few men who were still working dropped tools and rushed to the list, where Scarface, Jonfré, and Thienn stood.

Scarface watched them gather, feeling a strange sense of loss. When they'd assumed the air of men waiting for orders he raised his voice. It seemed weak to him, as though rusty from disuse. "I'll be leaving today. I've been honored to be your king, but—"

The words that came to him were puny things, unworthy of the occasion, explanations the men didn't need and might not understand. "I leave you, as king, my son Thienn. Obey him as you would me." He forced his voice into a shout, "Long live King Thienn."

After an awkward moment of silence, the men repeated the shout.

He glanced at Thienn, who stared coolly at the people shouting his name then he leaned toward Jonfré and whispered, "If he rules badly, if he misuses the people, kill him. Your last duty, Duke."

Jonfré said nothing and his nod was the merest flicker of movement but his eye glittered, as cold and hard as a blade.

Scarface strode to the stable. The boy who held his horse's reins was one of the urchins of Glangurrach. He stood stiffly but his eyes glittered with tears he was too proud to shed. On impulse, Scarface threw his arms around the boy and embraced him, then took the reins and climbed into the saddle, reached down, and took the lead line of the pack horse.

From his vantage on the back of his mount he looked around once at the castle, the hub of the city-to-be that had once been his then he urged the horse forward, toward the gate.

He made no attempt to press the horses faster than a trot, a gait they could maintain for days, and he avoided holdings or any other sign of human settlement. The pace he let the horses set demanded little attention from him, and so he sank deeper into depression as he rode.

He noticed daylight only when it was almost gone, and his avoidance of any kind of household became a habit, so the country through which he passed was an alien and unreal place to him. When it became too dark for the horses to go on safely he stopped, busied himself with tending the animals, then lay staring at the stars but not really seeing them, lost inside himself.

Days became a blur, one disappearing into another, the only marks of their passage being a slow dwindling of his provisions, so it was almost a surprise when he realized he was in the foothills of The Spine.

He stopped, wondering what had made him tug at his mount's reins then half-recalled that he'd seen a flicker of light atop one of the mountains. Some sentry might've used the polished center boss of his shield to signal other watchers.

When he halted at the end of the day he tried to estimate where he was. At a guess, a rough guess, he was still two days' ride from Cerco. Now that he was nearing his destination his nagging anxiety had risen to a belly-churning, nerve-fraying tension. Sleep eluded him for most of the night, and the night inside him was starless.

~ * ~

He rose late the next morning, saddled and loaded the horses, and set off at a walk. These trails were more taxing on the animals. He barely remembered having ridden other horses at a run in more treacherous terrain and weather. What drove him now wasn't the same urgency, had more than a tinge of reluctance. If he'd allowed revenge to become his reason for existence, the sooner he took vengeance, the sooner he'd again be without a purpose. And still his feelings refused to form neat ranks. Hate and love still wrestled within him.

Sunlight gleamed on polished metal, and he even caught a glimpse of the watcher ducking behind cover. If the man were a Dieri, Orhan was permitting his men to become lax. Or perhaps that sentry had wanted Scarface to know he was being observed.

After spending another restless night he rode through another gray morning he didn't really experience until another flash from ahead snapped him out of his reverie and reminded him, as he glanced about, that it was almost noon.

On he rode, toward the man or men watching him, waiting for a challenge or an arrow. Neither happened, and so he stopped at noon, hobbled the horses, and built a fire. The wineskin was still almost half full and he dug out journey cakes and dried meat. He was heating the venison when riders, half a score of them riding line-abreast, topped the rise a spear's cast from where he sat.

He loosened his sword in its scabbard and watched them with a sidelong stare but they didn't charge him, nor were bows drawn. They halted at the top of the rise and all but the rider at the center of the line waited with a patience that resembled boredom. Scarface recognized the man riding slowly toward him as Orhan, but didn't stand. A spear's length from the fire, Orhan dismounted, approached, and sat down within arm's length of Scarface. Both had chosen to be friends meeting on a journey.

Scarface took a long drink from the wineskin and handed it to Orhan, who also took a drink and handed it back. "I have orders not to allow you into Cerco."

Scarface handed him a journey cake and a piece of warm meat. "Does that mean you've come to kill me?"

"Only if there's no other way to stop you." Orhan tore off a piece of meat with his teeth and chewed it reflectively.

Scarface took another drink of wine. "It's really my own fault. I relied upon the faithfulness of an empress. Failing that, gratitude. Failing that, her wisdom."

Orhan finished chewing the meat, swallowed, and washed it down with wine. "Women don't understand honor."

"*Some* women don't," Scarface corrected.

Orhan nodded, accepting the distinction. "This one doesn't." Orhan stared at him until the silent scrutiny became burdensome. "So, are we going to fight until you kill me and my men, perhaps, kill you?"

"No." Scarface gazed at the last bite of meat and tossed it away from the camp, the customary offering to Father Wolf. If he couldn't kill his enemies, why battle his friends? Why hack and cut at Orhan and leave Marikaa to feel loss like his. Let the wheel of hurt and anger stop where it stood now. He glanced along the trail he'd taken to this place. "Are you familiar with the southern mountains?"

"Not so much. Why?"

"Is there a place back there a comfortable distance from Cerco with enough game to support a man into meditation?"

"No, but there's a place less than half a day's ride south where Cercan patrols are likely to lose supplies and where an enterprising hermit might find them."

"I'm in your debt."

"Not so. As long as you remain outside Cerco, I don't have to die fighting you."

"Very flattering, but I don't think the fight would be so easily decided."

"Ready?"

They both stood, Scarface to clear the camp and Orhan to signal his men to wait, then the two of them mounted and, with Scarface leading the pack horse, rode south,

In the early afternoon, as they followed a trail beside a deep gorge, Scarface drew rein and dismounted. He took the scepter from the top of his boot. In some ways, it was the cause of so much of the trouble. It attracted Mendarian's attention, and almost everything that had happened since seemed to be the result of that fateful meeting.

Pressing the head of the scepter against a boulder, he willed it to drain, drain totally. The boulder crumbled into dust, some of which was carried away on the wind then Scarface hammered at another boulder with the rod, beating the end into an unrecognizable blob. After staring at the battered metal for a moment, he flung it into the gorge. The thing had no value to him now, and it was too dangerous to leave it where it could be found.

Orhan eyed him sharply as he remounted but asked no questions, and in the late afternoon they arrived at a natural shelf slightly larger than the base of most keeps, and with an entrance to a cave near the far end.

Scarface twisted in the saddle and gripped Orhan's forearm, then tapped the Dieri's palm with his own, in the Cercan custom. "If you would, take my horses. As far as I know, they haven't been banished from Cerco and there's no forage for them here." He dismounted and unloaded the meager supplies from the pack animal, then handed the reins and the lead line to Orhan. "Thank you. Pleasant journey."

"More pleasant than the journey to where I met you today. May we meet again under happier circumstances." Orhan turned and rode a dozen paces, halted, and wheeled to face Scarface. "By the way, you have a friend who's asked about you—a woman named Topaz. She's at Stag Mountain, northeast of here. Do you have a message for her?"

After a heartbeat's hesitation, Scarface said, "Tell her I'm well. Or, at least, healing. Thank her for her concern." Scarface watched Orhan ride away, then he turned and regarded his new kingdom.

~ * ~

The guard's eyes and manner told Forgren the news was bad, even before the words were out. "Harma's dead!"

Forgren felt a hand of ice on the back of his neck. "How?"

"He was stabbed. He'd been in the tower two days. On the third day he didn't take his morning meal nor answer when the men shouted. Eventually, Filvin ordered them to break down the wall to the stairs. Most of Harma's spells must've died with him, because we didn't lose any more men when we broke through to his chamber."

"You said he'd been stabbed. Where and how?"

The man raised his arm and touched his right fingertips against the upper back ribs. "Right there. It looked like the blade might've been poisoned, because there wasn't much blood, but there was no one in the tower, nor had anyone but the guards left any tracks on the raked ground outside. There was a note—"

"—Nailed to his forehead, I know." He scowled at the table. "You're sure no one could've gotten into that tower?"

"No one, no way."

"Leave." As the man reached the door, Forgren stopped him. "Get me a messenger. And I want ten men ready to leave for a long ride the day after tomorrow." He waved a dismissal, then, at an afterthought, asked, "What was done with Harma's things?"

"Nothing. Three or four of the trunks are still sealed."

"Take them to the dungeon, but be careful of them. We don't know what traps or wards he may have set on him, and some of them might've survived their caster. I'll go over later today and put the other materials away and you can have them taken to the same place."

The man left and Forgren dropped into his chair and stared at the end of the table. The demon had done it again! How? Maybe there was some secret passage under the place Harma hadn't known about. Or maybe he'd just materialized out of thin air. He knew enough of magic, and with that damned strange mind of his—and maybe they were right. Maybe he wasn't quite human but some elemental force of vengeance. The shadows in the room seemed to darken and crowd closer.

He shook his head. Too many fancies. That was what Hadrian counted on, fear that was part of the revenge and which immobilized the victim. He wouldn't play that game. It was past time to put a stop to Hadrian. There was a way he might be drawn into the open and trapped, and Mendarian might have the key to that door. All he had to do was find Scarface.

~ * ~

Hadrian craned his neck and turned his head so he could look out the keyhole. Only darkness outside. He slid the pin free and lifted the lid of the trunk, climbed out, stretched cramped muscles. Almost three days of staying coiled in a trunk had been uncomfortable. He grinned at the story he could imagine was being told all around Gain.

Time enough to count scores later. He crept to the door, after he'd assured himself the next room contained cells but no jailor, he cast the spell of concealment, picked the simple lock to the door, and crept to the door on the opposite wall. Through the grating he could see a flight of stairs leading upward and a single guard stationed at the head of the stairs. The man had his back to the door and seemed to be dozing.

Hadrian slipped a vial out of his pouch and applied oil to the hinges of the door, waited until the oil had spread, then picked the lock and silently climbed the stairs, grateful they were stone. He carefully stayed in the center of the steps, where the dust had already been scuffed away.

Before sunset he'd enjoyed a meal at Forgren's expense and considered his next move. While it was dangerous folly to stay in Gain, with all its guards and magic protections making any simple mistake possibly fatal, it'd also be almost as difficult to escape from as it had been to break into. Still, bodies found far from his latest killing would cause more useless fear than to concentrate his revenge in one place, where he might be trapped.

He'd leave, but while he was inside enemy walls, he might as well learn as much as he could that'd be useful.

Chapter 13

Just come into my memory,
And I'll tear off your face.

Just come into my sight,
And my eyes will burn you.

Just try to speak to me,
And my silence will deafen you.

There's nothing between us now.

You thief!
You stole my spring,
Stole the stars from my night sky.

You took my brave banners,
You've stolen my gleam and shine,
And left me with rags.

Strip off that mask.
We know each other too well.

Do you hear me, liar?
Strip off that mask.
All the lies are empty now.

Don't try to scare me.

No knife sharp enough,
No poison strong enough,
To ever make me fear you.

Get out of my world,
Out of my heart,
Out of my hopes and dreams.

Get out of my thoughts and words,
Out of my silences,
Out of my aloneness.

How long must I scream, "Get out"?
Out of my seething mind.
Just get out.

Damn your eyes and smile.
Damn your empty soul,
Hungry for nothing.

I cast you down
Into the empty pit of you,
Into the remorse you don't know.

Damn that stone you call a heart,
Damn the dagger that hides in the stone,
Damn your ice-cold grave's breath.

Give me back my pointless life,
Or I'll tear your smile to shreds.
I'll stir the thin broth of your memories.

You have magic, have you?
I'll spit on your designs,
I'll crush your power like the hollow shell it is.

Run from me, you monster!
Even the sounds of our footfalls
Shout at one another.

Run from me, you monster!
You've made of me a monster, too,
With fangs and claws and burning hunger.

Let pain be your food and drink,
Let anguish be your pillow and blanket.
Let rest be denied you.

Let your world be silent;
Mute wind and water and hope.
Hear only the gnashing of my teeth.

I've wiped your face from my mind,
Your shadow from mine,
Burned the warmth to bitter ashes.

I'll be just what I am,
Rootless, baseless, hopeless.
I'll be my own crutches.

You could never have beaten me in open battle.
You chose the weapons: You picked guile,
A coward's game.

You drew the first blood.
Now fear me, for I still live.
You could not make me die.

Wait for my strike
Wait till the stars burn out,
Wait till the sun is as cold as your heart.

You cut me, tore me, burned me,
But you could not beat me.
I still love.

~ * ~

Morgan was suddenly wide awake; his heart pounding, his breathing rapid and shallow. He was drenched in his own sweat and trembling with a chill. He sat up, groped in the darkness for the wineskin, found it, and cleansed his mouth with a swallow of sour wine.

He still remembered the words, they still echoed in his memory. They held a strange truth. He wanted Mendarian out of his thoughts, wanted to stop talking to her in his mind, and still he loved her, and that was a victory of sorts. If she made him coldly hate her as she despised him, then she'd really beaten him, made him like herself.

What would revenge gain him? It wouldn't raise Martina or the others from the dead, nor would it pay the debt he owed his cousin—all his cousins, for they'd been giving, even if he'd been unable or unwilling to recognize it before.

At first, it didn't matter that his desire for vengeance had been as hollow and as pointless as his kingship. He could hate the Union utterly, make their destruction a goal that kept his chest pumping breath and heartbeats, and their motives were of no concern to him. They'd been the instruments of his loss and that, for a time, was sufficient. Now he could see it made him more like them. If he found reasons for despising them, what could the reasons be? That they killed and tortured? He'd left a broad trail of bodies in his wake, too, and most of them for no better reasons than they could give for the destruction of the clan.

He felt the terror of the dream fade away and something like peace enter the dark, empty corridors of himself. He tried to embrace the peace, to entice it to remain, but it tarried all too briefly then followed the fear, leaving him to wait for his next visitor. It was remorse.

He'd been as responsible as anyone for what had happened to the clan. A sudden flash of insight at another irony made his chest heave and, almost spasmodically, he laughed. The sound met its echoes in the cave and they became a chorus, and the laughter of the crowd of ghosts made him laugh even more, until his breath came in ragged gasps and tears slid down his cheeks.

In his arrogance, he'd made of himself almost a godling, and he'd played with the gods, cynically invoking their names to serve his own purposes, but he'd played without understanding the game, not even knowing when and how he'd been beaten. His cunning wasn't even the palest reflection of the subtlety of the gods, who could even manifest themselves through an unbeliever afflicted with the conceit he was using them.

He'd almost mocked Father Wolf with his masquerade at the Great Council, yet he'd done what Father Wolf would've wanted; he'd drawn the tribes together again. His gift to Mordach had been a war to build a kingdom and spread that realm with more war, then defend with arms what he'd taken by force. His reward for faithful service had been the need to keep offering at Mordach's bloody altar.

While he'd been deceiving himself that he was free to make his own decisions, he was, all unaware, only a tool of the gods.

Perhaps retreating to the cave was the best he could do, for himself and everyone else. What had he given? His kingdom had enjoyed a modicum of enforced peace within its borders but suspicious, angry neighbors at its boundaries. Annexing Gascolin would've put him on the southern marches of Bildesh and the western edge of Shatilla, just as joining with Glangurra had made him a neighbor of Pitlahsa. Each burst of growth had brought or would bring new enemies,

Had the people been brought trade? Not yet, but when it happened, what end would it serve? The people of Donradé were largely self-sufficient, and trade would bring luxuries that would be corrupting.

Had he started roads? Again, to what purpose? In an instant he could see into the future with icy clarity and he saw that growth was just the state that preceded decay, as the hungry became well-fed, then were replaced by others who were still hungry.

He hadn't been a bad king, but he'd been a king for the wrong reasons, and so his abdication was best for his people as well as for himself. All his building and striving had been without point or meaning. It'd all been an empty game, a diversion to hide the fact nothing was really changing.

And Mendarian?

He'd failed her and he'd failed himself. He'd been gone when she'd most needed him. If his kingdom hadn't meant so much to him, had he had the inner strength to bear her insults and cuts better.... But then, what was between Mendarian and himself was perhaps doomed from the start. His reasons for wanting her, for loving her, had become nebulous. That didn't diminish his wanting or loving, but he'd wanted—needed—something from her that she couldn't or wouldn't give, nor did she want what he had to offer.

What had he to offer? What would make him a better match than the lowliest swineherd? He had, without hesitation, assumed command of men, certain of his goals. Now he could, without wanting it, have a quarter of the women in Donradé, but he had no desire for them. He began to wonder why this was so, why Mendarian was so important to him.

He soon dropped the question. She was important to him, and that mattered, even if the importance were only a matter of personal preference. Beneath all the hardness and self-delusion, there was something of gold in her, something fragile, and that was what he'd wanted to reach out and touch, to point out to her the gold within her.

Then there were his needs. He perceived that he needed meaning and support, but it didn't matter whether he'd received what he needed, it mattered only that he hadn't been able to give enough. For all his skills and all his power, he'd never really been able to reach through the ice and the snarled web of lies and evasions to the woman beneath them, and that was his greatest failure.

Perhaps Poker had been right. His war-gods had brought him nothing but strife. Could a different god give him peace, and at what price?

He knew the answer and he shrank from it. The price was—everything. His own striving had given strength to the fears he'd fought, even as it'd stolen whatever gifts he had, made gold in his hands turn to mud. He could easily have what he didn't want, but the more he struggled for what he really wanted, the further he pushed it away. That had turned Mendarian against him. That might not have been the whole reason, but it was a part of it.

He noticed then the sky outside had become vivid with sunrise and, from where he sat on his rude pallet, he watched the day begin. He felt an almost forbidden pleasure in enjoying the sunrise.

If the lesson he had to learn was acceptance, now was the time to begin. He was alone and he had nothing.

~ * ~

Forgren paced between the rows of pallet racks, anxious and angry. Mendarian had treated him more as an ambassador or an enemy, or even as a prisoner, than as an ally. He'd been escorted by half a hundred Dieri to Crown Mountain, and the men with him had constantly been on edge, apparently expecting to have to defend, at any moment, themselves and their leader.

Forgren himself had been nervous. The messenger, whom he'd met on the trail, had brought a cool response from Mendarian, who seemed to feel the struggle between Forgren and Scarface, didn't involve her.

Then the armed Dieri had met him at the border of Cerco. They outnumbered his guards and he knew that even with his power, a massive attack could kill him as dead as any lesser man.

Finally, when he and his men reached Crown Mountain they were herded into the barracks and told to wait.

Two or three of his men sat on the wicker pallet frames, honing their weapons. The rest were either trying to sleep or playing at knucklebones. He glared at each of the men, wondering how much he could count on their loyalty if Mendarian turned against him now. He cursed his uncharacteristic impulsiveness that had led him to try this scheme and tried to guess if that weren't precisely the sort of ill-considered action Hadrian had intended to cause.

If Hadrian were plotting with Mendarian—

His musings were interrupted by the arrival of a Dieri soldier who apparently spoke only a few words of Ghiblin. "You," he said, gesturing at Forgren, "come."

One of the men watching the game of knucklebones and one of those putting an edge on his sword came to their feet, weapons ready. The Dieri glanced at them, shook his head. "You come. They stay."

Forgren tried to glower the man into submission but it was like trying to impress a storm cloud. Finally he stood. "Stay here," he said to the men, "I should be back soon."

His guide led him through a maze of corridors to what had to be the throne room. Mendarian sat in a great chair of jade, flanked by four men, armed and armored, with two rows of men standing against the walls.

He approached but stopped at the edge of of the dais and forced himself to bow deeply. "Greetings, Mendarian, Empress of Cerco. "As I said in my message, I'm here to destroy our common enemy."

Mendarian smiled. "Scarface, whatever his faults, is hardly common, and Hadrian even less so, but they are dangerous, and I can also sense a threat." She stared at the air over his head until he began to fidget then locked gazes with him again. "I've discovered where Scarface is hiding. I'll personally lead you there but I'll take no hand in the battle. And I'll have an escort of a score of my men." She gave him a frigid smile. "You see, I trust you as you trust me, which is to say, not at all. My soldiers are for my protection but they won't fight Scarface for you."

Forgren shrugged. "If my men and I can't take him, then a few odd troops would be of no use anyway."

"We understand each other, then. You may return to the barracks. We'll leave tomorrow morning."

"Very good." He bowed again then stared coolly at Mendarian. A day would come when those bows would be repaid. He needed her help now, but with Hadrian and Scarface no longer blocking him, nipping at his heels like the curs they were, he'd rebuild the Union, make it stronger than ever, and when that time came, Mendarian would learn what arrogance looked like from the other side of the throne.

He turned and stalked from the chamber, striding so rapidly that the Dieri supposed to guide him back almost had to trot to keep up with him.

He remembered the way they'd taken to the throne room from the barracks and now he followed that way back. When he entered the room, most of the men stood. He gestured a curt dismissal at the Dieri, then said, "We leave here tomorrow morning. You might all do well to look to your weapons then get a good night's sleep."

The men went to their pallets to follow his orders or broke into mutally congratulatory groups, less eager to face Scarface than to be out of what resembled a prison.

Forgren paced to the pallet he'd chosen, alone in a corner, and opened his saddle pouch. Unless Mendarian decided to feed them, he'd have to make do with trail rations. His hand dipped into the bag and emerged clasping a small brass bell, its clapper muffled with a scrap of silk.

He sat staring at the bell. He'd paid a heavy price for the spell that would be freed by ringing the bell, but it'd be well worth it. The men were only along as a precaution, in case Scarface was far more powerful than Forgren believed he could be.

He handled the bell carefully, almost reverently, for it was life and death. Once the bell was rung and the spell released, it meant death for the victim or the caster.

~ * ~

Mendarian watched Forgren strut out of the room, feeling a detached amusement at his barely suppressed fury. With luck, maybe he and Scarface would kill each other. It was too much to hope for that Hadrian might die trying to rescue Scarface, but it was a pleasant thought. He'd be the only danger left if Scarface and Forgren died. At least, this confrontation would lessen her enemies by one.

She leaned back into the throne, her hands flat on the curved ends of the armrests. Was there some stirring within her at the thought of seeing Scarface again? Almost certainly there was some fear. The message she'd sent him had been intended to cut him to the bone-marrow.

When Forgren had gone she stood and walked from the room. Tomorrow would begin a new time, a time of change. That was a dim, not-quite-seen truth. Or was it only foreboding? Scarface had made her rule secure throughout Cerco, but could that end when he died?

She paced slowly to her rooms, hardly aware of the corridors through which she passed, lost in memories of what had been and hopes of what could be. It was the might-have-beens that struck the deepest notes. Her rooms seemed to be crowded with ghosts that had never quite been real, and most of them hid in her bed.

Her sleep was fitful, as it had been since Hadrian's visit. That was one reason for her having taken bedpartners from among the warriors. She needed the excitement and sweating activity to bring on an exhaustion that let her sleep as though dead, and although the sex was seldom satisfactory and the sleep not much more so, it was better than nothing.

Not much better, she reflected. She'd taken only two men. The first was a very young man who'd been so in awe of her as his empress that he'd been unable to perform. The second had reminded her of Thienn, in temperament as well as body. He was a pretty boy, proud of what age would take from him, and with nothing that would grow and flourish with age. He'd given himself airs until Mendarian had been forced to point out to him that he was only a mount, that as a man he could never replace Orhan's lieutenants, much less Orhan himself.

Orhan, for whom she'd developed an almost grudging respect, had said nothing but had sent the young men to distant garrisons.

Mendarian returned to the matter at hand. She'd heard Scarface had abdicated. Perhaps that's what she should do, but she'd no idea what she'd do later. Roam again? There was no Arv to ride with her now, and she had the fear that someday she'd be left dead in a ditch. She needed all the power she had, but with power came weights, restrictions, enemies. She'd considered taking sides in the war between Ghiblein and Abaransa, but that might end her power as quickly as it ended her boredom.

Her sleep came in small, interrupted segments of deep slumber and she always knew she'd dreamed without being able to remember the dreams, only the faces.

~ * ~

She'd risen and dressed well before dawn, unable to stay abed any longer. It felt good to wear her traveling garb again, and the dagger strapped to her left forearm was an old friend she'd almost forgotten. The weight of it seemed right, and it brought back memories.

She wolfed down a meal and busied herself with supervising the loading of the provisions until Forgren and his men were ready. Orhan had already gathered his men for the journey.

Orhan had chosen carefully. All the men in his party were veterans. That was one reason, which she hadn't admitted to Forgren, why she wouldn't order her men to attack Scarface; most of them had served under him and she didn't know how well the order would be taken. Certainly, it wouldn't be carried out with enthusiasm, and she didn't want Forgren aware of the weakness. Better to put a distant face on it and remain aloof, not offering what her men wouldn't want to give.

As she mounted and rode out the Wolf's Gate she felt more at peace than she had in months, partly because she was taking action against a problem, partly because, while the saddle was more chafing to the body than a throne, it was more comforting to the spirit. Perhaps it was just that the responsibilities of rule had grown onerous. Whatever the reasons, the cool, open air was a tonic to her.

Her sense of freedom was short-lived. It was summer in the mountains but there was an autumn air to the journey, a sense of ending or, at least, of a beginning of an end.

She rode inside a circle of Dieri, who kept Forgren and his hirelings at a distance, and each of the Dieri kept a wall around himself, no unnecessary words being uttered. Either the same dour mood had infected Forgren's retainers or they were already in similar spirits, for there was no bantering or humming, no sign the party wasn't a funeral in the making.

The camp they pitched that night was equally grim, and she noticed Forgren posted his guards along with hers.

She stared at him across the fire. Most of his self-assurance seemed to have eroded and he was apparently lost in his own dark thoughts. She tossed a stick of kindling, brought from Crown, into the flames. "Afraid I'll have you killed in your sleep?"

His glower focused on her. "No."

He was disturbed about Hadrian then. Mendarian could understand that fear. If Hadrian were in these mountains, they'd need all their guards, and still no one was safe when he closed his eyes. She felt a little more secure, since Hadrian had once told her that her life belonged to Scarface, but she was uneasy, not sure he'd honor words once given, now that he was on a blood-trail.

She drew her cloak and blankets tighter about herself and tried to relax and sleep. She drifted into slumber, frequently interrupted by sudden starts of nervous wakefulness. Hadrian might be anywhere. He probably wasn't in Cerco but still he haunted her nights. Perhaps when it was all done she could find some way to rid herself of her nemesis. There must be some way to put restless spirits to unquiet rest.

She nodded off again but jerked awake with a sharp image in her mind of the clan dead, their heads impaled on spears. Several more times she drifted just near enough to sleep to run into the shoals of bitter, implanted memory.

~ * ~

At dawn the party gradually cleared the camp and prepared for the day's ride, with the final shift of sentries saddling the mounts and loading the pack animals. Tasteless trail rations were listlessly chewed and swallowed by sullen men. No one attempted humor or courtesy, knowing either would be rebuffed.

Orhan led the way, and his every line was a study in grimness. Had she not noticed his absence and asked the right questions, she might never have learned that he knew where Scarface had gone to ground, and she'd had to order him to tell her where he'd left Scarface.

Maybe he'd outlived his usefulness to her. Any loyalties other than to her could present difficulties, even dangers.

A reflective side of her noticed jealousy in her anger and uneasiness. She had the staff and crown, yet Scarface, without them, commanded more personal loyalty from the men. She dismissed it with the observation that she was a woman in a man's role, forever an outsider, and the facile answer let her put the question away without having to look more deeply into it.

She missed Arv. At least he could've been counted on to always take her side. Now she was alone.

Another restless night and anxious day began to wear deeply into her and on Forgren and his men. Twice he had to stop brawls between his soldiers, once after swords had actually been drawn. The Dieri remained taciturn but steady, as though they rode toward an unpleasant task, but one they'd accepted as their duty. Forgren's men, however, were on a haunted trail with an uncertain ending, each of them apparently seeing his own death a very real possibility.

On the morning of the third day, Orhan nodded toward the south. "We'll reach the place before noon."

Mendarian told Forgren what Orhan had said and he alerted his men, who seemed almost relieved the waiting was nearly done, although she noticed most of them touched amulets or made ritual gestures.

The morning seemed to last a year. Mendarian's hands were damp, and constantly twisted and knotted the reins. Her mount seemed to slow, then she realized she was keeping the reins drawn taut. She'd also become excessively cautious about the condition of the trail.

She was intelligent enough to recognize the signs of reluctance. It was as though she were riding to her own execution. Did she still have feelings for Morgan, or was it only fear that he'd take the life Hadrian had said was his to take or give? With Scarface dead, would Hadrian still feel bound by his given word, or would he feel free to stalk her? Sudden frights and wild fancies raced each other through her mind.

It almost came as a shock when Orhan stopped at the top of a knoll and pointed downward. She halted her mount beside his, and knew Forgren had drawn up on the other side of her. The gentle slope of the rise swept down to a wide, flat ledge in front of a squat hill with a gaping mouth of cave.

Forgren ran his tongue across his lips and stared down at the dark opening. He looked at Mendarian and gestured at Orhan. "Do you think he knows whether Scarface had a bow with him?"

She translated the question and the negative answer.

On sudden impulse, she rode back to the horse in whose pack rested the staff and the crown. She led the animal to where Orhan sat as still and imposing as a monument.

She spoke in Dieri. "Father Wolf has chosen you to be my successor. The last command I lay on you is that if Forgren or any of his men draw weapon against me, they die."

Orhan didn't seem pleased with the sudden honor shown him but made no objection. He gave a command to his men, who dismounted and strung bows.

Forgren watched these preparations with obvious misgivings. Three of his men also carried bows and he seemed to be calculating whether having his men follow the example of the Dieri would provoke a confrontation between the two groups. He hesitated but gave no orders; and his troops and Mendarian followed him as he led the way down to the rock shelf and stopped perhaps ten spear-lengths from the cave.

Forgren swung down from his saddle onto the rock. One of his men dismounted and the rest did the same. Standing at the head of his men, Forgren drew a small bell from his pouch and carefully unwrapped the clapper, then stood, legs apart, and shouted, "Scarface, come out."

Within the darkness of the cave mouth was a deeper darkness ending in blotches of lighter color. The shape moved and Scarface, clad in his grim black, stepped into the sunlight. His hair was longer than Mendarian remembered, past his shoulders, and his beard was long and wild-looking, but he moved with the familiar assurance of the old days. He advanced half a dozen paces from the cavern, then stopped, his arms crossed.

Forgren took a step toward him. "You're my prisoner. You'll come back to Gain with me."

Scarface stared at Forgren and suddenly he barked a laugh. "Forgren, you're a fool. Do you really think Hadrian would jeopardize his mission of vengeance just for me? No, he'll just add my corpse to your account. I suspect the only reason for this journey, if you think on it, is to avenge yourself on me, and I'm not going to give myself over to be tormented at your leisure. Nor have you the power to take me alive. I am a bit surprised you came for me yourself instead of just sending your toadies. It inspires in me a trace of something like respect."

Forgren thrust forward his lower jaw and his voice came out as a growl. "You're the cause of everything that's happened, and I consider seeing you die a special pleasure, one worth a few minor risks."

His arm whipped downward and the bell rang its note, then Forgren's glare at Scarface became more fixed. Scarface stared back with the same intensity.

Mendarian watched the two men, who seemed tensed as if in violent battle, but only glaring at each other. Then, though it might've been some trick of the light, she thought she perceived a bright line running from one man's eyes to the other's. The line appeared to pulse and throb, almost like heartbeats, and she noticed that Morgan's scars were also pulsing, turning a deeper black, then fading. Time almost ceased to exist, and she couldn't guess how long the men stood, crouched, bracing themselves for the effort. Soon it was no longer possible to dismiss the glowing line between the two men as a creation of mountain light. It had become almost palpable, and the throbbing and wavering was more frantic. Sweat ran down both men's faces and she wondered what would happen if either had to blink to clear sweat from his eyes.

Suddenly Forgren broke the silence. "Take him." His voice was a croak shoved out of a strained throat. "A hundred marks of silver to the man who kills him."

The men, who'd been standing as though captured by the same spell that bound Forgren and Morgan, surged forward then faltered. The two men in the lead collapsed, one with a spear in his back and the other pumping blood from a torn neck and clutching feebly at the knife that had bit him.

Mendarian saw a blade flash and another man fell. The killer snatched the sword his victim hadn't had time to draw and, with two swords, claimed three more lives before the last three of Forgren's men had turned to face their attacker. One of the men carried a spear and he cast it but a sword flicked out and almost effortlessly deflected the spear, then the swordsman was moving to his enemies' right and striking.

The man who'd flung the spear died before he could draw his sword more than a hand's width from its scabbard. The other two tried to attack together but the killer continued to move to their right so they were forced to face him one at a time. Almost instantly he cut down the nearer fighter.

The last man hid behind his shield but, at his first strike, saw his sword, his hand still wrapped around its hilt, tumble through the air across the shelf. He hadn't had time to recover from his shock before his head was cut open to the shoulders.

The man who'd killed his companions turned to face Forgren and his form shimmered, and Mendarian wasn't surprised to see the armor sagging on Hadrian's angular form. He glanced at her then faced Forgren.

"Forgren, this is one you'll have to finish yourself. If my brother doesn't kill you, I'll let you live, but I don't think I need anticipate any regrets." His head turned slightly, toward Morgan. "Brother, I leave these two to you. This is your battle now." His blades swept up in a salute then he stripped a sword belt and scabbard from a corpse, sheathed both weapons, and caught up the reins of a horse. He sprang into the saddle and guided the animal toward Mendarian.

She was transfixed, staring wide-eyed at him, almost certain that despite his words, one of his deadly blades would lick out and cut her down, but he only gazed at her with such withering contempt that she winced, then he was gone.

She watched him ride up the slope, saw the Dieri part ranks to allow him to pass, and saw Orhan wave him a salute.

Forgren's voice called her attention back to the struggle before the cave mouth. The strain was beginning to wear down both men, and she wondered if the spell could leave two dead bodies. "Mendarian," Forgren rasped, his voice rough and strained. "Mendarian, what's Scarface's true name?"

She looked at Morgan. His scars no longer throbbed as they once had and they appeared duller, as though something vital had been leeched from them. He looked as though the momentary respite offered by Hadrian's surprise attack was wearing off. His hair hung lank and wet with sweat, and his shirt was plastered to his body. He was obviously nearing the end of his reserves, and she remembered what Poker had said about his scars. He must've finally exhausted their power and was now holding on by will alone, and the slightest push....

"Mendarian, his name! Give me his name!"

Her own voice seemed to be made of broken glass tearing its way out of her throat. Mor – Mordaign. He used part of his own name in Donradé."

Forgren grinned, lips peeling away from teeth. "Mordaign, I thrice bind thee, once in breath, once in heart, and I bind thy eyes. This is my will and it shall prevail. Be thrice bound and die."

Morgan's eyes blazed briefly as he heard Mendarian and his stance shifted subtly. Some of the strain was gone but his intensity seemed to double. Forgren had hardly finished his spell when he began to weaken, doubt and fear pursuing each other across his face. Suddenly he screamed and fell to his knees as his eyes melted and ran down his cheeks then the top of his head disappeared in a red-gray mist. The corpse toppled onto what was left of its face.

Mendarian looked again at Morgan, who'd stumbled, then staggered to the mouth of the cave to lean against the rock wall. She moved slowly toward him. She still had the dagger hidden in her sleeve and he was obviously in no condition to fight. "Hadrian gave you my life. Are you going to take it?"

Color slowly returned to his pale face. "No." He made a gesture that obviously cost effort, indicating Orhan and the crown. "You have much less power to harm others now." He turned his head and stared with bloodshot eyes at the bodies. "What's been gained?" He stared directly into her eyes. "What have you gained from all this, Mendarian? Forgren— dead. Martina—dead, Poker—dead, Arv—dead. And Hadrian—as good as dead. He was really only alive when he was with his family, but your game has cost him that. He's become a soulless death-bringer. And what have you gained? A crown you've just given up? Your life, which no one in the clan ever wanted to take?"

"Martina threatened me once—"

"Did she threaten you or did she just refuse to bend to your threat? Was all this waste and carnage a game to you? Have you made a single friend, or even an ally? Have you made anyone happier, unless it was some dark power? Have you even made yourself happier? Did you have enemies, or did you make them?

"You and I have more power than most, and so our responsibilities are greater than most. We can see there are consequences to our actions. If I toss a rock from this ledge, am I not responsible for who or what it strikes?"

"People aren't rocks," Mendarian snapped. "They have free choice; they make their own decisions. Hadrian decided to 'die' the way he has."

Morgan brushed the damp hair back from his face with a gesture like Travesty's and his voice somehow reminded her of Poker's. "We have limited choice, Mendarian. It's possible that Hadrian would simply accept the deaths of his kin, but how likely was it? It's easy to say one is only responsible for one's own actions and the responsibility ends when another person reacts to those actions. It's much harder to bear the responsibility for or even watch the pain of others who've been hurt by the consequences."

"So," she sneered, "your goal in life is to feel all the pain of others. That's an exotic form of self-flagellation."

"And that's an easy excuse. No, life is precious, but it's precious to us all. I merely say we have foresight for a reason, to examine our actions in the light of their consequences, intended and unintended. Whether we then choose to act or not is our decision to make but if we choose to act, knowing that what we do will cause harm to another, then we're responsible for their pain. To detach ourselves from that pain; or to hide from it behind our own successes or rationalizations is simple cowardice."

Mendarian gestured at the bodies. "Do you accept responsibility for the deaths of Forgren and his men?"

"Ultimately, yes, I must. I'd thwarted and fought him so much that a confrontation was inevitable. More directly, it was a conflict of choices. He came here to kill me and I chose not to die. Some things can't be resolved with reason as long as one person refuses to accept reason."

"He chose death for one of us when he rang the bell. It's largely because of you that he died and not I. Why did you do it?"

"No good reason."

Morgan grinned. "And I still care for you for no good reason." The grin faded. "I wish we could ride away together, with no crowns, no thrones but saddles, but too much has happened, too much has changed. I've changed too much. Now it's your turn to change."

Mendarian turned her head at a sound and observed that the Dieri had gone. "So, you're deserting me?"

"No, I'm leaving you to yourself. You have the chance to grow and change, but that's your choice to make, just as it must be your choice how you will change and into what. I can't make those decisions for you." He turned and trudged into the cave. Mendarian stared after him, numb, devoid of feeling.

Morgan returned within moments, buckling on his sword belt, his cloak already clasped. Most of his color had returned and only a trace of weakness seemed to remain. "There are provisions enough to last a month; longer if you take the packs from Forgren's horses. I'll only need one." She watched as he caught up the reins of a bay gelding, then hauled himself up and dropped into the saddle.

Without, herself, knowing whether it was a desire or a threat, Mendarian said, "We'll meet again."

Morgan's lips twitched in the familiar way and he replied, "Perhaps. You do make life interesting." For a moment he gazed at the rocks around them as though seeking direction then turned his horse's head and rode to the northeast.